"*French Quarter Fiction* is a treasure. It is a gem of a collection that every New Orleans fan, from novice to aficionado, will be proud to place on their reading table, and reread every chance they get. It's a feast for the eyes, heart and soul."   —*CLARION LEDGER*

"The Vieux Carré unmasked by those who love her. This book breathes with the pulse of the fecund heart, sweat, tears, tragedy, and joie de vive of the French Quarter."   —*ALTERNATIVES*

"An eclectic collection of short fiction by some of our most prestigious writers, while introducing the work of promising new voices....Ellen Gilchrist's 'Sunday' offers you a line so perfect, it leaves you humble....Whatever your taste in fiction, you will find a story in this book to satisfy you, and some will inspire and enlighten you, just as some will challenge you."   —*PLANETWEEKLY*

"This is the Quarter with a volcano of smells and termite-infested buildings. Clark has amassed a powerful assortment of talented writers, whose smooth, elegant prose makes reading joyful. The stories are always cool and intellectual, and humorous without being intentionally funny."
     —*NEW ORLEANS MAGAZINE*

"In 2025 when every structure in the Quarter will be built out of copper plaques commemorating the people who once lived here, this book will be the first one the lit hounds pick up in search of *ur*-sounds."
     —*Andrei Codrescu*

"The colorful and eccentric residents of the Quarter swarm through these stories like fire ants.... Each story offers an evocation, a sharply drawn scenario that will transport the reader to a particular time and location in the French Quarter. Enjoy the trip."   —*SUNDAY ADVOCATE MAGAZINE*

"Penetrates, subverts and explodes the standard shopworn clichés that ride this city's ragged coattails... 'The Night Was Full of Hours' is a staggeringly personal peek into the life of this city's most famous writer, Tennessee Williams."   —*WHEREY'AT*

"Colors in the many-hued portrait of the most interesting, unusual, and beautiful neighborhood in the world."   —*DOUBLE DEALER REDUX*

"A grand undertaking...An excellent collection."   —*GAMBIT*

"A diverse literary anthem."   —*PRIME MAGAZINE*

FRENCH QUARTER FICTION

THE NEWEST STORIES OF

AMERICA'S OLDEST BOHEMIA

FRENCH QUARTER FICTION

EDITED BY

JOSHUA CLARK

FALL RIVER PRESS

Contents

Introduction

FIRES. FLOODS. PLAGUES. TEN WARS. SIX FLAGS. But we're still here and we still have stories to tell the world.

The French Quarter has crawled into its fourth century as the heart of a distinct star in the homogenized red, white and blue sky. And while it may not be the oldest neighborhood in America, it is arguably the oldest that has retained a true sense of its history and original culture, and it is as well the oldest bohemian village.

Every year the Quarter chews up and spits out a stream of eight million tourists, real estate investors, gutterpunks and celebrities. From the world over they funnel through this place, a thin, swift current along the steady, perpetual fall of the Mississippi. They leave a trace of themselves here and inevitably they add a short story or two to the anthology of their own lives. They come for jazz, some of the best food in the world, and 202 bars at last count. One could go on and on expounding the Quarter's virtues (vices?), but you're not holding a 384-page pamphlet from the Department of Tourism. Still, I would dare anyone to find a neighborhood in the core of a city with more "eccentric" characters than are to be found in every store, pub, and street corner of the French Quarter. Anywhere. Just go shopping at our one major food store, the miniaturized A&P of Marda Burton's "Making Groceries," and I promise seven out of the ten people in line with you will be… well, let's just say some of their screws will be "eccentrically" loose.

It is no secret that the French Quarter has inspired many a writer. From French Romanticists like Chateaubriand to Whitman to Faulkner to Robert Olen Butler, for almost three hundred years authors have penned tales with ink of the blood that flows from the heart of the Crescent City.

There have been local literary journals: from *Les Cenelles* in 1845, the first anthology of African-American poetry in the United States; to the *Double Dealer* of the 1920s; to the *New Laurel Review* currently working on its 22nd volume.

But never before has the combined merit of the Vieux Carré's uniqueness, and the plethora of living writers that has dwelled in it, been consolidated into one volume.

And so here it is.

The single criterion for stories was that they were anchored in the French Quarter of New Orleans, Louisiana—physically, spiritually.

However, by no means are these stories wholly trapped in this 13 x 6-block rectangle. The characters contained in these works also find themselves everywhere from Sarajevo on the eve of the First World War to Algiers Point just across the River.

Nor need these *Newest Stories* be confined to modern times. They wander from the 18th Century New World of John Verlenden's "Lost Text: The Hotel St. Pierre" to a rooftop view of Bourbon Street as we shoot into the third millennium of "S.I.N.ners" by Joe Longo.

It did not matter how long a writer had spent here. What *was* necessary was that their story penetrate the standard clichés that "N'awlins" evokes— Mardi Gras, voodoo, swamp, jazz, etc. Not to say that stories could not address these themes, but one would be hard-pressed to find voodoo captured with the cruel integrity of Jarret Keene's "Conjure Me."

We asked for work from some of the preeminent authors of our time and also scored through hundreds of unsolicited submissions from down the street to the Czech Republic to Australia. While some material was written exclusively for the anthology, some stories have been hitherto unpublished, others appeared in literary magazines, and still others selected and republished from authors' best work. They are stories of people who visit the French Quarter, people who have a home in the French Quarter, and those who make a home of the French Quarter. In them are all facets of Quarter life—from the homeless to the service industry to high society. Whether it's flash fiction, surrealism, or satire, when it comes down to it, these are simply great stories: exciting, beautiful, poignant, tragic and comic.

Hope, despair, and their fellow universal themes weave around these stories' common thread, the French Quarter—the one thread through to the end, the others woven around it until they are cut or knotted and the last period is placed after the last word of a story. Turn the page and follow the thread's flow into the next sentence of the book.

We created some semblance of method behind the madness of organizing the stories' order by splicing their groupings with local cocktail recipes—their ingredients or history eerily appropriate to the stories that follow them. Give them a taste if you haven't already.

The French Quarter is an American anomaly that has perhaps never truly pledged allegiance to any of the flags flown over Jackson Square. Trapped between Acadia and the Deep South, its heritage is Caribbean, African, French, Spanish, Irish, Italian and many other ingredients in the bowl of Gumbo that is its city.

Unlike the melting pot of other American cities, social and cultural identities have remained distinct in New Orleans, and for the most part still work in harmony with one another. And it is in the French Quarter that these groups collide. Only here could the native college kid of "Gregory's Fate" use *The Times-Picayune* stock exchange reports to shield himself from a right-wing Nicaraguan arms smuggler's daughter who had just finished shopping at the city's most expensive boutiques (in a café modeled after one operated by an East Asian family).

Add to this mix the tourists from across the globe, and it can make for one hell of an interesting talk around the bar. At one time I forced myself to carry a small notebook whenever I went out in order to write snapshots of the people I encountered. Within a week—somewhere between a man who was the fifth child of his family, born at 5:55 AM on 5/5/55 with five sons from five wives living in apartment #5; and a blind Mongolian whose lifelong ambition was to shoot heroin in William Burroughs' old house across the River—the pages were filled, and it was all too strange for fiction.

The short story, more so than the novel, replicates how we depict our lives, both to others and ourselves. No person can be encapsulated within the narrow confines of even an epic novel. Our lives are anthologies of experiences, a repertoire of stories—the same ones we spout off around a café table or belly up to a bar.

Since this neighborhood has the highest density of bars and cafés in the world there's likely more stories being told here at any given time than anywhere on Earth. And just as we fill it with our own stories, so too has its stories, and these are 37 of its best, the ones we dare unmask because we can call them fiction.

*   *   *

We live in the haunted ruins of a long lost Garden of Eden. And as Eden's living ghost too, our neighborhood bears an orchard of temptation—"the next more more," as Andy Young phrases it in "Go to Hell." Some merely gaze at the romantic gleam of the apples, some touch, taste, some escape, others fall prey to the snake's tongue, and a few, like many of the stories in this anthology, draw their sustenance from it.

"The past keeps rising up here," Tom Piazza writes, "the water table is too high." Characters now gone from our mortal world make their way around this neighborhood and across these pages. John Biguenet said it all when he once told me, "*Ghostbuster*-ing would not occur to a New Orleanian." Tennessee Williams believed it was some boy's lost spirirt that rang the wind-chimes in his second room, and for this it was the favorite of all his possessions.

It is the past, and occasionally the present, that concern this neighborhood, this city, as opposed to the future—"restoration rather than reinvention," as James Nolan has stated, "rather than the ongoing American frontier of endless self-invention." This is taken to a mania by Andrei Codrescu's antagonist from his upcoming novel *Fleeing the Restoration*, indicative of a paradoxical element here that is concerned with endless restoration.

Restoration of the soul also transpires. Renewed identities are realized through discovering those you had buried or forgotten, latent. Lee Grue's "Pretty Birdie and the Toy Pomeranian" exposes the inherent possibility of recognizing, as well as accepting, one's true identity in this place.

In "The New Orleans of Possibilities" the Quarter surfaces buried truths to the point where a character is unable to recall his own self. I remember sweating buckets in William Faulkner's backyard during a reception while David Madden told me he had written this story, in which something happens that has never happened before—"*Ever*," he said, leaning back, his forehead glinting in Mississippi's July sun, his index finger piercing the deep blue sky overhead. I wouldn't let him finish. I purchased his book at a used book store upon my return to New Orleans and read the story while sitting on the levee. I realized he had not let me down as I finally raised my stare back to the River.

Old Muddy himself is, of course, a theme of our stories, a theme as inevitable as its twisted current shaping the crescent arc of this neighborhood's belly. Its opaque surface hides a world below, a world that some vanish into and perhaps other appear from. Flat and deceptively composed in appearance, it is a colossal metaphor for the great story which intimates the hidden weight below its manifest surface.

And just as we feel the heft of hidden worlds, we are able to actually glimpse the characters herein behind the barriers—wooden shutters, stone walls, cast-iron fences—that shield them from the traveling masses (and each other) and peer into their courtyards, living rooms, bedrooms. No walking tours, nor photography books, nor history books of this neighborhood could hope to lift the veils of privacy so utterly. None has ever given us such an unabashed, intimate view into the mindset of Tennessee Williams in his later years as "The Night Was Full of Hours," and perhaps none of his other works have either.

This project was originally intended as a celebration of the living writers whom the Quarter has influenced. But, in keeping with theme of the Quarter's past inexorably rising into the present, two irresistible exceptions reared their heads.

Labeled "the greatest photographic son of the South,"[1] Clarence John Laughlin spent most of his life in New Orleans, and was a central artisitic figure in the Quarter. Those who made the trek up to his fourth story residence in America's oldest apartment buildings, the Pontalbas stretching along Jackson Square, found over 20,000 books; 15,000 magazines; and 10,000 photographs—between which he had manged to squeeze a cot for his bed. They were greeted with hour-long lectures in preparation for viewing a print (it was said that an original Laughlin had a button imprint on it since he would clutch it to his chest during this time), hot tea from the faucet, and maybe part of a leftover sandwich.

"The Land of the Poppies," unearthed by his agent Nancy Moss, is the only work of his short fiction ever to be published; this from a world renowned photographer who considered himself a writer first and foremost, then a book collector, and thirdly a photographer.

And while his story, inspired by Omar Khayyam's epic 12th Century poem *The Rubaiyat*, is the only piece that does not occupy the same physical space as the French Quarter, one could certainly make the case that the mystical world Laughlin depicts is in significant aspects similar to the Vieux Carré.

The Quarter and its people seem to defy time altogether—lost somewhere between the lack of seasonal change and the 24-hour bars—as Laughlin states of his land, "Time has no triumph here.... The swift birds of the hours fly lightly by." And it seems our neighborhood imitates his land's natural restoration: "For as fast as the poppies whither, new ones, exactly like the dead in every particular, spring up in their stead."

He continues, "And the sum of all their song is to make merry while we may, before age destroys Life's sweetness; to seek, above all, forgetfulness of the dark curse laid upon the race of men." Comparison to Bruce Henricksen's "The Last Bijou" is irresistible: "Life's sweetness" is embodied in the peach Andre holds as he marvels at a smear of bubble gum on the Riverwalk, and later that "dark curse" of mortality is defied as he offers to push that peach through the I.V. bag for his dying mother. Andre lives without concern for change, wholly in the present.

Again, Laughlin:

> *They think not of the future and so do not dread it.... Living and delight with them are one. They seize without hesitation, without fear, the momentary span Life allots them, implicitly knowing it eternal. And that living knowledge— better than all our crumbs—renders them intoxicated and superb.*

As Tennessee Williams said, "I've never known anybody who lived in, or even visited the Quarter who wasn't slightly intoxicated—without the booze."[2] Remy Benoit's "Annie," the character herself a personification of the Quarter, is someone in whom living and delight are still, after our age and in the echo of disaster, one. It is a celebration of life that is always prevalent here.

Laughlin touches a similar sentiment familiar to anyone who has spent time in the Quarter, a more colloquial sense of intoxication—"Ah wine! Would Life be possible without it? Would Life be endurable? Does it not alone redeem us from Time and make us akin to the flowers?"—a sentiment celebrated in Ellen Gilchrist's "Sunday" and the recipe of a Ramos Gin Fizz.

And when he speaks of "the priceless gift of Joy and Death made into one," a better description of jazz funerals may never have been written.

But Laughlin's eden must come to an end though forces of nature that the Quarter itself has faced many a time, yet thus far defied. And his characters rest eternally—"this the method by which death comes, softly and by stealth, in this slumberous land.... to slip easily and without any previous knowledge thereof, just as you would fall asleep, into the deep dark grave." He ends, "Subsequent to this a joyful death among the races of men has not been known . . ."

"I hope to die in my sleep, when the time comes," said Tennessee Williams, "and I hope it will be in the beautiful big brass bed in my New Orleans apartment."[3] Unfortunately, death did not find him in restful unconsciousness, nor did his soul at times. Like much of his writing in *Memoirs,* "The Night Was Full of Hours" was likely composed in the graying, sleepless void of pre-dawn.

Concerned with a plane of reality far closer to the pitted streets of the French Quarter, Tennessee Williams grants us this last piece of the anthology, a prose poem that like Laughlin's is previously unpublished.

Williams once listed his favorite things as (1) New Orleans, (2) the human animal, (3) New Orleans, (4) Ernest Hemingway, (5) New Orleans.[4] He often described it as his favorite city, the Quarter being "his spiritual home"[5] where he had done much of his best writing. Upon exposure to uptown society, that world past the business district, Williams reflected, "I love to visit the other side now and then, but on my social passport Bohemia is indelibly stamped, without regret on my part."[6]

As W. Kenneth Holditch points out in *The Last Frontier of Bohemia*, it was the Quarter that turned him from a "proper young man in a neat conservative suit, polished shoes, dress shirt, and tie, into a Bohemian, wearing a sport shirt and sandals on his way to California with a clarinet player in a decrepit Chevy."[7] And it was here that Thomas Lanier Williams found independence, here that he took his new name.

He called this a place where poets "huddle together for some dim, communal comfort—I have been a part of their groups because of the desperate necessity for the companionship of one's own kind."[8] This is the flesh and blood over the bones of affordable living that is Bohemia, and these are stories from our country's oldest. Enjoy.

—*Joshua Clark*

---

[1] D. Eric Bookhardt, *Gambit Weekly*, March 2, 1998

[2] Interview with Dick Cavett, New Orleans, 1974 (as quoted in *The Last Frontier of Bohemia* by W. Kenneth Holditch, 1987)

[3] Tennessee Williams, *Memoirs*, Garden City, NY: Doubleday, 1975

[4] 1955 newspaper interview with Pen Wilson as cited in *The Last Frontier of Bohemia* by W. Kenneth Holditch, 1987

[5] William S. Gray as interviewed by W. Kenneth Holditch

[6] Tennessee Williams, *Memoirs*, Garden City, NY: Doubleday, 1975

[7] Nancy Tischler as quoted in *The Last Frontier of Bohemia* by W. Kenneth Holditch, 1987

[8] Tennessee Williams, *Where I Live: Selected Essays.* NY: New Directions, 1978

"*The basis of bohemia is cheap rent, and New Orleans is still a cheap place to live. So young people from across the country can come here, rent an apartment for three or four hundred dollars a month, work part-time day-jobs and practice their arts. That's simply not possible in New York or San Francisco anymore, because rents there are astronomical. You'd have to marry a corporation to afford fifteen hundred dollars a month for a studio apartment. With the bohemia here comes an incredibly broad mix of people, of ages, classes, races, sexualities, backgrounds. This isn't possible anymore in more stratified cities like San Francisco and New York, where you literally have to buy into the "right neighborhood," the one that fits your narrow social identity. So bohemia there is just a fashion show, where people pay enormous rents to live in formerly hip neighborhoods like North Beach or the Village. But they're working for corporations and don't have time to be artists...*

For a long time, probably since the turn of the century, anybody who was a misfit in the South ended up in the French Quarter. You know, drunken debutantes from Mississippi, flamenco dancers from small Texas towns, people like that. We still have rigid social classes in the South, particularly in New Orleans, but in the French Quarter social distinctions have always melted away. So a Delta debutante shacks up with a pool-shark whose father was a sharecropper. Invite them both over for spaghetti. What was the question again?"

—James Nolan

QUARTER RATS

by James Nolan

I COME FROM A LONG LINE OF QUARTER RATS. We inhabit crumbling buildings, seldom poke our snouts out of the French Quarter, and like our distant cousins the cockroaches, can stay up all night and will eat anything. Of the five generations of my family in New Orleans, only my mother has never lived here, but her first job was as a secretary in a dress factory located three blocks from my apartment. As a child, when I'd present her with some loopy drawing, she'd exclaim, "Why, that's so good you could take it to Jackson Square." That was her ambition for me, to become a painter on Jackson Square, but perverse as ever, I became a writer instead. You see, everything and everyone in this neighborhood has a story: art, buildings, bars, restaurants, shops, rats, even writers and their mothers.

A favorite daydream of mine takes place at my great-grandfather's to-bacco shop, at the corner of St. Louis and Chartres. It's 1885, let's say, the year my grandmother was born. The family was still living above the shop, as Creole merchants did at the time. My great-grandfather is speaking French with a dwarfish Quarter rat in a wide round hat that makes him look like an ambulant mushroom. Lafcadio Hearn switches into English to welcome George Washington Cable. Back from a lecture tour with Mark Twain, Cable has stopped in for a cigar. My great-grandfather abruptly turns his shoulder: Cable slandered the Creoles in *The Grandissimes*, and nobody speaks to him anymore.

An imposing woman in a red tignon passes the shop, carrying a basket of roots. Is that the Widow Paris from rue St. Ann, they whisper, or her daughter Marie Glapion, also known as Marie Laveau? The light-skinned voodooienne is walking with an ancient African wearing a gris-gris neck-lace, Jean Montanet, a.k.a. Dr. John from Bayou Road. Both Hearn and Cable have written about Dr. John, so they rush outside to greet him. Then up walks Pére Roquette, a parish priest from the Ursuline convent who dresses like a wild Indian. He's known as Chahta-Ima among the Choctaws in St. Tammany Parish. Hearn quizzes the priest about his interviews in *The New Orleans Bulletin*, done by someone called Walt Whitman. "That name," Hearn says, "rings a bell."

My grandmother, on the balcony in her mother's arms, is staring down wide-eyed at the characters on the corner. Then suddenly it is 1963 and, already an old lady, she's sitting with her 16 year-old grandson at the kitchen table, reminiscing about the "old neighborhood," which took the place of the Old Country. Why should she care if Jimmy goes to the French Quarter? They say it's wild and bohemian down there, but what are guitars and longhair to her, after the world she grew up in?

"Now you get home early," Mémère says.

But, of course, I never did.

As the busiest port in the country, New Orleans reached its apogee of wealth and power in the 1840s. And it's been downhill ever since. A decadent port is the perfect place to foment a literary bohemia, providing the three essentials: cheap rent, creative misfits, and a window onto the world. The French Quarter has possessed that magic combination of ingredients during several distinct eras. The first was the world that I daydream passed through the family cigar store. Local colorists such as Cable, Hearn, and later Kate Chopin, wrote vivid portraits of the Creole neighborhood, a previously unmapped enclave of French Caribbean culture entrenched north of the Canal Street "neutral ground," at war with the money-mad Americans on the other side.

The Americans won. And by the first World War, the Creoles were in retreat, and most had abandoned the Quarter for Esplanade Avenue. Their shops and homes had fallen into disrepair, and were taken over by Sicilian immigrants who set up groceries on almost every corner. This was the slum that William Faulkner discovered in 1924, when he rented an apartment in Pirate's Alley and described the Quarter as "this courtesan, not old yet no longer young." Sherwood Anderson, already ensconced in the Pontalba Building, had put out a call to young writers to come to the "most civilized place I've found in America."

And they did come. Faulkner, Anderson, John Dos Passos, and Anita Loos met up with locals such as Lyle Saxton and William Spratling to form a bohemia often described as Greenwich Village South. They came for the ambience, each other's inspiration, and—make no mistake about it—the booze that kept flowing during Prohibition. In no way were the Puritan restrictions of Anglo-America enforced in an Italian neighborhood with

Spanish architecture, French culture, and African streetlife. The Quarter was one big speakeasy.

By the beginning of the Depression, most of these writers had scattered, as the local colorists had by the turn of the century. Who remained in the Quarter were artists applying the folkloric concept of local color to painting, a bold breakthrough at the time. Their realistic canvasses of Louisiana life, of its swamps, plantations, and street scenes, appealed to visitors, so they began to take their work to sell in Jackson Square. This was the era that fostered such a great photographer as Clarence John Laughlin, although the regional esthetic later degenerated into the tourist schlock sold today.

Curiously, most American bohemias have taken root in immigrant Italian neighborhoods—Greenwich Village, North Beach—and this was also true of the French Quarter. Quarter-rat painters became honorary Mediterraneans, donning berets, downing espressos and Dago red, and scraping by on pasta in tenement rentals. Ever since, painters have formed the backbone of Quarter bohemia. They can both live here and make their living "on the fence," as they call Jackson Square. When Tennessee Williams arrived in the French Quarter in 1938, he carried a letter of introduction to two such painters, Knute Heldner and Colette Pope.

Williams' Quarter of the 40s and 50s was a brawling seaport filled with foreign sailors, pimps, hookers, burlesque clubs, and the first gay bars. During his stay, William Burroughs—"author of *Junkie* and *Queer*," as a marker proudly proclaims in front of his former house—no doubt found everything he needed here. This was when the neighborhood acquired its enduring reputation for vice, the Quarter of my parents' generation. My father warned me in high school about "getting rolled" down here, afraid someone would "slip a mickey" in my drink. My grandmother may have fancied I was going to the Quarter to mourn the French Opera House of her youth, just as my father figured I was heading to the Hotsy Totsy Club of his, but neither was the world I was searching for.

Where I was going were the integrated coffeehouses and blues clubs, not to mention the uproarious Discussion Group, a monthly get-together of painters, poets, and other ranting eccentrics. During the 1950s and early 60s, the Quarter was part of what was called the Golden Triangle between here, the Village, and North Beach for everyone "on the road." The local scene was energized by the civil-rights movement, and the arrival of Beat writers and jazz musicians from New York and San Francisco. Folksingers wailed Odetta from coffeehouse stages, demonstrations were plotted, jazz-

and-poetry collaborations filled the air, and magazines such as Gypsy Lou Webb's *The Outsider* published Bukowski and Ferlingetti, who were often in town. A young native named John Kennedy Toole was taking all this in, and certain sources swear that miscreants were conspiring inside courtyards to assassinate another Kennedy, the President.

Then the Quarter was still home to a working port, and seedy bars along Decatur Street were blaring Greek and Latino music that lured both foreign sailors and local bon vivants. Drinking in those dives formed my first contact with the world at large. But when gigantic modern freighters no longer fit inside the wharves, and the port was moved upriver, the Quarter lost its connection to the vital grit of marine commerce, and the legitimate businesses and shadowy demimondes that fed off of it vanished from the neighborhood. The truth is, the Quarter isn't as wicked as it once was, but mainly only pretends to be, and now makes much of its living off of conventioneers so drunk they can't tell the difference.

Fortunately, preservationists quashed plans to erect an elevated freeway over the Quarter and to install a sound-and-light show in Jackson Square. But the 1984 World's Fair ushered in the final stages of waterfront redevelopment, and the decaying port was transformed into a theme park, an international design echoed in San Francisco's Fisherman's Wharf and New York's South Port. It's as if Faulkner's aging courtesan had closed the shutters, taken a long look in her vanity mirror and decided, honey, it's time to live off your reputation.

Once again the French Quarter is a walled city, enclosed not by colonial ramparts to thwart invasions but by a glittering ridge of highrise hotels to house the invaders. Alone in the urban museum, we Quarter rats wander a ghost town of tastefully restored vacation condos, time-shares, and bed-and-breakfasts. Block after block of T-shirt shops blasting Zydeco peddle voodoo dolls, whorey boas, and hokey hot sauce, marketing local color like an aisle at Walmart. Mass tourism inspires an ironic self-consciousness about who we are that, as a writer, I find difficult to ignore. It makes me want to place quotation marks around words like Creole, Cajun, and voodoo. On a bad day, I creep out to the street and feel as if I'm living in Disneyland, surrounded by Haiti.

Yet on good days, I crack open the gate of the ramshackle fence that hides the courtyard where I live, and step into the only place that has ever felt like home. Like layers of paint peeling from an old building, history reveals itself at every turn of my stroll. And then the living Quarter rats emerge from behind their shutters. Interrupting my reveries, I always run into a friend, often one of the writers represented in this anthology: Lee Grue, Andrei Codrescu, Andy Young, Julie Smith, Marda Burton, Utahna Faith, Josh Clark, all fellow Quarter rats. We stand gabbing on the corner about who is reading at the Dragon's Den or Café Brasil, who's moving, who's in love again, and perhaps repair for a drink to Molly's. Walking home, the decades scrambled in my head, the living with the dead, I think *plus ça change, plus c'est la même chose.*

Despite Disneyfication, the Quarter has three guarantees of its survival: architecture, transience, and terrible weather. What you see on the street is not what the Quarter really is. Our lives—more like our short stories than we'd care to admit—take place behind the anonymous walls and gates of courtyards, marking the Mediterranean separation between public and private. This labyrinth of inviolate worlds, which has repelled Spanish, British, and American incursions, also keeps at bay the hordes of tourists wearing balloons on their heads. Lindy Boggs, for example, that grande dame of Louisiana politics and octogenarian former ambassador to the Vatican, lives on Bourbon Street.

Lured by the romance, people continue to arrive. And most eventually go, either straight into rehab, or because they become weary of crime, noise, and the banana-republic economy of this town, where you can find anything you want except a job. Like wisteria vines around a wrought-iron fence, only the truly twisted stay rooted here. The neighborhood certainly will outlast the current plague of tour-promoters and real-estate developers selling "charm" by the hotel-bed or square-foot. The French Quarter feeds on the flesh of its strangers, and never grows old.

And after a few years of hurricanes, torrential rains, and steaming summers, even the snazziest renovations will soon look like one of Clarence John Laughlin's phantasmal ruins. But don't be fooled. These few blocks of moldering buildings aren't the French Quarter. Turn these pages, and you're holding it in your hands. Thanks to the writers and artists who have passed through here, the eternal Quarter exists as a place in the imagination that imbues these worn bricks and rotting boards with magic. Only occasionally, and at unexpected moments, can you catch bewitching glimpses of the real Quarter. Lafcadio Hearn, one of the first Quarter rats, got it right long ago when he compared the neighborhood to "one of those phantom cities of Spanish America, swallowed up centuries ago by earthquakes, but reappearing at long intervals to deluded travelers."

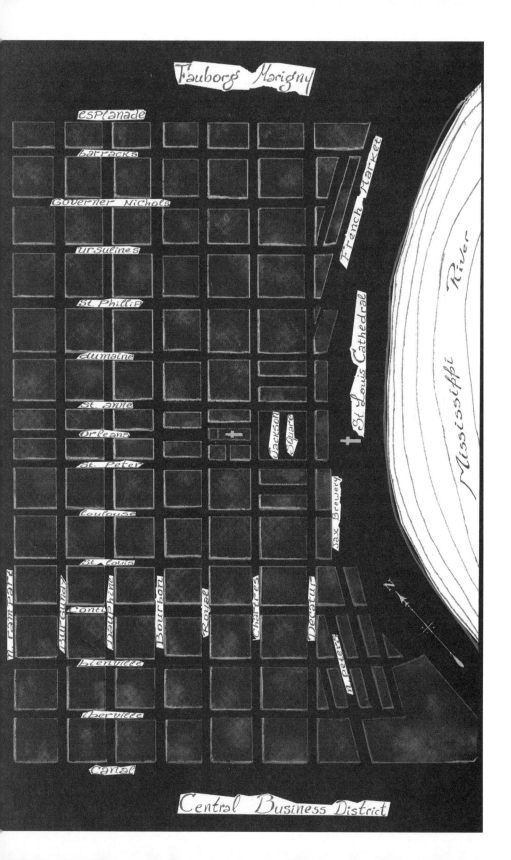

ramos gin fizz

Henry C. Ramos came to New Orleans in 1888 from Baton Rouge and purchased the Imperial Cabinet Saloon, where he invented this cocktail. He bought the Stag Saloon on Carondelet Street in 1907 and the drink became so popular that people often waited an hour to be served one. During the 1915 Mardi Gras, he employed 35 "shaker boys" and still could not keep up with the demand. After prohibition, the Hotel Roosevelt acquired the rights to the name of this cocktail which has been equated to drinking a flower.

1 tablespoon powdered sugar

3 drops orange blossom water

juice of half a lime

juice of half a lemon

$1\,^1/_2$ oz. dry gin

1 egg white

$1\,^1/_2$ oz. milk or cream

squirt of soda

2 drops vanilla extract (optional)

Pour into a shaker with ice in order given.

Shake long and steady.

Strain into a Collins glass to serve.

BRUCE HENRICKSEN

THE LAST BIJOU

ANDRE LOVES NEW ORLEANS AND ESPECIALLY THE VIEUX CARRÉ. It is delightful to lie in bed on a Saturday night, safe behind burglar bars, savoring the call of trombones, trumpets, clarinets, and drums drifting from the open doors of Bourbon Street's Dixieland clubs—a gumbo of tempos and tunes spiced with shattering glass, with shouts and screams. Sometimes a gunshot, a siren. The sound of the Quarter on a Saturday night is Spike Jones in spades, an outrageous overture to a new week. And soon, as the din of the Quarter withdraws in waves and Andre falls asleep, he is again sitting cross-legged with his sister, Ruby, on the living room floor of the house on Chestnut Street, sitting among mountainous bowls of popcorn Mom has made as they watch Spike and his band on Milton Berle or Ed Sullivan.

Then, as the lights go up on a Sunday morning, it is delicious to awaken and don his red beret and freshly laundered shirt and slacks and step out onto the stage to commence his rounds, marshaling an appetite for coffee and a pastry at the Croissant d'Or. And if the cleanup of the streets has been delayed, Andre loves to breathe the scent of urine and stale beer, to bask in a panorama of abandoned Lucky Dogs, regurgitated oysters, and discarded napkins stained with various coagulated residues of vice, gluttony, and disease. Loves to play again the connoisseur of decadence amid smashed bottles, crumpled wrappers and bags, an occasional needle, a tampon, and blood stains on a wall. He strides across Bourbon Street and pauses for a moment to gaze down toward Canal, the bespattered pavement stretching away like a mammoth slab of super-delux, all-the-toppings Big Foot Pizza.

Always in Andre's mind there is music, an orchestra in the pit or a juke box in the corner, and as he turns toward Ursulines Street his insides swell with the strains of *Oh What a Beautiful Morning*. Certainly something wonderful is coming his way!

Then to order a cup of French roast, to linger over his choice from the Croissant d'Or's exquisite cast of fresh pastries—almond croissants, chocolate croissants, croissants dusted with sugar, éclairs with chocolate ready to ooze, Danishes with an array of fillings, trays of variously concocted muffins, a banana bread to die for, something with crumbs sparkling on the outside and mush of peach inside, and even long-gone childhood's favorite, the incomparable cream puff. The pudgy lady behind the pastries has served him often, though not so often as his mother. And she is usually patient like Mom, unless, as sometimes happens, a hungry crowd behind him resorts to muttering.

And how thrilling to play the man of leisure on the patio by the marble fountain with its lilies and goldfish, a fresh bouquet on the table, with coffee, a chocolate croissant or cream puff, and the Sunday *Times-Picayune*, to read of public officials and their latest scams, or of David Duke throwing his hood into the ring again. And after the golf news and the anti-climactic funnies, to step out onto Ursulines, the pavement steaming at the end of a morning shower, when the last raindrops are children on holiday skipping down the street, and to pause and admire the buildings that are like the stubby, exposed ganglia of something huge and maimed, something opened to the sun that is quickly dispatching the remaining clouds like so much lint. Oh what a beautiful morning! Andre loves New Orleans, but especially the Vieux Carré.

On Sundays, after his coffee and pastry, he strolls to the flea market to muse among the costumes and props of past lives, to finger faded shirts, cracked cups and saucers, and vinyl records in disintegrating jackets. Perhaps a music lover has died, and Andre imagines a deathbed scene where a loved one places a favorite album beneath the needle of an ancient stereo for the last time. Sometimes Andre buys an album to add to his own collection, maybe one picturing Frank Sinatra with a jaunty hat and one arm raised in the body language of song, or Doris Day gazing at a sunset, or maybe he'll choose Joan Baez barefoot at Big Sur with her guitar. For half an hour each Sunday, he is an archeologist of life's dreams, brooding over tables and tables of tools and artifacts, sensing the mystery of others' stories, hearing their soft, sad melodies.

But soon it is time to walk the center aisle of the Farmers Market, stopping to talk with bucolic venders about oranges, to inquire about grapefruit and peaches. As he walks, the produce displayed in long tables on either side of the aisle, he hears in his mind Rosemary Clooney's song about lovely bunches of coconuts. Many of the venders know him by sight and call to him until he settles on his choice of fruit for the bench by the river, and this time for Mom as well.

Next he passes the Café Du Monde, jammed with tourists eating beignets and rubbing powdered sugar from sleeves and shirt fronts, some then heading out to tour the French Quarter in one of the many donkey-drawn carriages waiting by Jackson Square, others strolling off with cameras and children dangling.

On this particular Sunday, Andre notices a familiar carriage and crosses Decatur to say hello. He often takes Leon's tour of the Quarter, always asking for the patter, enjoying to hear again the history of the Cabildo, of the Old Mint, or the Ursulines Convent. Although Leon speaks the mainstream dialect, Andre always hears him in the black dialect of old movies, and later Andre remembers bows and shuffles that hadn't been.

"How is business today, Leon?"

"Oh, it be berry good Mr. Bijou, sir. And how is you? I sees you doan got yo camera t'day."

"The camera is being repaired, Leon. Other than that I'm tip-top, thank you. Tell me, Leon, because I can never remember, is your trusty steed a donkey or a mule?"

"This one be a mule, Mr. Bijou."

"And what exactly is the difference between a donkey and a mule?"

"Well, sir, a mule it come from matin' a ass wid a horse, and a mule doan make no other mules—he what you call sterile."

"I see. Miscegenation, Leon. Let that be a warning. By the way, does it have to be a male ass and a female horse, or can it be the other way around?"

"No sir, Mr. Bijou. No other way 'round. It always got to be a boy ass an' a girl horse. Dat fo' sho'."

"But mules themselves can be either sterile boy mules or sterile girl mules?"

"Well, I reckon dey can, but dey doan pay each other no nevermind. No sir."

"Well, I'm sure your mule has a good life anyway, Leon. I'm sure he enjoys taking people around the Vieux Carré."

"Oh, he get plenty hay an' water. But as to enjoyin' . . . well, he just a mule, Mr. Bijou. He just turn de same corner ev'y day."

"Well in that case, I hope that you at least enjoy your day, Leon. Thank you for sharing your barnyard biology. Everyday is an education."

"An' de berry same to you, Mr. Bijou."

Andre crosses the street and climbs the steps to the top of the levee, away from the turbulence of tourists eddying about balloon-twisting mimes, street musicians, and panhandlers. There is time before the second Mass in St. Louis Cathedral to sit on his usual bench and meditate. He thinks about Mom as his hand gropes in the bag from the Farmers Market. There is just time for a peach, which he eats while admiring the pink smear of abandoned bubble gum on the walkway. Two yards further off a pigeon is eating pizza. Do they still have those nuggets of Double Bubble, he wonders, with the paper twisted on both sides of the savory cargo? Or is it always a slab now, next to some absurd baseball cards? Minutes pass. Then, as he stands, he sees on the branch of a crepe myrtle the trembling wings of a bronze butterfly, asleep in the lavender shade.

The walk past Jackson Square to the St. Louis Cathedral is cluttered today with all of Indiana, corn-fed folks with voices all chippered-up for vacation, and with all of Tokyo, well-cameraed people with sing-song voices and skin the color of French fries.

And after Mass a stroll to Canal Street to catch the streetcar, to enjoy the rattle and sway up St. Charles Avenue to Foucher. Peering out the window, he is joyously in the center of a Spike Jones production of *Clang, Clang, Clang Went the Trolley,* a drama of Buicks and Pontiacs and Toyotas stopping and swerving, snagging at intersections, left-turning and right-turning, all stuffed with people on their way to Sunday visits, to an early afternoon movie, to cheer Jimmy's softball team, or to cruise the shops in the Riverwalk. Smiling, he remembers his father's Ford, unused and dusty now in the garage, still bearing the license plate that reads DR WHIZ.

Then the walk to Touro Infirmary, where Mom, who had once starred at the Southern Rep, is playing her final scene. She is bivouacked among the usual accessories of disease, and today Andre finds that tubes have been added, tubes coming from her nose like long noodles of snot. She is being given oxygen, Nurse Wilfred explains before continuing her rounds of mercy. The roses Andre sent are on the night stand, and as he inhales their fragrance Mom's hand struggles heroically with bedding and tubing, emerging at last to where he can fondle her ancient knuckles as duty and affection dictate. He snatches the red beret from his head and perches on the edge of the bed, his feet dangling above the tile floor. He takes her hand and fumbles in the pungent silence for a topic.

"Mom," he asks finally, "remember when Grandma died? They used oxygen tents then, and the first time you took me to see her I thought she was in a big bubble of snot. Remember?"

Her face scrunches, perhaps into a smile. He continues:

"And the way she was propped at that odd angle and doing those funny things with her eyebrows, she looked just like that William F. Buckley guy you and Dad always admired! We could have put her in a talent show right there in the hospital, and she would have won hands down—Buckley in a Bag! Then, when she'd pout, she looked just like a little fishy in a baggy ready to come home from the pet store. But I don't know what you look like with all your tubes. Maybe like something served with spaghetti . . . or pasta. I wish I had my camera so I could get a picture of myself beside you!"

She gurgles, apparently appreciatively, until a bubble grows from around the noodle in one nostril. Andre weighs her gnarled hand in his for many minutes, not knowing what to say next, watching Mom's nose through many eruptive cycles. It is time for words of love and consolation, time to return ancient favors, nose-wiping favors and everything-will-be-all-right favors.

"It's okay Mom. You've had a good life, and now you're gurgling and melting. But the docs here at Touro will do their best. I'm going to talk to Doc Melville, ask him to slip something into your I.V. to sort of grease the slide, so to speak. Sort of speed things up. No fun just to linger in the noodles, right? And I called Bultman Funeral Home. I told them that it's two outs and two strikes in the bottom of the ninth. And guess what? They're ready anytime. How's that for service? And I got Benny—remember Benny, who wrote that poem when the car dealer's race horse died? I got Benny to write a eulogy. So don't worry, Mom. I'll say Benny's eulogy, then whoosh! Mom among the Noodles is Ashes in an Urn. It's truly amazing, Mom!"

He feels like an actor who has barged into the wrong play, but it is too late to stop. He shifts his weight on the edge of the bed, still clutching the hand.

"And then you've got eternity. Just think of it, blessed eternity! Do you know how long that is? Have you heard the one about the bird carrying one grain of sand per trip to the moon—no, make it the far side of Andromeda? By the time he gets all the sand in the world up there, eternity is still a party waiting to happen. Do you know how much sand there is? Think sandbags on the levee. Think hacky-sacks. And beaches and bunkers. Nevada and New Mexico! And all that time is yours! With nothing to do! You'll just sit there like the head official in tennis and look down on all the future. You'll know what incredible things people think thousands of years from now. How they like their eggs. Will it still be Protestants and Catholics, Tulane and LSU? You'll know all the mysteries of space and time— like, do they have Ground Hog Day in foreign galaxies?

"Now stop blowing bubbles like that, Mom. I know you're excited, and as I said, I'll talk to Doc Melville, slip him a twenty for alacrity—for wings for my angel! Because you have been an angel, Mom, and next time you go to sleep, you might wake up flapping feathers right along with that little bird. Maybe you'll even get to carry a grain of sand!"

Then, placing her hand in the bedding and stroking her head, he adds, "Still, you better fix your hair. There might be reincarnation."

With her tubes and her hair in tangles, with the bedding rumpled about her, her small face, pale and pocked, is like a Maxfli in the rough. He remembers the peaches.

"By the way, Mom," he says, bringing her back from a distant shore, "I brought you some peaches, but it looks like they drip everything into you now, so I'll just leave one here on the night stand by the roses as a symbol. Unless you want me to mush it up and put it in your I.V. bag? No? Well then, I'm off. What's that? Your swan song lacks articulation. You're just snorting away at the gates of hog heaven. But if you could talk, I bet you could tell some stories now—or soon!"

He slides down off of the bed and places his ear close to her scrunching face.

"Oh that's all right, Mom. Think nothing of it. Kiss, kiss, you old slugabed you."

I'm truly insane, he thinks as he walks down the corridor toward the elevator, appreciating as always the smell of medicine and chemicals, the sweet smell of doctoring. Hanging like a gargoyle on the side of the bed, he had babbled of cremation and eternity. Truly insane, but Mom understands.

He dodges traffic across Prytania, still clutching his beret in his hand, to linger over lunch at the Bluebird Café. In the ashtray on his table, a half-smoked Virginia Slim, crushed and crumpled, languishes like a cripple in a doorway. Andre wonders if the smoker was a sleek, fast-lane type out of the ads? Or an uptown matron of much rouge and girth? Perhaps a desperate boy in drag? Like Keats's urn, the ashtray won't tell. Then, drifting among his neurons, an old song about foolish things rises to consciousness, even though the cigarette that bears lipstick traces reminds Andre of no one. The waitress cleans the ashtray, wiping the song away. Then Andre savors the day's single glass of chardonnay, a small salad with Italian dressing, and a blackened breast of chicken garnished with parsley and a lemon slice. He muses long over coffee. A woman Andre remembers from the neighborhood branch of Hibernia enters with her flashing emerald eyes and hair red as a sports car. Andre looks away, then leaves to catch the streetcar on St. Charles back to the Vieux Carré.

The streetcar jostles up memories of childhood in the family house in the Garden District, especially the games of hide-and-seek in the tropical yards and gardens. As a young adult he had longed for his childhood, for the coloring books and the songs of school, for the romps under the sprinkler in nothing but his underwear. But longing has ceased its bittersweet crawl beneath the skin, and nostalgia isn't what it used to be. Now his childhood friends have run off to hide in their grownup careers, families and distant homes, and Andre is still "It."

Last week, before her speech became swamped in mucus, before becoming be-noodled for her final curtain call, Mom had made him promise to move back to the family house. Years ago, when Andre had already passed the age at which other young men were earning incomes and starting families, Dad, himself a wealthy urologist, had insisted that Andre take his own apartment, that he learn "to connect with the world." Often Dad would become angry, shouting, "Normal up, Buddy!" The issue had been marriage, and Andre remembers Dad's counsel, offered as they waited on the fourth fairway for the green to clear at Lakewood Country Club:

"Don't be ashamed to trade your wealth for beauty, my boy. Guilt and fine sentiments are thugs out to mug the genes. A woman's beauty guarantees reproductive health, and reproductive health cooks the goose of death. So check her teeth, the curve of her thighs and ass. Check her hips and hooters. You want a babe who'll throw good pups. And remember, Buddy, the eyes are windows to the sinuses. Now step back, son, and let Dr. Whiz show you how to knock down a six iron into the wind."

Dad had called him Buddy in the early days, before he switched from supporting actor to chief critic of Andre's life. The night before Dad died in the front bedroom, the oak tree had rapped its old knuckles against the house in the wind like some gnarled and ghastly messenger. That night Dad had told Andre that he must eventually come back to be the last Bijou to live in the Chestnut Street house. And now, as the streetcar sways down St. Charles, Andre sees it coming to pass. Looking out of the window at the sky, he imagines his father's soul ejaculated from his body at the moment of death, ejected like a terrified pilot, only to settle under a billowing chute onto eternal fairways where all the lies are good, all the bunkers raked, and duffers never slow you down.

Andre knows, as the streetcar clatters past the Pontchartrain Hotel, that he will miss the Quarter. But Commander's Palace is near the house on Chestnut, and Magazine Street is reputed to have some new restaurants that will do nicely for everyday. And he will be able to keep a dog, perhaps the Alsatian that he had always been denied as a child. Yes, the house on Chestnut Street, with its ancient oak, its crepe myrtles, and its rose bushes and azaleas, will do just fine. And the weeks will continue to morph their gentle loops from Sunday to Sunday.

To his left in the distance, as the streetcar approaches Lee Circle, he sees the Superdome like a mammoth skull (or is it a testicle, a snot bubble, a hooter?) erupting from beneath the city. In a few minutes, exiting the streetcar at Canal, he meanders among the bars and restaurants that populate the way back to the St. Louis Cathedral. He loves the tranquility of the cathedral, whispering its eternal *holy-oly-oaks in free* amid the noise and clutter of the Quarter, and he sits alone in its coolness with his beret resting on his knee and his rosary cycling slowly through a small hand. As the beads slip through his fingers, he imagines *Ave Maria* sung by Frank Patterson, the tenor voice floating like Spanish moss among thoughts of his impending role, the Garden District Gentleman. He is about to become the last Bijou.

His younger sister, Ruby, died several years ago in a flaming car wreck, just three months after her breast implants. Andre had thought at the time that it is a great risk to your health to alter yourself that way, and what if they poked someone's eye out? Perhaps Dow-Corning had implanted napalm left over from Vietnam, and Ruby had burst into flame during heavy petting at seventy miles per hour. And now Mom's soul was about to rise like smoke to heaven. Now Ruby, Dad, and Mom would all nestle down in their alabaster jugs, marshaled in a row on the mantel beneath the portrait of Grandfather Bijou in the house on Chestnut Street. He imagines shaking the jugs on quiet nights and hearing them whisper inside.

Outside the cathedral, some of the artists who set up camp around Jackson Square each morning are now packing their things, although tourists and sunlight remain in abundance. Mary, from whom Andre has purchased many charcoal drawings, is one of those calling it a day. Her brown hair falls softly, like rain, toward the sidewalk as she bends to gather and fold the tools and paraphernalia of the street artist. He will enter offering fruit.

"Good afternoon, Mary. You look rosy today. Would you care for a peach?"

"Peaches today? Thanks, Mr. B. You and your fruit are as inevitable as baseball scores this summer. By the way, how is your mother doing?"

"Putting on the eighteenth green," Andre says, making a sad, philosophical smile. "But what about you, have you made a solid day's worth of likenesses?"

"Likeness-wise, it's been a swell day, Mr. B," she replies, running fingers through her great festoonery of hair.

"I enjoy being able to glance up at a wall and see my own likeness, especially those you've made. It's comforting to have one's likeness about the house . . . a sort of verification. But tell me, Mary, why do we enjoy so much a charcoal and pastel drawing made by a single hand? Why are these more prized than snapshots, which are remarkable things? Centuries of science and genius have gone into the evolution of the camera—Newton's optics, the emulsion film, and now the mini-computer. Truly remarkable. And yet some charcoal applied to paper by a single hand, nearly in the same manner as the cave artists of 40,000 years ago, commands a higher price than an entire roll of snapshots."

Mary flashes her usual lovely, crooked smile, considering for a moment as she collapses her tripod. Then she replies:

"But all the people who collaborated down the years on the camera are not here in Jackson Square as Johnny snaps the shutter at Mom and Dad. Sure, mistakes and hesitations and choices went into the evolution of the camera, but all that creativity is now hidden in history."

She leans back, drifting further into the issue, giving her festoons a toss and placing one foot up against the iron fence that protects the cluster of petunias behind her and that surrounds Jackson Square's small park.

"On the other hand, my customers see choices, accidents, and corrections as I draw. The drawing is connected to human fallibility and to the moment. There are surprises waiting to happen with every drawing, and waiting to be discovered later by the viewer. So it's like life. It can always be changed in the process, and is never really finished . . . just sort of left off. Anyhow, I try to picture the customers in ways they'll like. I cook the books in their favor the way snapshots don't. Now tell me, Mr. Bijou, if you don't care for my drawing, why did you buy so many?"

"Oh, I *do* like your work. That is not what I meant at all, not at all. And now I see why I love them so. The sketch I take home is the memory of a performance."

"Well thank you! Listen, Mr. B, I gotta run. By the way, if I don't see you again I want to thank you for buying all the drawings."

"What do you mean not see me again?"

"I'm getting married, Mr. B. We're moving to Boston. Dave is finishing a degree in archeology."

"But . . . what if there's a fire, or a car wreck?" Again he feels like a blundering actor inventing lines.

"What?"

"What I mean is, Mary, you were *born* in New Orleans."

"Things change, Mr. B. Life goes on."

"But are you sure it's the right decision, Mary. How will you know what to do there?"

"Well, we make it up as we go. You know what Roethke said: *I learn by going where I have to go.* I love that poem. Anyway, listen, thanks for your concern, but I gotta run. I've really enjoyed our swell talks."

Andre works his face into a goodbye smile, a smile that remains for many moments, as though fixed with grade-school paste.

On Sundays Andre usually buys a muffuletta at the Central Grocery to enjoy while watching *60 Minutes*. But today he forgets his muffuletta and walks, deep in thought, through the half-deserted streets of a late Sunday afternoon toward his apartment on Burgundy Street. In the distance he hears the clop of a donkey—no, a mule—perhaps Leon's, pulling the day's last gaggle of tourists. Andre's morning rounds had commenced beautifully with pastries and peaches, but then there had been Mom's face invaded by noodles, her arm by an I.V. tube, and then the memory of Grandma drifting away in her bubble. And now Mary singing the praises of change.

Of course some things change. Interest rates fluctuate and microbes mutate. Somewhere around 1980 Datsuns became Nissans, and then a few years later spaghetti became pasta. And one day out of nowhere there was Velcro and missing kids on milk cartons. Even in his own home, before the breast implants and car wreck, Ruby had talked of marrying Sidney and moving to his house on Octavia Street, more than a mile away. But Andre has never known anyone who simply announced that she was moving to Boston. Hasn't she heard the song? Doesn't she know what it means to miss New Orleans?

Mary's decision to leave mingles with what she said about drawings. What is so interesting about fallibility, about the possibility of choices and mistakes, about accidents and making it up as you go along? The good in life is constancy, always finding the Croissant d'Or open in the morning, its full cast of pastries posed naughtily before you. It is seeing tourists emerge from the Café Du Monde, each in a reverie of powdered sugar, and always listening again to Leon's patter behind the clip-clop of his trusty steed. It is always finding one's bench on the levee, one's place in the scene. The art of living is nothing like Mary's precarious, slap-dash drawing, and if things change and mistakes get made, such smudges are certainly nothing to celebrate. The good life stays the same, like Coca-Cola. He is disappointed in Mary.

He locks his apartment doors behind him, the deadlock of the metal door snapping into its frame and the bolt of the wooden door sliding smoothly into its housing. He loves the Vieux Carré, but when evening comes it is best to be safely inside and merely listen.

After hanging his red beret on the coat rack, Andre holds each of his three peaches to his nose, then arranges them in a row on top of the piano. He thinks of the three urns that will soon stand guard beneath Grandfather's portrait on Chestnut Street. Standing in the middle of his living room, he is circled by pictures like the beads of a rosary. It is the gallery of his life, and the walls are crowded with Andre, each photo framed and blurred by dusty glass, blurred like Grandmother in her plastic bubble. Some are mere snapshots, others studio portraits. The exhibition has been arranged as a quasi-cinematic narrative, a montage timed to the pace of one's steps, which Andre has dubbed "Andre on the March" after the newsreel in *Citizen Kane*.

The wall right of the front door is a bustling nursery—a spanking new Andre seen through the glass of the hospital viewing room; baby Andre biding time in his mother's arms; Andre in his crib on Chestnut Street, reaching for a dangling mobile; Andre with a pacifier plugged in his mouth. As today's Andre moves along the wall, the pictured Andre grows older— Andre under the live oak with his first red wagon, Andre and Ruby at the beach with buckets and shovels; Andre and a neighbor girl by the crepe myrtles wielding two of his father's golf clubs, "playing doctor" he used to like to say to tease his father. And many more. Each picture is a shaving of time nicked off by the camera and preserved under glass.

Andre pauses by the stereo, lowering the needle to his recording of Moussorgsky's suite. Then he continues to the back wall, which offers pictures of Andre at Jesuit High School, where the priests had filled him with visions of Andre lifting a chalice before a throng of the faithful. And there are two blowups of Andre at Loyola University, one in which a grinning Andre holds his trophy for third in intramural golf, the other in which an Andre in green tights plays Puck in Marquette Theatre. Then, coming up the adjacent wall toward the front, the age of the pictured Andre approaches that of the viewing Andre. There are many scenes with elderly parents, two of him beside the coffin at Dad's funeral. Andre pauses to recall his father's dying words, his last performance. He had raised himself on one arm in the bedroom by the oak tree, had lifted the other into the air, and intoned in his deepest register:

"Marriage, my son! Marriage! You must look to the future. You must marry and play golf. Golf recapitulates our ancestral past, the wielding of weapons and the flight of projectiles. But the thrill of the sight of the flight of the ball also embodies our drive toward transcendence. The long ball hanging in the air is a figure of the future. Golf is the ultimate image of evolution, making copulation coherent. Like the next champion on the tee at Augusta, we must blast our genes through the winds of change, beyond the hazardous *fin de siécle*, and into the fresh and beckoning fairway of the new millennium. 'Tis generation only that dulls the Grim Guy's sickle and frosts the baleful balls of Death. So normal up, Andre! In the words of the immortal Dr. Freud, tee it up and get laid!"

Two days later Dad lay in a lacquered coffin, straight and proper as an Oscar—or a King Cobra driver.

After the funeral pictures, in a special place to the left of the front door, Mary's charcoal drawings converse among themselves. He enjoys the fact that Mary has found various poses for him. In one, for instance, his head is bare and he cradles his camera artistically, in another he wears his red beret at a jaunty angle, like Frank Sinatra, and in a third he carries his Sunday bag of fruit. But in each drawing, Andre sits in a chair on the sidewalk by Jackson Square, the shops and restaurants receding into a background where people seem to hurry about their various lives. Some of these people may be the accidents of composition Mary had spoken of—smudges turned into art. In any case, the people and the doorways trouble him now, as though the doorways are mysteries that others explore as he, quietly seated in the foreground, smiles blithely out into another world.

His thoughts of Mary mingle with a melody. Will he, too, be seeing her in all the old familiar places?

Stepping back to view the charcoals as a group, it occurs to him that the smudged background people are Andres he never became, parts that he turned down in life's drama. There, in one drawing, is Andre the business-man, scurrying along the street with a briefcase; there in another strolls Andre the lover, arm in arm with reproductive perfection. And perhaps that dark blur by the doorway in a third is Father Andre Bijou, S.J. In each drawing, lurking behind the central image of himself, he now sees a small gallery of once possible Andres.

As Moussorgsky ends, he realizes that his day and also his life have spi-raled toward a still center like the grooves of a phonograph record. Would it have been worthwhile to have been more like others, like those who colored outside the lines in school and who ran off to hide in grownup jobs and families? If other lives mutate and morph, why has he always just been Andre? And are these thoughts the surprises Mary said were hidden in every drawing?

Sometimes Andre likes to reverse the gallery tour, running the movie backwards to his birth. And often he thinks how sweet it would be to un-learn words and the world and gently dwindle down and back into his young mother's arms, warm as morning pastry. But today there is no plea-sure in this thought. Although *60 Minutes* has commenced, he merely stands for a long time, still in his living room, framed by the doorway and sur-rounded by his likenesses dozing in their frames. His film is over, and the moment flickers. Then it begins to darken around him and his newly dis-covered other selves, as twilight returns to the Vieux Carré like an old song.

Fairy Tale

I like the way fairy tales start in America. When I learn English for real, I buy books for children and I read, "Once upon a time." I recognize this word "upon" from some GI who buys me Saigon teas and spends some time with me and he is a cowboy from the great state of Texas. He tells me he gets up on the back of a bull and he rides it. I tell him he is joking with Miss Noi (that's my Vietnam name), but he says no, he really gets up on a bull. I make him explain that "up on" so I know I am hearing right. I want to know for true so I can tell this story to all my friends so that they understand, no lie, what this man who stays with me can do. After that, a few years later, I come to America and I read some fairy tales to help me learn more English and I see this word and I ask a man in the place I work on Bourbon Street in New Orleans if this is the same. Up on and upon. He is a nice man who comes late in the evening to clean up after the men who see the show. He says this is a good question and he thinks about it and he says that yes, they are the same. I think this is very nice, how you get up on the back of time and ride and you don't know where it will go or how it will try to throw you off.

Once upon a time I was a dumb Saigon bargirl. If you want to know how dumb some Vietnam bargirl can be, I can give you one example. A man brought me to America in 1974. He says he loves me and I say I love that man. When I meet him in Saigon, he works in the embassy of America. He can bring me to this country even before he marries me. He says he wants to marry me and maybe I think that this idea scares me a little bit. But I say, what the hell. I love him. Then boom. I'm in America and this man is different from in Vietnam, and I guess he thinks I am different, too. How dumb is a Saigon bargirl is this. I hear him talk to a big crowd of important people in Vietnam—businessman, politician, big people like that. I am there, too, and I wear my best aó dài, red like an apple, and my quân, my silk trousers, are white. He speaks in English to these Vietnam people because they are big, so they know English. Also my boyfriend does not speak Vietnam. But at the end of his speech he says something in my language and it is very important to me.

You must understand one thing about the Vietnam language. We use tones to make our words. The sound you say is important, but just as important is what your voice does, if it goes up or down or stays the same or it curls around or it comes from your throat, very tight. These all change the meaning of the word, sometimes very much, and if you say one tone and I hear a certain word, there is no reason for me to think that you mean some other tone and some other word. It was not until everything is too late and I am in America that I realize something is wrong in what I am hearing that day. Even after this man is gone and I am in New Orleans, I have to sit down and try all different tones to know what he wanted to say to those people in Saigon.

He wanted to say in my language, "May Vietnam live for ten thousand years." What he said, very clear, was, "The sunburnt duck is lying down." Now, if I think this man says that Vietnam should live for ten thousand years, I think he is a certain kind of man. But when he says that a sunburnt duck is lying down—boom, my heart melts. We have many tales in Vietnam, some about ducks. I never hear this tale that he is telling us about, but it sounds like it is very good. I should ask him that night what this tale is, but we make love and we talk about me going to America and I think I understand anyway. The duck is not burned up, destroyed. He is only sunburnt. Vietnam women don't like the sun. It makes their skin dark, like the peasants. I understand. And the duck is not crushed on the ground. He is just lying down and he can get up when he wants to. I love that man for telling the Vietnam people this true thing. So I come to America and when I come here I do not know I will be in more bars. I come thinking I still love that man and I will be a housewife with a toaster machine and a vacuum cleaner. Then when I think I don't love him anymore, I try one last time and I ask him in the dark night to tell me about the sunburnt duck, what is that story. He thinks I am one crazy Vietnam girl and he says things that can burn Miss Noi more than the sun.

So boom, I am gone from that man. There is no more South Vietnam and he gives me all the right papers so I can be American and he can look like a good man. This is all happening in Atlanta. Then I hear about New

Orleans. I am a Catholic girl and I am a bargirl, and this city sounds for me like I can be both those things. I am twenty-five years old and my titties are small, especially in America, but I am still number-one girl. I can shake it baby, and soon I am a dancer in a bar on Bourbon Street and everybody likes me to stay a Vietnam girl. Maybe some men have nice memories of Vietnam girls.

I have nice memories. In Saigon I work in a bar they call Blossoms. I am one blossom. Around the corner I have a little apartment. You have to walk into the alley and then you go up the stairs three floors and I have a place there where all the shouting and the crying and sometimes the gunfire in the street sounds very far away. I do not mix with the other girls. They do bad things. Take drugs, steal from the men. One girl lives next to me in Saigon and she does bad things. Soon people begin to come in a black car. She goes. She likes that, but I do not talk to her. One day she goes in the black car and does not come back. She leaves everything in her place. Even her Buddha shrine to her parents. Very bad. I live alone in Saigon. I have a double bed with a very nice sheet. Two pillows. A cedar closet with my clothes, which are very nice. Three aó dài, one apple red, one blue like you see in the eyes of some American man, one black like my hair. I have a glass cabinet with pictures. My father. Some two or three American men who like me very special. My mother. My son.

Yes, I have a son. One American gives me that son, but my boy is living in Vietnam with my mother. My mother says I cannot bring up a child with my life. I say to her that my son should have the best. If Miss Noi is not best for my son, then my son should be someplace different. When the man brings me to America, he does not want a son either, and my mother does not talk to me very much anyway except to say my son is Vietnam boy, not American boy. At least my mother is my blood, though sometimes she is unhappy about that, I think. I do not think they are happy in Vietnam now, but who can say? You have a mother and then you have a son and then boom, you do not have either a mother or a son, though they are alive somewhere, so I do not have to pray for their souls. I do not have to be unhappy.

I pray in my little room in Saigon. I am a Catholic girl and I have a large statue of Mary in my room. That statue is Mary the mother of God, not Mary Magdalene, who was a bargirl one time, too. My statue of Mary the mother of God is very beautiful. She is wearing a blue robe and her bare feet are sticking out of the bottom. Her feet are beautiful like the feet of a

Vietnam girl, and I pray to Mary and I paint her toenails and I talk to her. She faces the door and does not see my bed.

I sleep with men in Saigon. This is true. But I sleep with only one at a time. I do not take drugs with any man. I do not steal from any man. I give some man love when he is alone and frightened and he wants something soft to be close to him. I take money for this loving, but I do not ask them to take me to restaurants or to movie shows or to buy me jewelry or any gifts. If a girl does not make money but makes him take her to a restaurant and a movie show and buy her jewelry and then gives him loving, is this different? I would not take a man to my room and love him if I did not want to do that. The others could buy me Saigon tea in the Blossoms bar. The men would water the blossoms with Saigon tea. I talk with them and they put their arm around me and play music on the jukebox, but I do not take them to my room unless I would like them to be there. Then they would give me money, but I ask for nothing else. Only when they love me very much I ask them to get me something. In the place where the GI eats, they have something I cannot get in Saigon. This thing is an apple. I only ask for apples. I buy mangoes and papayas and pineapples and other sweet things to eat in the market, but in South Vietnam, an apple is a special thing. I hold an apple and it fills my hand and it is very smooth and very hard and it is red like my favorite aó dài. So red. I bite it and it is very sweet, like sweet water, like a stream of water from a mountain, and it is not stringy like a pineapple, and it is not mushy like a mango or papaya.

In New Orleans I buy many apples. I eat them in America whenever I want to. But is that memory not better? A GI who loves me brings me an apple and I put it on the table where Mary sits and after that man is sleeping and the room is dark, I walk across the floor and I am naked and the air feels cool on me and I take that apple and go to the window and I watch the dark roofs of Saigon and the moon rising and I eat my apple.

In New Orleans, there are apples in the stores and I buy them and I eat too many. The taste is still good but it is not special anymore. I am sometimes very tired. I take off my clothes on the stage of the club. I am not a blossom in New Orleans. I am a voodoo girl. The manager of the club gives me a necklace of bones to wear and the faces of the men are raised to me and I am naked. Many eyes see me. Many men want to touch Miss Noi, and I sleep with men in New Orleans. I still do not take them to my bed if I am not ready to like them. When they get up in the morning I always make sure they shave right. Many of the men miss a place at the back of their jaw or under their bottom lip. I make sure they have a clean shirt. I am ready to wash their shirt if they want me to. But they pay me money and they go, and they do not let me clean their shirt. Sometimes they go before the night is done. These are the men who have wives. I can see the place on their fingers where the sun has tanned around the ring which they took off to come to the bar. Their finger is dark skinned, but the band of flesh is white and they look naked there, even more naked than I must look to them on the stage. Their ring is in some pocket. I worry about their rings. What if the ring is to fall out on my floor and get kicked under the bed? What do they say to their wife when she sees their naked hand?

How does a life change? You meet some man who says he will take you away across the sea and he will marry you. A blossom and even a voodoo girl gets many men who talk about love and some of them talk about marriage. You are very careful about that. Many girls on Bourbon Street tell stories and laugh very hard about the men who say they want to marry them. I do not tell the story about the embassy man and the sunburnt duck. They would not understand. I dance naked on the stage and one night the announcer makes a big deal about Miss Noi being Vietnam girl. Sometimes he does this, sometimes Miss Noi is just some voodoo girl. But this night he sees some men in the audience with jackets on that says they were in Vietnam, so he says I am from Saigon and I am ready to please.

After I dance and put on my clothes and go and sit at the bar, these men in the jackets do not come near me. But one other man comes and stands beside me and he calls me "Miss." He says, "Miss, may I sit down?" If you want to sit next to a bargirl and hope that she will think you are an okay man, this is a good way to start, with "May I sit down, Miss." I look at this man and he is a tall man with a long neck so that he seems to stretch up as high as he can to see over a fence. His skin is dark, like he's been in the sun too long, and he is wearing a plaid shirt and blue jeans and his hands are rough, but there is no white band where a ring has been taken off. I look at his face and his eyes are black, but very small. His nose is long. Vietnam noses are not long, and though I know many Americans in my life and some French, too, I still lean back just a little when there is a long nose, because it seems to be pointing at me.

This man is not number one for looking at him, but he calls me "Miss" and he stands with his eyes looking down and then he peeks at me and then he lowers his eyes again as he waits for me to say if he can sit down. So I say yes. He seems like a nice man.

"You are very beautiful, Miss Noi," this man says.

This is 1981 and Miss Noi is thirty years old and I am glad to hear some man say it this way. I am not sexy bitch, wiggle it baby, oh boy oh boy it's hot, it feels good. These are okay things, too, for Miss Noi. These men give me money and they love me. But this man says I am beautiful and I say, "Thank you. You buy me a drink, okay?" I say this to all the men who sit next to me at the bar. This is what I am supposed to do. But I want this man to buy me a drink because he thinks I am beautiful. So he buys me a drink and I say he must buy one, too, and he buys a Dr Pepper, even though it is the same price as a drink of liquor. My drink is supposed to be liquor but it is mostly water, like Saigon tea. They make it the same in New Orleans, the New Orleans tea.

We sip our drinks and he does not have many words to say. He sips and looks at me and sips and I have many words I use on men. You from this town? You in New Orleans for long? You like Bourbon Street? You listen to jazz music? What is your work? But I do not use these words. I tell you I am sometimes very tired. This man's long nose dips down toward his Dr Pepper like he's going to drink through it, but it stops and then he lifts his chin a little and sips at his straw. His face seems very strange-looking and his hair is black but a little greasy and I just let him be quiet if he wants and I am quiet, too. Then he says, "It was nice to see you dance."

"You come often and see me dance and buy me drinks, okay?"

"You look different," he says.

"Miss Noi is a Vietnam girl. You never see that before."

"I seen it," this man says. "I was in Vietnam."

I have many men say they were in my country and they always sound a little funny, like they have a nasty secret or a sickness that you should be careful not to catch. And sometimes they just call it "Nam," saying that word with broken glass in their voice or saying it through their noses and their noses wrinkle up like the word smells when it comes out. But this man says the name of my country quiet and I don't always understand what American voices do, but he sounds sad to me. I say to him, "You didn't like being there? It makes you sad?"

He lifts his face and he looks at me and he says, "I was very happy there. Weren't you?"

Well, this is something for me to think about. I could just answer this man, who is only one more man who saw me dance naked. I could just say yes or no and I could talk about reasons why. I am good at bargirl bullshit when I want to talk like that. But this man's eyes look at mine and I look away and sip my drink.

What do I know about men, after all? I can't tell anything anymore. I take men to my bed and I save my money and there have been very many men, I guess. It's like eating too many apples. You take a bite now and you can make yourself remember that apples are sweet, but it is like the apple in your mouth is not even there. You eat too many apples and all you can do is remember them. So this man who comes with his strange face and sounds sad when he talks about Vietnam because he was so happy there— I don't know what to make of him and so I take him to my room and he is very happy about that.

He tells me his name is Fontenot. He lives far away from New Orleans. He owns a little boat and he works fixing car engines. He was in Saigon one year working on car engines and he loved that city very much. I ask him why but he can't really explain. This is all of our talk, every bit of it, except before he makes love to me he says he is sorry he can never get his hands clean. He shows me how the grease from the car engines gets around his fingernails and he can't get them clean. I tell him not to worry and he makes love to me, and when he gets off me and lies down, he turns his head and I think that is because he does not want me to see that he is crying. I want to ask if he is very sad again, but I don't say anything. His face is away from me and he wants it like that and so I say nothing. Those are all the words of that night. In the morning I go into the bathroom and he is in the tub and I kneel beside him and take his hands and I have a cuticle file and I clean the grease away. He kisses my hands when he leaves.

What do I know about men anymore? That is not much to say about Mr. Fontenot. He came to see Miss Noi on a Saturday night and left on Sunday morning. Then the next Saturday night I was naked on the stage and I saw his face at the foot of the runway, looking up with his long nose pointed at my special part, and I felt a strange thing. My face got warm and I turned my back to him and danced away. After I finished my dance, I got dressed and came out to the bar, but he was not there. I asked the guy behind the bar, "Did you see that tall man with the thin neck and the long nose that I had a drink with last week?"

This guy says, "The one who looks like a goddamn goose?"

I don't like this guy behind the bar. I never even learn his name. So I say, "Go to hell, you," and I go outside and there is Mr. Fontenot waiting on the sidewalk. I go to him and I take his arm and we go around the corner and down the block and he says, "I couldn't hang around in there, Miss Noi. It makes me uncomfortable to talk to you in there."

I say, "I know, honey. I know." I see all types of men, though I realize I don't understand any of them deep down. But I know some men feel nervous in a bar. They come there to meet me but then they tell themselves that I really don't belong there, it's not worthy of me. And if I take this type of man to my room, they give me money quiet, folding the bills and putting them under a vase or somewhere, like it's not really happening. I know that kind of man. They can be very sweet sometimes.

We go up to my apartment again. It is a small place, like Saigon. I am comfortable there. Outside my window is a phony balcony. It looks like a balcony but it is only a foot wide, just a grill on the window. But it is nice. It looks like lace, though it is made of iron. I close the shade and turn to Mr. Fontenot and he is sitting on my bed. I go and sit next to him.

"I've been thinking about you," he says.

"You drive all the way back to New Orleans just to see Miss Noi again?"

"Of course," he says. His voice is gentle, but there's also something in it that says I should know this already. This is plenty strange to me, because I know nothing about Mr. Fontenot, really. A few words. He's a quiet man. I know nothing more about him than any man.

Then he says, "Look," and he shows me his hands. I don't understand. "I got one of those things you used on me last week." I look closer and I see that his hands are clean.

This makes me feel one more strange thing, a little sinking inside me. I say, "See? You have no need for Miss Noi anymore."

He takes me serious. He puts his arm around my shoulders and he is right to do this. "Don't say that, Miss Noi."

So then we make love. When we are finished, he turns his face away from me again and I reach over and turn it back. There are no tears, but he is looking very serious. I say, "Tell one thing you like in Saigon."

Mr. Fontenot wiggles his shoulders and looks away. "Everything," he says.

"Why should I not think you are a crazy man? Everybody knows Americans go to Vietnam and they want to go home quick and forget everything. When they think they like Vietnam while they are there, they come home and they know it was all just a dream."

Mr. Fontenot looks at me one more time. "I'm not crazy. I liked everything there."

" 'Everything' means same as 'nothing.' I do not understand that. One thing. Just think about you on a street in Saigon and you tell me one thing."

"Okay," he says and then he says it again louder, "Okay," like I just push him some more, though I say nothing. It is louder but not angry. He sounds like a little boy. He wrinkles his brow and his little black eyes close. He stays like this for too long.

I ask, "So?"

"I can't think."

"You are on a street. Just one moment for me."

"Okay," he says. "A street. It's hot in Saigon, like Louisiana. I like it hot. I walk around. There's lots of people rushing around, all of them pretty as nutria."

"Pretty as what?"

"It's a little animal that has a pretty coat. It's good."

"Tell me more,"

"Okay," he says. "Here's something. It's hot and I'm sweating and I'm walking through your markets in the open air and when I get back to my quarters, my sweat smells like the fruit and the vegetables in your markets."

I look at Mr. Fontenot and his eyes are on me and he's very serious. I do not understand a word he's saying now, but I know he's not saying any bullshit, that's for sure. He sweats and smells like fruit in Saigon. I want to talk to him now, but what am I to say to this? So I just start in about fruit. I tell him the markets have many good fruits, which I like very much. Mangoes, mangosteens, jackfruit, durians, papaya. I ask him and he says he has not eaten any of these. I still want to say words, to keep this going, so I tell him, "One fruit we do not have in South Vietnam is apples. I loved apples in Saigon when GI bring me apples from their mess hall. I never have apples till the GIs give them to me."

As soon as I say this, Mr. Fontenot's brow wrinkles again and I feel like there's a little animal, maybe a nutria, trying to claw his way out from inside Miss Noi. I have made this man think about all the GIs that I sleep with in Saigon. He knows now what kind of girl he is talking to. This time I turn my face away from him to hide tears. Then we stop talking and we sleep and in the morning he goes and I do not come and help him bathe because he learns from Miss Noi already how to clean his hands.

Is this a sad story or a happy story for Miss Noi? The next Saturday Mr. Fontenot does not come and see me dance naked. I sit at the bar with my clothes on and I am upon a time and I wonder if I'm going to fall off now. Then boom. I go out of that place and Mr. Fontenot is standing on the sidewalk. He is wearing a suit with a tie and his neck reaches up high out of his white shirt and I can bet his hands are clean and he moves to me and one of his hands comes out from behind his back and he gives me an apple and he says he wants to marry Miss Noi.

Once upon a time there was a duck with a long neck and a long beak like all ducks and he lives in a place all alone and he does not know how to build a nest or preen his own feathers. Because of this, the sun shines down and burns him, makes his feathers turn dark and makes him very sad. When he lies down to sleep, you think that he is dead, he is so sad and still. Then one day he flies to another part of the land and he finds a little animal with a nice coat and though that animal is different from him, a nutria, still he lies down beside her. He seems to be all burnt up and dead. But the nutria does not think so and she licks his feathers and makes him well. Then he takes her with him to live in Thibodaux, Louisiana, where he fixes cars and she has a nice little house and she is a housewife with a toaster machine and they go fishing together in his little boat and she never eats an apple unless he thinks to give it to her. Though this may not be very often, they taste very good to her.

DAVID MADDEN

THE NEW ORLEANS OF POSSIBILITIES

RIND MIST PRICKLING HIS NOSTRILS, he crushed the orange slice against his palate, constricted his gullet to keep from swallowing too much of the surging juice at once, enjoyed even the sting where his new pipe had burnt the tip of his tongue.

"Where did you get this orange?" Kenneth asked the woman at the next table whose smile as she had offered him the fruit had enhanced the shockingly sudden deliciousness of the juice.

"At the produce market down the street," said the man, realizing the woman had not heard Kenneth, enrapt as she obviously was in the first hour of the Sunday morning of lovers.

"I haven't had a real orange in years," Kenneth said to the woman, who turned toward him, the breeze blowing her hair across her eyes. She smiled again, for *him* now.

Eating the orange, section by section, Kenneth glanced at the lovers who in their felicity had chosen more strawberries, bananas, black cherries, peaches, and oranges than their stomachs could hold, whose overflow of felicity and fruit had touched him. So it was not only in balmy breeze and Sunday morning sunlight that they basked.

New Orleans, the most romantic city of his imagination, the city in which he had once expected to realize so many possibilities, had become so routine. He had awakened in the Royal Sonesta this morning to a palpable, almost urgent impulse to do something slightly unusual. Having supper alone at Begue's last night, on the occasion of his thirty-sixth birthday, he had realized that except for Charleston he had seen—though only as a salesman can see—every American city he had ever wanted to see. Doubting there would ever be a necessity to go to Charleston and failing to imagine it as a vacation attraction for Helen and John made him sad. But up in the room, looking down on Bourbon Street, where he no longer felt safe walking at night, he had realized too that New Orleans, his favorite city even over San Francisco, had in his routine become almost as bland as an airport layover. And when the morning light woke him, he knew he had not felt merely the blues of a man away from home on his mid-passage birthday. He had projected his life to live in cities, and the cities were gone. Sipping café au lait with fifty tourists outside the Café Du Monde and eating beignets had not quite met his criterion for something slightly unusual. The gift of the orange, the woman's smile, had.

The lovers left their table littered with fruit peelings, seeds, rinds, pits. Unable to sustain the shared moment in the breeze and sunlight, Kenneth walked toward the produce market, his system so unused to juice straight from the rind that he felt nauseated.

The second time he had come to New Orleans the heat, humidity, and pollution had been so powerful he had seen the market from an air-conditioned touring bus with Helen and John. The first time, he had come alone to handle a new account and had confined his walking to Bourbon Street.

The mingled odors of fruits and vegetables were so intense that he tasted the market before he smelled it.

Walking under the long open-sided shed, down the narrow aisle between the stalls, Kenneth felt as if the bodies, faces, hands, and the fruit and vegetables were a palpitating morass that excited and delighted him, reminding him of his childhood birthday parties in Indiana. He bought pears, apples, peaches, bananas, a pineapple, strawberries, oranges, and tomatoes, and wondered what he would do with them. Appointments in Houston and Dallas lay between New Orleans and home. I may never *see* stuff like this again in my lifetime, he thought, smiling condescendingly at his isolated gesture.

Entering the lower end of the shed, he saw that this section was given over to a flea market. He wished Helen, who loved garage sales, could be there. The intriguingly slummy atmosphere of this part of the French Quarter, of the market, drew him among the tables, some of which were set up in the parking spaces. Bright old clothes hung from the barred windows of a discarded streetcar with Desire as its destination. Inside a high iron fence, tourists were being guided through the vast Old Mint building, recently restored after decades as a prison.

His mood fluctuated between revulsion at the sleaziness and excitement at possibilities. Looking at objects that ranged from cheap new pseudocraft products to genuine antiques, from trash to bizarre oddities of some value to collectors, he forgot the queasiness that café au lait, powdered-sugar-sprinkled beignets, and orange juice had induced. Realizing that he had fully acted on impulse to break routine and open himself to possibilities made him feel a sense of adventure, and a little anxiety made him reach for objects he had never imagined he would ever want to look at, much less buy and use and enjoy.

"For the man who has everything," Helen had said, presenting the pipe three days before his birthday. Now he had twelve pipes, only one of which got the use and care a pipe demands. And here, too, among the disgorgings of New Orleans attics were discarded pipes that perhaps someone here would be glad to smoke.

That a buyer had been imagined for each likely and unlikely object on disarrayed display intrigued him as much as the objects themselves. The snaggle-toothed old woman, who looked like a caricature of a witch, had sat in a foul-smelling room somewhere in this sprawling city and imagined a buyer for those rusty iron pots. Kenneth paid her three-fifty for the cast-iron corn-stick mold, so heavy it almost balanced the load of fruit in his other hand.

And that bearded man who reached across the table, his underarm stench palpable as flesh, had stooped among those coils of barbed wire and anchors and canoe paddles, seeing buyers clearly enough to load it all into the back of his VW van and haul it down here at daybreak. Kenneth passed on by the barbed wire.

And this spaced-out girl, dark circles under her eyes, veinless smooth hands trembling more visibly than the old woman's, had squatted in some chairless, mattress-strewn, windowless slave quarters off a courtyard as sump-smelling as a Venice canal, convincing herself someone would buy one or two or three of the old photographs she had foraged out of attics and basements and rooms of abandoned houses, old houses torn down, and trash cans where she had hoped perhaps to find edibles. Too flummoxed by such incomprehensible assumptions to move on, Kenneth stopped, stared down into the lopsided cardboard box into which the girl had dumped thousands of photographs, mostly snapshots muted in time's sepia tone.

The moist fruit had dampened the bag. He lifted and hugged it, damp side against his coat, and walked on among the 78-rpm records, the fabrics and shirts and blouses and dresses, the rings and buttons, the glass insulators, the Mississippi driftwood and cypress knees, the old comic books, the tables of unfocusable clutter, the neater displays of antique toys, the moldy books and *National Geographics* dating from the twenties, that Kenneth was too burdened to leaf through.

He made the rounds, continuing long after fatigue and nausea and the increasing heat and humidity had made him sluggish, as if to miss even scanning sight of any of this stuff would wake him in the middle of the night in Houston or Dallas or home in Chicago, regretful, with that gnawing sense of unfinished business. The peculiarity of such a premonition making him feel a need to assert his own control over his behavior, he turned away from the flimsier tables lined up alongside the streetcar named Desire, and with the phrase, *he retraced his steps*, consciously in his mind, went back the way he came.

Kenneth waited for a young man in overalls and wide-brimmed leather hat to pay for the photographs he had stuffed into his pockets.

"May I set these down a moment?" Kenneth looked at the dark circles around the girl's eyes. She nodded rapidly, unblinking.

He reached into the bulging box, asking, "How much are these?" to make conversation, for the girl made him uneasy. He picked one of the photographs gently from the clutter, as if handling someone's personal effects.

"Fifty cents a handful."

"You don't sell them one by one?"

"Fifty cents a handful."

Imagining the young man in overalls grabbing two fistfuls, cramming his pockets, crushing some of the photos, shocked Kenneth.

"Get out the pictures, Granny." His grandmother used to imitate the way he had said that when he was a boy. Then she would honor his new request and take the hat box down off the shelf in her closet and sit beside him on the couch and gently pick them one by one from the loose pile. He felt an urge to tell this girl what his grandmother said, to imitate *her* voice imitating his own, but even had she not stared at him, seeing nothing, he knew he wouldn't have told *anybody*.

His fingers webbed together to cradle his head, a man leans back in a high-backed straight chair, his foot braced on a white railing that runs blurred out of the edge of the photograph toward the end of the porch, getting thinner as it reaches his foot, the toe of the other foot touching the floor almost delicately. Someone caught his semicandid pose at the turn of the century. The locale was possibly the Garden District. Smiling, imagining his grandmother's response, Kenneth placed the photograph back on top, trying to put it where he found it.

He picked up a raw recruit of the forties, saluting, mock-serious, his billed cap resting on his ears. On V-J Day was he in Times Square or beneath a white headstone in France? He laid it down. Propped up in a hospital bed, a young woman in a lace-trimmed nightgown holds her newborn baby. The kind of shot Kenneth had once snapped himself.

A plump man in suspenders sits in his favorite chair under a fringed lamp on a stand, his delicately smoking cigar held between the fingers of his upraised hand, at the ready.

An old man changes a tire on a road in arid hills, a little boy sitting on the running board. The man's wife probably took this one. Out West, on vacation.

An elementary school class against a freshly washed blackboard, half of the children smiling, half tight-lipped. Losing their baby teeth?

A child sits on a table, a birthday cake with three candles between its legs, presents heaped on both sides. Kenneth had one of himself at four, a similar pose.

A young man in a jogging outfit, his arms full of old record albums, stopped to glance over Kenneth's shoulder at a family in their backyard under a mimosa tree, a man in a hammock, a child in diapers wearing a sailor hat, lifting the long handle of a lawn mower, a woman taking a bite from a piece of cake, an old man reaching for an apple from a tree, smiling for the camera.

"You want that one, sir?"

"I'm just looking."

"Mind if I take it?"

"No, go ahead."

"Fifty cents a handful," the girl said, with no more response to the young man than to Kenneth, who was feeling older than thirty-six the longer he stood there.

The young man obediently grabbed "a handful" and carefully slipped them into the pocket where he had found the fifty-cent piece.

Kenneth wondered whether older people had bought any of the pictures. As he picked them up at an increasingly faster tempo, his assumption that they came from many sources was confirmed. The faces from picture to picture bore no resemblance to each other, although a few that turned up in succession were in a sequence. They seemed to span decades, with many settings beyond New Orleans. Kenneth looked at her. Maybe she wanders in a trance like a gypsy from city to city, rummaging in trash cans. A free romantic life, for which he felt a fleeting envy, irrational not only because she looked like death warmed over, but because "wandering from city to city" described his own life.

A young man and his date pose in formals at a prom. Kenneth wondered whether the slim young man now had a pot belly.

A telephone operator of the forties, surprised, ruins a candid shot, shouting no, her hand thrust out to blot the camera eye.

Children, perhaps a Sunday school class, at a picnic, one boy in a swimsuit, looking straight up into the sky. Kenneth imagined an airplane.

A grinning young man opens the door of his new, perhaps his first, car, early fifties model.

A man behind a soda fountain, his hand on the nozzle, two girls having turned from their sodas to smile at—good ol' George, Kenneth imagined. I can remember cool soda fountains, said Kenneth, almost aloud. Helen would get a kick out of this one. They were just going out when we came in.

"I'd like to buy this one."

"Fifty cents a handful."

"No, just this one. Glad to pay fifty cents for this one."

"Look, man, I'd like to dump all of this, save me the hassle of lugging it back to the room. Take a handful, will you?"

"Why not?" He pushed together, like strewn bridge cards, enough to stack on his right palm.

As he slipped the stack into his coat pocket, she said, still not looking at him, not seeing him, "Take two—no extra charge."

That would be greedy, he started to say, but the comment seemed inappropriate even for her benumbed ears. He started aligning another stack.

"Look, man, like they aren't going to bite you."

"No, I just. . ." He wondered how, in such situations, such marginal people manage to make one feel inept, inferior.

Digging down with a kind of venal abandon, Kenneth dredged up an overflowing handful, noticing that one of those that spilled was a snapshot of a young man sucking in his belly, flexing his muscles, letting his pants drop over his hips below his navel, clenching teeth and bugging eyes that were the spitting image of his own. He smiled self-consciously, as if the girl, her hand still held out for the fifty cents, had discerned the resemblance in the same instant of surprise.

Now what do you know about that? Amazing. He'd always heard that by the law of averages there must be somewhere on the earth someone who exactly resembles yourself, and in all time and all the universe, someone who is your exact duplicate, or your *doppelganger*, a scary concept that had universal appeal. And once, he had picked up the newspaper, startled at the face of a bush pilot who had crashed in the Alaskan wilds, survived subzero weather for five weeks, and lay in the hospital. Even with a tube up the nose, the frost-bitten face against the white pillow was so obviously his own, he called Helen out of the shower, dripping, to look at it. "That's Kenneth Howard all right," she corroborated.

Picking it up, recalling the girl's assurance it wouldn't bite, Kenneth started to slide it beneath the deck as a novelty item to startle Helen and John and party guests. Within the magnifying range of his first pair of glasses, the face proved to be Kenneth's own.

The exhilarating moment of discovering a wild coincidence faded quickly into reasonable doubt. He put the second deck in his other coat pocket and looked closely at the face. Holding his breath, his teeth clenched in a jack-o-lantern grin, his eyes bulging like Peter Lorre. Who could—could even he?—say whether the face was his.

When? When he was about seventeen. Where? Against the side of a garage, the white paint peeling badly. He remembered his severe sunburn peeling that summer. But that was not his father's garage. Perhaps a neighbor's. He tried to remember, and couldn't. He looked for a scar or some revealing mark on his naked chest. All his scars dated from college football. Was that black spot the size of a nickel his navel? How does one recognize one's own navel? He laughed. But it didn't seem as funny as on the surface it ought to have. Well, it's not me.

Imagining the girl scrutinizing him for his strange behavior, Kenneth looked up. Still, she saw nothing—catatonic—her palm open, not impatiently. Indifferently.

Not possible. Not possible? Hadn't he always thought of New Orleans as the city of possibilities? In New Orleans, what was not possible? Uneasily, he smiled, shrugged it off as a wild coincidence, the kind of experience you come to New Orleans for, even if you're coming anyway for routine reasons, and slipped the photo into his coat pocket with the others, wondering who had snapped this shot.

Idly, as he felt in his pocket for a fifty-cent piece, he pushed his fingers through the box, stirring up images. He handed her two quarters and picked up the corn-stick mold. As he lifted it, the bag broke, and he had to chase the fruit down the aisle among shuffling feet. People helped him. It's the business suit. He remembered reading an article that answered the question, Who gets helped, where and when, if somebody drops something in a public place? Noticing that the oranges rolled the greater distance gave him a comforting sense of workaday reality. And there were the bananas lying where they had landed. None of the fruit was ruined except for several squashed peaches; rising imperceptibly, bruises would show hours later.

He eased his armload onto the table and walked briskly to the fruit and vegetable stalls and paid a dime for a paper bag. Walking back, the possibility struck him that if there was *one*, there could be another, perhaps others, in the bulging shapeless box, and he hurried to her table, afraid his fifty cents added to the day's take might have given her enough for a fix and she would be gone.

The girl, the box, the fruit were still there. He offered her an orange. She shook her head in revulsion.

The back of a man's head, severely barbered, as he leans away from the camera to kiss a woman, blotting out her face.

A woman smells a rose on a bush, wearing a flared hat of the forties.

A girl wearing a Keystone Cop hat and coat, a moustache pasted under her nose, thrusts herself toward a boy behind bars in a gag shot at an amusement park.

A formal gathering at an outdoor celebration of some sort—no, a funeral. Photographs *are* deceptive, Kenneth thought decisively.

Practicing, a majorette twirls her baton, fractioning her face.

A man washing his car. I think I know that guy. Kenneth set it aside.

A man working at his desk, looks up, smiles quizzically at the camera.

A sober-faced little girl pushes a toy, no, a regular baby carriage down a cracked sidewalk. Empty, or occupied?

His head turned, his eyes half-closed, his mouth oddly ajar, Kenneth, in an ambiguous setting, caught in a Polaroid shot, the surface poorly prepared by the chemical substance he almost smelled now. Cracking, scratched, perhaps by fingernails pawing over the contents of the box. Kenneth licked his lips. The eyes blurred, closing. Perhaps another—no, not another coincidence. He rejected the possibility that some submerged need in him was looking for resemblances. Letting the picture drop on the cast-iron corn-stick mold, he dug further.

Firemen pose in front of a fire hall, standing, hanging all over a new engine, perhaps only freshly washed—yes, water sparkles, drips from the fenders.

A man, leering, pretends to sneak into an outhouse marked WOMEN.

A businessman, perhaps a government official, presents a check and a handshake to a well-dressed middle-aged woman.

A man strides down a crowded sidewalk, caught unaware in a shot obviously snapped by a sidewalk photographer.

A young man poses with his parents at a high-school graduation ceremony, the mother blurring herself as she moves toward her son, as if to kiss him.

A young woman sits in a swing, empty swings on each side, blowing cigarette smoke toward the camera.

If I find one more, just one more, then . . . The third was clear, his face quite natural, the suit his first job suit, the setting unmistakably the front of the building, at the curb, beside the red, white, and blue mailbox and the *Keep Chicago Clean* courtesy trash receptacle. What was the occasion? Probably not his first day because he stood there (waiting for the light to turn green) with such aplomb, one hand in his pocket, the other casually holding a cigarette at ease—obviously between puffs, not in a hurry, looking straight into Kenneth's New Orleans stare, but not into the camera's lens. Looking, like the girl, at nothing in particular, but unlike the girl, so young and vibrantly alive and receptive, he struck Kenneth as a charming, likable young man in his early twenties. He couldn't see the street sign but he knew it was Halstead and Grand. When was it taken? Who took it? The questions drew such total blanks, he didn't start going over the possibilities. He wanted to dig for more.

One impression held his attention on the picture already in his hand—he didn't seem to realize he was being photographed. He looked at the Polaroid. Obviously candid. He pulled out the muscle-flexing shot—even around this classic exhibitionist pose hovered a sense of privacy violated. The show-off eyes were introspective. He set the three aside, neatly together.

A man driving a tractor looks up as if responding reluctantly to a request.

A stiffly posed, badly retouched color shot of a married couple.

An infant wearing a knitted tam manages a brilliant smile with only a single tooth. The brilliance in the eyes. Was it still there?

A teen-age boy strains to pose for a self-portrait as he presses the shutter release lever on the camera, seen in the lower right-hand corner of a bathroom mirror.

People in tennis togs crowd around as a man in a suit presents a trophy to another man. Kenneth thought one of the spectators resembled a man he knew years ago.

Through glass from the rear, a shot of himself standing in an empty room, his back to the camera, looking out a tall window in an old house, wearing his football jersey, number 8. The stance, one foot cocked back, his body leaning, his elbow propping it against the window frame, his arm bent back so he could palm the back of his head, the other hand in his pocket, was obviously not a conscious pose for a photograph. He seemed to have been shot through a side window at an angle that caught him looking out a front window.

The possibility that anyone he knew had taken these pictures without his knowledge as a joke—they were not, except for the muscle-flexing pose, gag pictures, and he remembered none of the situations or occasions—was so remote, he left himself open to a joking assumption the CIA had had him under surveillance since he was seventeen—or maybe younger. He looked for younger shots.

A teen-age girl in shorts strikes a pinup pose against sheets on a clothesline.

A man sets his face in a mindless expression for a passport or an ID photo that has turned yellow.

Kenneth looked for someone he might know, even vaguely, in a family-reunion grouping on steep front porch steps.

A woman and a boy pose in front of a monument, looking so intimately at the photographer, Kenneth lucidly imagined the photographer himself.

A woman has turned from the trunk of a car, a sandwich held up to her open mouth, four other people bent over, their backs toward Kenneth, who, unable to see their faces, feels uneasy.

A double-exposed shot of Kenneth reading a newspaper on a train, so intent upon a particular article he holds the paper and thus his body at an awkward angle, giving the photographer an opening. On the train window, as if it were a reflection, a child sits on a Shetland pony. A Chicago train? Nothing showed to answer his question. He had ridden hundreds of trains, perhaps thousands.

He looked at the girl, wondering whether she might not suddenly recognize him as a recurrent image in her scavenged collection. She was still in a hypnotic world of her own making or of some chemical's conjuring. He took off his jacket, lapped it over the bag of fruit, picked his sweat-saturated polyester shirt away from his skin, wiped his hands along the sides of his pants, licked his lips again. His mouth was too dry.

Kenneth began to dig into the box, shuffling quickly past the little brown studio portraits of the 1860s whose edges crumbled, leaving his fingertips gritty, past the baby pictures—in his mother's collection, he had never recognized himself—past the group pictures that obviously excluded him, past the ones with Spanish-moss backgrounds, New Orleans settings, nothing specific to look for, his breathing fitful against the expectation that each movement of his hand would turn up out of this deep box his face. The savage's fear that cameras snatched the soul and photographs held it captive made Kenneth laugh at his own fearfulness.

A young man of the seventies sits in the grass on the levee playing a guitar, a barge passing behind him.

The rim of a pale shadow in bright sunlight smokes on a stucco wall, the partial outline of a camera looking as if it is attached to the photographer's hip.

A couple sit on a New Orleans streetcar, having exchanged hats, exhibiting beer cans.

A company picnic. Kenneth looked anxiously for someone he may have known at some phase of his life.

A man sleeps, perhaps pretends to sleep, in a fishnet hammock.

Kenneth is having lunch with a man whose fork obscures his face. Kenneth sits before his own plate as if wondering whether he can eat it all. Between himself and the man—he tried to recognize the ornate cuff links—communication has visibly ceased or not yet really begun, perhaps was never resumed. What restaurant was that? His memory responded to nothing in the decor. *November 1972* printed in the white margin stimulated nothing. It did not appear to be one of those restaurants where girls come around taking pictures of moments to be treasured forever. No third party had said, "Hold it! Smile! That's terrific!"

"Say, miss . . . Say, miss?"

"Fifty cents a handful."

"I know, but I just wanted to—I just wondered—could you tell me where you collected these photographs?"

"I don't remember."

He showed her one of the pictures. "Do you have any more of this fellow here?"

He showed her the one of his back in the empty room.

"I don't know."

He showed her the one on the street corner. "Him. Recognize him?"

"No."

"Him?"

"No."

"How about him?"

"No."

"They're me. They're all me." He looked into her lackluster eyes. "See? Each one of them resembles me to a T. I mean, they *are* of me. Somebody took . . . Do they look like me?"

She nodded, expressionless.

"Then do you remember where you first found them?"

"No."

"Do you remember when?"

"No."

Pigeons perch on a woman's arm, tourists feeding pigeons behind her, a European cathedral in the background.

A boy stands at attention to show off his new scout uniform.

An elderly couple stands in front of a tour bus, the letters spelling its destination backwards.

A religious ceremony, ambiguous.

A man shows a string of fish, a river flowing in the background.

A young man and woman sit on a diving board, in profile, looking away from the camera, squinting into the sun.

A little boy sits on a plank placed across the arms of a barber chair, obviously captured on the occasion of his first haircut.

Kenneth stands in line at an airport, the destination on the board unclear. He is lighting his pipe, his lips pursed on the stem. Another Polaroid. Between himself and the woman in front of him, a fat boy in shorts takes snapshots with a mini-camera. In the picture the boy snapped—of his mother, his father, his sister, his aunt, his teacher, his friend, a stranger who caught his eye—one could see perhaps the person who had taken Kenneth's. The combination of images—in hand and imagined—made him aware of the nausea again. He had to make it to a bathroom quick.

He riffled through the box, thinking, I'm missing some, I must be missing some—there's no system to what I'm doing. The pictures, too quickly scanned, spilled from his hands back into the shifting clutter out of which he had fished them. The sun, the nausea, the eyestrain in the bright polluted air made him too weak for the task of sorting them all out on the cramped table.

"Will you be here all day?"

The girl shrugged her shoulders, "Man, how do *I* know?"

"Here, I'll pay for these—I'm—I'll come back right away—here, let me take some more handfuls." He shoved a handful into his right pants pocket, spilling, another into his left pants pocket, spilling, into both his back pockets, his inside breast pockets, his shirt, worrying about the effect of his sweat on them, stuffed some into the bag with the fruit, picked up the ones he had spilled, and gave her five dollars.

"Keep the change and try to stay around awhile, I'll come right back." He turned, hugging the bag of fruit, carrying the corn-stick mold out through the stalls, the parking spaces, and then went back to her. "Well, did you get them all in the same place?"

"No, man."

"The same town? New Orleans?"

"Yeah. Maybe. Take another handful at a discount. Only a quarter."

"I just hope you're still here. I want to go through them one by one, systematically."

He made a final effort to see a glimmer of recognition in her eyes, and failing, turned away again, feeling distance increase between himself and the box hunched on the table.

In the dirty narrow street he flagged a taxi.

Lying stripped to his briefs, on his bed in the Royal Sonesta, the nausea ebbing, the photographs spread around him, he said over and over, Who took these pictures?

As he named his brother, his sister, his mother, his father, his other relatives, Helen, John, and a combination of them to account for the variety, each possibility struck him as so absurd, the rapidity with which he rejected them made him pant in exasperation with himself for even considering them.

He scanned the pictures slowly, hoping to stop short at the face of someone who might have become somehow obsessed, a creepy childhood friend, a spurned sweetheart, an oddball relative, or a deranged business associate.

Looking up at the ceiling, he saw himself in many places, at many periods in his life, all past his seventeenth year, but he saw no faces of likely secret photographers.

What happened to the people who had taken them, causing the pictures to end up in the New Orleans flea market?

Was this person or persons male or female? Young or old? A contemporary? Known to him? Known well? A mere acquaintance? A business rival? Or a stranger? Friend or stranger, loved one or enemy, his frustration, his helpless astonishment had a quality of zero that he felt in his bones.

In the batches he had snatched up at the last moment, he had found other shots of himself. He is gassing up the car at a self-service island. Sitting on the bench as a player. Having a drink, sitting on the patio. Waiting for his bags to show up at a carousel in an airport. Walking the dog. Looking at stills outside a movie theater. Sitting in a lobby, his face hidden by a newspaper, as if he were a private eye, but obviously himself. Caught taking trash down a driveway to the curb. Lighting a cigarette in a stadium with friends, their faces turned away from the camera. Doing what people in the other photographs did. Sometimes strangers in the frame with him, but most often alone. As if he were being contemplated.

Each of the snapshots declared at a glance that he had not posed the image he held in his hand. Several types of cameras had taken the pictures, a range of paper sizes, shapes, stocks had been used.

The quality of the photography ranged from awful to professional. A few were dated by the processors, a few had been dated in pencil, perhaps by the same hand but not one he recognized. Age or neglect had yellowed some. The negatives of some had been scratched. Some were soiled, damaged. A few had tabs of fuzzy black paper or smears of rubber cement on the backs as if they had been preserved in a scrapbook, then ripped out and put away or discarded.

Some of the places he recognized but couldn't fix in time. For some, he determined a time, but was at a loss to name the place.

Perhaps he, she, they had kept a record of the dates and the places.

Sometimes, he even remembered generally how he had felt, once specifically (melancholy), but not the context.

Lying on the double bed as if on a rubber raft at sea, he tried to go over every possibility again, imposing a kind of system. But each sequence to which he tried to adhere was besieged by so many unaccounted-for possibilities and sheer impossibilities, he abandoned them and gave himself up to chance. If a photo was worth a thousand words, he needed the words for these, because, as a neutral voice told him, "The camera never lies."

He scrutinized each picture of himself for the third time, straining his eyes to detect ghost images such as spiritualists and UFO enthusiasts claim to see, or as religious fervor discerns Christ's visage in commonplace photographs. He remembered reading about a news photographer who happened upon a wreck on the highway and who shot the scene too fast to distinguish faces until his own seventeen-year-old son's face became more and more distinct in the developing tray.

The bounce of the springs as he jumped off the bed spilled some of the pictures onto the carpet. As he picked them up, he realized that the almost reverent care he used came not from narcissism but from respect for the feelings of the person or group who, he was inclined to conclude, had pursued through the years an obsession to chronicle his life.

Returning to the Market, he caught a glimpse of the Sunday-morning lovers, hoped they would wave to him, but more than a hundred people milling about the flea-market tables distracted them.

The girl was gone, but behind the box a little black boy's head was visible from the eyes up, his hands clutching the top, as if he were guarding.

"Where's the lady?"

"You the man?"

"Yes, where did she go?"

"She split, man. Said, give me a dollar for this box of pictures and a man come in a business suit give you a million dollars for this ol' box of trash."

"Here's two tens. Okay?"

"Man, that trash belong to *you*." He took the two tens and shoved the box toward Kenneth.

Kenneth picked up the box, looked around for any strays, and turned, lifting his knee to balance, as he embraced the shifting bulky sides of the torn cardboard box, feeling mingled awe and anxiety, remembering the two men who had bought pictures, feeling an impulse to track them down, wondering whether and from what angle sudden light was for a fraction of an instant flooding a dark chamber, etching his struggle on sensitized paper.

JOSH RUSSELL

TWO PHOTOGRAPHS BY WALKER EVANS

THERE IS A WALKER EVANS PHOTOGRAPH THAT NO ONE save my family and those who visit us has ever seen. In it a man stands in a barbershop doorway, his face half-covered in lather, half-shaved. The pole bisects the image. Captured in the bold tones of all of Evans' work, it looks like peppermint candy. The barber, his name on the plate glass like a caption, is perplexed as he holds his razor over an empty chair. The harlequin man in the doorway looks right into the lens. His hands rest on his hips. He glares. The man is my father and this is the story.

Evans took a photograph of my sister Lillian, at seventeen. In it she lies nude on a bed covered with a simple white sheet. Her hair is a crazed dark crown on the pillow and her foot casts a shadow like an ink stain. Her legs are parted and her vulva is captured in those wonderful gradations of black and white of which Evans was a master. She showed the picture to me the day she packed, though I was a thirteen-year-old boy and knew nothing. The sight of her naked was shocking and beautiful. While she filled a musette bag with her things she told me how the photograph came to be taken. She and Evans were lovers, and one morning when my father and I had assumed she was shopping in the Quarter, Evans had simply taken a playful snapshot of her as she lay in his bed. They had just made love and she pointed to the smile she wore in the picture as proof that she was happy there with Walker. Evans had left shortly after the photo was taken, and she was supposed to catch a bus on the sly and meet him in Valdosta, Georgia.

The last days he was in New Orleans, Evans had feared murder by my father's hands. Searching her bureau for forbidden Lucky Strikes, my father had happened upon the photograph of his daughter basking in a bliss whose source no one could fail to recognize.

The next day, mid-shave in a Royal Street barber's, he spotted Evans as he snapped shots of a grocery. He raced to the door and yelled Walker's name. Evans turned with his camera to his eye and saw my father through the lens. He snapped the shutter reflexively; the composition was too good to waste—a cat sat on the edge of the frame, in the window combs and scissors swam in a jar of antiseptic, the daddy of his lover stood scowling with his face half-masked by shave cream. The next moment my father was sprinting across the narrow avenue and Evans was running for his life, cutting down Pirate's Alley and ducking inside the St. Louis Cathedral on Jackson Square.

This picture of my father hangs tacked to the wall in the front room of his small house uptown on Magazine. A Western Union boy brought it to him the day after Lillian was gone, two days after he'd received half a shave. There was no note, only Evans' studio stamp on the back of the print. As far as I know, I am one of only four people who have ever seen the picture of Lillian—Evans, my father and herself being the other three.

Why show it to me? I asked, amazed that she had. Love, she told me, is the most important thing in the world. Everyone will admit to this, but I want to tell you something they won't: Love is the body. Believe the body, she said. That's why I'm showing it to you.

BLUE ELEPHANT

PAUL WATCHED HIS WIFE EMERGE ON THE ARTIST'S SKETCHPAD: the oval of her face, the light and shadow of her nose, the feathered lines of her eyebrows.

The artist, an old black man in a dingy thermal shirt and Indian sandals, dried his fingers on his jeans and smudged the pencil strokes he'd just made, softening Helena's jaw line. His hands moved with a fluid confidence; there was no hesitation, no stuttering of graphite against the milky vellum. A few simple curves and an ear appeared, elegant as a seashell. A quick erasure and the man caught the sheen of Helena's dark hair, the way the sunshine cast a ribbon of light across her bangs.

Paul and Helena had come to New Orleans to get pregnant. Neither of them said so, or even alluded to the fact, but Paul knew they both hoped that what would not take root in domestic territory might blossom on foreign soil. They weren't desperate, not yet, but desperation loomed on the horizon. It had announced its intention to visit on Helena's fortieth birthday.

The trip was going beautifully except for one thing: Paul could not perform. It didn't matter that it had never happened before, not in his twenty-plus years of experience with a half-dozen women. It didn't matter that he'd been drunk most of the time or stuffed with crawfish or etouffeé. What mattered was that awful moment, repeated three times, when he lost it. The momentum. The feeling. The erection.

Helena understood. She was so understanding in fact that Paul suspected it was something of a relief. No matter how they tried to pretend otherwise, every moment of their lovemaking these days seemed grave, fraught with significance. Like it was being conducted at gunpoint.

A kid flew by on a bicycle, stirring the pages of the artist's sketchbook. The old man sat up straight and arched with his hands on his lower back. Paul heard his vertebrae crackle, like the sound of kindling snapping in their hotel room fireplace.

The old man sighed. "*C'est mauvais*. Everyone in a hurry."

Helena shifted in her seat and looked up at Paul. "How does it look?"

"Beautiful," he said, and he was telling the truth. On the page was Helena, but softer, more relaxed. A Helena before college politics forced her out of a job, before her mother remarried her alcoholic father. This was a rounder, more supple Helena, with light in her face, with the frown lines bracketing her lips shaded to flattering indentations. It wasn't that she looked younger in this picture, really, or that the artist had taken any liberties with her features. It was simply as though he was drawing the person she'd be if her life had taken another—better—path.

That night he and Helena wandered the French Quarter, Hurricanes in hand, and stared into the windows of voodoo museums and souvenir shops. They didn't say much, and neither pointed out that the souvenir they most wanted could not be found in any of these places.

They came to a strip club on Bourbon Street. A midget in top hat and tails stood out front, exhorting passersby to come inside. "A little something for everyone," he said, stepping across their path to shove a neon blue flyer into Paul's hands.

"Do you want to go in?" asked Helena.

Looking at her, Paul wasn't sure what answer she wanted. He shrugged. "Why not?"

They stepped through the double doors where men were shunted to the left, women to the right. Helena kissed him wetly before they parted. "Enjoy, tiger," she said and fleetingly squeezed his crotch before slipping through a curtain made of what looked like leather shoelaces.

But Paul didn't want to enjoy, at least not without his wife. Somehow, having her permission made it all worse, took the titillating edge off of things. He felt obligated to respond a certain way because of it, and the results were about the same as what had been going on in bed.

He switched to whiskey sours and watched the pale women scissor their legs beneath a purple strobe. Young men crowded the stage, passing fistfuls of bills toward the bar. The song blaring from all corners said something about wanting to feel someone from the inside.

Paul's attention wandered to a man sitting behind the stage. He looked shrunken, cowed by the whole experience. He sat low in his seat, as if ready to slide under the table. It was only when the man lifted his drink at the same moment Paul lifted his that he realized he'd been looking in a mirror.

Angry with himself, he bought a lap dance in a back room. He felt a few promising stirrings when the stripper settled her plump ass on his thigh and squeezed her breasts with both hands.

"Do you like these?" she asked.

Paul would have answered except that it seemed she was speaking not to him, but to some pinpoint horizon behind him. After that, it was all about feigning interest. He didn't want to hurt her feelings.

He left the club and stood against the building, waiting for Helena. A bedraggled horse clopped by, dragging a carriage with squeaking wheels. It had rained, and the streets were slick and dappled with neon puddles. Sometimes after rain things felt new, Paul thought. But here they just felt wet.

Helena joined him after a while. Her cheeks were pink, and her lips looked wet and tender, as if someone had kissed her. Before she could say anything, he kissed her himself, easing her back against the building, the purple strobe still flashing behind his eyes, the scent of whiskey and cigarette smoke and sweat flooding the space between them.

"Let's go," she said, breathlessly.

"Where?"

"Back to the room."

"No," he said, not knowing why. Except that perhaps he didn't want to revisit the scene of past failures. "Let's go somewhere else. Somewhere . . ."

"Close?"

"Yes, close," he said. Close. While he was still mindless, while it was still about her body and his and the alcohol on her heated breath and her pores and their fingers and tongues . . .

No, not babies. Not babies. Damn it.

Paul gripped Helena's arm and led her around to the side of the building, to the L-shaped alley between the club and a small bodega, preposterously Hispanic in this town of Boudreaux and beignets. The alley smelled of piss and wet cardboard. On the ground lay a condom like the cast-off skin of a small pink snake.

The condom made him think of their early days, their first joyful couplings, sunk together on a narrow bed in his dorm room or in his car, parked behind the Academic Center. They were careful then. Always. Both of them carried condoms so there would never be a moment, not one instant, when they let fate and biology stand in the way of the lives they were meant to live.

"I can't even think about it until I'm thirty," Helena had said, and Paul admired her prepossession. From their very first encounter, she seemed to be someone who'd seen the map of her life, who'd traced the route, and who had no doubt whatsoever of reaching her final destination.

Only there had been detours, disappointments, and now a major breakdown. All he wanted was to help her get back on the road, to give her the life she'd imagined, unspoiled and glittering with hope.

He became dimly aware, as though swimming up through a murky lake, that Helena was on the ground in front of him, that she'd bunched newspapers beneath her knees and was fiddling with the zipper of his trousers. Her attention was on her task, both hands working, the incline of her head suggesting the posture of someone bent over a set of blueprints.

He saw her suddenly then, saw her in a new way, and he began to cry. Every part of him went limp.

Helena looked up. "Honey, what's the matter?" Her tone made him cry even harder, feel more ashamed. It was the careful tone she would have used with a child.

Would have used. Would use.

He helped her up and she put her arms around him. Her body was chilled now; her hands on his back felt like ice. "What is it?" she asked. "What can I do?"

But there was nothing she could do and nothing, it seemed, that he could do either.

On the way back to their hotel, the word "inconceivable" drifted through his mind. He thought of it as meaning something that couldn't be born: an idea, a hope, and now, particularly, this baby. This baby was inconceivable. It would not be fathomed.

He felt angry at this shadow being who so stubbornly refused their efforts to mold it into life. Did it have any idea what it was missing? Rain on windows. Blowing bubbles into its milk with a straw. Handshakes. The small of its mother's back in a white slip as she dressed for an evening out. So much, so much. And all of it a clear trajectory from this one elusive moment, this intersection of flesh.

*   *   *

Back in their room, Paul said, "It's like the blue elephant thing."

"What is?" asked Helena.

"It's like when someone says, 'Whatever you do, don't think about a blue elephant.' Well, of course that's the only thing you're going to think about."

Helena sat on the bed and slipped out of her shoes. She pulled off her earrings and dropped them onto the nightstand. "And the blue elephant is . . . ?"

"I guess . . . I guess the baby."

She smiled in that blurred way she had, an expression between real amusement and pain. "At this point, I'd settle for a blue elephant." She slouched back on the pillows, knees bent, and looked up at the ceiling. "At this point I'd settle for just getting laid."

He went into the bathroom and ran the shower until the room filled with steam, until he couldn't make out his own features in the mirror. He stepped beneath the scalding water and let it slice through him, let his dried tears and anger and sweat run down the drain. He stood, one hand on the cool tile and one on his cock, and tried to bully himself into arousal. It worked, but it left him feeling grim, strangely unreal.

When he came back out, naked and erect, Helena was asleep on the bed, her knees still bent, one hand on her throat. He slid beneath the sheets and touched her hair. But he didn't kiss her. He didn't try to press against her or even wake her so she could get properly undressed. He left her there, above the blankets, while he burrowed deeper into the cool space beneath. He lay on his side in the darkness and listened to the *plink-plink-plink* of water hitting the shower drain.

Paul woke to find Helena's side of the bed empty. She was gone, but her suitcase still rested by the door, trailing the sash of her peach satin robe. On the nightstand, her hairbrush, with its filaments of black hair glinting in the sunlight, held a certain kind of eloquence.

He was surprised by how quiet the room was, how, without Helena, without her nose-blowing and the delicate chafing of her legs beneath her robe, the air seemed somehow less diffuse. He listened for a moment, expecting something. Street noises, perhaps, or just an echo of last night's recriminations.

Finally, he dressed and went, barefoot, out into the inn's small court-yard. He brushed leaves off a wrought-iron chair and sat down, rubbing his heels against the smooth stone paver.

Another couple sat nearby, clad in matching white robes, a carafe of coffee on the table between them. There was something furtive in the way they sat without really looking at one another, both of them intent on the tendrils of steam wafting from their mugs. Maybe they were married to other people, thought Paul. Or maybe they had engaged in some kind of unseemly and—in the light of day—embarrassing sexual behavior. He heard New Orleans could do that to a person.

An old man entered the courtyard and began to hose down the cobble-stone steps leading to the inn's main building. He wore blue coveralls and a baseball cap and performed his task with a kind of measured reverence, as though preparing a place for God himself, first wetting the stairs, then scrubbing them with a wide horse brush.

When he removed his cap to mop his brow, Paul recognized him as the man who had drawn Helena's portrait. Perhaps attracted by Paul's atten-tion, the man turned around to look at him.

"Mornin'," he said, smiling. "Where's that lovely wife of yours?"

Paul shrugged and spread his hands.

The old man chuckled and aimed his hose at a patch of moss growing up between the stones. "Well, you wouldn't be the first young man come to *Naw'leans*, lose his woman."

"I don't suppose I would," said Paul. It made him feel better, somehow, to have Helena's absence treated lightly, to feel as though he was just one of a hundred husbands who had sat in this courtyard: shoeless, wifeless. An-other character in what would hopefully become a comical story told years later.

"Not like these two," the man said, flipping his hose in the direction of the young couple. "Joined at the hip, ain't that right?" He winked, and Paul couldn't help smiling in response.

The man turned back to his work, stooping to pull weeds from the fissures in the cement, pushing mulch back into the flowerbeds with his big, graceful hands.

It occurred to Paul then that perhaps that was the best he and Helena could hope to do: create a space for their child, something sacred and wel-coming, something they needed to tend the way the old man tended to this landscape. Beyond that, he realized, it was out of their hands.

A shadow moved across the table, and Paul looked up. Helena stood there, a wax paper bag in her hands. She tipped the leaves off the chair across from him, sat down, and slid the bag over to his side of the table.

"Beignets?" he asked.

She smiled, shook her head. "Open it."

Conscious of her eyes on him, Paul opened the bag and withdrew a wad of tissue paper. He peeled back the layers to reveal a porcelain figurine in the shape of an elephant. It was blue with tiny octagonal mirrors set in its flanks. He looked at her.

"Now you don't have to think about it anymore," she said.

He thought about the serendipity of her finding the figurine, imagined her delight, and knew, in that telescoping way the truth has of striking home, what it meant for her to give it to him.

She drew her chair close to his, and he took her hand. They sat together quietly, watching the old man minister to his small patch of earth.

Paul thought about all the ways they had been together like this, wordless but companionable. Doctor's appointments. Movies. In the car for hours at a time, playing CD's, her hand on his leg or the back of his neck. All the things they had gone through together, side by side. His father's funeral. The farewell party her students had thrown for her a few years before.

"This isn't so bad, is it?" he asked. "Just this."

"No," she said. "It's not."

He wasn't sure she meant it, but for the moment Paul was content to let it go. In the sunshine, the suggestion of a breeze stirring her hair, Helena looked like the image of herself in the portrait. It was a trick of the light, no doubt, or their soulful environment, but real enough that Paul wished he could preserve it forever.

He picked up the elephant figurine and slipped it into his breast pocket. "Let's go home," he said.

"I want to do something first," Helena replied. She called to the old man who propped his broom against a chair and came over.

"Will you draw another portrait for us?" she asked.

"Of course," said the artist. "You'd like one of your husband?"

"No, I'd like one of both of us, together."

"*Mais naturellement.*" He grinned. "The family."

"Right," she replied and put her arms around Paul. "The family."

Mary Elizabeth Gehman

Trompe l'oeil

Fidel castro was drawing tourists' portraits on Jackson Square in New Orleans that summer of 1971. He sat hunched over a tray of colored chalk and worked on large sheets of cheap manila paper attached to an easel. Black and white charcoal portraits went for ten dollars, while those in chalky pastels brought fifteen. It was too hot for his usual fatigues—instead he wore a sleeveless dirty white T-shirt and cutoff jeans, but the cigar dangling from his clenched teeth as he concentrated on the curve of an eyebrow or the shape of an ear was the real thing. Almost. Cuban cigars had been outlawed, but Castro claimed to have his own supplier straight out of Havana. I never believed him though.

No one much suspected him of being a dictator or anything else that summer on the square. New Orleans has always had its share of strongmen, being the unwitting gateway to the Caribbean and Central America. Thus Castro languidly cultivated his wavy beard and a penchant for catching people's likenesses on cheap manila paper all through the infernally hot summer afternoons.

I'd stop by now and then when business was slow to see what he was up to. The portraits were his day job. At night and late into the dawn he worked in his apartment on mammoth canvases painting what he called his "classics"—wonderfully crowded scenes of surreal humans and animals, some with faces or bodies interchanged. I could never tell which. A very discreet wolf, for example, had human hands extended into a woman's purse lifting her wallet, or an old man leaned on a cane made of a live snake. None of these were centaurs or unicorns or recognizable fairy tale characters—they all flowed from Castro's deft strokes with an ease and originality reserved for geniuses, or at the very least much more serious artists than the

71

other dozen or so denizens of Jackson Square. Castro knew how to paint, and he would show the world one day.

Our friendship was elusive. He'd invite me up the creaking stairs of his apartment that ran along a balcony overlooking Decatur Street just down the block from the Seven Seas Bar. The door downstairs was never locked.

"Just push it hard; it'll give," he'd tell me. And it always gave after two or three shoulder heaves. The hinges were a cranky alarm of sorts. Castro would hear the commotion and come out to lean across a wooden railing as I made my way up the two stories of winding stairs around a series of obstacles, bags of garbage, a lone boot, an ancient auto battery, that sort of thing. It was obvious only men inhabited the old, unkempt building, though a scanty pair of panties hung incongruously from a wash line strung across the landing like a booby trap in Vietnam.

Castro had been to Vietnam, he once told me. He had served a tour of duty with the Viet Cong incognito and sans beard, he said, and considered re-enlisting but nightmares of buddies disintegrating in rice paddies had riddled his brain, and it was time to turn the thick marijuana smokes in for some home grown cigars.

He always greeted me warmly at the top of the stairs, staring long into my eyes and grinning with childish amusement as though each time anew my interest and perseverance surprised him. Amenities were few. There was no furniture to speak of in the cavernous rooms of his apartment or studio—I could never tell which. Paints, canvases in all states, some stretched partially over wooden frames, and easels dominated the place. A mattress was slung in one dark corner as an afterthought, and the kitchen, obviously with its original plumbing and cabinets, sagged with disuse. An old refrigerator sputtered its electrical obligations and yielded from its half cool interior an occasional beer or partly opened can of tuna fish. The pungent smell of overage garbage kept that part of the place off limits. Strains of it mixed at times with that of turpentine and oil paint gave the front rooms a distinct gallery feel.

Castro appreciated my being a young, attractive woman but never alluded to it. He assumed I knew he tolerated my evenings spent crouching on the only seat—a bar stool filched from the Seven Seas nearby—watching him paint because of my looks. Brains in women had probably not occurred to him. This is not to say he underestimated me. We'd banter back and forth like tennis players on topics of the day. He never read the newspapers or watched TV, while I had a distinct advantage for doing both, but he knew intuitively what should be going on in the world, though most of the time his moral compass was askew from reality.

"Why don't you ever feed that mangy cat out on the stairwell?" I'd ask absentmindedly during a particularly long lull.

"What cat?"

"The one that's crying—can't you hear it meowing?"

"You can take it with you."

"I don't want a cat," I'd say for at least the third or fourth time. "My landlord won't allow it."

"If you don't want to take care of it, what makes you think I do?"

I had no quick response. Nothing was quick in the tall room with a ceiling fan set on low. Not set there, just not working on medium or high.

"Too many mangy cats in the world," Castro said. "Nature should do them in, but you come along and want to prolong their misery."

He turned his head ever so slightly as to seem immobile, but I caught the glance aimed at me in the silence and chose to ignore it.

As he mixed paints and tested brushes on a fresh canvas it was like his world took on a whole new vista. Some colors and images evoked the bustling traffic of Decatur Street below, but suddenly the sweeping expanse of the Malecón along Havana's seaside weaseled its way in. A hint of colonial arches on a beige plaster building could have been the Cabildo two blocks away on the square where he painted every day or the National Archive building in Havana. I never knew which.

The cigars disappeared in his apartment. I never saw Castro chew on one there, nor did I ever see stashes of them among the mélange of clothes, old magazines and half-eaten hamburgers that cluttered the floor near his mattress. Actually, I never thought about it in those days when smoking among artists was as natural as breathing, but looking back now it occurs to me that he never lit one in my presence. The cigars could have been a ruse, or perhaps, in fairness to the man, a marker between his personal world and the social-commercial world of the square where he was forced to interact with tourists and honeymooners for whom he had little regard.

"That couple will stay together less than a year," he'd predict after finishing a very presentable portrait and counting over and over the dollar bills they had given him before stuffing the cash into his shorts pocket. "Then what becomes of my art work? That's why I don't bother to sign it. Here today, gone tomorrow," he sighed, stroking his tapered beard.

He said all this without the tinge of a Spanish accent. I didn't notice that either at the time. If others noted a foreign sound to his conversations, they never spoke of it. He was a large man with a large presence punctuated with fiery black eyes, and no one ventured to doubt his passion about the French Quarter art world nor his tenuous place in it.

As the hours passed and my bar stool became uncomfortable, I'd make motions to leave; Castro would always rebuff such a notion by fetching another tepid beer from the gurgling refrigerator or changing the long play jazz record on the turntable. Sometimes he'd reverse the record and set the needle down on the other side so that the whole night passed with the same music coming round and round like our conversations and the images on his canvases. It was, however, never monotonous nor even repetitious, because each time the same musical number came by it had something interesting that had escaped my untrained ear the first time.

Castro never commented on the jazz records, only once stating a dislike for rock and roll. He considered Elvis Presley an impostor, he said, and since I wasn't quite sure what the word meant nor in what context Presley was one, I chose to agree with him.

Finally, no longer able to amuse myself while Castro sank into total concentration on his painting, I'd slip out silently, shadowlike, and let myself out onto the early morning street below. Something was inevitably still going strong at the Seven Seas with its juke box spilling out on the street from the open French doors. The bartenders all knew me and whoever was on duty would set me up with a fresh foaming draft.

"How's Castro?" the regulars would ask grinning, as if no matter where I'd been nor how long, I had to have just emerged from the painter's bed. It bothered me, but how to correct them? I was his woman—old lady was their term for it—and that was that. That was my place in their world. Castro himself rarely showed his face in the Seven Seas, though everyone there knew him from the square and from his marathon stints in his studio nearby. It was up to me to represent him here, to say he was doing O.K., still had a bad cough, had finished another large painting or whatever. They in turn never hit on me, reserving for painters' old ladies the same respect as for their own mothers.

So it went, humid sweaty night after night. Sometimes I didn't see Castro for a whole week, but something pulled me back to the heavy door on Decatur Street, the loud creaking hinges, his tousled head peering over the wooden balustrade above, his amused look welcoming me, the occasional hug on my arrival and distracted kiss on the lips on my leaving.

Toward the end of August Castro became visibly agitated. There had been something in the news about the U.S. blockade against Cuba. He needed to get back to his people, he said, donning a fatigue jacket with its short sleeves rolled up to his armpits. A pair of scuffed Army boots sat at the ready.

That night his painting took on a bizarre military cast not present in his earlier work. Muscular reindeer strained to pull a huge anti-ballistic missile through a cobalt blue sky, and human men sat on haunches as though they were German shepherds. The colors were all brown, khaki and olive green. Even the long play record had changed to something he muttered about being Delta blues, whatever that meant.

He had run out of beer and made no motion to go out for more. The fan in the floor-to-ceiling window that looked out over the balcony churned but hardly cut through the humidity.

It was time for me to go. Castro turned from the canvas, his hands glistening with dark paint, and embraced me, holding me tight against his chest and thighs as he had never done before, running his left hand over my cheek, leaving rivulets of dark painted tears. He studied my face with a fierce stare that could have betrayed anger, though I chose not to see it that way.

"You leave tonight and you'll never see me again," he said at last and turned abruptly away from me. I had to go, I explained: my job—my apartment—my life—my friends. It sounded like an oddly plaintive litany unrecognizable even to myself. He didn't look back at me. His hand had already resumed the brush on canvas.

At the Seven Seas, Curt was behind the bar and handed me my usual draft.

"Guess Castro's flipped, huh?"

I looked up from the glass, my eyes heavy with sleep.

"Flipped?" The word hung over the bar between us.

"Yeah, the guys in white coats are gonna have to come for him," Curt continued as if he had no idea how the words pained me. "You didn't see him flippin' out yesterday on the square? Didn't hear how he took all his clothes off and was drawing a self-portrait on his chest? "

I made no response. I felt numb.

"Cops told him to go home. Some dudes from his building took him back."

"He's going to Cuba," I said as if I had all the answers. "He told me they need him there."

"Yeah, sure. What's the Cubans going to do with a freaked out Italian, huh? You know his name's Joey Trevino. Fidel Castro? Shit! Joey went to school with me at Warren Easton."

The juke box surged with a Latin beat. I could hear bongos and maracas and feel the breezes off the ocean. It was 4 a.m. The cobalt blue sky had muscular reindeer pulling Fidel Castro on a gurney high over Decatur Street, headed across the mighty Mississippi River and down toward the Gulf.

I hoped to hell they'd make it.

new orleans mint julep

The word julep can be traced back to the year 1400, defined as "something to cool or assuage the heat of passion." Many variations of this drink exist across cultures. Louisiana's original mint julep came in 1793, after aristocrats were expelled from Santo Domingo during the slave revolt there. Bourbon whiskey eventually took the place of sugar cane rum.

$2\,^1/_2$ oz. bourbon whiskey

powdered sugar

mint leaves and sprigs

Refrigerate large highball glasses
or metal goblets overnight.

Drop a layer of mint leaves in the
serving glasses, fill 1/4 full with
shaved ice, then add 1 teaspoon
of powdered sugar.

Repeat this layer &
then add a jigger of Bourbon.

Repeat this process one more time.

Garnish with mint sprig and
serve with a straw.

THE PASSION OF HYPOLITE CORTEZ

the passion

PARSHAL LEE CRACKED OPEN THE MONKEY'S SKULL with a ball peen hammer, picked it up, and drank the fluid from the deceased simian's hypothalamus gland. He was a determined individual. If this was what it took to regain the exclusive affections of Hypolite Cortez, damn straight he'd do it. It and anything else that seemed logical to Miss Consuelo Yesso, Parshal's advisor in matters involving love and finance.

Parshal Lee was an artist, a portrait painter who set up shop daily next to the north fence of Jackson Square in New Orleans. He was thirty-eight years old, a native of Meridian, Mississippi, a place to which he had no desire to return. Parshal had not been in Meridian since his mother, Zolia Versalles Lee, was buried four years before across the street from the Dixie Boys Field. He had no living relatives that he knew of other than an eighty-four-year-old bastard uncle named Get-Down Lucky, who was part Gypsy and sold Bibles door-to-door in Dothan, Alabama. It was this uncle who had informed Parshal at Zolia Lee's funeral that the meaning of life was based on a simple concept. "It ain't what you eat," said Get-Down Lucky, "it's the way how you chew it."

Parshal's father, Roy L Lee, had disappeared the day before his son's fourteenth birthday. Roy L—he had no middle name, only an initial he'd taken himself so that he would have something to write in on forms that requested one—was believed to have fled Meridian in order to avoid prosecution for grave robbing. He and a one-armed Salvadoran refugee named Arturo Trope, who had worked as an undertaker's assistant in a Meridian funeral parlor, had been apprehended exhuming newly buried bodies in order to steal rings, necklaces, and other valuable items decorating the corpses. Both men had skipped town on bail, and two months later Arturo Trope had been shot to death during the commission of an armed robbery of a jewelry store on Capitol Street in Jackson. Roy L had not been seen or heard from since the cemetery scam. Parshal considered his daddy dead and himself a free agent. All he had to make his way in the world was his God-given artistic talent. Roy L, Parshal figured, had nothing to do with that.

Parshal sat on the porch of his rented bungalow on Spain Street in the Marigny, chasing the bitter taste of monkey gland fluid with Rebel Yell. His brain was obsessed by thoughts of his erstwhile girlfriend, Hypolite Cortez, and the fact that she had abandoned him in favor of a woman. Hypolite now lived with an exotic dancer named Irma Soon, a Panamanian-Chinese who simulated copulation with a rock python six nights a week at Big Nig's Gauchos 'n' Gals Club on Pelican Avenue in Algiers. Parshal was hoping that Miss Yesso's prescription would inspire Hypolite to return to her senses and to him. She had given no reason for her defection, merely left a note on her red sateen pillow embroidered in yellow with intertwined initials *P* and *H*, that said: "Parshal you took care of me best you could but I have fallen for Irma Soon who I believe is my destiny. Our two years together have been good however love is got to be better than good and only with Irma Soon have I felt what is commonly called ecstasy. I hope one day you will know for yourself with someone the way I feel with Irma. Luv to you and I mean it, Hypolite."

Parshal Lee had given Hypolite's note to Consuelo Yesso, who rolled the paper into a tiny ball, dipped it into a powder made of flywings and lizard tongues, and told Parshal to swallow it, which he had. By ingesting Hypolite's note, garnished with these purposeful ingredients, Miss Yesso explained, Parshal would cause his beloved to dream of him and force Hypolite to reconsider her situation. Miss Yesso had handed him the monkey's skull wrapped with aluminum foil and promised to continue her efforts toward accomplishing Hypolite and Parshal's reconciliation. Parshal paid the *bruja* what she asked, and tried to put a hopeful spin on his thoughts, but he knew that it would take more than Miss Yesso's powers to bring back Hypolite Cortez.

"Hey, Parshal! Parshal Lee!"

Parshal broke out of his trance and saw Avenue Al, a neighbor, standing on the sidewalk. Al was wearing a dyed-purple mohair suit, which he called his "goat coat," and was propped up on crutches, necessitated by his having taken a hard fall and broken both knees while leaving Teresa's Tite Spot Lounge in the Bywater two months before. Avenue Al, a sixty-year-old former professional wrestler whose claim to fame was that he had bitten off one of Dick the Bruiser's earlobes, was suing Teresa for damages. His plan, he told everyone, was to take the money and retire in Cebu City, the Philippines, where he had once wrestled an ape. "Fell in love a dozen times in six days," he claimed, "and never even got the clap."

"Come on, Parshal," Avenue Al shouted, "let's go! Trumpet Shorty havin' a funeral for his pit bull, Louis Armstrong, jus' passed. Be the firs' dog have a second-line since dat rabid Airedale, Dagoo, hads to be put down in '71."

great expectations

"Nobody cares *what* you do in New Orleans, but everyone wants to know what it is."

"I like for folks to know what I'm up to, so they know what to *expec'*."

Parshal Lee sat at the bar in Teresa's Tite Spot, nursing a Bombay on the rocks, half-listening to Beverly Waverly and Caspiana Pleasant, two café-au-lait transvestites, converse. Mostly, he contemplated his unhappy circumstance.

"Parshal. Parshal, baby," said Caspiana. "Why you so morose?"

"What's morose?" asked Beverly.

"Unnormally quiet and broodish," Caspiana answered. "What's up, Parshal? You might can tell us girls."

"Hypolite left me."

"Aw, honey," said Beverly, putting a meaty, hairy forearm around Parshal's neck, "ain't that a bitch. Some women just don't got good sense. No man she could get better'n you."

"Didn't leave me for a man. Took up with an exotic dancer over in Algiers. Woman name Irma Soon."

Caspiana gasped. "You mean the China girl porks her ownself with a snake? Used to she work at Tickfaw Fouquet's Crawl Inn?"

"Half Chinese. Half from Panama."

"Shit, baby," said Caspiana, "that's rough. You need it, me an' Beverly, we zoom ya."

"Ain' be pussy, 'xactly,'" said Beverly, "but it defi'tely da nex' bes' thing."

" 'Preciate your concern, ladies, but I'm workin' on this in my own way."

"Okay, baby," said Caspiana, "but we here for ya."

"I hoid such a terr'ble thing today," Beverly said. "Was on the TV news."

"What dat?"

"Russian man was sentence to death for killin' more'n fifty people. Men, boys, women, an' girls. Ate parts their bodies, mostly tips of their tongues and genitalia."

"Saint Rose of Lima!" cried Caspiana, crossing herself.

"Man was fifty-six years old, and impotent. Only way he could complete a sexual act was by torturin' an' killin' someone. Russian papers called him the 'Forest Strip Killer,' after the place where he dump mos' the bodies."

"Lord have mercy. He jus' cut folks apart, huh?"

"What da news say."

"An' some people thinkin' *we* weird!"

"If everyone was so well adjusted as you two," said Parshal, "wouldn't never be no more wars."

Caspiana smiled, leaned over, and kissed him on the left cheek.

"Bless you, baby," she said. "But you jus' seen us on our best behavior. We might can be some tacky bitches sometime."

"You want Hypolite back," said Beverly, "best you stay in her face. Let her know you there for her."

Caspiana shook her curly gold wig. "Don't believe it, sugar. Liable push the lady further away. Besides, she an' this snake charmer in the first flush of their love. No way to buck that. My advice, darlin', wait it out. You a good *man*, after all. Hypolite come back aroun'. She don't, somethin' turn up."

Parshal finished off his Bombay, thanked Caspiana and Beverly for their commiseration, and walked outside. It was a hot night; the air was even heavier than ordinary in July. He went to his car, a two-year-old blue Thunderbird, unlocked the driver's side door, and was about to get in, thinking to cruise over to Algiers, check out his rival Irma Soon's terpsichorean snake act, when Parshal felt a cold, hard object enter the outer part of his left ear.

"Y'all don' min'," a high-pitched voice said, "my name is Carjack Jack an' I gon' be y'all's designated driver tonight."

Out of the corner of his left eye, Parshal saw a skinny, balding white man in his mid-thirties, wearing a blue Hawaiian shirt decorated with yellow parrots and red flowers. A bright purple scar the width of a trouser zipper ran down the center of his nose from bridge to tip. Parshal started to turn toward him but as he did the man inserted the gun barrel deeper into Parshal's ear, forcing his head away, then removed the weapon briefly before bringing the butt down hard on the soft spot at the back of Parshal's head. Parshal collapsed against the car and the man opened the door, shoved Parshal's limp shape into the backseat, took the keys from the door lock, climbed behind the steering wheel, and closed himself inside. He cranked the engine and grinned, exposing a row of rotten teeth.

"Hellfire!" Carjack Jack screeched, shifting the T-Bird into gear and tearing away from the curb. "We got us some *miles* to go before we sleep. *Miles*. Course, y'all're already sleepin', ain't ya? Well, as them pussies out in California say, this here's the first day of the rest of our lives, an' a life is a terrible thing to waste. Or is that a mind is bad to waste? Hell, *I* don't mind! Waste not, want not. Two peas in a pod. Damn the *Defiant!* Ain't *no* business like *show* business. Fasten your seatbelt, buddy, this gon' be a *bumpy* fuckin' ride."

the big bite

Hypolite Cortez sat at a ringside table in Big Nig's Gauchos 'n' Gals Club, sipping sparkling water through a straw. She was twenty-two years old, a smidge more than five foot two, had never weighed a hundred pounds in her life, had huge black eyes, severely arched Chinese eyebrows, and permitted her midnight black hair to fall slightly below her seventeen-inch waist. Above the nipple of her left breast was a three-quarter-inch in circumference dark blue, star-shaped mole that Hypolite referred to as "where the Arab bit me." This mole Hypolite had inherited from her maternal grandmother, Ephemere Plaire, who told Hypolite that her own paternal grandmother, Pilar LaLa, had borne this identical mark. The first time Irma Soon saw it, she experienced a spontaneous orgasm.

The lights dimmed, a drum rolled, and from offstage a husky female voice, that of Bruma "Big Nig" Goma, the proprietress herself, announced: "Get ready, Eddie! Chase dat frown, Miz Brown! You ain't seen poon 'til you seen Miz Soon! Here she be, di-rek from Mandinga, Panama, da soipent princess, doin' an exclusive performance of 'La Gran Mordedura'—a specialmost dance she create herself that been banned in most parts da Orient—Miz . . . Oima. . . Sooooonnn!"

The lavender curtains parted, revealing a diminutive woman whose body was crisscrossed with several rivet-studded black leather belts. Miss Soon's most intimate part was fully exposed, however, while stretched across her tiny breasts and relaxed around her neck was a reticulated creature the color of Delaware River mud. The patrons of the half-filled Gauchos 'n' Gals Club howled and applauded at this sight. A slow version of "Little Egypt" emanated from the band pit, prompting the lithe Filipina to begin her routine, which consisted mostly of waving arms and undulating hips. This tepid dance continued for several minutes, during which time the reptile remained composed, placid, unstirred; until Irma Soon gently but firmly grasped its head with her right hand and placed it directly between her legs.

At this point the patrons, some of whom gasped audibly, froze in their seats. The dancer closed her eyes, thrust her pelvis forward, and bent backward incrementally, slowly, tortuously, or so it seemed to those in rapt attention, until her head touched the floor. To all appearances, the python's head had disappeared inside Irma Soon. Hypolite Cortez shivered as she watched her lover manipulate the reptile. As easily as Miss Soon had accommodated it, she withdrew the lubricated cranium and with an agonizing absence of haste, sinuously resumed an upright position. Holding the python by her right hand just behind the head, Irma positioned it face-to-face and flicked her own pointy tongue toward it. The music reached a crescendo and Irma twirled with the snake, the two creatures' tongues darting at one another until the dancer whirled them offstage.

The audience whistled and clapped their hands, hardly believing what they had just witnessed. Hypolite smiled demurely and sat still, proud and deeply in love, thoroughly enchanted.

"Dass it, gauchos 'n' gals," boomed Bruma Goma. "Ain't another performer like Irma Soon this side o' Subic Bay! Let her know y'all appreciate her art! Open up fo' dis Filipina baby!"

The patrons continued to shout, whistle, and applaud until the curtains closed. It was not Irma Soon's habit to take a parting bow. She had explained to Hypolite that once the connection with her audience had been made, she preferred to leave it unblemished, having no desire to break the spell or alter the feeling she had engendered. To her fans, Irma remained forever in character.

The band segued into a waltz-like treatment of "The Fat Man" and several couples, some of the same or similar sex, rose to dance. Hypolite dipped a hand between her gooey thighs and closed her eyes as she massaged herself, holding in her mind the impossibly beautiful image of Irma Soon and the python locked in their forbidden embrace.

two for the road

"You gonna harm me?"

Carjack Jack looked back over his right shoulder at Parshal, wrinkled his lips toward his zipper-nose, and laughed.

"Hell, pardner," he said, returning his eyes to the road, "I ain't no demon. Don't do no brutalizin' 'less it's essential. Sorry I had to sock you back there, but a man has to know what he has to do when it has to be done. Mack Daddy of all Mack Daddies told me that ten years ago. City jail, Montgomery, Alabama. Copperhead Kane was his name. Famous man, famous. Had him a escort network from Alabama to Illinois. Copperhead Kane, yeah. The man invented phone sex. That's a fact."

Parshal lay on the backseat, still woozy from the blow to his head. He noticed that neither his hands nor his feet had been bound. Carjack Jack sped the blue Bird along Chef Menteur Highway.

"What're you gonna do with me, then?" Parshal asked him.

"Ain't quite decided. You want me to drop you someplace in particular? I'm thinkin' on headin' up north, myself. What's your name, anyway?"

"Lee. Parshal Lee."

"Just call me C.J. Best you don't know my family name."

Parshal thought about Hypolite Cortez. He wondered whether the years she had worked as a teenage prostitute for the Hilda Brausen Charm School had unduly influenced her gender preference. He had to admit that despite his unselfish efforts of a sexual nature, Hypolite had never really responded to him as did other women. Something had been missing in their relationship. Parshal watched the blackness pass for a minute before he spoke.

"You don't mind, C.J., maybe I'll just tag along with you. Need to put some space between me and a kind of unhealthy situation here, anyway."

"Guess I could do with some comp'ny, Parshal. Ten to one it's a renegade female messed up your mind."

"How'd you guess?"

C.J. laughed. "It's a epidemic. Happenin' all over the so-called civilized world. Copperhead Kane predicted it back when. The people ain't starvin' for food are starvin' for answers. Things is got too complicated for words, or ain't you been payin' attention?"

"Not close enough, I guess."

"Take this show I seen on TV one night in the joint, called *Down to Earth*. You ever watched it?"

"No," said Parshal. "What is it?"

"See, these couples go out on a date for the first time, and one of 'em thinks it's the greatest thing. Usually they had sex of some type on the date. So they bring on the one of 'em thinks the date was great, all that. Then the other one comes on and totally tears up the date, hated it, had bad sex, bad breath, bad manners, the guy's hairpiece fell off while he was performin' cunnilingus on her. They'll say anything."

"Prob'ly it's in the script. They just sayin' what was wrote for 'em to say and ain't none of it happened."

"Wrong, Mr. Lee. Nobody could make up this stuff. This guy had eyebrows took up half his face won with the best story."

"Wha'd he tell?"

"You won't believe it. Said he and this girl go out to a nice dinner. She has the lamb chops, eats the parsley, so he figures she's both classy and healthy, yeah?"

"Oh?"

"Yeah. So, they go to a movie."

"What movie?"

"A Spanish picture, somethin' European, where all the women got long noses and by the end the men are wearin' spike heels and lipstick and complainin' how they don't get enough sex."

"Ho!"

"They go next to the girl's apartment, where the guy says she's all over him like an electric blanket. Get this, the guy actually says this: 'I got my eel out and she's doin' the popsicle!' That's what he says! The audience is dyin'!"

"He got his eel out."

"His eel, yeah. Then it comes."

"His eel?"

"No, no. The good part of his story."

"The good part."

"He grabs her crotch, and guess what?"

"She's a guy, too."

"Right! Right! Of course, she's really a guy!"

"Is the guy who was supposed to be a girl on the show?"

"Yeah, yeah. And guess what? He comes on after Eyebrows gives his version and denies everything! You believe that, Mr. Lee? Completely and entirely says Eyebrows is out of his goddam mind!"

"Jesus."

"Now, here's the killer."

"Don't tell me."

"Shit, Parshal, can you guess? Can you?"

"She offers to prove she's a woman."

"Correct! Yeah, yeah! Right on the air! She pulls up her skirt an' shows her pelt! The audience is goin' batshit. The host is lyin' on the couch, chokin' to death. This Nancy starts paradin' up an' down the stage, like on a runway, got his jewels tucked up so nothin' shows. Man, you never, *never* seen nothin' like this."

"What's Eyebrows doin'?"

"Okay, get this: Eyebrows attacks Nancy."

"Eyebrows *attacks* Nancy?!"

"Tries to get at his dick."

"Holy shit."

"Nancy karate chops him in the back of the neck, and Eyebrows goes down hard on his nose, which bleeds."

"Holy shit."

"The security guys come out an' separate the two. Nancy is outtahermind handsdown havin' the greatest time of her life! She's smilin', throwin' kisses to the audience."

"You have to admit, C.J., it's a special place would allow a program like that on the air."

Carjack Jack nodded his red crew-cut head several times and laughed.

"Mr. Lee," he said, "I got no doubt in my mind but that there ain't never been and won't never will be another country like this one in the history of planet earth."

ANDREI CODRESCU

From *FLEEING THE RESTORATION:*
A NOVEL WITH ARCHITECTURE

the insane man next door

IT STARTED SMALL, JUST BEFORE THE WAR. It was a restlessness at first, an inability to be happy unless one placated the gods with loud noises or getting totally blotto. Good people made loud noises, the tender and artistic got blotto. Wakefield did neither. He was a man of moderate habits and a diligent worker. Wakefield was a traveler with his ear to the ground. He had flown and driven for more than thirty years and had made good money. At some point, toward the end of the century, he had sensed the coming of something monstrous. He had been woken one morning by a noise, but not just any sound. An insistent hammering. At the time, he was living alone in the old quarter of an indulgent Southern port city with a nightlife. His small apartment had no television, only books and various objects he had picked up in the cities and countries where he'd done business. He looked forward to slowing down and spending the rest of his life reading. He looked forward to a bourgeois schedule of walks along the river, a fresh newspaper at the neighborhood coffee house, regular Sunday appearances at a favorite bar where acquaintances would comment on the state of the world—which was benign and solid—and a sexual adventure now and then.

Precisely at the moment when all this appeared possible, an insane man started hammering on the other side of his bedroom wall. The insane man was certified by the city to restore the old house adjoining his apartment. Built in the 18th century, this crumbling cottage had served, respectively, as the birthplace of a famous musician, a bordello, and a flophouse. When the madman bought it, the old quarter was already going high rent, and the flophouse was destined to become "studio apartments," like so many of its neighbors. The madman thought that he was "rescuing" the house, and pledged to restore it brick by brick to the original 18th century splendor into which the bawling baby musician had been born, ready to give a certain musical style to his epoch. The city agency charged with historical authenticity applauded.

It was unfortunate that the man's plan for the future of the house was so implacably opposed to Wakefield's plan for his own future. Plans for the future did not come easily to Wakefield. In fact, he had always had no plans, relying on circumstances for most of his life. Very slowly, however, over a period of years that allowed for the luxury of inner exploration in a climate of general prosperity and peace, Wakefield had conceived an ideal retirement for himself. That conception was now under attack by a force he had not provoked in any way he could think of. Still, a cloud of unexplained guilt dogged Wakefield. Was he responsible for the renovating madness that had seized the people of his city? No. Did he set the prices of real estate? No again. Was he encouraging the cult of history and the worship of old houses? Most emphatically no. Then why? Why was his tranquil future targeted for destruction?

On the street, the madman was just a guy who went to the gym early in the morning and always greeted him politely. But inside the unfinished house, he was an insane man obsessed by bricks. What he had embarked on wasn't just renovation of the kind practiced by the nouveau-riches who wanted to live in old houses with modern amenities. Those people hired lazy carpenters who started drinking around ten a.m. and quit working around noon. That kind of renovation seemed to Wakefield an unattainable ideal when compared to the activities of the insane man. The drunks, whatever their flaws, managed to finish the job, eventually. At most, in a year they actually got it done.

The madman involved himself with each brick as if it was a sacred object, a rare book. First, his workers carefully took down the walls, including the one adjoining Wakefield's bedroom. When the walls were down, each brick was scraped clean with historically correct rusty tools. Then walls went up again, only to be taken down a month later, and then the process repeated itself.

About the time of the second rebuilding, Wakefield, who could no longer take the incessant scraping, troweling and hammering, opened the small window between his bathroom and the courtyard next door, and shouted at the crew.

"Stop! Just stop that infernal noise! I live and work here! I must have quiet!"

The madman appeared on the scaffolding. "Don't you swear at them!" he shouted back. "They are master bricklayers!"

Wakefield was amazed. Master bricklayers! Perhaps Italian Renaissance craftsmen just arrived by packet boat from Carrara! "I work here and I need peace!" he lamely rejoindered.

"Get a job!" shouted the madman.

That was the declaration of war. Wakefield had a job. He worked in his home, when he wasn't traveling. Just because his schedule didn't coincide with that of people who worked eight-to-five jobs, did not mean that he was a bum. The madman was going to pay for his hubris.

Oh, my poor casa, lamented Wakefield. He never called his dwelling his "house," because he did not like the English word "house." This particular word was a perfect case for the impossibility of translation. An American "house" was not a French "maison" or a Spanish "casa." He had lived in both ranch-style suburbs and Parisian apartments. He preferred the walled-in Moorish casas of Cadiz. That was his idea of home. Not only was his peace shattered now, but his own sweet illusion of elsewhere. Under other circumstances, he would perhaps have shared his neighbor's passion. Houses, he believed, embodied local culture more than anything else, even more than human beings themselves. Humans adapted easier to new conditions and had more "universal" mechanisms than houses which, in their commitment to geography, weather, history, and the humans who lived in them were utterly and wholly specific. This was no longer the case in America and efforts at "restoration" were perhaps laudable. Maintaining an illusion of "home" as a cultural expression had become more and more expensive. Wakefield had an acquaintance, raised in Manhattan, who now lived in Prague and paid thousands of dollars per month in order to inhabit a New York-style apartment in the Old City. For that same amount, he could live in an historic Czech palace. But Benjamin didn't want Czech, he wanted built-in microwave and butcher-block kitchen counter, loft areas, sanded wooden floors, and modern art on the walls. He wanted his own culture, his "pad," and he paid for it.

The "master bricklayers" were dismissed after ten months. He heard the insane man fire the crew, screaming like mad King Ludwig of Bavaria, except that King Ludwig eventually finished his famous castle. He called his "master bricklayers" dreadful names for refusing to take down the walls for the fifteenth time. After they were gone, the madman started going it alone, accompanied sometime by a woman who hammered alongside.

The insane man wasn't Wakefield's alone. On the other side of the house were the bedrooms and studios of other neighbors also being driven insane by the insane man. In the beginning, everyone had been tolerant. They imagined, like most reasonable people, that the "renovation" would one day come to an end. They warned the insane man that his hammering, chiseling, and scraping kept them from sleeping or working. Ha! Then they tried to get tougher. They made calls to the city agency in charge of permits, calls that, curiously, were never returned. Then there was talk of a lawsuit, but the man's building permits, renewable every six months, were always in order. Then the police were called. What could the police do? According to the permits, work could begin at 7 AM and cease by 4 PM. Everyone (but Wakefield) became resigned to the hammering. Most of the neighbors worked days anyway, and some of them kept their city apartments only for weekends. They simply stopped hearing the insane man. In this, thought Wakefield, they were like the rest of America. Hear no evil, see no evil, speak no evil.

There is no way to describe to a calm person living in a quiet neighborhood, by an unruffled lake perhaps, what such unending racket meant to Wakefield. And how long had he lived with it? Long enough for him to become Wakefield. Thinking that far back, Wakefield had the feeling that the insane man with the hammer had always been there, that he was the constant soundtrack of his entire existence, that his entire life had been a dream punctuated by the Hammer.

spy in the sauna

Wakefield did some research. The sicko had powerful friends. The Chairman of the Old Quarter Commission-on-Insuring-the-Authenticity-of-Facades was the insane man's sauna pal. Wrapped in a towel, with sunglasses on, Wakefield stalked the two of them at the city's premier Club for Naked Fat White Men. They seemed to be laughing at the torments they dreamed up for citizens of the district and, Wakefield thought, directly at his predicament. Hidden in the protective steam of the sauna, Wakefield listened to them try to outdo each other creating restoration horrors: dogs trained to sniff doorknobs for inauthenticity, spies in every courtyard who reported any intrusion of disallowed materials, walking patrols by plainclothes commission employees to test peeling paint to make sure that it was peeling and not just faux-peeling. Their imagination for restoration was as endless as the sauna steam.

Sitting in the sauna shriveling slowly, Wakefield heard other monsters, judges and bar owners, liquor distributors and contractors trading professional favors in the steam. Their bellies drooped in folds over stubby penises, their breathing was labored from smoke and drink, and their hearts hung by a thread over a vat of boiling cholesterol, but their bravado was breath-taking. Sometimes a young hustler, all muscles and with a full head of hair, would sit between these tubs of lard and make a furtive buck letting himself be stroked or fellated. These men indulged such whims without breaking their wheeling and dealing for a second.

The club had been founded one hundred years before in the heart of the red-light district. Though the district no longer existed, the city's powerful still came here for assignations and dirty deals. Membership was exclusive. Once one belonged, one could not resign. The contract with the club was for life. To resign was only possible by showing proof that one had moved to another country and become the citizen of a hostile foreign power. If one did not have such proof, one had to have a friend or a family member present a death certificate. Wakefield, who had paid for the membership in order to spy on his enemy, was intoxicated and nauseated by the psychic energy of these men.

Once, Wakefield concealed a small tape recorder in his towel. Unfortunately, the machine failed. A few days after that, the Commissioner renewed the madman's permits. The renewal was supposedly contingent on making progress. Not only had the sicko made no progress, but his mission was the complete destruction of intelligent life around him. Making complaints had been useless, because all complaints were shredded at the commission offices. Something stronger was needed.

occult interventions

There were a great number of practitioners of the occult in the city at that time. In a certain neighborhood, African voudouin, Catholic exorcists, shamans, and musical magicians could be hired for almost any job. For Wakefield, it was simply a matter of harnessing enough magic to begin his assault.

No matter how gloomy he might have felt in the pre-madman days, all he had to do was walk out of his house and head for the square, where amusing and often spontaneous spectacles instantly regenerated him, providing tonic to his soul. He listened to the street musicians, scanned the tables of the fortune tellers, and watched tourists trying to make "living statues" laugh. But this therapy no longer worked. Now when he went to the square he saw only the broken paving stones and the panhandlers. He remembered that this square had once been used for whippings and the occasional hanging. Instead of vivacious eccentrics, he saw the outlines of ancient gallows. Even the tourists looked to him like spectators to terrible and bloody events. The history of his city, which had once intrigued him, now appeared riddled with small black holes through which the past poured poisons thin as smoke. He heard many times people from Japan or France remark at how "European" the city was. Now Wakefield could see that they were unaware that the source of their delight was the smoke of a murderous history entering through their nostrils when they inhaled. He could hear the ghosts laughing.

Wakefield wasn't quite sure what sort of occult specialist to hire. Perhaps, in a manner befitting the science, one would just manifest. He sat at the window at his favorite café and watched the life in the square carefully. Directly in front of him was the courtyard of a small museum where a mysterious object had been displayed for a century. It was an iron blimp, a Surrealist dumpling, that was thought to be the world's first submarine. It had been fished from the bottom of a lake, but no one knew how it had gotten there. Nobody could explain it and it didn't matter. The thing had once made him happy. It had a childlike quality, like an onion. Wakefield had often inhaled its rusty iron aroma and felt as if he was smelling an onion. Today, it looked ominous.

An angel with big white wings crossed the square and leaned casually against the sub. She wore a short white skirt and golden sandals. Wakefield hadn't seen her around before. She was not one of the regular "statues," who made their living standing still with wings and horns. She looked directly at him, an ice-blue gaze. Wakefield would not have been startled if the new angel doubled as a prostitute, but the gaze was not mercenary. He waved her over. For a minute it appeared as if he had grievously insulted her. Embarrassment flooded him, but at the very moment he was ready to sink into the cobblestones, she smiled faintly, crossed the street, and sat down at his table.

"Reverend Telluride." She wiggled a wing. "Occult specialist."

They left together. Wakefield helped Reverend Telluride into the driver's seat of her Volkswagen Rabbit. One of her wings caught slightly in the door and Wakefield gently freed it. Then he sat in the passenger seat and they drove silently to the shoddy neighborhood adjoining his. She parked in front of a door painted with blue snakes and unfamiliar symbols. The narrow house sat in an unassuming block of 19th century houses. Inside the dark room, lit only by the nubs of two sputtering black candles, Wakefield made out various items, herb packages, oils, incense, candles, salts, jewelry, and statues of saints and animals, all of which had handwritten price tags attached.

Reverend Telluride asked him to sit down on a low stool. She took off her wings, lit a stick of incense, and sat at a tiny desk in front of him. Behind her was a heavy blue velvet curtain.

"I'll be frank with you," Wakefield said, "There is a man who won't stop hammering on my wall. He must be stopped."

The angel agreed that it might be possible to stop the man, but it was difficult work. It involved the making of a wax likeness of the insane man, and a great deal of patience, up to a year. She had not come upon a similar case, since she dealt mainly with ghosts, not living beings. She had been born Jewish in New Jersey, had traveled to Haiti where she had been initiated, and was now ministering to a voodoo congregation plagued by ghosts.

"What's with the ghosts?" asked Wakefield

"There are more uneasy ghosts now," she said, moving her thin arms, setting in motion a mysterious vibration. "I recently exorcised three ghosts from a house where three wives of one man committed suicide. In this town, even the bars are haunted." This she knew because she moonlighted as a cocktail waitress, the voodoo business not being sufficient to pay all the bills. Even that job did not pay all her bills, which is why she had decided to also work as an angel in the square.

Wakefield said that a year was much too long to wait, even if he did obtain a picture for her to make a wax statue. The Reverend sympathized, but did not want to give him false hopes. Wakefield bought several packages of powder, but the Reverend confided that their efficacy was doubtful. When he made ready to leave, she said: "I know someone who might help you." She wrote an address on the back of a flier announcing, "Spiritual Readings by Reverend Telluride, Ten Dollars."

occult interventions, cont.

Papa Ram agreed to meet him at the city's oldest bar, a ruin that had been once used as a pirate pawnshop and a whorehouse. The owners kept it in a state of careful decay. Papa Ram had warned him on the telephone that everything depended on his mood of the day. Some days he was extremely tired and cranky from dwelling in the world of spirits. On days like that it was better for prospective clients to buy him very strong drinks and make no attempts at frivolous conversation.

Wakefield ordered an Irish Coffee. He noticed the uneven floor of rough wooden planks. Underneath there was pirate treasure. And skulls. He could smell them.

Wakefield had no difficulty recognizing Papa Ram. He was pine-tree straight and skinny, prairie-tan, Cheyenne brave-braided, surrounded by an aroma of tobacco and burning sage. He carried a staff carved with snakes. He sat down and called to the bartender, "Brandy Alexander!" He then looked Wakefield up and down and asked him if he had participated in any Native American ceremonies.

"No, I haven't. To my regret."

"Any ceremonies at all?"

"Only the ones where I lost my innocence, and, most recently, my cool."

Papa Ram laughed. "When I was twelve years old I was hanging with a couple of teenyboppers backstage with Muddy Waters, cause we were really into the blues, and Muddy Waters looks at us and goes, 'Y'all are ram!' And I said, 'Yes, sir, I are am'! And that's how come I'm Ram. And I'm Papa because I have six kids and a Yaqui Holy Man named me."

Papa Ram led an all-women congregation of Black women on the path of spiritual healing. When his Brandy Alexander came, he poured a few drops from a tiny bottle in his pouch. "That makes it Papa Ram Alexander. What can I do for your soul?"

Wakefield explained his plight. As he talked, ectoplasm, which is the substance ghosts are made of, thickened in the air. A man who tried to use the public telephone behind their table dropped the receiver with a curse. It had slipped out of his hand, as if coated with ghostly viscera.

"You want this dude rubbed out, or just slowly peeled?" Papa Ram asked practically.

"No, no," Wakefield was alarmed. "I just want him to stop."

Papa Ram frowned, trying to understand the difference.

"You need to put him on pause. Cessate his music." he said at last.

"Exactly."

"That calls for the bone harp." Papa Ram explained. On Thursdays there was open mike at the "Butt Pillory," a music club in the city. Papa Ram would compose a "Cessate the Hammer" piece and perform this on his bone harp. Wakefield should show up for a brief purification ceremony before the performance, Papa Ram would see to the rest.

cessate the hammer at the butt pillory

Papa Ram cleansed Wakefield with bundled sage a few blocks away from the club, at the spot where a Catholic priest had once seen a vision of the White Buffalo. After the vision, the priest began ministering to Native Americans. A brass circle was imbedded in the sidewalk, commemorating the vision, and now Wakefield sat inside it, with his eyes closed, trying to feel the energy. "Suck the energy, suck the energy!" urged Papa Ram. As Wakefield sucked the energy into his body, he began to feel floaty. His toes plumped up like little balloons and started curling upwards.

Aficcionados cut the rug until the wee hours at the "Butt Pillory," but Thursdays were relatively quiet. The club had a deep, sultry, sexy, atmosphere. A few people holding instruments were there for open mike. The audience consisted entirely of their friends. Wakefield absorbed the vibrations of the place like a cocktail through a straw. He was very receptive.

The program started around ten. The Madame Palmetto Amusement Company put on a variety show of poetry and acrobats. Then Papa Ram took the stage, holding the bone harp. He explained the instrument. It was made from the vertebrae of a Cheyenne warrior who had left all his bones to musicians.

"Music can bring peace to the soul, storms to the heart, new thoughts to the head. This song is for peace. Peace for a man haunted by another man." He struck the bone harp, which gave forth an anguished cry.

"Stop the man with the hammer
Stop the demon of the wall
Help his neighbor find peace.
Help us all."

And so the song went, through several stanzas, each one more forceful, demanding the cessation of the insane man's hammer. Wakefield basked in the attention of the crowd, tried to identify in his own bones with the bone harp, but the skeptic in him kept putting ironic question marks after each one of his sincere attempts to be wholly present.

Papa Ram came off the stage glistening with sweat, and hugged Wakefield. The infinitely sad hug lingered, and Wakefield knew that the sweetly romantic palliatives of sorcery wouldn't work. The man with the hammer was oblivious to such things.

Next morning, half expecting to rise into the unaccustomed quiet of a hammerless day, he woke up violently when the wall started shaking.

Despair invaded him.

LEE MEITZEN GRUE

PRETTY BIRDIE
AND THE TOY POMERANIAN

PRETTY BIRDIE CARRIED THE WINE and Benito carried the wine glasses to Jackson Square for the caroling. It was near Christmas, but there had not been a freeze. The air was thick and humid—New Orleans Christmas weather—like a swim in warm water. Birdie's pink tee shirt stuck to his thin shoulders, and Benito had wet, dark circles under the short sleeves of his khaki shirt. His large features glistened with sweat.

Hundreds of people moved through the Quarter to the four iron gates that led to the center of the Square. Each holding a lighted candle, they poured through the gates to form a living cross of light. Music swelled up in the night like a great bonfire of voices. Benito didn't sing, but listened attentively to Birdie. In the dark, Birdie's flushed face was illuminated by candlelight—a thin handsome face suffused with happiness and wine, head thrown back, singing with great feeling. His voice sometimes slipping up to the highest notes of the carol, sound drifting up through the humid night over the river to the anchored ships blacked out in fog. "O, come all ye faithful, joyful and triumphant . . ."

Later at dinner, Birdie stood, wine glass in hand and said, "Listen you Cratchits. I want to say something serious: God bless us every one—and your Mother—Cabrini."

"I'll drink to that," laughed Patrick, Birdie's best friend. They toasted each other with champagne, ringing the Waterford glasses together like chimes while Benito carved the turkey. Behind the chair sat Von Stroheim, the Weimaraner, like a statue of blue granite. Patrick and a tall boy called Kitty sang their own version of Pogo's "Deck the Halls with Boston Charlie." Benito served each of them perfect slices of white meat, and Birdie spooned out oyster dressing. Eric, the other man, drank Scotch on the rocks, and leaned back in a chair of beige leather and chrome.

Pretty Birdie floated on pink champagne and the success of the evening. She was house-proud. Their creole cottage had soared in value since she and Benito had bought it ten years before, and Birdie had decorated in her own style, which she called "Early Volunteers of America." Her taste, except for a few good pieces, tended to the slightly rococo, but Benito's room was set with heavy furniture of dark mahogany. Bold in brown and brass, the room had a heavy masculine smell like smoke from a meerschaum pipe. Birdie burned a little pipe tobacco in an ashtray to keep up the aroma, but Benito didn't sleep there. He slept with Birdie. He kept the room as a study and as his bedroom to show off when his sister and mother came to visit.

Birdie had spent most of the week before the Christmas party planning decorations and flowers. He had used his best Havilland—gold rimmed—the baccarat like paperweights at the right of each plate, and Grand Baroque silver knives heavy as hammers. The company was less precise, each person dressed according to fancy, the light conversation reminiscent of that in a B-movie bordello. After dinner, the stereo blaring *Gaite Parisienne*—the boys linked arms in an unsteady can-can around the two men and half-eaten food. Benito sitting at the head of the table smiled and called "Bravo. Bravo." Only Eric, Patrick's friend, was glum.

"Why don't they shut up?" he snapped at Benito.

"They do no harm," said Benito. "They're happy. Let them dance."

"They're gay all right. What's happy?" said Eric, throwing his hand out and knocking over a glass. Scotch spilled on the white tablecloth. Birdie rushed off to get a dish towel while Kitty and Patrick whisked away the flowers and after-dinner coffee cups.

Benito sat very still, his large face troubled, a pulse like a blue caterpillar crawled across his right temple. Eric made no move to help clean up. He sat back in the chair with one leg cocked up, his dark suit fitting sleek as cat fur, his beautiful mouth molded as the lips in a portrait in the Uffizi Gallery, curving down. A hawk on his shoulder would have placed him among the Medici. He was impatient, scornful, and beat Patrick for nothing, not lightly with the baton for good reason ending in love as Benito switched Birdie, but cruelly, so that twice Patrick had come to Birdie for comfort with a black eye and welts across his ribs.

Eric's company was tolerated for Patrick's sake. Patrick of the bright blonde hair and long, thin fingers, who played organ at St. Cecelia's Church and Mozart after dinner at Birdie's. Patrick who always dressed for carnival in a black strapless evening gown, rouged and powdered, wearing a powerful aphrodisiac, the outer-skin of a woman. Eric had met Patrick at carnival under the colored lights of the Parade dance floor where her beauty shown incandescent for one night. The affair had lasted longer than most of Patrick's affairs, but the fights were fiercer now, each waiting for something—some change as profound as the change effected by the magic light of the bar, the under-glow of Mardi Gras midnight. Birdie there too swimming through the murky light, her white plumes spreading from her thin hips, lifting from her small, elegant head, the tiny body sheathed in sequins catching the red light from the juke box, the green of the beer clock, the long mirror behind the bar—a fire bird led through the crowds by the patient hand of Benito who escorted her through the gawkers, the oglers—the feather pluckers, bird-wounders, and if he protected the beautiful night bird, it was the plain-skinned boy of morning he loved as well. Not Eric, who loved a fantasy—Patricia—the beautiful pretend who danced in the dark and swimming light of the jukebox. That creature disappeared in daylight replaced by Patrick, a small, drab man who tolerated beatings—craved beatings since he had been beaten all his life, and felt uncared for if no one beat him.

After the table had been cleared, the boys began to chatter again. As they talked they glanced nervously at Benito and at Eric, who lounged back in the chair, his taut body implying menace.

"Don't you queers ever get tired of twittering?" he asked. In the sudden silence his words were naked as the sudden bone of a compound fracture.

"You insult my house," said Benito, getting up from his chair.

And this was when the terrible thing happened. Both men standing—a visible pulse pushing against the skin of Benito's forehead—his fist raised in anger—Benito took a step toward Eric, a sudden look of surprise crossing his face, he sank to his knees saying, "I have a terrible headache."

They helped him to the couch and called 911. When the police arrived with their oxygen he was dead.

Shock put Birdie in the hospital. His father, his lover—everything had been lost in Benito. Birdie had no other family, and after ten years, their house, the dogs, the cages of brilliant love birds, had been his life. The two of them had known their rolls perfectly. Birdie kept house and cooked. Benito worked as a brick-layer.

The body went with the police and never returned to Birdie for the full expression of his grief. Benito's Mama Grazione and his sister Filomena gave Benito a large and beautiful funeral with pearl-gray limousines and oceans of flowers. Birdie attended as the roommate, still shaking, but so sedated he looked as dead as the corpse. Birdie wore a borrowed suit, his hair cut for the occasion. He wore no make-up and stayed far removed from the veiled and weeping women. Benito's ex-wife was there with their twelve-year-old son. Birdie sat in the back pew of the church permitting himself no tears.

He stood when the others stood, knelt when they knelt. He followed the priest in his benedictions out the door of the church following the swinging censer and the crying relatives to the cemetery where he was not even among those who dropped earth upon the casket.

Mama Grazione and Filomena swept into the house like furies. Things went: the china, the crystal, the silver, the heavy bed from Benito's study. Anything that might be considered personal went: the pajamas, the silver backed brush engraved with BG, given by Birdie to Benito for Father's Day. The women were fair, but heavy suspicions hung unmentioned in the air. They left Birdie's bedroom intact. The great tester bed with its crown of melon velvet was left for the "roommate," and whatever clothes fit Birdie were left untouched. They also left the birds. Von Stroheim was taken away and Mama Grazione claimed the house. "We give you a month to find a place," said Mama.

After they were gone, Birdie lay dry-eyed in the tester bed. Patrick, alone now since his lover had disappeared before the police arrived at Christmas, tried to make conversation. All Birdie's young giddiness had vanished, and he lay upon the bed like a man in a hospital kept alive by some mechanical support system that might be disconnected at any minute.

"He was a good man," said Patrick soothingly.

Birdie roused slightly, answered, "I know."

"His mother didn't mean to hurt you, Birdie. She thought everything was his."

"I know that—the house was terrible when we bought it," said Birdie.

"It's beautiful now," said Patrick.

"We stripped the old wallpaper," said Birdie turning to stare at the French wallpaper.

"You did?" said Patrick, pleased at so much conversation.

Birdie remembered Benito standing in the patio holding the hose, spraying the roses, and then suddenly turning and spraying the bedroom's flowered wallpaper through the open window.

Birdie had screamed, "You're ruining the plaster. It won't work."

But it did. They pulled wet wallpaper off in long strips unveiling solid plaster walls. It took them all day, laughing and working together. By evening they were soaked, tired, and smelling of wallpaper paste. After the work, they sat together in the patio eating a supper of boiled crawfish, washing it down with Dixie beer.

Birdie wanted to cry. The damp cold of January hurt his knees with an ache like growing pains. There was no smell of sweet olive in the patio. Birdie felt as if his strength had been borrowed from Benito. He was still a child, but his father was dead. There was no one who wanted spaghetti for supper, no one who said, "We are going to the opera. *Don Pasquale* is playing." No one to correct him, forgive him with love.

Patrick took Birdie's arm as if he knew what Birdie was thinking; when Patrick played music it was always as if he knew the mind of the composer.

The rain stopped. They went out into the patio where a glass atrium housed the birds. Colors—cobalt blue, a bright chartreuse, colors as strong as flower paintings by Monet fluttered across the bamboo perches. Birdie opened a cage. He put his index finger to the breast of a bright blue parakeet which hopped on, riding out of the cage.

"This is Piaf, the little sparrow," he said

"Piaf never wore anything that bright in her whole life," said Patrick.

Birdie tossed the parakeet through the open door up into the wind.

"Oh, no," said Patrick, with a swift intake of breath.

The bird sailed up, then back down into the cage.

"This is Pierrot," said Birdie taking out a white male.

"That fits," Patrick answered.

Birdie tossed Pierrot into the air. He flew off into the dry branches of a Poplar tree.

"He'll die, Birdie."

"How do you know? Maybe he can make it on his own," Birdie said with a wry smile.

"Come on, Birdie. It's January. No parakeet from South America is going to make it in New Orleans in January."

"I'm old, Patrick."

"You look good, Birdie. Nobody would guess how old you are."

Birdie looked at his friend. At a distance he too looked like a boy, but up close there were dry laugh lines around his eyes, and his blonde hair was cut close to his head to hide the balding top.

"Two little old boys. That's what we are, Patrick."

Birdie took a long stick from the corner and pressing gently against the breast of the parakeet was able to coax him back into the cage. It began to sprinkle. The momentary sun had vanished again.

"Know anybody wants to buy some birds?" asked Birdie.

Birdie, still sedated—homeless—loverless—went to the bars. He made the rounds nursing one beer until someone bought him another. He went to the Parade; he even went to Jewel's where the sidewalk out front was crowded as a buzzard pen with men in black leaning against the building, where other men in leather jackets with handcuffs hanging from their belt loops sat astride motorcycles holding drinks. Music roared out the door like a jet engine taking off. Birdie, chilly and contained, carried his feelings like a gin and tonic in a tall glass. Once he went into the damp, black cave of the back room at Jewel's and he went home with a man in jack boots— who yelled "Take that, Mama!" when he came.

Everyday Birdie danced at the Parade—open twenty-four hours—under the strobe lights, his arms jerking to the heavy metal sounds of Billy Idol, living off electric guitar, ethyl chloride and strangers. A couple he met liked him so well they sent him a submit postcard from L.A., but he never replied. One afternoon he went to a bar called Paw Paw's where the sign in the window read "Desade men welcome," where the bartender, who gave him a paper cup full of pills like jelly beans said, "Come back tonight. Here they don't care how old you are."

Birdie took his go cup. He went to DeeTee's which catered to Quarter types of any persuasion. Kristina was there. She looked like a butch girl— no makeup, her long, blonde hair tucked up in a cool cap. "Jesus, Birdie you look like the wrath of God."

"Nobody loves a fairy when she's forty," Birdie said.

Still tranquilized, walking like a zombie, Birdie went to stay with Kristina who had been Birdie's friend since she first came out. Kristina had a long term gig at the club My-O-My as a female impersonator. Kristina's specialty was Marlene Dietrich. The apartment was filled with black and white photographs of Marlene's high cheekbones. Marlene as the Blue Angel; Marlene with Cary Grant; Marlene in an ape costume, blonde kinks sticking out, the ape head in her hands. There was a war snapshot of Marlene being lifted up by her famous legs to kiss a soldier on a train. There were other photos—Kristina's high cheek bones, Kristina as Marlene, and the rooms were draped with heavy beaded gowns on padded satin hangers. "Falling in Love Again" played constantly on a tinny record player. It was the late thirties in the boudoir, the early forties in the kitchen, the living room was Las Vegas and it all smelled of rice powder and heavy perfume.

Birdie never went out except to shop at the all-night A&P. She zipped up the beaded gowns, cooked delicate breakfasts for Kristina when she awoke at noon, her voice husky from last night's cigarettes and too much champagne. Kristina got a seven dollar cut on each twenty-five dollar bottle of champagne she drank with a John. It was cheap champagne and she poured it in the bucket, in the plastic flowers, and once in some John's shoe. "Jee-sus Christ," he yelled as champagne wet his crotch and ran down his pant leg into his orthopedic shoe.

The next morning, telling Birdie, Kristina said, "Isn't that too much, darling?" as she buttered her French toast.

Kristina did coke, but only enough to keep her up for work. Birdie stayed so well sedated that Kristina called her "Miss Walgreen, anything you want on the shelves."

Kristina confined her lovers to Texans in large hats. Texans with money who treated her well and bought her jewelry which she examined with a jeweler's loop. In the late afternoon, piling rings and necklaces on her dressing table, she examined each one for minute flaws in her security.

On Tuesdays when she arose from her darkened bedroom, she lifted her black eyeshade and began singing Dietrich's songs in a harsh, guttural voice. At five, her hair still in rollers, six rings on her fingers, she welcomed a square-shaped graduate student from Tulane University who taught her German. Birdie fancied Kristina in love with her German teacher, but Kristina never spoke of love, preferring control, she thought only of her career which was impersonating Dietrich, and of her beauty which might fade.

At six o'clock one morning Kristina came staggering into the house in full drag.

"Birdie," she screamed, "where the hell are you?"

"I'm in bed." Birdie answered groggily. "Where did you think I'd be?"

Kristina limped into Birdie's bedroom, the high heel of one satin shoe broken, her wig tilted crazily to one side, lipstick smeared up to one thin eyebrow.

"I brought you a present, Birdie, but it cost me a lot."

Kristina threw a cloth covered basket onto the bed. The cloth wiggled, whimpered a bit, then lay still except for a slight trembling.

"It must have. I've never seen you trashed so bad. What happened?"

"Well, I picked up this Texan. At least he fooled me. I thought he was an oil gusher. He had on a Stetson, lit my cigarettes with dollar bills, and had *that* with him. We drank champagne at the club and everything was rosy. Then we went out after hours to the Dew Drop Inn and he tried to pick up some black queen who already had a friend. There was a hair-puller. I was able to haul ass out the back door because Saloo knows me, but the police took the Texan away. Saloo set bail for him, and guess what, darling?" She laughed huskily. "That kinky piece of trash is some Medieval Studies professor from Harvard." She straightened her wig and staggered off to bed.

Birdie uncovered the basket. A little dog stared up into her face. The muzzle was sharp—a fox face—bright black eyes shone in a fluff of caramel colored fur. The dog was a Pomeranian; the kind the breeders call Toy. Still trembling, the little dog examined Birdie's face and tentatively licked her fingers. Birdie's stomach felt warm as if she'd just eaten. She patted the dog's ears, and gently rubbed the light, soft fur behind them. As if reassured, the dog turned around three times on the comforter, then curled up in a ball to sleep. Birdie had always wanted a little dog, but Benito liked big dogs. Over the years they had a Great Dane, two shepherds, and the Weimaraner, Von Stroheim. Birdie enjoyed being seen with the strong, stern Benito, and the various big dogs that followed at heel and sat before crossing streets. They were attentive to the baton. Precise as parade soldiers, they were the decorations of Benito's lost military career.

Birdie put her hands behind her head. She lay there staring into the shadows behind the light pooled around the lamp. She remembered the girl in a story which had frightened her when she was a boy. It was a Hans Christian Andersen story his mother always read to him on dark, rainy days in February. The Snow Queen, a terrible lady, had cast a spell upon a boy. It had all come from a splinter of broken glass. The devil made a mirror which distorted everything, for a short time you could see the world and how all the people really looked, but as the devil flew with it to Heaven, the grinning mirror slipped and fell shattering into millions of bits. Each fragment flew off into someone's eye. Once there the fragments distorted everything, a few people got fragments in their hearts. That was how Birdie felt, as if he had a large splinter in his heart. As if, like the boy in the story, he had shifted flat pieces of ice to and fro trying to fit them into every possible pattern; he arranged them all in a game of ice cold reason. He had arranged the pieces to spell many words, but he could never find the way to make them spell the one word he wanted.

He thought the word had been spelled in the Royal Street house, but now that was over, and Birdie's heart had ingrown around the splinter. But something had happened tonight like the story where the hot tears of Gerda had gone directly to the boy's heart, melted the lump of ice, and burned away the splinter of glass—releasing him from the terrible lady who imprisoned him. As Birdie drifted into sleep he put his right hand on the dog and called her, "Gerda."

The next day Birdie changed the record on the stereo to "They All Axed For You" and he did a few dance steps while he made Kristina's breakfast. Gerda followed every step; he fed her tidbits of brioche which she ate daintily. Many of her mannerisms were cat-like. Birdie found her fascinating. He watched everything she did with enormous pride.

Kristina lurched out of the bedroom in a green negligée.

"My God, what time is it?"

"One o'clock."

"One o'clock! It's got to be seven. You've been futzing around in here since daylight, banging pots and pans. What's that?" She pointed an accusing finger at the dog which, at the loud, raspy sound of Kristina's voice, had hunkered down on the white rug.

"That's Gerda."

"Well, for God's sake, take her for a walk. She's going to ruin the carpet."

Birdie picked the dog up, and went out into the sunlight. It seared her eyes. It was the first time in months she'd been out in sunlight. She'd been shopping at the all-night A&P where she pushed her basket along with a strange assortment of night creatures, who crept from doorway to doorway when the sun came out.

Gerda shivered in her arms. Birdie thought of the Weimaraner and how he'd sit at the curb waiting for Benito's signal to cross. Twice a day Benito had walked the dogs down the neutral ground on Esplanade Avenue. He always took the leash off and held it doubled in his hands, slapping it against his jeans as the dogs bounded ahead. Benito carried a leather crop under his arm. It was supple from use.

Birdie put Gerda down on a worn patch of grass near the curb. The dog lay there miserably, watching Birdie's face for some indication of what was wanted of her. Birdie didn't know how to teach any signals or commands.

After awhile, when Gerda continued to lie there, Birdie broke off a thin switch from the crepe myrtle tree. She tried holding it under her arm as Benito had held his leather baton, but it had leaves, and didn't fit.

"Come on, Gerda," Birdie called, but the little dog rolled over exposing the sparse, pale hair of her white belly. Birdie felt an unreasonable anger with the dog—her weakness—her submissive pose. Birdie brought the thin switch down across Gerda's stomach. With a yelp the dog scrambled to her feet and ran into the street directly into the path of a taxi turning onto Dauphine Street. The cab driver slammed on his brakes, as Gerda stood transfixed in the middle of the street. Birdie ran out and grabbed her.

"HEY," yelled the cab driver leaning out the car window, "you better watch your dog. Ain't everybody going to stop."

Birdie hugged Gerda to her thin chest and threw the switch away. She wondered why the sight of the dog's belly, the dog's small size—why Gerda's weakness had made her so angry. Was there something in weakness that called for force? Birdie saw her own thin body lying in the street. Even in the hot sunlight she shivered. Still holding the dog she walked into DeeTee's Bar.

The air-cooled dark loomed in her face. The bartender remained a shadow in the depths of the room.

"Draft," she called to him. Like a white fish he swam toward her from the murky recesses of the room, but when he stood before her he was a large, solid figure in a white apron.

"What kind of dog?" he asked.

"Pomeranian," said Birdie. "She's still shaking. She nearly got run over by a taxi."

"Here, I've got part of a Po' boy sandwich—roast beef. Maybe that'll make her feel better." He put out a saucer with bits of roast beef and gravy. Delicately the dog began to sniff, then lick the gravy. Birdie was happy to see Gerda eat, relieved to see that she had forgiven Birdie for using the switch.

Gerda was not like the birds. As beautiful as they were, Birdie had never loved them, theirs was a closed society—subject to terrible diseases like "scaly face" and tumors which she had tried with little success to cure. When they were well, they were self-absorbed—two being their most generous number. Birdie had always wanted a little dog to care for. When she though of the switch on Gerda's white belly she whispered, "I'll never beat you again, even in love," and love was what she felt in the tips of her fingers as she scratched the dog's ears. Gerda, full of Po' boy sandwich, snuggled up and went to sleep in Birdie's lap. For the first time since Benito died, the heaviness went out of Birdie's chest with a long sigh like a tide.

"Hey," she said to the bartender, "you know of any apartments where they take dogs? I've got to make a move."

RICHARD FORD

PUPPY

EARLY THIS PAST SPRING SOMEONE LEFT A PUPPY inside the back gate
of our house, and then never came back to get it. This happened at a time
when I was traveling up and back to St. Louis each week, and my wife was
intensely involved in the AIDS marathon, which occurs, ironically enough,
around tax time in New Orleans and is usually the occasion for a lot of
uncomfortable, conflicted spirits, which inevitably get resolved, of course,
by good will and dedication.

To begin in this way is only to say that our house is often empty much of
the day, which allowed whoever left the puppy to do so. We live on a corner in the fashionable historical district. Our house is large and old and
conspicuous—typical of the French Quarter—and the garden gate is a
distance from the back door, blocked from it by thick ligustrums. So to set
a puppy down over the iron grating and slip away unnoticed wouldn't be
hard, and I imagine was not.

"It was those kids," my wife said, folding her arms. She was standing
with me inside the French doors, staring out at the puppy, who was seated
on the brick pavements looking at us with what seemed like insolent curiosity. It was small and had slick, short coarse hair and was mostly white,
with a few triangular black side patches. Its tail stuck alertly up when it
was standing, making it look as though it might've had pointer blood back
in its past. For no particular reason, I gauged it to be three months old,
though its legs were long and its white feet larger than you would expect.
"It's those ones in the neighborhood wearing all the black," Sallie said.
"Whatever you call them. All penetrated everywhere and ridiculous, living
in doorways. They always have a dog on a rope." She tapped one of the
square panes with her fingernail to attract the puppy's attention. It had

begun diligently scratching its ear, but stopped and fixed its dark little eyes on the door. It had dragged a red plastic dust broom from under the outside back stairs, and this was lying in the middle of the garden.

"We have to get rid of it," Sallie said. "The poor thing. Those shitty kids just got tired of it. So they abandon it with us."

"I'll try to place it," I said. I had been home from St. Louis all of five minutes and had barely set my suitcase inside the front hall.

"Place it?" Sallie's arms were folded. "Place it where? How?"

"I'll put up some signs around," I said, and touched her shoulder. "Somebody in the neighborhood might've lost it. Or else someone found it and left it here so it wouldn't get run over. Somebody'll come looking."

The puppy barked then. Something (who knows what) had frightened it. Suddenly it was on its feet barking loudly and menacingly at the door we were standing behind, as though it had sensed we were intending something and resented that. Then just as abruptly it stopped, and without taking its dark little eyes off of us, squatted puppy-style and pissed on the bricks.

"That's its other trick," Sallie said. The puppy finished and delicately sniffed at its urine, then gave it a sampling lick. "What it doesn't pee on it jumps on and scratches and barks at. When I found it this morning, it barked at me, then it jumped on me and peed on my ankle and scratched my leg. I was only trying to pet it and be nice." She shook her head.

"It was probably afraid," I said, admiring the puppy's staunch little bearing, its sharply pointed ears and simple, uncomplicated pointer's coloration. Solid white, solid black. It was a boy dog.

"Don't get attached to it, Bobby," Sallie said. "We have to take it to the pound."

My wife is from Wetumpka, Alabama. Her family were ambitious, melancholy Lutheran Swedes who somehow made it to the South because her great-grandfather had accidentally invented a lint shield for the ginning process which ended up saving people millions. In one generation the Holmbergs from Lund went from being dejected, stigmatized immigrants to being moneyed gentry with snooty Republican attitudes and a strong sense of entitlement. In Wetumpka there was a dog pound, and stray dogs were always feared for carrying mange and exotic fevers. I've been there; I know this. A dogcatcher prowled around with a ventilated, louver-sided truck and big catch-net. When an unaffiliated dog came sniffing around anybody's hydrangeas, a call was made and off it went forever.

"There aren't dog pounds anymore," I said.

"I meant the shelter," Sallie said privately. "The SPCA—where they're nice to them."

"I'd like to try the other way first. I'll make a sign."

"But aren't you leaving again tomorrow?"

"Just for two days," I said. "I'll be back."

Sallie tapped her toe, a sign that something had made her unsettled. "Let's not let this drag out." The puppy began trotting off toward the back of the garden and disappeared behind one of the big brick planters of pittosporums. "The longer we keep it, the harder it'll be to give it up. And that *is* what'll happen. We'll have to get rid of it eventually."

"We'll see."

"When the time comes, I'll let *you* take it to the pound," she said.

I smiled apologetically. "That's fine. If the time comes, then I will."

We ended it there.

I am a long-time practitioner before the federal appeals courts, arguing mostly large, complicated negligence cases in which the appellant is a hotel or a restaurant chain engaged in interstate commerce, and who has been successfully sued by an employee or a victim of what is often some terrible mishap. Mostly I win my cases. Sallie is also a lawyer, but did not like the practice. She works as a resource specialist, which means fundraising for by and large progressive causes: the homeless, women at risk in the home, children at risk in the home, nutrition issues, etc. It is a far cry from the rich, arriviste-establishment views of her family in Alabama. I am from Vicksburg, Mississippi, from a very ordinary although solid suburban upbringing. My father was an insurance-company attorney. Sallie and I met in law school at Yale, in the seventies. We have always thought of ourselves as lucky in life, and yet in no way extraordinary in our goals or accomplishments. We are simply the southerners from sturdy, supportive families who had the good fortune to get educated well and who came back more or less to home, ready to fit in. Somebody has to act on that basic human impulse, we thought, or else there's no solid foundation of livable life.

One day after the old millennium's end and the new one's beginning, Sallie said to me—this was at lunch at Le Perigord on Esplanade, our favorite place: "Do you happen to remember"—she'd been thinking about it—"that first little watercolor we bought, in Old Saybrook? The tilted sailboat sail you could barely recognize in all the white sky. At that little shop near the bridge?" Of course I remembered it. It's in my law office in Place St. Charles, a cherished relic of youth.

"What about it?" We were at a table in the shaded garden of the restaurant where it smelled sweet from some kind of heliotrope. Tiny wild parrots were fluttering up in the live-oak foliage and chittering away. We were eating a cold crab soup.

"Well," she said. Sallie has pale, almost animal blue eyes and translucently caramel northern European skin. She has kept away from the sun for years. Her hair is cut roughly and parted in the middle like some Bergman character from the sixties. She is forty-seven and extremely beautiful. "It's completely trivial," she went on, "but how did we ever know back then that we had any taste. I don't really even care about it, you know that. You have much better taste than I do in most things. But why were we sure we wouldn't choose that little painting and then have it be horrible? Explain that to me. And what if our friends had seen it and laughed about us behind our backs? Do you ever think that way?"

"No," I said, my spoon above my soup, "I don't."

"You mean it isn't interesting? Or, eventually we'd have figured out better taste all by ourselves?"

"Something like both," I said. "It doesn't matter. Our taste is fine and would've been fine. I still have that little boat in my office. People pass through and admire it all the time."

She smiled in an inwardly pleased way. "Our friends aren't the point, of course. If we'd liked sad-clown paintings or put antimacassars on our furniture, I wonder if we'd have a different, *worse* life now," she said. She stared down at her lined-up knife and spoons. "It just intrigues me. Life's so fragile in the way we experience it."

"What's the point?" I had to return to work soon. We have few friends now in any case. It's natural.

She furrowed her brow and scratched the back of her head using her index finger. "It's about how altering one small part changes everything."

"One star strays out of line and suddenly there's no Big Dipper?" I said. "I don't really think you mean that. I don't really think you're getting anxious just because things might have gone differently in your life." I will admit this amused me.

"That's a very frivolous way to see it." She looked down at her own untried soup and touched its surface with the rim of her spoon. "But yes, that's what I mean."

"But it isn't true," I said and wiped my mouth. "It'd still be the thing it is. The Big Dipper or whatever you cared about. You'd just ignore the star that falls and concentrate on the ones that fit. Our life would've been exactly the same, despite bad art."

"You're the lawyer, aren't you?" This was condescending, but I don't think she meant it to be. "You just ignore what doesn't fit. But it wouldn't be the same, I'm sure of that."

"No," I said. "It wouldn't have been exactly the same. But almost."

"There's only one Big Dipper," she said and began to laugh.

"That we know of, and so far. True."

This exchange I give only to illustrate what we're like together—what seems important and what doesn't. And how we can let potentially difficult matters go singing off into oblivion.

The afternoon the puppy appeared, I sat down at the leathertop desk in our dining room where I normally pay the bills and diligently wrote out one of the hand-lettered signs you see posted up on laundromat announcement boards and stapled to telephone poles alongside advertisements for new massage therapies, gay health issues and local rock concerts. PUPPY, my sign said in black magic marker, and after that the usual data with my office phone number and the date (March 23rd). This sheet I xeroxed twenty-five times on Sallie's copier. Then I found the stapler she used for putting up the AIDS marathon posters, went upstairs and got out an old braided leather belt from my closet, and went down to the garden to take the puppy with me. It seemed good to bring him along while I stapled up the posters about him. Someone could recognize him, or just take a look at him and see he was available and attractive and claim him on the spot. Such things happen, at least in theory.

When I found him he was asleep behind the ligustrums in the far corner. He had worked and scratched and torn down into the bricky brown dirt and made himself a loll deep enough that half of his little body was out of sight below ground level. He had also broken down several ligustrum branches and stripped the leaves and chewed the ends until the bush was wrecked.

When he sensed me coming forward he flattened out in his hole and growled his little puppy growl. Then he abruptly sat up in the dirt and aggressively barked at me in a way that—had it been a big dog—would've alarmed me and made me stand back.

"Puppy?" I said, meaning to sound sympathetic. "Come out." I was still wearing my suit pants and white shirt and tie—the clothes I wear in court. The puppy kept growling and then barking at me, inching back behind the wrecked ligustrum until it was in the shadows against the brick wall that separates us from the street. "Puppy?" I said again in a patient, cajoling way, leaning in amongst the thick green leaves. I'd made a loop out of my belt, and I reached forward and slipped it over his head. But he backed up farther when he felt the weight of the buckle, and unexpectedly began to yelp—a yelp that was like a human shout. And then he turned and began to claw up the bricks, scratching and springing, his paws scraping and his ugly little tail jerking, and at the same time letting go his bladder until the bricks were stained with hot, terrified urine.

Which, of course, made me lose heart since it seemed cruel to force this on him even for his own good. Whoever had owned him had evidently not been kind. He had no trust of humans, even though he needed us. To take him out in the street would only terrify him worse, and discourage anyone from taking him home and giving him a better life. Better to stay, I decided. In our garden he was safe and could have a few hours peace to himself.

I reached and tried to take the belt loop off, but when I did he bared his teeth and snapped and nearly caught the end of my thumb with his little white incisor. I decided just to forget the whole effort and to go about putting up my signs alone.

I stapled up all the signs in no time—at the laundromat on Barracks Street, in the gay deli, outside the French patisserie, inside the coffee shop and the adult news on Decatur. I caught all the telephone poles in a four-block area. On several of the poles and all the message boards I saw that others had lost pets, too, mostly cats. *Hiroki's Lost. We're utterly disconsolate. Can you help? Call Jamie or Hiram at . . .* Or, *We miss our Mittens. Please call us or give her a good home. Please!* In every instance as I made the rounds I stood a moment and read the other notices to see if anyone had reported a lost puppy. But (and I was surprised) no one had.

On a short, disreputable block across from the French Market, a section that includes a seedy commercial strip (sex shops, T-shirt emporiums and a slice-of-pizza outlet), I saw a group of the young people Sallie had accused of abandoning our puppy. They were, as she'd remembered, sitting in an empty store's doorway, dressed in heavy, ragged black clothes and thick-soled boots with various chains attached and studded wristlets, all of them—two boys and two girls—pierced, and tattooed with Maltese crosses and dripping knife blades and swastikas, all dirty and utterly pointless but abundantly surly and apparently willing to be violent. These young people had a small black dog tied with a white cotton cord to one of the boys' heavy boots. They were drinking beer and smoking but otherwise just sitting, not even talking, simply looking malignantly at the street or at nothing in particular.

I felt there was little to fear, so I stopped in front of them and asked if they or anyone they knew had lost a white-and-black puppy with simple markings in the last day, because I'd found one. The one boy who seemed to be the oldest and was large and unshaven with brightly dyed purple and green hair cut into a flattop—he was the one who had the dog leashed to his boot—this boy looked up at me without obvious expression. He turned then to one of the immensely dirty-looking, fleshy, pale-skinned girls crouched farther back in the grimy door stoop, smoking (this girl had a crude cross tattooed into her forehead like Charles Manson is supposed to have) and asked, "Have you lost a little white-and-black puppy with simple markings, Samantha? I don't think so. Have you? I don't remember you having one today." The boy had an unexpectedly youthful-sounding, nasally midwestern accent, the kind I'd been hearing in St. Louis that week, although it had been high-priced attorneys who were speaking it. I know little enough about young people, but it occurred to me that this boy was possibly one of these lawyers' children, someone whose likeness you'd see on a milk carton or a website devoted to runaways.

"Ah, no," the girl said, then suddenly spewed out laughter.

The big, purple-haired boy looked up at me and produced a disdainful smile. His eyes were the darkest, steeliest blue, impenetrable and intelligent.

"What are you doing sitting here?" I wanted to say to him. "I know you left your dog at my house. You should take it back. You should all go home now."

"I'm sorry, sir," the boy said, mocking me, "but I don't believe we'll be able to help you in your important search." He smirked around at his three friends.

I started to go. Then I stopped and handed him a paper sign and said, "Well, if you hear about a puppy missing anywhere."

He said something as he took it. I don't know what it was, or what he did with the sign when I was gone, because I didn't look back.

That evening Sallie came home exhausted. We sat at the dining room table and drank a glass of wine. I told her I'd put up my signs all around, and she said she'd seen one and it looked fine. Then for a while she cried quietly because of disturbing things she'd seen and heard at the AIDS hospice that afternoon, and because of various attitudes—typical New Orleans attitudes, she thought—voiced by some of the marathon organizers, which seemed callous and constituted right things done for wrong reasons, all of which made the world seem—to her, at least—an evil place. I have sometimes thought she might've been happier if we had chosen to have children or, failing that, if we'd settled someplace other than New Orleans, someplace less parochial and exclusive, a city like St. Louis, in the wide Middlewest—where you can be less personally involved in things but still be useful. New Orleans is a small town in so many ways. And we are not from here.

I didn't mention what the puppy had done to the ligustrums, or the kids I'd confronted at the French Market, or her description of them having been absolutely correct. Instead I talked about my work on the Brownlow-Maisonette appeal, and about what good colleagues all the St. Louis attorneys had turned out to be, how much they'd made me feel at home in their understated, low-key offices and how this relationship would bear important fruit in our presentation before the Eighth Circuit. I talked some about the definition of negligence as it is applied to common carriers, and about the unexpected, latter-day reshapings of general tort law paradigms in the years since the Nixon appointments. And then Sallie said she wanted to take a nap before dinner, and went upstairs obviously discouraged from her day and from crying.

Sallie suffers, and has as long as I've known her, from what she calls her war dreams—violent, careering, antic, destructive Technicolor nightmares without plots or coherent scenarios, just sudden drop-offs into deepest sleep accompanied by images of dismembered bodies lying around and explosions and brilliant flashes and soldiers of unknown armies being hurtled through trap doors and hanged or thrust out through bomb bays into empty screaming space. These are terrible things I don't even like to hear about and that would scare the wits out of anyone. She usually awakes from these dreams slightly worn down, but not especially spiritually disturbed. And for this reason I believe her to be constitutionally very strong. Once I convinced her to go lie down on Dr. Merle Mackey's well-known couch for a few weeks, and let him try to get to the bottom of all the mayhem. Which she willingly did. Though after a month and a half Merle told her—and told me privately at the tennis club—that Sallie was as mentally and morally sturdy as a race horse, and that some things occurred for no demonstrable reason, no matter how Dr. Freud had viewed it. And in

Sallie's case, her dreams (which have always been intermittent) were just the baroque background music of how she resides on the earth and didn't represent, as far as he could observe, repressed memories of parental abuse or some kind of private disaster she didn't want to confront in daylight. "Weirdness is part of the human condition, Bob," Merle said. "It's thriving all around us. You've probably got some taint of it. Aren't you from up in Mississippi?" "I am," I said. "Then I wouldn't want to get *you* on my couch. We might be there forever." Merle smirked like somebody's presumptuous butler. "No, we don't need to go into that," I said. "No, sir," Merle said, "we really don't." Then he pulled a big smile, and that was the end of it.

After Sallie was asleep I stood at the French doors again. It was nearly dark, and the tiny white lights she had strung up like holiday decorations in the cherry laurel had come on by their timer and delivered the garden into an almost Christmas-y lumination and loveliness. Dusk can be a magical time in the French Quarter—the sky so bright blue, the streets lush and shadowy. The puppy had come back to the middle of the garden and lain with his sharp little snout settled on his spotted front paws. I couldn't see his little feral eyes, but I knew they were trained on me, where I stood watching him, with the yellow chandelier light behind me. He still wore my woven leather belt looped around his neck like a leash. He seemed as peaceful and as heedless as he was likely ever to be. I had set out some Vienna sausages in a plastic saucer, and beside it a red plastic mixing bowl full of water—both where I knew he'd find them. I assumed he had eaten and drifted off to sleep before emerging, now that it was evening, to remind me he was still here, and possibly to express a growing sense of ease with his new surroundings. I was tempted to think what a strange, unpredictable experience it was to be him, so new to life and without essential defenses, and in command of little. But I stopped this thought for obvious reasons. And I realized, as I stood there, that my feelings about the puppy had already become slightly altered. Perhaps it was Sallie's Swedish toughmindedness influencing me; or perhaps it was the puppy's seemingly untamable nature; or possibly it was all those other signs on all the other message boards and stapled to telephone poles which seemed to state in a cheerful but hopeless way that fate was ineluctable, and character, personality, will, even untamable nature were only its accidental by-products. I looked out at the little low, diminishing white shadow motionless against the darkening bricks, and I thought: all right, yes, this is where you are now, and this is what I'm doing to help you. In all likelihood it doesn't really matter if someone calls, or if someone comes and takes you home and you live a long and happy life. What matters is simply a choice we make, a choice governed by time and opportunity and how well we persuade ourselves to go on until some other powerful force overtakes us. (We always hope it will be a positive and wholesome force, though it may not be.) No doubt this is another view one comes to accept as a lawyer— particularly one who enters events late in the process, as I do. I was, however, glad Sallie wasn't there to know about these thoughts, since it would only have made her think the world was a heartless place, which it really is not.

The next morning I was on the TWA flight back to St. Louis. Though later the evening before, someone had called to ask if the lost puppy I'd advertised had been inoculated for various dangerous diseases. I had to admit I had no idea, since it wore no collar. It *seemed* healthy enough, I told the person. (The sudden barking spasms and the spontaneous peeing didn't seem important.) The caller was clearly an elderly black woman—she spoke with a deep Creole accent and referred to me once or twice as "baby," but otherwise she didn't identify herself. She did say, however, that the puppy would be more likely to attract a family if it had its shots and had been certified healthy by a veterinarian. Then she told me about a private agency uptown that specialized in finding homes for dogs with elderly and shut-in persons, and I dutifully wrote down the agency's name—"Pet Pals." In our overly lengthy talk she went on to say that the gesture of having the puppy examined and inoculated with a rabies shot would testify to the good will required to care for the animal and increase its likelihood of being deemed suitable. After a while I came to think this old lady was probably completely loony and kept herself busy dialing numbers she saw on signs at the laundromat, and yakking for hours about lost kittens, macramé classes, and Suzuki piano lessons, things she wouldn't remember the next day. Probably she was one of our neighbors, though there aren't that many black ladies in the French Quarter anymore. Still, I told her I'd look into her suggestion and appreciated her thoughtfulness. When I innocently asked her her name, she uttered a surprising profanity and hung up.

"I'll do it," Sallie said the next morning as I was putting fresh shirts into my two-suiter, making ready for the airport and the flight back to St. Louis. "I have some time today. I can't let all this marathon anxiety take over my life." She was watching out the upstairs window down to the garden again. I'm not sure what I'd intended to happen to the puppy. I suppose I hoped he'd be claimed by someone. Yet he was still in the garden. We hadn't discussed a plan of action, though I had mentioned the Pet Pal agency.

"Poor little pitiful," Sallie said in a voice of dread. She took a seat on the bed beside my suitcase, let her hands droop between her knees, and stared at the floor. "I went out there and tried to play with it this morning, I want you to know this," she said. "It was while you were in the shower. But it doesn't know *how* to play. It just barked and peed and then snapped at me in a pretty hateful way. I guess it was probably funny to whoever had him that he acts that way. It's a crime, really." She seemed sad about it. I thought of the sinister blue-eyed, black-coated boy crouched in the fetid doorway across from the French Market with his new little dog and his three acolytes. They seemed like residents of one of Sallie's war dreams.

"The Pet Pal people will probably fix things right up," I said, tying my tie at the bathroom mirror. It was still unseasonably chilly in St. Louis, and I had on my wool suit, though in New Orleans it was already summery.

"If they *don't* fix things up, and if no one calls," Sallie said gravely, "then you have to take him to the shelter when you come back. Can we agree about that? I saw what he did to the plants. They can be replaced. But he's really not our problem." She turned and looked at me on the opposite side of our bed, whereon her long-departed Swedish grandmother had spent her first marriage night long ago. The expression on Sallie's round face was somber but decidedly settled. She was willing to try to care about the puppy because it suited how she felt that particular day, and because I was going away and she knew it would make me feel better if she tried. It is an admirable human trait, and how undoubtedly most good deeds occur— because you have the occasion, and there's no overpowering reason to do something else. But I was aware she didn't really care what happened to the puppy.

"That's exactly fine," I said, and smiled at her. "I'm hoping for a good outcome. I'm grateful to you for taking him."

"Do you remember when we went to Robert Frost's cabin?" Sallie said.

"Yes, I do." And surely I did.

"Well, when you come back from Missouri, I'd like us to go to Robert Frost's cabin again." She smiled at me shyly.

"I think I can do that," I said, closing my suitcase. "Sounds great."

Sallie bent sideways toward me and extended her smooth perfect face to be kissed as I went past the bed with my baggage. "We don't want to abandon that," she said.

"We never will," I answered, leaning to kiss her on the mouth. And then I heard the honk of my cab at the front of the house.

Robert Frost's cabin is a great story about Sallie and me. The spring of our first year in New Haven, we began reading Frost's poems aloud to each other, as antidotes to the grueling hours of reading cases on replevin and the rule against perpetuities and theories of intent and negligence—the usual shackles law students wear at exam time. I remember only a little of the poems now, twenty-six years later. "Better to go down dignified / with boughten friendship at your side / than none at all. Provide, provide." We thought we knew what Frost was getting at: that you make your way in the world and life—all the way to the end—as best you can. And so at the close of the school year, when it turned warm and our classes were over, we got in the old Chrysler Windsor my father had given me and drove up to where we'd read Frost had had his mountainside cabin in Vermont. The state had supposedly preserved it as a shrine, though you had to walk far back through the mosquito-y woods and off a winding loggers' road to find it. We wanted to sit on Frost's front porch in some rustic chair he'd sat in, and read more poems aloud to each other. Being young southerners educated in the North, we felt Frost represented a kind of old-fashioned but indisputably authentic Americanism, vital exposure we'd grown up exiled from because of race troubles, and because of absurd preoccupations about the South itself, practiced by people who should know better. Yet we'd always longed for that important exposure, and felt it represented rectitude in practice, self-evident wisdom, and a sense of fairness expressed by an unpretentious bent for the arts. (I've since heard Frost was nothing like that, but was mean and stingy and hated better than he loved.)

However, when Sallie and I arrived at the little log cabin in the spring woods, it was locked up tight, with no one around. In fact it seemed to us like no one ever came there, though the state's signs seemed to indicate this was the right place. Sallie went around the cabin looking in the windows until she found one that wasn't locked. And when she told me about it, I said we should crawl in and nose around and read the poem we wanted to read and let whoever came tell us to leave.

But once we got inside, it was much colder than outside, as if the winter and something of Frost's true spirit had been captured and preserved by the log and mortar. And before long we had stopped our reading—after doing "Design" and "Mending Wall" and "Death of the Hired Man" in front of the cold fireplace. And partly for warmth we decided to make love in

Frost's old bed, which was made up as he might've left it years before. (Later it occurred to us that possibly nothing had ever happened in the cabin, and maybe we'd even broken into the wrong cabin and made love in someone else's bed.)

But that's the story. That was what Sallie meant by a visit to Robert Frost's cabin—an invitation to me, upon my return, to make love to her, an act which the events of life and years sometimes can overpower and leave unattended. In a moment of panic, when we thought we heard voices out on the trail, we jumped into our clothes and by accident left our Frost book on the cold cabin floor. No one, of course, ever turned up.

That night I spoke to Sallie from St. Louis, at the end of a full day of vigorous preparations with the Missouri lawyers (whose clients were reasonably afraid of being put out of business by a 250-million-dollar class action judgment). She, however, had nothing but unhappy news to impart. Some homeowners were trying to enjoin the entire AIDS marathon because of a routing change that went too near their well-to-do Audubon Place neighborhood. Plus one of the original marathon organizers was now on the verge of death (not unexpected). She talked more about good-deeds-done-for-wrong-reasons among her hospice associates, and also about some plainly bad deeds committed by other rich people who didn't like the marathon and wanted AIDS to go away. Plus, nothing had gone right with our plans for placing the puppy into the Pet Pals uptown.

"We went to get its shots," Sallie said sadly. "And it acted perfectly fine when the vet had it on the table. But when I drove it out to Pet Pals on Prytania, the woman—Mrs. Myers, her name was—opened the little wire gate on the cage I'd bought, just to see him. And he jumped at her and snapped at her and started barking. He just barked and barked. And this Mrs. Myers looked horrified and said, 'Why, whatever in the world's wrong with it?' 'It's afraid,' I said to her. 'It's just a puppy. Someone's abandoned it. It doesn't understand anything. Haven't you ever had that happen to you?' 'Of course not,' she said, 'And we can't take an *abandoned* puppy anyway.' She was looking at me as though I was trying to steal something from her. 'Isn't that what you do here?' I said. And I'm sure I raised my voice to her."

"I don't blame you a bit," I said from strangely wintry St. Louis. "I'd have raised my voice."

"I said to her, 'What are you here for? If this puppy wasn't abandoned, why would *I* be here? I wouldn't, would I?'

" 'Well, you have to understand we really try to place the more mature dogs whose owners for some reason can't keep them, or are being transferred.' Oh God, I hated her, Bobby. She was one of these wide-ass, Junior League bitches who'd just gotten bored with flower arranging and playing canasta at the Boston Club. I wanted just to dump the dog right out in the shop and leave, or take a swing at her. I said, 'Do you mean you won't take him?' The puppy was in its cage and was actually being completely quiet and nice. 'No, I'm sorry, it's untamed,' this dowdy, stupid woman said. 'Untamed!' I said. 'It's an abandoned puppy, for fuck's sake.'

"She just looked at me then as if I'd suddenly produced a bomb and was jumping all around. 'Maybe you'd better leave now,' she said. And I'd probably been in the shop all of two minutes, and here she was ordering me out. I said, 'What's wrong with you?' I *know* I shouted then. I was so frustrated. 'You're not a pet pal at all,' I shouted. 'You're an enemy of pets.' "

"You just got mad," I said, happy not to have been there.

"Of course I did," Sallie said. "I let myself get mad because I wanted to scare this hideous woman. I wanted her to see how stupid she was and how much I hated her. She did look around at the phone as if she was thinking about calling 911. Someone I know came in then. Mrs. Hensley from the Art League. So I just left."

"That's all good," I said. "I don't blame you for any of it."

"No. Neither do I." Sallie took a breath and let it out forcefully into the receiver. "We have to get rid of it, though. Now." She was silent a moment, then she began, "I tried to walk it around the neighborhood using the belt you gave it. But it doesn't know how to be walked. It just struggles and cries, then barks at everyone. And if you try to pet it, it pees. I saw some of those kids in black sitting on the curb. They looked at me like I was a fool, and one of the girls made a little kissing noise with her lips, and said something sweet, and the puppy just sat down on the sidewalk and stared at her. I said, 'Is this your dog?' There were four of them, and they all looked at each other and smiled. I know it was theirs. They had another dog with them, a black one. We just have to take him to the pound, though, as soon as you come back tomorrow. I'm looking at him now, out in the garden. He just sits and stares like some Hitchcock movie."

"We'll take him," I said. "I don't suppose anybody's called."

"No. And I saw someone putting up new signs and taking yours down. I didn't say anything. I've had enough with Jerry DeFranco about to die, and our injunction."

"Too bad," I said, because that was how I felt—that it was too bad no one would come along and out of the goodness of his heart take the puppy in.

"Do you think someone left it as a message," Sallie said. Her voice sounded strange. I pictured her in the kitchen, with a cup of tea just brewed in front of her on the Mexican tile counter. It's good she set the law aside. She becomes involved in ways that are far too emotional. Distance is essential.

"What kind of message?" I asked.

"I don't know," she said. Oddly enough, it was starting to snow in St. Louis, small dry flakes backed—from my hotel window—by an empty, amber-lit cityscape and just the top curve of the great silver arch. It is a nice cordial city, though not distinguished in any way. "I can't figure out if someone thought we were the right people to care for a puppy, or were making a statement showing their contempt."

"Neither," I said. "I'd say it was random. Our gate was available. That's all."

"Does that bother you?"

"Does what?"

"Randomness."

"No," I said. "I find it consoling. It frees the mind."

"Nothing seems random to me," Sallie said. "Everything seems to reveal some plan."

"Tomorrow we'll work this all out," I said. "We'll take the dog and then everything'll be better."

"For us, you mean? Is something wrong with us? I just have this bad feeling tonight."

"No," I said. "Nothing's wrong with us. But it *is* us we're interested in here. Good night, now, sweetheart."

"Good night, Bobby," Sallie said in a resigned voice, and we hung up.

That night in the Mayfair Hotel, with the window shades open to the peculiar spring snow and orange-lit darkness, I experienced my own strange dream. In my dream I'd gone on a duck hunting trip into the marsh that surrounds our city. It was winter and early morning, and someone had taken me out to a duck blind before it was light. These are things I still do, as a matter of fact. But when I was set out in the blind with my shotgun, I found that beside me on the wooden bench was one of my law partners, seated with his shotgun between his knees, and wearing strangely red canvas hunting clothes—something you'd never wear in a duck blind. And he had the puppy with him, the same one that was then in our back garden awaiting whatever its fate would be. And my partner was with a woman, who either was or looked very much like the actress Liv Ullmann. The man was Paul Thompson, a man I (outside my dream) have good reason to believe once had an affair with Sallie, an affair that almost caused us to split apart without our even ever discussing it, except that Paul, who was older than I am and big and rugged, suddenly died—actually in a duck blind, of a terrible heart attack. It is a thing that can happen in the excitement of shooting.

In my dream Paul Thompson spoke to me and said, "How's Sallie, Bobby?" I said, "Well, she's fine, Paul, thanks," because we were pretending he and Sallie didn't have the affair I'd employed a private detective to authenticate—and almost did completely authenticate. The Liv Ullmann woman said nothing, just sat against the wooden sides of the blind seeming sad, with long straight blond hair. The little white-and-black puppy sat on the duckboard flooring and stared at me. "Life's very fragile in the way we experience it, Bobby," Paul Thompson, or his ghost, said to me. "Yes, it is," I said. I assumed he was referring to what he'd been doing with Sallie. (There had been some suspicious photos, though to be honest, I don't think Paul really cared about Sallie. Just did it because he could.) The puppy, meanwhile, kept staring at me. Then the Liv Ullmann woman herself smiled in an ironic way.

"Speaking about the truth tends to annihilate truth, doesn't it?" Paul Thompson said to me.

"Yes," I answered. "I'm certain you're right." And then for a sudden instant it seemed like it had been the puppy who'd spoken Paul's words. I could see his little mouth moving after the words were already spoken. Then the dream faded and became a different dream, which involved the millennium fireworks display from New Year's Eve, and didn't stay in my mind like the Paul Thompson dream did, and does even to this day.

I make no more of this dream than I make of Sallie's dreams, though I'm sure Merle Mackey would have plenty to say about it.

When I arrived back in the city the next afternoon, Sallie met me at the airport, driving her red Wagoneer. "I've got it in the car," she said as we walked to the parking structure. I realized she meant the puppy. "I want to take it to the shelter before we go home. It'll be easier." She seemed as though she'd been agitated but wasn't agitated now. She had dressed herself in some aqua walking shorts and a loose, pink blouse that showed her pretty shoulders.

"Did anyone call," I asked. She was walking faster than I was, since I was carrying my suitcase and a box of brief materials. I'd suffered a morning of tough legal work in a cold, unfamiliar city and was worn out and hot. I'd have liked a vodka martini instead of a trip to the animal shelter.

"I called Kirsten and asked her if she knew anyone who'd take the poor little thing," Sallie said. Kirsten is her sister, and lives in Andalusia, Alabama, where she owns a flower shop with her husband, who's a lawyer for a big cotton consortium. I'm not fond of either of them, mostly because of their simpleminded politics, which includes support for the Confederate flag, prayer in the public schools and the abolition of affirmative action— all causes I have been outspoken about. Sallie, however, can sometimes forget she went to Mount Holyoke and Yale, and step back into being a pretty, chatty southern girl when she gets together with her sister and her cousins. "She said she probably *did* know someone," Sallie went on, "so I said I'd arrange to have the puppy driven right to her doorstep. Today. This afternoon. But then she said it seemed like too much trouble. I told her it *wouldn't* be any trouble for *her* at all, that *I'd* do it or arrange it to be done. Then she said she'd call me back, and didn't. Which is typical of my whole family's sense of responsibility."

"Maybe we should call her back?" I said as we reached her car. We had a phone in the Wagoneer. I wasn't looking forward to visiting the SPCA.

"She's forgotten about it already," Sallie said. "She'd just get wound up."

When I looked in through the back window of Sallie's Jeep, the puppy's little wire cage was sitting in the luggage space. I could see his white head, facing back, in the direction it had come from. What could it have been thinking?

"The vet said it's going to be a really big dog. Big feet tell you that."

Sallie was getting in the car. I put my suitcase in the back seat so as to not alarm the puppy. Twice it barked its desperate little high-pitched puppy bark. Possibly it knew me. Though I realized it would never have been an easy puppy to get attached to. My father had a neat habit of reversing propositions he was handed as a way of assessing them. If a subject seemed to have one obvious outcome, he'd imagine the reverse of it: if a business deal had an obvious beneficiary, he'd ask who benefited but didn't seem to. Needless to say, these are valuable skills lawyers use. But I found myself thinking—except I didn't say it to Sallie—that though we may have thought we were doing the puppy a favor by trying to find it a home, possibly we were really doing ourselves a favor by presenting ourselves to be the kind of supposedly decent people who do that sort of thing. I am, for instance, a person who stops to move turtles off of busy interstates, or picks up butterflies in shopping mall parking lots and puts them into the bushes to give them a fairer chance at survival. I know these are pointless acts of pointless generosity. Yet there isn't a time when I do it that I don't get back in the car thinking more kindly about myself. (Later I often work around to thinking of myself as a fraud, too.) But the alternative is to leave the butterfly where it lies expiring, or to let the big turtle meet annihilation on the way to the pond; and in doing these things let myself in for the indictment of cruelty or the sense of loss that would follow. Possibly, anyone would argue, these issues are too small to think about seriously, since whether you perform these acts or don't perform them, you always forget about them in about five minutes.

Except for weary conversation about my morning at Ruger, Todd, Jennings, and Sallie's rerouting victory with the AIDS race, which was set for Saturday, we didn't say much as we drove to the SPCA. Sallie had obviously researched the address, because she got off the Interstate at an exit I'd never used and that immediately brought us down onto a wide boulevard with old cars parked on the neutral ground, and paper trash cluttering the curbs down one long side of some brown-brick housing projects where black people were outside on their front stoops and wandering around the street in haphazard fashion. There were a few dingy-looking barbecue and gumbo cafés, and two tire-repair shops where work was taking place out in the street. A tiny black man standing on a peach crate was performing haircuts in a dinette chair set up on the sidewalk, his customer wrapped in newspaper. And some older men had stationed a card table on the grassy median and were playing in the sunlight. There were no white people anywhere. It was a part of town, in fact, where most white people would've been afraid to go. Yet it was not a bad section, and the Negroes who lived there no doubt looked on the world as something other than a hopeless place.

Sallie took a wrong turn off the boulevard, and onto a run-down residential street of pastel shotgun houses where black youths in baggy trousers and big black sneakers were playing basketball without a goal. The boys watched us drive past but said nothing. "I've gotten us off wrong here," she said in a distracted, hesitant voice. She is not comfortable around black people when she is the only white—which is a residue of her privileged

Alabama upbringing where everything and everybody belonged to a proper place and needed to stay there.

She slowed at the next corner and looked both ways down a similar small street of shotgun houses. More black people were out washing their cars or waiting at bus stops in the sun. I noticed this to be Creve Coeur Street, which was where *The Times-Picayune* said an unusual number of murders occurred each year. All that happened at night, of course, and involved black people killing other black people for drug money. It was now 4:45 in the afternoon and I felt perfectly safe.

The puppy barked again in his cage, a soft, anticipatory bark, then Sallie drove us a block farther and immediately spotted the street she'd been looking for—Rousseau Street. The residential buildings stopped there and old, dilapidated two- and one-story industrial uses began: an off-shore pipe manufactory, a frozen seafood company, a shut-down recycling center where people had gone on leaving their garbage in plastic bags. There was also a small, windowless cube of a building that housed a medical clinic for visiting sailors off foreign ships. I recognized it because our firm had once represented the owners in a personal-injury suit, and I remembered grainy photos of the building and my thinking that I'd never need to see it up close.

Near the end of this block was the SPCA, which occupied a long, glum red-brick warehouse-looking building with a small red sign by the street and a tiny gravel parking lot. One might've thought the proprietors didn't want its presence too easily detected.

The SPCA's entrance was nothing but a single windowless metal door at one end of the building. There were no shrubberies, no disabled slots, no directional signs leading in, just this low, ominous flat-roofed building with long factory clerestories facing the lot and the seafood company. An older wooden shed was attached on the back. And a small sign I hadn't seen because it was fastened too low on the building said: YOU MUST HAVE A LEASH. ALL ANIMALS MUST BE RESTRAINED. CLEAN UP AFTER YOUR ANIMAL. IF YOUR DOG BITES A STAFF MEMBER YOU ARE RESPONSIBLE. THANKS MUCH.

"Why don't you take him in in his cage," Sallie said, nosing up to the building, becoming very efficient. "I'll go in and start the paperwork. I already called them." She didn't look my way.

"That's fine," I said.

When we got out I was surprised again at how warm it was, and how close and dense the air felt. Summer seemed to have arrived during the day

I was gone, which is not untypical of New Orleans. I smelled an entirely expectable animal gaminess, combined with a fish smell and something metallic that felt hot and slightly burning in my nose. And the instant I was out into the warm, motionless air I could hear barking from inside the building. I assumed the barking was triggered by the sound of a car arriving. Dogs trained themselves to the hopeful sound of motors.

Across the street from the SPCA were other shotgun houses I hadn't noticed. Elderly black people were sitting in metal lawn chairs on their little porches, observing me getting myself organized. It would be a difficult place to live, I thought, and quite a lot to get used to with the noise and the procession of animals coming and going. Sallie disappeared into the unfriendly little door, and I opened the back of the Wagoneer and hauled out the puppy in his cage. He stumbled to one side when I took a grip on the wire rungs, then barked several agitated, heartfelt barks and began clawing at the wires and my fingers, giving me a good scratch on the knuckles that almost caused me to drop the whole contraption. The cage, even with him in it, was still very light, though my face was so close I could smell his urine. "You be still in there," I said.

For some reason, and with the cage in my grasp, I looked around at the colored people across the street, silently watching me. I had nothing in mind to say to them. They were sympathetic, I felt sure, to what was going on and thought it was better than cruelty. I had started to sweat because I was wearing my business suit. And I awkwardly waved a hand toward them, but of course no one responded.

When I had maneuvered the cage close up to the metal door, I for some reason looked to the left and saw down the grimy alley between the SPCA and the sailors' clinic, to where a round steel canister was attached to the SPCA building by some large corrugated aluminum pipes, all of it black and new-looking. This, I felt certain, was a device for disposing of animal remains, though I didn't know how. Probably some incinerating invention that didn't have an outlet valve or a stack—something very efficient. It was an extremely sinister thing to see and reminded me of what we all heard years ago about terrible vacuum chambers and gassed compartments for dispatching unwanted animals. Probably they weren't even true stories. Now, of course, it's just an injection. They go to sleep, feeling certain they'll wake up.

Inside the SPCA it was instantly cool, and Sallie had almost everything done. The barking I'd heard outside had not ceased, but the gamy animal smell was replaced by a loud disinfectant odor that was everywhere. The reception area was a cubicle with a couple of metal desks and fluorescent tubes in the high ceiling, and a calendar on the wall showing a golden retriever standing in a wheat field with a dead pheasant in its mouth. Two high-school-age girls manned the desks, and one was helping Sallie fill out her documents. These girls undoubtedly loved animals and worked after school and had aspirations to be vets. A sign on the wall behind the desks said PLACING PUPPIES IS OUR FIRST PRIORITY. This was here, I thought, to make people like me feel better about abandoning dogs. To make forgetting easier.

Sallie was leaning over one of the desks filling out a thick green document, and looked around to see me just as an older stern-faced woman in a white lab coat and black rubber boots entered from a side door. Her small face and both her hands had a puffy but also a leathery texture that southern women's skin often takes on—too much sun and alcohol, too many cigarettes. Her hair was dense and dull reddish-brown and heavy around her face, making her head seem smaller than it was. This woman, however, was extremely friendly and smiled easily, though I knew just from her features and what she was wearing that she was not a veterinarian.

I stood holding the cage until one of the high-school girls came around her desk and looked in it and said the puppy was cute. It barked so that the cage shook in my grip. "What's his name?" she said, and smiled in a dreamy way. She was a heavy-set girl, very pale with a lazy left eye. Her fingernails were painted bright orange and looked unkempt.

"We haven't named him," I said, the cage starting to feel unwieldy.

"We'll name him," she said, pushing her fingers through the wires. The puppy pawed at her, then licked her fingertips, then made little crying sounds when she removed her fingers.

"They place sixty-five percent of their referrals," Sallie said over the forms she was filling out.

"Too bad it id'n a holiday," the woman in the lab coat said in a husky voice, watching Sallie finish. She spoke like somebody from across the Atchafalaya, somebody who had once spoken French. "Dis place be a ghost town by Christmas, you know?"

The helper girl who'd played with the puppy walked out through the door that opened onto a long concrete corridor full of shadowy metal-fenced cages. Dogs immediately began barking again, and the foul animal odor entered the room almost shockingly. An odd place to seek employment, I thought.

"How long do you keep them?" I said, and set the puppy's cage down on the concrete floor. Dogs were barking beyond the door, one big-sounding dog in particular, though I couldn't see it. A big yellow tiger-striped cat that apparently had free rein in the office walked across the desk top where Sallie was going on writing and rubbed against her arm, and made her frown.

"Five days," the puffy-faced Cajun woman said, and smiled in what seemed like an amused way. "We try to place 'em. People be in here all the time, lookin'. Puppies go fast 'less they something wrong with them." Her eyes found the cage on the floor. She smiled at the puppy as if it could understand her. "You cute," she said, then made a dry kissing noise.

"What usually disqualifies them?" I said, and Sallie looked around at me.

"Too aggressive," the woman said, staring approvingly in at the puppy. "If it can't be house-broke, then they'll bring 'em back to us. Which isn't good."

"Maybe they're just scared," I said.

"Some are. Then some are just little naturals. They go in one hour." She leaned over, hands on her lab-coat knees and looked in at our puppy. "How 'bout you?" she said. "You a little natural? Or are you a little scamp? I b'lieve I see a scamp in here." The puppy sat on the wire flooring and stared at her indifferently, just as he had stared at me. I thought he would bark, but he didn't.

"That's all," Sallie said, and turned to me and attempted an hospitable look. She put her pen in her purse. She was thinking I might be changing my mind, but I wasn't. "Then that's all you need. We'll take over," the supervisor woman said.

"What's the fee?" I asked.

"Id'n no fee," the woman said and smiled. "Remember me in yo' will." She squatted in front of the cage as if she was going to open it. "Puppy, puppy," she said, then put both hands around the sides of the cage and stood up, holding it with ease. She made a little grunting sound, but she was much stronger than I would've thought. Just then another blond helper girl, this one with a metal brace on her left leg, came humping through the kennel's door, and the supervisor just walked right past her, holding the cage, while the dogs down the long, dark corridor started barking ecstatically.

"We're donating the cage," Sallie said. She wanted out of the building, and I did, too. I stood another moment and watched as the woman in the lab coat disappeared along the row of pens, carrying our puppy. Then the green metal door went closed, and that was all there was to the whole thing. Nothing very ceremonial.

On our drive back downtown we were both, naturally enough, sunk into a kind of woolly, disheartened silence. From up on the Interstate, the spectacle of modern, southern city life and ambitious new construction where once had been a low, genteel old river city, seemed particularly gruesome and unpromising and probably seemed the same to Sallie. To me, who labored in one of the tall, metal and glass enormities (I could actually see my office windows in Place St. Charles, small, undistinguished rectangles shining high up among countless others), it felt particularly alien to history and to my own temperament. Behind these square mirrored windows, human beings were writing and discussing and preparing cases; and on other floors were performing biopsies, CAT scans, drilling out cavities, delivering news both welcome and unwelcome to all sorts of other expectants—clients, patients, partners, spouses, children. People were in fact there waiting for *me* to arrive that very afternoon, anticipating news of the Brownlow-Maisonette case—where *were* things, how were our prospects developing, what was my overall *take* on matters and what were our hopes for a settlement (most of my "take" wouldn't be all that promising). In no time I'd be entering their joyless company and would've forgotten about myself here on the highway, peering out in near despair because of the fate of an insignificant little dog. Frankly, it made me feel pretty silly.

Sallie suddenly said, as though she'd been composing something while I was musing away balefully, "Do you remember after New Year's that day we sat and talked about one thing changing and making everything else different?"

"The Big Dipper," I said as we came to our familiar exit, which quickly led down and away through a different poor section of darktown that abuts our gentrified street. Everything had begun to seem more manageable as we neared home.

"That's right," Sallie said, as though the words Big Dipper reproached her. "But you know, and you'll think this is crazy. It *is* maybe. But last night when I was in bed, I began thinking about that poor little puppy as an ill force that put everything in our life at a terrible risk. And we were in danger in some way. It scared me. I didn't want that."

I looked over at Sallie and saw a crystal tear escape her eye and slip down her soft, rounded, pretty cheek.

"Sweetheart," I said, and found her hand on the steering wheel. "It's quite all right. You put yourself through a lot. And I've been gone. You just need me around to do more. There's nothing to be scared about."

"I suppose," Sallie said resolutely.

"And if things are not exactly right now," I said, "they soon will be. You'll take on the world again the way you always do. We'll all be the better for it."

"I know," she said. "I'm sorry about the puppy."

"Me too," I said. "But we did the right thing. Probably he'll be fine."

"And I'm sorry things threaten me," Sallie said. "I don't think they should, then they do."

"Things threaten all of us," I said. "Nobody gets away unmarked." That is what I thought about all of that then. We were in sight of our house. I didn't really want to talk about these subjects anymore.

"Do you love me," Sallie said, quite unexpectedly.

"Oh yes," I said, "I do. I love you very much." And that was all we said.

A week ago, in one of those amusing fillers used to justify column space in one of the trial lawyers' journals I look at just for laughs, I read two things that truly interested me. These are always chosen for their wry comment on the law, and are frequently hilarious and true. The first one I read said, "Scientists predict that in five thousand years the earth will be drawn into the sun." It then went on to say something like, "so it's not too early to raise your malpractice insurance," or some such cornball thing as that. But I will admit to being made oddly uncomfortable by this news about the earth— as if I had something important to lose in the inevitability of its far-off demise. I can't now say what that something might be. None of us can think about five thousand years from now. And I'd have believed none of us could *feel* anything about it either, except in ways that are vaguely religious. Only I did, and I am far from being a religious man. What I felt was very much like the sensation described by the old saying "Someone just walked on your grave." Someone, so it seemed, had walked on my grave five thousand years from now, and it didn't feel very good. I was sorry to have to think about it.

The other squib I found near the back of the magazine behind the Legal Market Place, and it said that astronomers had discovered the oldest known star, which they believed to be 50 million-light years away, and they had named it the Millennium Star for obvious reasons, though the actual Millennium had gone by with hardly any change in things that I'd noticed.

When asked to describe the chemical makeup of this Millennium Star—
which of course couldn't even be seen—the scientist who'd discovered it
said, "Oh, gee, I don't know. It's impossible to reach that far back in time."
And I thought—sitting in my office with documents of the Brownlow-
Maisonette case spread all around me and the hot New Orleans sun beaming into the very window I'd seen from my car when Sallie and I were
driving back from delivering the puppy to its fate—I thought, "*Time?* Why
does he say *time,* when what he means is space?" My feeling then was very
much like the feeling from before, when I'd read about the earth hurtling
into the sun—a feeling that so much goes on everywhere all through time,
and we know only a laughably insignificant fraction about any of it.

The days that followed our visit to the SPCA were eventful days. Sallie's
colleague Jerry DeFranco did, of course, die. And though he had AIDS, he
died by his own dispirited hand, in his little garret apartment on Kerlerec
Street, late at night before the marathon, in order, I suppose, that his life
and its end be viewed as a triumph of will over pitiless circumstance.

On another front, the Brownlow appellants decided very suddenly and
unexpectedly to settle our case rather than face years of extremely high
lawyers' fees and of course the possibility (though not a good one) of enduring a crippling loss. I had hoped for this, and look at it as a victory.

Elsewhere, the marathon went off as planned, and along the route Sallie
had wanted. I unfortunately was in St. Louis and missed it. A massacre
occurred, the same afternoon, at a fast-food restaurant not far from the
SPCA, and someone we knew—a black lawyer—was killed. And, during
this period, I began receiving preliminary feelers about a federal judgeship
which I'm sure I'll never get. These things are always bandied about for
months and years, all sorts of persons are put on notice to be ready when
the moment comes, and then the wrong one is chosen for completely wrong
reasons, after which it becomes clear that nothing was ever in doubt. The
law is an odd calling. And New Orleans a unique place. In any case, I'm far
too moderate for the present company running things.

Several people did eventually call about the puppy, having seen my signs,
and I directed them all to the animal shelter. I went around a time or two
and checked the signs, and several were still up along with the AIDS marathon flyers, which made me satisfied, but not very satisfied.

Each morning I sat in bed and thought about the puppy, waiting for
someone to come down the list of cages and see him there alone and staring, and take him away. For some reason, in my imaginings, no one ever

chose him—not an autistic child, nor a lonely, discouraged older person, a recent widow, a young family with rough-housing kids. None of these. In all the ways I tried to imagine it, he stayed there.

Sallie did not bring the subject up again, although her sister called on Tuesday and said she knew someone named Hester in Andalusia who'd take the puppy, then the two of them quarreled so bitterly that I had to come on the phone and put it settled.

On some afternoons, as the provisional five waiting days ticked by, I would think about the puppy and feel utterly treacherous for having delivered him to the shelter. Then, other times, I'd feel that we'd given him a better chance than he'd have otherwise had, either on the street alone or with his previous owners. I certainly never thought of him as an ill force to be dispelled, or a threat to anything important. To me life's not that fragile. He was, if anything, just a casualty of the limits we all place on our sympathy and our capacity for the ambiguous in life. Though Sallie might've been right—that the puppy had been a message left for us to ponder: something someone thought about us, something someone felt we needed to know. Who or what or in what way that might've been true, I can't quite imagine. Though we are all, of course, implicated in the lives of others, whether we precisely know how or don't.

On Thursday night, before the puppy's final day in the shelter, I had another strange dream. Dreams always mean something obvious, and so I try as much as I can not to remember mine. But for some reason this time I did, and what I dreamed was again about my old departed law partner, Paul Thompson, and his nice wife, Judy, a pretty, buxom blond woman who'd studied opera and sung the coloratura parts in several municipal productions. In my dream Judy Thompson was haranguing Paul about some list of women's names she'd found, women Paul had been involved with, even in love with. She was telling him he was an awful man who had broken her heart, and that she was leaving him (which did actually happen). And on her list—which I could suddenly, as though through a fog, see— was Sallie's name. And when I saw it there, my heart started pounding, pounding, pounding, until I sat right up in bed in the dark and said out loud, "Did you know your name's on that goddamned list?" Outside, on our street, I could hear someone playing a trumpet, a very slow and soulful version of "Nearer Walk with Thee." And Sallie was there beside me, deep asleep. I of course knew she'd done it, deserved to be on the list, and that probably there *was* such a list, given the kind of reckless man Paul Thompson was. As I said, I had never spoken to Sallie about this subject and had, until then, believed I'd gone beyond the entire business. Though I have to suppose now I was wrong.

This dream stayed on my mind the next day, and the next night I had it again. And because the dream preoccupied my thinking, it wasn't until Saturday after lunch, when I had sat down to take a nap in a chair in the living room, that I realized I'd forgotten about the puppy the day before, and that all during Friday many hours had passed, and by the end of them the puppy must've reached its destination, whatever it was to be. I was surprised to have neglected to think about it at the crucial moment, having thought of it so much before then. And I was sorry to have to realize that I had finally not cared as much about it as I'd thought.

JULIE SMITH

HOUSE OF MISCHIEF

IT IS A FACT UNIVERSALLY ACKNOWLEDGED—like the one made famous by Ms. Austen—that the very walls have ears. What is not so generally known is that we also have eyes.

If you have ever lived in a historic house, especially in New Orleans, you are well aware that such a building is an entity unto itself, with a personality and a way of expressing it.

Normally, we do not give up our secrets. But, my darlings—this one is so delicious! And harmless—truly harmless. Dreadful things can happen in houses, and amusing ones as well. But nothing unusual ever does.

Or hardly ever.

Death, birth, cruelty, laughter, drama—these things are everyday occurrences. But in my entire hundred and fifty years, I never witnessed a scene such as the one played out last summer by Mr. Leo Becnel and Ms. Francine Delahoussaye.

Mr. Becnel lives under my roof, which in fact has sheltered generations of Becnels in comfort and in rather, if I say so, splendor. The Becnels are a fine old family, extremely sensitive and ever alert to the privileges of rank, in whatever form it might arrive. The Delahoussayes, I believe, are from somewhere in southwest Louisiana.

Leo has raised six children here, two from each of his wives. Georgina, the third wife, left after that scandal at the law school involving the sexual harassment complaints. A bit hasty, in my opinion. No one has known Leo longer than I have, and I am quite sure he never meant to break any rules. On the contrary, I should say that in all probability, it simply never occurred to him they were meant to apply to him. This is a family characteristic; and the family being what it is, they are nearly always able to squirm out of a scrape. That is what Leo did on that occasion (though it did cost him Georgina).

By profession, he is a professor of law, as you may have gathered. And despite the self-involvement characteristic of all the Becnels, he isn't that bad a sort in the long run. The things some of his forebears did to their slaves—especially the female ones—were infinitely worse than anything poor Leo would dream of.

He's a jolly sort, actually, and not bad looking. He's getting on towards fifty now, when I think of it, and his hair has turned a pleasing sandy gray. In the summer he wears seersucker suits, which look quite dapper with his moustache and bow ties. They have a forgiving way, as well, with his portly conformation. In fact, I would go so far as to say he cuts quite a figure, and certainly he never lacks for feminine companionship.

He likes a good joke and a good glass of wine and of course he adores the fine cuisine for which our town is famous. He also likes a lovely woman—for a time. And after that he likes another.

Nor is he incapable of true friendship, and it is through this vehicle that I have been vouchsafed access to the inner workings of his mind. But on to the story. It began prosaically enough with a phone call. Gordon was in the kitchen that day. Gordon is Leo's one true friend, an old army buddy, one evidently the worse for wear (much like me)—and he is my savior. Leo lets him live in the old slave quarters in return for which he "works on the house." Lovingly, he sands and paints and inspects; he cleans gutters and replaces shingles; he is ever on the alert for the scourge of my kind—the Formosan termite. If not for his eternal beer breath, I would worship the dear man.

On the afternoon of the call, Gordon was popping a brew, as he is wont to say, slouching about in ragged jeans, with Leo dapper in khaki shorts and white polo shirt, a roll of lovely, jiggling fat clearly visible. When Leo hung up the phone, he seemed a little dazed, as if he had stared too fixedly into the sun. This prompted Gordon to say, "What's up, bro'? You look like the cat that swallowed the canary."

"That was one of my former students," Leo answered. "She said she's never forgotten me. She's giving a talk here."

Gordon shrugged. "You musta' taught her good. Sounds like she got to be a lawyer, accordin' to the plan."

"A judge, Gordon, a judge. The judge. That was Francine Delahoussaye. Franny to her old pedagogue."

"Git outta' here!"

"But I remind you, Gordon—I can't. This is my house."

"Wow. Hangin' Franny. Toughest broad in the world."

From this exchange I gathered that Judge Delahoussaye had done something to elicit fame—if Leo said she was *the* judge, that was one thing. If Gordon had actually heard of her, that was proof positive. For let us face it, those outside the legal profession know nothing of those inside it, however distinguished they may be. Gordon seemed to admire her, which was interesting. You do not get to be a hundred and fifty years old without noticing that men do not usually admire women for their toughness. I suspected there was more.

Gordon took a swig of his beer. "Know who she used to hang with? Alec Banks. Swear to God. What a babe. You watch the Oscars? She was his date."

Leo seemed surprised. "Banks the actor? I wouldn't think she'd go in for that sort of thing."

"Hey, man—she's a star. Makes Oprah look like a piker."

Leo stroked the neat little beard that hid his double chin. "I suppose she is."

"So when's she coming over?" Gordon, normally a quite respectful person, executed what could only be called a leer.

Leo acquired once again his canary-feathers look. "In about two hours. I invited her for drinks."

"Damn! You're killin' me, man! You know I got a class." Gordon was studying something or other at night school, though I believe "adult education" is the preferred term today.

Leo said, "Gordon, please. The woman's only coming to pay respects to her old professor—it isn't an autograph session." And he went up to make his toilet.

When the doorbell rang, he was a study in splendor—white shirt, gray suit (though it was far too hot for such a caparison), silk tie, and strong cologne. (Yes, we can smell too. And given that, my only regret is that we cannot taste—ah, the aromas that come from kitchens!)

Judge Francine Delahoussaye entered the house as if she owned it and the rest of New Orleans as well. And well she might have! I have been host to hundreds of women over the years, but none more magnificent than this one. She moved as sinuously as the bayou itself, and in her face was reflected the dusky mystery of all Louisiana, and all France, and probably all Africa as well. She had the dark heavy hair and languid eyes for which Cajun women are justly renowned, and the sensuality of Ava Gardner (who once was a guest here). I knew instantly that if this woman's face was not her fortune—if she was indeed the "toughest broad in the world"—she must surely be as remarkable a combination of qualities as I had seen in a century and a half.

She did not disappoint me.

For the first ten minutes or so, Leo could barely stammer. Francine, as he chose to call her, lost no time in putting him adeptly at his ease.

She let him go on a bit about her television show (which I gather accounted for her fame), and then she said, "For heaven's sake, Leo, it's just me, Franny—the kid who flunked con law."

"But, Franny, I had to fail you. You never came to class."

"I did. Once. But I was busy that semester—working on a campaign, if I remember."

"Bigger fish to fry—I gather that's your m.o."

She shrugged. "Anyway, I made an A the next time I took it."

"That was a B, I believe."

"Just testing." She laughed, opening her lips wide and showing beautiful teeth, leaning towards him a bit. Flirting.

Leo noticed it too. Something happened to his body, something sharp and sudden, as if he'd received an electric shock, or possibly a revelation—a vision of possibilities he hadn't dared to dream of. He looked at his watch and stammered again. "Are you hungry at all? I mean, I was just wondering . . . if I called now we might be able to get into Arnaud's." (Where he was so well known he could probably walk in on a Saturday during a cardiologists' convention.)

"I'm ahead of you, professor. I made reservations at Emeril's."

"Oh, did you now? What made you think I'd be available?"

"I took a chance. Remember Katie, my roommate? She said it might be interesting to get to know you better."

"Oh, Katie—uh, yes." He was blushing and stammering both.

"Don't worry, she's fine now. You can barely see the scars on her wrists."

"Now, Franny, it was nothing like that and you know it. The merest dalliance—on both our sides."

She raised an eyebrow. Leo freshened the drinks and, after much reminiscing and merriment, they departed arm-in-arm and staggering a bit.

I was, of course, not privy to the occurrences of the next few hours, but I can report that the next morning Leo was fairly blanketed in canary feathers, and gloating to Gordon at the breakfast table. ". . . so I said, 'Can I see you again before you go?' And she said, 'Thought you'd never ask.' You believe that?"

"Gimme a break."

"So I said, 'Which night would be best for you?' and I swear to God she gave me The Look, Gordon. No, come on, I know it when I see it. She stared me straight in the eye and said 'Every night, darlin'.' "

"You're lyin'," Gordon protested. "You're makin' this stuff up."

But he was not, to that I can attest. At any rate, he did see her every night, and every night after that first, she spent under my roof. What the two of them did is something into which I would rather not go, but I can tell you that it was enthusiastic and varied. Indeed, for Leo, it seemed quite the rejuvenating experience. Of late, I have witnessed all too many a bedroom scene that seemed lacking in—how shall I phrase this?—the necessary manpower, shall we say.

I also began to notice a certain youthful glow, an unaccustomed spring in the step, an unconscious whistling of sprightly tunes. This I have seen many times, both with Leo (when he first met Georgina), and with so many others I can barely count them. If anyone in the world is qualified to judge when someone is falling in love, certainly I am. And most assuredly, Leo was.

And why not? The lovely Judge Delahoussaye was a temptress of world class ability. Not only was she able to rejuvenate Leo in the bedroom, she knew things that even I had not seen before. She was beautiful. She was famous—star of a television show, it developed, that featured actual court cases. She was also a woman of substantial means. And though Gordon did his best, I was starting to need shoring up in ways Leo really wasn't able to manage. What with his being on probation at the law school . . . well, things were very precarious indeed. Alec Gates had fallen, and he was a matinee idol (or whatever it's called these days). Why not Leo?

Franny, for her part, seemed no less enchanted. On their last day together, she burbled like a brook. "You know, darlin' we really haven't had enough time together. You must visit me in New York." She snapped her fingers. "Better yet, I have a place in the Florida keys. Let's go there next, shall we?"

Leo tried to sound casual. "Any old time."

"Next weekend?"

They kissed on it.

The next day before noon, two dozen white roses were delivered to Leo. Why not red, I thought? But the white did look lovely in the front parlor. Leo read Gordon the card: "Thanks again for a marvelous time—I'll call you soonest. Love, F."

"She'll call me!" Leo crowed. "I don't even have to pick up the phone—have you ever heard of a woman like this?"

But two days later, she hadn't called, and Leo had taken to smoking again. To pacing and biting his fingernails. I'd seen that one before too, though never in quite this form.

Finally, he called her, a most embarrassing procedure since, in the heat of passion (and complacency, I might add), he'd forgotten to get her home number. At last, someone at her office seemed to recognize his name. "Oh, Mr. Becnel, of course! The judge is taping right now, but she said to tell you she'll call you back tonight." (Or so he told Gordon.)

She didn't, however.

I don't know how he did it, but Leo actually managed to wait another full day to phone again, by now having lost five pounds, at least.

When he finally caved in, I heard only his side of the conversation, which went something like this: "It's Leo Becnel. Yes. Judge Delahoussaye invited me to her Florida house for the weekend and . . . well, yes, I know. I'm starting to wonder if she meant next weekend. But in case she didn't, think how embarrassing it would be . . . yes, of course." He waited awhile, and then perked up when someone came back on the line. "I see. Thanks so much for giving her the message."

Telling Gordon the tale, he said, "Yes, of course I'm sure she got the message. The flunky said, loud and clear, 'She's terribly sorry, but she's been swamped and she'll call me as soon as she gets out from under.' "

By now, of course, I had caught on, even if Leo and Gordon had not. I'd certainly seen it often enough. I knew as well as I knew my address that Leo was never going to hear from Francine Delahoussaye again.

Since then, the two men under my roof have spent endless nights drinking beer (Gordon) and gin (Leo) and trying to get to the bottom of what to them is one of the big mysteries of the universe. Gordon's solution, I believe (though he won't come out and say it), is that Leo is lying, or at least that he misread the situation—that Franny was never very interested in him in the first place, that she was merely being friendly to her old professor. The nights in bed, he seems to think, were emblems of her boundless gratitude for his tutelage and nurturing.

Leo, on the other hand, has turned to psychology. He thinks that Franny, finding herself falling in love—really truly in love—experiencing the genuine article perhaps for the first time in her fast-paced life, simply spooked.

Couldn't face up to the reality, couldn't handle the life changes such a realization would bring, couldn't commit, just got scared and backed off.

Ah, it is to laugh, it is to giggle! How delicious it is to listen to the two of them, especially, if I may say so, Leo.

How often have I listened to women having these conversations, coming to these conclusions? Dozens, perhaps hundreds if you count the little talks that take place at parties. And yet it does not occur to either of these paragons that Francine Delahoussaye deliberately set out to seduce and abandon Leo Becnel, just as millions of men have done with millions of women throughout the ages (or at least for the century and a half for which I can vouch).

But why? you may ask. Why would she do such a thing?

Perhaps it had something to do with the roommate, or perhaps she told herself it did. But I very much doubt it.

I believe this is a harbinger of changes more profound than those wrought first by the industrial revolution and then by the silicon chip. I believe feminism has at last come full circle. I believe this is something we will begin to see again and again, and, really, as an impartial observer, I cannot but smile.

I believe Franny's old pedagogue taught her more than he knew.

I think she did it just because she could.

And you know the part I like best? "I'll call you soonest." Really, I'd split my sides if I thought Gordon could fix them.

ANNIE

I AM OLD, SO OLD. RUST ON MY HANDS. I am so old that I have rust on my hands. Age spots, indeed. No, just rusting out, creaky boned, and clogged arteries.

Anyway, that is what shows.

Ah, I remember when I could devour half a Po' Boy in minutes; shrimp jumping out of it for their lives at the life eating chomp of my jaws and my shiny white teeth.

Now I put fixative on the rims of the false ones in the morning after their swim in the glass on the night table. A quarter of a Po' Boy is hard work getting down, hard but delightful. Shrimp and crawdads smile at me; no threat here anymore, holding no grudges—like me, just happy to be, at least, a while longer.

Ah, but who they see, who I see in the old tarnished mirror in my apartment down the street is not the *real* Annie.

Yes, I am old, weathered, much traveled, much mellowed, but inside, inside how Annie chews up shrimp and dances to the life, to the pulse of this place. Oh, I have been so many, so very many places.

But now, for a long time, I am this place and it is me and both of us have so many secrets; some to share, some to hold close for only those who really want to and are able to see. Funny thing about secrets, Mr. Duck Head Man, is that most of them are out in the open, right there in front of us and we just can't seem to grasp 'em.

Most people just call me Miz' Annie. I like that. At least they see part of me, of who Annie really is. They know that I know. It is just that they are not quite sure what I know, or what I am about. But, in some of their eyes, I have seen them come close to truly knowing, and that pleasures me.

Oooh, how I love secrets, and secrets there are aplenty here. All is not as it seems here. It is more, so much more, and so much of it is etched into these old bones that perhaps will one day be on display. Look, here, this tiny healed crack in the left femur is from the first Mardi Gras when lights went on again after the Big One. Slipped just a little, bumped it into the light stand; hurt, sure, but went on dancing.

Hat? How long have I had you, Hat?

You with your silly wilted and frayed flowers; you with your silly flocked duck head peaking out from behind them laying on the wide brim; tattered ribbons tied around my scrawny neck and dry, wrinkled throat.

I remember the day I found you, someone hawking summer hats on Jackson Square. Sun was real warm that day, but nobody cared 'cause they were there in Jackson Square, and where else would you want to be?

Didn't have you, my little duck friend, then. You came later. In fact, you came the day the Soviets blinked and I stopped imagining mushrooms topping the steeples of St. Louis.

Lord? How are we expected to keep up with it? Russians as Allies; then Soviets as Allies; then Evil Empire and enemies; now Russians again.

But where was I? I do ramble sometimes. Oh yes.

We would go on; we would keep squawking our delight in dancing in the streets. Then I saw you. There you were, peeking out at me from a shop window, part of some kid toy. And I knew, no matter how wrinkled, dry, creaky and bent over I might become, I would never let go of that kid in me. And you wouldn't either.

Have you looked at yourself, Mr. Duck Head Man? Have you looked at yourself lately and seen that your glorious sun-yellow flocking is all gone missing or dingy? Your dark eyes all faded to almost nothing?

Well, buddy, my hair is not dark, long and lustrous anymore; it doesn't cascade over my shoulders, falling on either side of a soft deep cleavage anymore either. It is grey now, not even silver, and the cleavage is all crinkly and the bosom all wrinkly.

Ah, but the eyes can still be twinkly.

Okay, so it's terrible rhyming. Who cares. It just shows that a lot of the synapses are still snapping.

Did you notice, Mr. Duck Head Man, that everybody has been looking pretty glum? Well, they have reason to be. Nasty piece of work up New York City way. Buildings crumbling, people dying, terrible, terrible, inexcusable thing it is.

Lived through a lot of inexcusable things, I have. You too. Gonna make it through this one too. Did you notice the people filing into the Cathedral? Did you see all the flags about; the red, white and blue ribbons?

No, no thank you, John. No more coffee. Yes, box it up as usual, I'll eat it later. Or tomorrow. Don't get hungry much for food anymore, you know? Hungry instead for each next breath. Keep the change. Thanks.

A little boost onto the old legs always helps. No, I'll be fine. The Duck Head Man and I have to go out and be about; thinking the city people need to see things endure despite all the troubles of the world, and we sure are things of endurance, he and I.

Steamy today.

Which way do you want to go? Tired are you? Well, I'll lean on this cane for both of us. But we are going out and about, so make a decision. Which way do you want to go?

What do you mean, where are we? You know exactly where we are. Orleans and Royal.

Okay, since you are not all there today, I shall make the decision. Seems a good day to walk down St. Ann. It is a good day to be near a patron saint. Maybe St. Anthony too, for something great has been lost, again.

Peace, you foolish duck. We have been violated. No, *not* Pearl Harbor. Oh, you *are* getting senile. Well, of course I remember all the soldiers here then, all ready to go fight; all seeking a few last minutes pleasure and life here on these streets.

Different music then pouring out of the buildings: jazz, swing.

We looked different then. Well, no you weren't born then, but my pretty hair was all done up in a pompadour and when my feet walked the Quarter through those years they were in little white anklets and sturdy tie shoes.

And there were no lights at night. Everything blacked out. But there will be lights on tonight, despite those terrible tumbling towers. We are not quitters; we are a peaceful people, but you can't be backing us up against a wall without our standing up.

Look up there, your faded eyes still good enough to see the rampart? See us holding back the very water that wants this city?

Wasn't any real Quarter that first year when it flooded back in '19. No, not 1919, *1719*. What *was* there then, three houses and another building? *What* was it? Ah, the Mississippi Company Store. See, I still have some memory facilities.

Afternoon, Jake. I know it is a terrible thing. But you are the lawyer man, not me. How do we get, how do we deliver, Justice without delivering more terrible things? Ever wonder about that lady who is supposed to be Justice? Is reality so bad she has to be blindfolded; or is that her way of saying let my ears hear and judge what my eyes cannot bear to see?

Jake, before you go back to work, do you think you could be opening a door and settling us into a pew at St. Louis? I need a rest, need some quiet time. At my age things all start tumbling around and I get kind of confused.

Thanks.

Sure, go on. We will be fine now, and the Lord will be sending someone to get me out of this pew when the time comes.

Now listen good, Mr. Duck Head Man, 'cause I have to whisper in here. You see that up there? They call it the Passion. A passion is a thing that is so important to you, so throbbing with life and meaning and purpose that you are willing to die for it.

He did.

He had, and has, both that kind of Passion for us, and compassion too. Now there is something we so often deny ourselves, giving it to others, keeping it from ourselves. Thinking today is a day to be learning about compassion too. How do we know if we have compassion? We feel it; we feel it in our middles. Lots and lots of middles hurting worldwide today. How do we know if we have passion? You feel it, goose. You feel it in every single thread of you. They have fancy words for it now; seem to like chemical words for it now. They talk about endorphin things flowing about your body, sparking your writing, your painting, your singing, your lovemaking.

That is what this whole city is about you know: a great, great, great passion for life building itself right in the midst of the amniotic womb of the great river. Well, of course, it is called Old *Man* River; but did you ever know a male without female balance of one sort or another? I like to think of the river's flowing as the *he* part, of what it is flowing over as the *her* part.

And we pushed the river back and we built on her womb. No, I don't care who likes or dislikes my interpretation of things. It is my interpretation and that is what this city is about. Think about it, Mr. Duck Head Man, you goose. That too is what the Quarter is about. Having, and saying, and yes, even *showing our own feelings* about things.

Is all of our history real? Well, *yes* and *no*. Memory, time, disintegrating brain cells, molding, distorts all those things. But maybe the *real* is in the *essence* of what happened; the feel of what happened that leaves a special legacy in its wake.

You know Mr. Duck Head Man, you aren't *really* real, but I have made you that way. Most of the people who live here know you, through me. *Hee, hee,* guess that means I sort of made myself a twin, or alter ego, or something.

What is real? Lafitte was real and very attractive to the ladies. Well, yes, we do have a real sense of the bawdy, of the sensual. Part of us too often denied, but also part of us to be lived with that great passion.

But did the Lafittes, Jean, or his brother, Pierre, ever own what is supposed to be their blacksmith shop? Probably not. Old, old building it is; earliest record of ownership I've heard of is 1772. No Lafitte names showing up anything connected with it. So, no, they probably did not do any smithing there, but it doesn't matter because the Lafittes did help forge this city, and this *Vieux Carré*, into what it is.

They lived with passion and they fought next to Andy Jackson with passion in a rag tag army of pirates, Free Men of Color, Native Americans, Irish, Germans, Italians, Spaniards, you name them. And it doesn't make a tinker's damn worth of anything if they fought that Battle for New Orleans and the control of this river after the war was over. They didn't know that; they fought as men protecting a way of life.

So yes, Mr. Duck Head Man, *laissez les bon temps rouler,* because every time we have needed we have fought for the right to. Doesn't mean we were always right, always perfect, or always compassionate. But we fought for our passion for freedom.

On the corner of Bourbon and Conti, in the Old Absinthe Bar, you can tack your business card up on the wall and sit down at the bar. That bar top went traveling during the years when drink was forbidden. Ended up there a block or so from its original home.

And you can say, "Well, the card I put up there says what I do to put bread and butter on a table with a roof over it; but it doesn't say who I am. So . . . so if you want to know *who* I am, sit down with me here at this water-pocked bar top and I'll buy you a drink. I'll tell you about the smell and flow of the river running through me . . . and why I think all of this Creation came about. Do we have time? *Of course we do*; this is *Nouvelle Orléans* and here we have life enough and time to know ourselves."

And think too about all those lovely open louvered shutters letting in the air, gift of the Spanish occupation. Everyone who comes here gives us something; and oh, yes, we give them something special too.

So *who* is the Quarter? *What* is the Quarter?

It is all of us.

What, you are thirsty from all this mindwalking? Me too. Let's see, who is about to help us up out of this pew? *Be patient.*

See, I *knew* there would be someone to help us.

The woman with the dark hair, over there lighting a candle. Probably for those who went on today so unsuspectingly. God help them home. Is she a Cajun woman? No, an import from up north. Came here with a special fella, fell in love with the city. Now, after a long time, makes it and him, her home. Name is Dr. Melanie Gratton-Irons.

No, not a medical doctor; a Doctor of Archaeology. She restores things, she does, and that special fella who she married, well, he is a journalist who records all her work for the rest of us to know about. Seems to work for them and certainly works for me.

Long time for their coming together, but *that* is a story for another time. Oh yes, I am just filled with stories. Not much went on, or goes on, that I don't know something about.

Hey, they think I am just a silly old goose, but I know lots and lots of secrets. Watch over those secrets I do, and them too.

I hear we have something in common, Miz' Melanie and me, and that is a sweet tooth; hers for éclairs, and mine for beignet. Now *there* is an idea.

Sit up now, she is coming this way.

Afternoon, Miz' Melanie.

Well, thank you for asking. As a matter of fact we do need some help. Do you have time to get us up out of here and settled in the Café Du Monde? We are getting kind of thirsty and there is always room for some hot sugared donuts.

Oh, you *are* a dear. Sit just a moment with a cup of café au lait, indulge in a beignet or two? Wonderful. Tell me, how is Jesse taking this terrible thing?

Oh, as I expected. Once they have been to war, once they have seen the elephant, it all must just come flooding back. But he is strong, honey, you know that. Just be holding him and letting him hold you. This is too awful, too unclear for us to be doing anything too rash right now. What we *need* is praying, lots of praying from all over. I think it is to be coming soon. It is in the air.

But what is my point? Oh, yes, all of us are, or were, all women of men who knew war—husbands, fathers, lovers, brothers, and sons too, my dear, sons too. These streets have known war, Melanie, but you know that. Many of the men who walk them have known some war or other, just like your Jesse.

You look surprised. Not much Annie doesn't know about, my dear, not much. But he was worth waiting for, isn't he? Of course, he is. Lot of years he went about looking for himself through all that traumatic stress. But he found him, and he found you, eh? Gonna be lots of stress around from this. We are all in shock now. Maybe that is why this old mouth is running so today. We can bottle it up, we can try to let it out. But do we dare put into words all the emotions that are tumbling about in us? Do we want to acknowledge the parts of us that want revenge? Can we control them, push them down through reason into compassion and right judgments?

That perhaps is the difference between those who have been to war and those who haven't. They didn't have time to reason, only to try to stay alive, and some of the parts of them they had to bring up to stay alive, well, let's say they didn't make the good times or the good feelings roll. And they were buried so deep, so very deep. This today will bring some of them up and out. It all takes time.

But Melanie, what is time? Look at me. I am old, rusty, creaky and old and yet yesterday is as clear to me, often more clear, than the real yesterday of twenty-four hours ago.

Want to know when I first came here, or what I wore, and I can tell you. What I ate yesterday? Well, not so sure. So what *is* time? I suppose it is how we relate to it. And how we relate to it, well, I suppose that is in the intensity of the emotions at a particular time and how deeply they are stamped into our psyches. So Pearl Harbor was yesterday to me, just as Cu Chi is yesterday to Jesse.

What do we do with that knowledge? Ah, that remains to be seen today and tomorrow, but how soon, how soon tomorrow will be today, and today will be yesterday. And we look back with, with what—emotions at how we handled ourselves?

Oh, Melanie, you are so patient with an old rusty woman. Here, please finish this last beignet for me. My capacity is not what it was yesterday, though my heart is bigger than ever. And maybe, maybe, Melanie, that is what they mean by growing old gracefully. Your heart gets bigger, just like the heart of this city, the heart of the Quarter, always making room for people from a new place, permanent stayers or visitors. Yes, maybe that is this. We may have peeling paint on the buildings, rusty age spots on our hands and on our twisted iron, but look past the exteriors and there are luscious, green, growing and expanding gardens and hearts thriving. Someone plants a hibiscus; someone cultivates a trailing Mandeville and helps expand the Quarter's heart.

That is our Quarter, Melanie, and I think it is what you fell in love with. The old always expanding its heart to take in the new and growing with it into something that speaks to those of all time. That is the pulse of the Quarter, flow as great as the river's. The Quarter is each of us spreading our roots into the womb of the below sea level Crescent City.

Here, give me your hand. Let me feel your pulse beat through it, and I will take you time traveling.

Relax, dear. Close your eyes.

Can you *feel* the intense clinging heat? Heat that is continual with no lessening by air-conditioned buildings, or cold drinks? Heat that is wet and hot and feels like a second skin?

Can you *feel* that skin under constant attack by thirsty, sharp-toothed mosquitoes?

Can you *feel* the heat as you lift a shovel? Can you feel yourself inside a man's sweating, heaving body building the first of the levees only by the power of your own arms and back?

Can you *feel* the determination to make a place of this place? A place where river trade could flourish, where your fortune might be made if you could make this place a place out of the river's hold?

Can you *smell* the smell of fires burning down what you have built up?

Can you *hear* tongues of fire eating noisily and hungrily the few places of comfort you have raised?

Can you *smell* the smell of death from plague? Licking the tongue of its hungry maw through doorways and windows, eating flesh and devouring dreams?

Can you *feel* the intensity of the *passion* to go on with the building of this place *no matter what*?

If you can *feel*, *smell*, and truly *know* these things, then you can begin to know the French Quarter. If you can *feel* the determination to go on when the dreams of gold and pearls are gone, when the air is laden with the scent of alligators, and the snakes slither wherever they will, then you can *know* the real history of the Quarter.

Can you get yourself to a place where you can taste the salt of tears and your own sweat droplets as they drip down your face and tumble off your body?

Can you *feel* the burn of the salt-sweat in your eyes?

Then you can truly *feel* the Quarter.

Can you read, plan, dream, and build a city where the heat sucks your brain almost right out of your head?

Then you can live in the Quarter.

But you knew that, didn't you, Melanie? You felt that when you first came here. You knew its water, hope, pain, its sensuality and joy. And you knew, too, that you *belong* here. Um, be . . . long . . . yes . . . long to be here. Must be here.

One day someone comes here, expecting to have a good time. *Ah*, but he or she finds that life has changed, sweetened in some indiscernible way. The Vieux Carré has touched something in them.

They come from all over. They come with bits of hayseed in their hair, with the scent of the northern Atlantic about them. They come with fancy suits and silk ties that are soon shed. They come with sand in their shoes from our own deserts and they come speaking many different tongues.

But they come and they will continue coming. To let down their hair and open their hearts and souls, even if just a tiny bit. Some are meant only to visit, to briefly touch and just begin to know our music, our pulse, then take it back home with them. They go back, but home will never be quite the same again, nor will they. Their life music plays to just a slightly different tune from then on. Some, like you, are meant to come and stay, becoming part of the music, adding to the pulse of the city. Those who stay drink something in with those hurricanes, and they can't go home again, because now home is here. And they find that New Orleans, notice the feminine, *Nouvelle Orléans*, has become a sort of midwife to a new birthing of their soul, with music, sunlight, heat, flowers, the river. Whatever it is that speaks to them says something that wasn't living for true in them, wherever they came from, and can live for true here.

Each of you who come, well, you add something new to us—a new dish, a new thought, a new word. You become one of us. Hey, maybe there was something in Jesse that knew of all the girls up north, that you were the one to bring south. Perhaps he sensed that your soul would fly open to our music, our heat, humidity, and yes, oh, yes, my dear, our *passion*.

You know that your heart has been captured, that you will always lie in the arms of the Live Oaks and delight in the rains tumbling down over you, soaking you through and dancing with delight on the banquettes. Our skies have become your skies—pearled, pinked, blued, grayed, sweetened frothy, or crashing stormy. And then you can lift another hurricane in a glass and drink it down with a toast: Here's to living with *passion*.

Oh, my goodness! You wouldn't think after all these years a crash of thunder would startle me! You have been so indulgent, Melanie. Letting me go on and on. Ah, how sweet, dear. I love you too. I am a little weary. Do you think, could I impose just a bit longer? Can you help me the few blocks to my apartment? I will move, of course, Mr. Duck Head Man, *we* will move as quickly as we can so you don't get drenched.

Thank you, dear. Would you like a cup of . . . ? Oh, yes, of course, you did mention you had a class late this afternoon. Well, run along, dear. And thank you, Melanie, just for being Melanie.

Ah . . . I do so love hugs. Later, I'll talk with you later.

Well, Mr. Duck Head Man, ready for kicking off these shoes a bit? What shall we do for a couple hours to rest? But you *already* know everything about everything in this room. Why would you want to hear the story again? And besides, the whole story is just too long!

Okay, okay. I'll tell you what. You pick any two things from this room and I will tell you how they came to be here. And then when the storm lets up, and the shiny, wet sunlight slips in the late afternoon window we will watch it dance on the red walls until it lulls us to a little nap.

Now, which two pieces is it to be?

Ah, the knitting needles that my hands can't hold anymore. Yes, they do look pretty sitting there. Sometimes I wonder if they know how many hands and feet were warmed because of them coming to life in my fingers.

Coming to life, now there is a phrase that has often intrigued me. *When did the Quarter come to life?* When the first building was built? When the first baby was born here? When the curve in the river was first seen as a good place to put it? Did you ever wonder, Mr. Duck Head Man, why so many live, and never *come to life?*

But coming to life comes from a deliberate motion. The kids put a hat on the Frosty fellow and he came to life. I picked up those knitting needles because the Sisters taught us, and visiting women from Britain taught us, how to knit.

Before Pearl Harbor became an Infamy day, we were "knittin' for Britain." So with the yarn, with those very needles sitting over there, still so many years now, with my once very agile—and I might add long and pretty—fingers, socks and gloves came to life and went to battlefields of cold death to keep still live soldiers warm.

Come to life they did for our men who sailed the seas once more for Britain and France, all the others, and for ourselves too. Those needles came to life again for our men in Korean snows. They weren't needed by Joe and his buddies in that Vietnam place. Too hot it was.

You *know* who Joe is. We see him every Tuesday night. He is there every Tuesday night, even if it is raining, blowing his horn, looking for one of his buddies who is still trying to come home. Why is he there? Ah, because one night someone else was there to help him come home.

And so he makes his horn come to life with the life of the Vieux Carré all around him making it hard for anybody, no matter how big the hurt they are carrying, to not feel the pulse and joy of life.

Maybe, maybe they are not ready to let it all in. But it does make cracks in shells, and that is the beginning of healing of whatever kind is needed. That is why on that awful Tuesday night, knowing that music is the song of the heart and soul, Joe played *Manhattan Serenade*. Somehow he knew the folks up in New York would hear and feel his healing music.

The Quarter is a good place for healing.

Now, what is the second thing you want to know about?

shot of bourbon*

straight

Early Times if you got it

CHRISTINE P. HORN

BURGUNDY

In some old charters they were called the "seigniors della Catene," in others "Herren von Ketten," both of which mean, "of the chains." They had come down from the North, stopping at the very threshold of the South. They proclaimed their loyalty now to the Guelph, now to the Ghibelline cause as it suited them, and at bottom regarding themselves as owing no allegiance to anything or anyone but themselves.
—Robert Musil, from "The Lady of Portugal"

THIS IS NOT FOR THEE, ye curious travelers and wonder-weary readers, but for the brave meandering all-timers abound the empty slabbed and hot cracked streets of the New Orleans summertime and to each and every puddle in the French Quarter, or, where you got your shoes.

To the poorly dressed impresarios of 19th century plantation dreams hawking shrimp, crawfish and bottomless girls. To the littlemen from Iberville, not Storyville, the bottlecap sneaker stompers, shirtless and wry. To the lonesome lover on the barstool and the would-be-loved in the toilets shooting coke. To elephant-eared, faulty-fountained garden cafés and two-for-a-dollar-ten-cent-au-laits. To the donkey-cart drivers and Luckydog teamsters, to the shopkeepers, knifesharp'ners, shisters and rats, and to the endless chronology of handsome delivery boys, twenty-four hours a day.

Up Chartres, down Toulouse, the proliferation of balconies is attributed to architectural ancestry, but those banquette topcovers serve all the souls who have no umbrellas, and the rains fall every day. With it the cloak of newness and order, the ritualized hosing down by both city and heavens to clear the way for another day's fresh revile, as each morning's awakening forgets the hope that was, and tonight will be, further obscured.

There where goes the Calliope sound, halls wet dripped and moaning damp down, sad corner smiles and churchbell hollers late in Jackson Square, where Pontalba ladies never tip their hats, yet tight beyond grasp of iron romeo-holds, follow oil-slick rainbows to croissants of gold (and shimmy the sliver-spiked balcony poles).

Or Burgundy, Burgundy, gaped lit Burgundy!
From the Black & Gold over monkeywalls
when Sicilian spaghetti and poker halls
saw red lights flash and heard siren calls
Oh the end of desire's the levee wall . . .

And tomorrow your ship will come in.

So we sit on the wharf and peek between the fog, hoping to glimpse a little red steamboat that can't take the river rocking. Rocking as the trawlers, the tankers, give sensations of movement. Tied to the dock, we toss to and throe, convinced we are not chained on the Mississippi.

Drowned for the sake of feeling anything at all.

S. I. N. NERS

RATS ARE A FACT OF REALITY AT THE CAJUN COOKHOUSE, rats and Bonnie, the bitch-dyke general manager who sucks the limp-ass dick of Boss Man the alcoholic owner. Every gin-soaked proclamation he makes gets woven into the Gospel According To Bonnie. Nothing is irrational to her if it's contained in his drool. Her favorite line is "He says it, you do it." Once he came crashing back to the dishwashing station to present Ivory with a dirty butter knife that a customer sent back. "Get this clean or stick it up your ass!" Saliva and Beefeater spewed on Ivory's workshirt. When Boss Man walked off, Ivory followed both orders. He wiped away the incriminating evidence, but that was a seriously stinking knife he tossed into the silverware tray.

But compared to the rock smokers he works with, Ivory's got himself a live and let live thing going on with Bonnie ever since he spotted her getting a pussy fix at the Rubyfruit Jungle. It was in no one's best interest to trade stories of why each of them was there, so Ivory gave the coolest of "whassup" nods and let her business resume unregulated. Ever since that night Ivory's assumed as much privilege as he feels is appropriate: selling rocks out the side door in Rat Alley; taking righteous helpings of Jambalaya (rule #43 of the Cookhouse's 86 Rules: no eating); negotiating a mutual hook-up with the bartenders (rule #42: no drinking); and generally making his work environment as comfortable as possible given the poor hand he's been dealt as a child of the Iberville Projects, thank you.

The rats are another matter. Pied Piper these motherfuckers and you can rule the world. They hold the deed on this restaurant. Waiters working the courtyard have to play like they're part of the decor, give them pet names like Mickey (those honeymooning fools wished they were at Disney!).

Every couple weeks, Boss Man's redneck nephew takes a pistol out after closing and shoots up the courtyard. (Is it even required to alphabetize the Boss Man's greasy relations with the Board of Health?) Nephew's got a pretty good eye when he leaves alone the Crown Royal. Gets four or five on a good night. ("Ivory, scrape 'em up and sell 'em to Prudhomme," he'll say. Ivory can fake laugh all he wants but he still does the scraping.) Fuck tonight's millennium action, bullets in the sky. There's frequent New Year's Eve gunfests at the Cookhouse.

But Redneck Nephew can click on those rodents all he wants. They keep coming. True soldiers.

No rat shooting tonight, though, at least as far as Ivory's business is concerned. Bonnie's in the house, conducting inventory the way Nino Brown surveys his freebasing factory. So her and Redneck Nephew send him home at quarter to the millennium. They act like it's a favor. Sure, I'll make the Iberville scene just as they're blasting out the security lights with semi-automatics. Blackout like my ass locked in a closet. No thank you. Ivory will hang with reliable electricity until the sun comes up, sip a few cocktails and kiss on some dykes maybe.

He turns up toward Bourbon Street and ducks into Kiwi Cruz Daiquiris. Ivory's been working next door since this slush house dropped two years ago. He's graciously sampled every mix of frozen, weak-ass poison they push, but the frozen shit gives him headaches. Most nights after punching out Ivory gets himself a Hennessey-and-Pineapple on the rocks. And after all this time, not once has any motherfucker hooked him up. Fact of the matter, they still measure his Hennessy shot, and if he's had a night of particular stress and needs an extra shot, they double the price. And measure it again. When the Arab owner is around, all Ivory gets in the range of recognition is "When is that motherfucker going to call an exterminator? They're getting on my roof."

That's cool. Ivory understands how respect is gotten and not gotten. He's got a keen awareness of the time. And it's no Klan secret that your average Bourbon merchant—Arab, Redneck, Viet—is in the business of keeping the Brotherhood Ratio to a minimum. We've developed a reputation. Hell, Ivory's abandoned the black trade himself, having discovered what the white man will shell for convenience. He can take an afternoon cruising Calliope, Desire, O.C. Haley, MLK, (he stays clean in his own backyard—you don't shit where you barbecue) and compile an impressive bag of rocks that he can sell in the Quarter to all manner of white humanity. Fag waiters, Eminem-looking whiteboys, wild-ass truckers.

S.I.N. night at the House of Blues is particular big business. It's not in Ivory's nature to laugh too hard at white people, but the existence of a Service Industry Night is just too much foolery, like you need an ordained occasion to get fucked up because you hate your bitch-ass job, call it "S.I.N." like it's real bad behavior. They ought to call it Bitch Worker's Night. Fuck it, whatever they want to call themselves is cool with Ivory. Fools fall for the bit that a rock dissolved in gin and juice is like ten Ruphies. Whiteboys love their women in a coma, sing songs about it even. Ivory triples his money every night out. Better than Microsoft.

Business is business, but every time Ivory orders his Hennessy-and-Pineapple, they want to make him feel like some farm nigger from Schriever living high off his Pick 3 winnings. Ivory is well aware that cognac is a sipping drink, but just because you want to do me for $8 a shot don't make Hennessy a cognac worth sipping on. Don't play like it don't need a little sweetener. And who the fuck are you to comment on my mixing habits? I didn't mix the blues with Elvis, or hip-hop with heavy metal. And who fucked up whose bloodlines? Who mixed Tang into our premium dark rum, called it Creole?

What are brothers doing running around with a name like Ivory? It's the question he's waiting to hear, that he'd rather not hear, the one that makes him the silent type, one who keeps his flow to a minimum, the question that he knows might make him click on a motherfucker. But he still wonders who put the notion in his momma's head. Yeah, it's supposed to give props to the motherland, but why get named after a color? Was it her ambition that he whiten up, give him a name to live up to, the way some mommas name their boys Lawyer?

Fact of the matter, Ivory doesn't all that much care for straight cognac.

It's not as if Ivory catches any serious beef, not from the Kiwi Cruz people or anyone. Like right now, with the crowd bouncing to some Middle East Arab techno shit, he's still given a smooth path to the bar. And when they take his order, their disapproval never comes out verbally. Ivory's been God-on-my-side lucky when it comes to staying far and wide from Central Lockup, but he knows how dangerous looking he is. No one gives him a chance to commit a hard crime. They're too busy making his personal space ample. Even when he's out in player mode, mostly in and around the Rubyfruit Jungle, with dykes who mistake him for one of their own, for a Queen Latifah gone hardcore instead of R&B, he gets it done mostly with body language.

If you were any kind of a television freak, you might notice that Ivory's got a kind of Shirley Hemphill thing going on, and if you were the first person to speak to him in the range of this fact you might also get clicked on.

The bar is full of fools, but Ivory decides to wait out midnight right where he is. Guns ought to be firing any minute, and he likes his chances surrounded by bricks and neon, with the rats scurrying over his head.

Matt promised himself years ago, when the subject first came up, that when the new millennium struck he'd be shooting off into something. He never would have figured on turning the world's odometer alone on the roof of Kiwi Cruz Daiquiris on Bourbon Street, mixing drinks by the gallon load. He'd complain if there was someone to complain to, but only for the pleasure of complaining, for the invocation of blue-collar privilege. In Matt's heart he knows this is the way to live, to always be somewhere you never planned to be.

Another way to live is to keep your own promises, and Matt distinctly remembers saying "something" and not "someone." And up here on the roof, the erections come easy. The conditions are always ripe. Matt shuttles between the walk-in cooler and the sticky-hot mixing room. The moisture level in his boxers bobs and dips like NASDAQ on a Monday morning, not to mention he's leaning dick level against the sink, mixing powder and water with a two foot wisk, a steady whirlpool rhythm.

I'll fuck anything, was his freshman year mantra, chanted nightly as he walked from his Tulane dorm to The Boot or Waldo's. This was when the subject of the millennium was first discussed, and among his friends a plan emerged that, when the time came, they would be doing exactly what they were doing now, only more of it, the adrenalized belief that the future will give you what you want.

And there are plenty of women on Bourbon. He sees them milling the street from up above, through a window with half the glass punched out. Southern divorcées, jailbait, bitches in their prime. Sultry redheads, bangin' black chicks, Tulane debs, trailer trash, trophy wives. Asian hip-hop whores. Matt seduces and fucks every one of them ten times a night in his head, wins them over with bold, articulate declarations of what they desire.

Objectifying gave Matt an edge, a necessary confidence. I'd fuck that. Would you fuck that? I can't believe he's fucking that. His older brother Ron, a junior at the time, gave him the sage wisdom when Matt first got to

New Orleans. Any given night, ask fifty women straight up to go home with you, and you'll never have to jack off again.

But unlike his brother, who moved to Brooklyn, freelances for Computer Associates and makes side bank through online trading, Matt fails more than he succeeds, so never jacking off again is just another investment scheme only his brother can seem to make work.

Matt's masturbation fantasies run like PG-13 movies, improbable flirtatious dialogue followed by a straight cut to the bedroom, strategically placed sheets, the soul baring and plot exposition. Stirring with one hand a five-gallon bucket of Piña Colada, Matt thinks about the Goth nympho at Molly's last night who rubbed glitter on his forehead as he polished off pints of Harp.

"You're Catholic," she said.

"Do I look Catholic?"

"It's more than that. It fills the air around you."

"Are you in a cult? Are you going to follow me home and brainwash me?"

"No."

"It's okay if you do. I've fucked stranger girls than you."

It was a high-risk line, but Matt was running out of money and was going home with or without her. She didn't say anything back, just twisted the cap back on her glitter and moved on to someone else.

On the roof, Matt plays it out a different way.

It's okay if you do. I've fucked stranger girls than you.

No. No, you haven't. You have not fucked stranger girls than me.

Then her loose black clothes strewn around his one-room above Chris Owens' Club, fucking her while house music shakes the building, every bass thump a new surprise for her, funky, a life-affirming fuck, a fuck that makes the mopey skinny pale industrial Anne Rice vampire death fucks that run her life look stupid, a fuck that brings her back to her senses, to the little girl she tried to make disappear, the little girl with her glitter.

He wasn't really aiming, but Matt scores a direct hit into the bucket of Piña Colada, similar in color and consistency. A few turns of the wisk and it's nothing more than an extra shot of love.

Fireworks pop over the Mississippi River. Maybe a gunshot. The air compressor kicks on.

Matt wipes up, washes his hands, checks the clock (12:01), and looks down on Bourbon Street. No mass acknowledgement or celebration, the fireworks unnoticed. He's been part of the crowd other years and knows they're not very good at synchronizing, no ball to stare at. It's the charm of the city, really, the indifference to time, the joyful decay. Still, you'd think on this occasion they'd make a concerted effort to promote group euphoria, a where-were-you-then-we-were-there-too camaraderie. But no, it all looks and feels the same, the business of a busy night: titty bar barkers pull guys in by the arm, beggars missing limbs shake their cups, Texans whoop, couples fight, black dudes put everyone on edge, and Matt knows he can't be disappointed. Yet another charm of the city. Everybody is on their own.

If he were watching it on a Webcam, he'd wish he were there. His women have receded into the crowd, anonymous.

He carries the bucket of Piña Colada into the walk-in cooler, where he dumps the liquid into the twenty-gallon reserve tank, careful not to spill any because it's a bitch to mop up.

Garnet knew the millennium would be a fizzle when she watched the earlier time zones on CNN. No glitches, no terrorism, no anarchy. Just fireworks and warmth. Bored, serving tray crossed over her chest, she saw an interview with a German pilot named Klaus who was going to be in the air over Africa when the aircraft controls rolled over. She only had closed-captioning to go on, "Livin' La Vida Loca" blared Surroundsound over the empty dance floor, but Garnet could hear Klaus' accent in her mind's ear. He reminded her of Torsten, her first gymnastics coach, all dumb and earnest confidence, a concentration camp guard cheerfully putting in his hours, and Garnet found herself wishing for the plane to go down.

No such luck. It was a smooth flight all the way, all part of the evening's predictable flow.

The only people who spill into Waikiki East are the ones desperate for a bathroom; they come in, get stuck for a $4.50 Budweiser, bitch, piss, dump their beer into a plastic cup, and leave.

Garnet jumps at the chance to cut out early. She's pulled fifteen hours and has to be back by ten a.m. to do it again. Hussein, her boss, gives her a complimentary glass of Korbel for the road, which she uses to wash down a pair of Darvocets she stashed in her apron. She's proud of her discipline, waiting for her shift to end. They take a half-hour to kick in, but the psychological effect is immediate. Yes, indeed, she thinks, in the manner of Kermit Ruffins, jazz trumpeter and Garnet's favorite black man in the world. Ye-es inde-ed.

Happy embryonic fluid. The millennium can go on without me.

Bourbon Street is more packed than Garnet imagined from the inside looking out, and she has to zig and zag to keep moving forward. Sugar Bowl crowd mostly, Virginia Tech hicks, Florida Gator rednecks, and their wives who have too much enthusiasm for college football. Garnet spent most of her life in Houston, to the extent that you could call it a life, and never could figure out how these women could be brainwashed into becoming football boosters. Her early years in New England must be all that gives her any perspective, though she's sure that women up north acquiesce in other ways, just with a touch more flair and dignity. Kitty Dukakis shotgunning perfume while her husband runs for President.

Bad tips and a grab-and-go crowd have conspired to leave Garnet with nothing but survival income. Hussein has a special talent for keeping the crowds away. He'd as soon sell ten people nine dollar drinks than bring twenty in with reasonable prices and basic human decency. Garnet will have to lend her ear to a sad, lonely man to get her evening nightcaps.

Like most of the Turkish owners Garnet has worked for and gotten drunk with, Hussein is a people person only where dollars and his dick are concerned. On the night when he took his shot at Garnet, feeding her Cosmopolitans and chunky lines of coke at The Whiskey Bar, all he got out of her was her life story, the highlights of which run this way: a foliage-filled childhood in Holly, Massachusetts, skillful cartwheels through fallen leaves; a father who slips in the tub when Garnet is eight, in that perfect way that kills you, a loophole in the adage that God looks after drunks; an impressive life insurance policy which her mother, who has no real hobbies, uses to finance Garnet's dreams of Olympic gymnastics glory, dreams which were expressed when Garnet was five, watching Mary Lou Retton on TV, dreams more or less forgotten about by Garnet but held in a death grip by her mother, who was willing to sacrifice . . . well, there wasn't much to sacrifice by leaving Holly and setting up in Houston, where Garnet spent twelve hours a day in several gymnastics concentration camps, before finally getting called into Bela Karolyi's Auschwitz (this is pretty much the way it went from Garnet's mouth to Hussein's ear, that night in The Whiskey Bar: impersonal, emphasizing the typical), training like Rocky, throwing up, and eating laxatives for dinner until finally, in 1995, at age sixteen, the sum total of the sacrifices of her mother and the hard work of Garnet culminate in an awkward vault landing, awkward in that perfect way that sends your calcium-starved shin bone through your skin and out into the world like an unwanted child. The pain was tremendous, and her early flirtation with painkillers has since blossomed into true love.

Not that Garnet makes it easy on anyone, but a small, vital part of her craves a little sympathy whenever she trots out the story of her life, even if the concern is fake, even if they just want to fuck. All Hussein offered, predictably, was, "You could have made millions selling cereal," an attitude which, oddly, makes Hussein an easy man to work for.

Garnet peeks in Pizzazz, always booming, millennium, Sugar Bowl, or average Wednesday. She doesn't expect to be able to see Sal behind the bar through the mob—rednecks, ravers, girls with fake ID's and low self-esteem—but the density of the people lets her know how many precious hours she'll be able to sleep alone, if she so desired.

She moved in with Sal out of convenience: he was the guy she met the night she spotted a rat in her $400-a-month studio apartment in the Lower Garden District. Since Garnet moved to New Orleans to go to and quickly drop out of Loyola, her apartments have marked a steady slide down the neighborhoods along the Mississippi River, and now she finds herself in an antiseptic one-bedroom job in the French Quarter. When Garnet gave Sal the life story routine, he laughed, savoring every tragedy. In the moment, it struck Garnet as the proper response.

Once, on a night she can no longer locate along the time line of her life, Garnet smoked a joint she later found out was laced with heroin. She sat in her bedroom, paralyzed, alone, for god knew how long. All that got in the way of her desire for more was the digital clock in the corner, telling her she had to be at work in two hours. The day she waits for and the day she's afraid of is the day she doesn't have to work anymore. But for now, she takes pills.

Ivory's seen enough convention fools slipping drag queens into their hotel rooms to know that plenty of the dykes he kisses on know what time it is. It ain't like all those white dudes don't know. When the wife is a thousand miles away, you can work around the dick. Drink beer and Everclear, you can ignore the dick. Ivory figures that ladies must sport the same sort of confusions.

Or maybe it's the dick you're looking for in the first place. White dudes are daily leaving their families to bite on pillows. One woman Ivory did a month back, a bloodshot redhead from the Rubyfruit who dragged him out to her pickup, told him black dick was her weakness.

Ivory hears that shit and isn't about to believe it. All boozy redheads look alike to Ivory, and too many of them got a liking for him. Nothing personal, for them it's a business move. They all got a break-daddy's-heart thing in effect, been playing it for years, old as some of them are. Brothers, dykes, anything to violate the code. Nothing weak about that weakness. It's a player strategy.

But Ivory's more than graciously willing to be played. He scans the Rubyfruit scene, clocking the dance floor, making his presence known, a black bull dyke looking for a pale waif. Ivory's gotten himself to like this gay techno. He respects the efforts of the starving diva backup singers, sisters playing fag hag, who disappear and have nine kids, who don't even rate a "Where Are They Now?" or props on Old School radio.

Most of the ladies are wearing silver Happy New Year cone hats. Ivory senses Ecstasy in the atmosphere, synthetic love, a serious point in his favor. Pretend the dick is a hallucination.

Ivory spots a lone cone hat dancing by the poker machine, shaking out a rhythm of her very own. It's nothing close to dignified to be hanging with yourself and sporting a hat like that.

She's got glasses, hair tied back all loose. White like Idaho. Ivory slides into her personal space, gets in the way of her blank stare. Her long dress gives up nothing. He waits on a reaction. If the proper vibes don't transmit in the first ten seconds Ivory will cut out and move on. Take or leave is the preferred style. He's not about to try relentless pursuit.

She gives him shy like they're waiting on a bus at Canal Street, like she wants their time together to be as noneventful as can be arranged. Her dancing loses its individuality and falls in line with the rhythm of the fag techno. Ivory holds his ground, puts it across to her that she's not in his way but is the reason he's here in the first place. Then he gives her the shoulder touch, a soft hand on the tricep, eyes putting the word on the street that I'm here for you. It's the defining move, meant to bring on the sensitive, Oprah getting the back of a wounded sister.

She leans in. They dance together. Ivory keeps his moves minimal, the self-conscious sway of a strong, silent butch-type.

It ain't like Ivory's always fixing to whip the dick out. There's whores for that sort of business. Ivory scouts for a little more than that, something in the range of warmth, hugs and nuzzles, something the skeleton rock whores can't put on the market. Quality time with some warm ass flesh, thirty seconds of soft.

Ever since Torsten, the coach who sold her into little girl slavery by praising her skills to her mother, Garnet has always drawn the attention and affection of rich foreign men. Something in her face—purity? sadness?

bewilderment? anger? Garnet has no idea—must scream America so loudly that guys making their fortune in the States desperately want to bring her back to their mothers in their home country, a totem of success, a claim on the land. It also helps that she's a soft touch for drugs and booze.

Garnet finds herself in Kiwi Cruz, sharing a bottle of Dom Perignon with a man from Sydney, Australia, who claims to be here to buy the place.

"When I take over." He has to shout over the snake-charm rhythms of absurd foreign music, the strain on his voice turning his Australian accent into something Kennedy-related. "This is the kind of shit I will sell." The Australian sips alternately from the champagne and a bottle of San Pellegrino mineral water. He makes no attempt to hide his wedding ring. "Upscale. Class. You know about San Pellegrino?"

Garnet guesses the singer is emoting in Arabic, spiteful "achs" and quavering vowels. A cab driver on the saddest day of his life. Who among us can ever get near his pain?

"What's to know?"

"A Sicilian chef told me one time. He said, when you drink Pellegrino, your sperm comes out like the ocean. Sicilians know how the world is run."

"Like the ocean?"

"It's true."

She scans the out-of-towners for any sign of incredulity, a fraction of comprehension that they've come to the Birthplace of Jazz to listen to this.

"What does that mean? Like the ocean?"

"His English wasn't up to snuff, but I knew what he was telling me. Like I said, it's true."

The good feeling that Garnet has floated on for the past hour has peaked, the genital tingle of cresting on a roller coaster. She only has the decline to look forward to, the stomach lurch. "Can I ask you something?"

He refills her glass. "Ask."

"Has anything remotely intelligent ever come out of Australia?"

"How do you mean?"

"Maybe my English isn't up to snuff, but I think you know what I'm telling you. Mel Gibson, INXS, Natalie Imbruglia. AC/DC. Rupert Murdoch. Taking the America's Cup seriously." Garnet drains her glass. "Bar fights. Greg Norman. You walking around with your own champagne."

" 'Bout Kate Winslet?" he asks, not at all defensively, a man impervious to the opinions of women. "And the Olympics this year. Would you like to come to the Olympics with me? I've got a house in the Olympic Village."

Garnet couldn't blame him for bringing up the Olympics. How could he have known? But there he is, promoting Australia's finest hour, hosting a colony of sixteen year old girls who haven't menstruated.

She takes the bottle of Pellegrino. "What does this do for women?" she says, taking a long sip, cheeks expanding.

"I might imagine it would—"

Garnet sprays his face with her mouthful. She intended to make it look like an accident, get away with it by spinning it into something sexual, lament her gag reflex. But the move had none of the subtlety she was hoping for. It was an act of aggression.

"Bloody bitch," he says, kicking over his bar stool. This gets the attention of one of the bartenders, out on the floor changing trash bags, his grey shirt tie-dyed with Daiquiri colors. He gets in between the Australian and Garnet, who is pleased that she could evoke an unselfconscious 'bloody.'

"Everyone relax," the bartender says. He turns to Garnet, makes a move for the Pellegrino bottle, gives her a wink. "Bottles are weapons." It embarrasses Garnet that the scene she's created is so typical as to barely concern him. He turns to make a move on the bottle of Dom, but the Australian snatches it and backs away, tripping over the fallen bar stool and onto the tiled floor, muddy with footprints and spilled drinks.

The scene earns the notice of all disinterested parties. Garnet smiles to balance the horrible feeling that suddenly overcomes her. If she could name it specifically it would no longer be an issue, but the general theme is mechanized adult behavior, how a show of humanity in disarray will always draw attention.

The stool doesn't seem to want to let go of his legs. It's a one-man melee, a display of diminished motor skills that is the unofficial ritualized dance of Bourbon Street.

When the Australian gets up in a rage the tie-dyed bartender pushes Garnet backwards out the side exit onto Conti Street. She watches two other bartenders push the Australian out onto Bourbon. Kiwi Cruz will not be sold.

"You okay?" the bartender says. He's a face she recognizes. They've been in rooms together before. He's short enough to look into her eyes without leaning over.

Garnet has developed a new thought.

"Am I the only person who wants to see the world end before I die?"

$*$ $*$ $*$

Matt pegs her look as Classic American Girl—Cindy Crawford hair, brown eyes. She puts him in mind of wheat fields, amber waves of grain. A tight body without obnoxious proportions, nothing to get her hooted at by construction workers. Product-endorsement smile. Jesus, she is smiling, isn't she, as she tells me she wants the world to end. What a strange thing to say, a line out of time and place. What's the answer that gets her into bed?

"Who doesn't want the world to end?" Matt says, and he can tell he fucked up right away, his what-else-is-new dismissal, seen-it-all irony. Stupid ass. What the fuck am I talking about, anyway? Plenty of people do not want the world to end. There goes her smile. He hated when women made him think about his words, their insistence on being more than one of fifty.

She sighs and starts searching her purse, the aura of onto other things. "I hate rhetorical questions. Give me facts and ideas."

"Imagine the sex." Matt can taste the bad timing on his tongue. His peripheral vision fuzzes over. "Like a plane going down but with more people to choose from."

"What I meant was I thought the millennium was something special, something we were privileged to be alive to see. Some great reckoning."

Matt is spared from having to respond when a purse snatcher hooks the corner around Bourbon and whizzes past them, an overweight cop chugging pathetically behind. Those on Bourbon who are curious begin to encroach on the privacy of their side street, and Matt remembers he's working. He has a notion to invite her into the mixing room, reveal behind-the-scenes machinations, the view from above. It impresses visitors, but Matt knows she's local. How did the Goth chick put it? It fills the air around her.

"But I appreciate you telling me what's on your mind," she says. "I'm always up for listening."

"I'm always up for talking." Matt wants to blow himself he's so ashamed. Is there anything more annoying than half-ass cleverness?

And then there's her shirt, with the Waikiki East emblem on the breast pocket.

The fat cop has given up. He leans against a parking sign down near Royal Street, talking into his radio.

"This is when I say I'll see you around," she says.

"And leave me to wonder if you mean it." He swears her smile returns as she dissolves into the crowd on Bourbon.

Matt is so impressed with his reply he can't wait to invent a response for her.

"This don't taste right. I want my money back."

Motherfucker. You're so fucked up you don't know what you're drinking. "What is it you ordered?"

"Supposed to be a kamikaze. It tastes like ass."

You want to taste ass, I'll shove your fucking face down the bitches' room toilet. "It sure doesn't look like a kamikaze. It's too green, probably Midori." A crazed, service industry smile. "I'll make you another one."

Friends pull on the motherfucker's jacket. "Let's go."

"I don't want another drink. You fucked it up. I want my money back."

Cocksucker. You need cab fare, don't you? You picked that fucking drink up off a table. "I can't give you money back. I'll be happy to make you another drink." And then get your golf visor-wearing wigger ass out of here.

"Aiight."

Sal has to turn his back on the wigger boy, mix the drink well away from him. Aiight. What a fucking disgrace. Sal used to hate blacks worst of all, but these Limp Bizkit Kid Rock motherfuckers have been burning him up lately. He can see where blacks don't know any better, especially in this shithole city, but what the fuck is the matter with these kids? What's their excuse? Sal could appreciate white trash when it was white—KISS, Van Halen, Metallica—but now there's no more pride even in that. Who's left carrying the white banner? Rednecks? NASCAR fans? Sal would rather be black. Almost.

Sal returns to the wigger boy, gives him a weak kamikaze. "Here you go."

The kid raises his glass. "Thanks, nigger."

Sal is over the bar, the Midori drink in his hand. He waits for wigger boy to turn around before winging the plastic cup at his face. Good, sticky liquor. Then Sal has got two hands around the wigger's throat, dragging him out onto Bourbon. It happens fast. Friends, bouncers, and the crowd that remains don't register the situation until wigger boy is rolling off the sidewalk into the gutter.

The bouncers take care of wigger boy's friends when they start to make a stink, but Darren, the manager, takes Sal into the back courtyard.

"What the fuck, man?" Darren says.

"Prick called me a nigger. I'm supposed to take that?"

"An eighteen-year-old punk with twenty shots in him calls you a name. Who would be left in here?"

Darren is good for this line at least once a week.

"C'mon Darren, I lost it. Kill me. You never lost it on someone?"

"There's a time and a place." This was another of Darren's favorites, the distilled essence of his managerial style. When he's full of coke instead of Valium, that's the time and place. Tonight he's all about getting along. "But Sal, man, you're flipping out once a weekend."

"Bullshit. Did I even raise my voice during the Bayou Classic? Did I flinch when that Grambling nigger threw his pint of Courvosier at me? Did I panic when his friend pulled a gun?"

"You told him to shoot you."

"I was calling his bluff. He was holding the gun sideways. He would have shot the mirror."

Darren rubs his chin, an obsessively groomed goatee, takes off his glasses and cleans them on his white silk shirt. "Sal, maybe you've got a little post-traumatic stress from that whole weekend."

Post-traumatic stress. This was new, and Sal has to give credit. Darren could pull up the perfect words every now and then. Sal has done three tours of duty at The Bayou Classic. A Thanksgiving weekend football tradition. Grambling vs. Southern, two black colleges vying annually to see who has the cheapest and most ignorant student body in Louisiana. This past year Pizzazz tried to close, "catch up on some maintenance," but the NAACP threatened a lawsuit. Sal loved the logic of their crusade. We will force you to take our money, it is part of our civil rights to be overcharged for piss liquor and treated like shit by a resentful service staff. We'll sue you if you refuse to screw us like you screw white tourists.

"You've got to learn to go easy." Darren puts a sympathetic hand on Sal's shoulder, rekindling his suspicion that Darren wants to fuck him.

The first time Garnet came in while Sal was working, Darren suddenly got football-buddy gruff. "Great to meet you, Garnet. We were worried that Sal here was a fag"

"Worried or wishful, you blow-dried coke whore," Sal replied, laughing, chummy ball-breaking.

Now Darren tells him to go home, rest, catch a blow job, get something to eat. "You gotta relax, man. We're in Sin City. It's a new millennium. We're making money. You got a girl who can put her leg behind her head. Where's the problem?"

Sal has never seen Garnet put her leg behind her head, the detail sudden news.

The sun is still down when Sal hits the street, and half a block down Bourbon he remembers he left his shades behind the bar. Fuck 'em. He knows who would steal them should they come up missing. Jorge the klepto barback. Let the dirty spic try.

Sal marches straight up the middle of Bourbon to his apartment, the only sober motherfucker on the street. People around him stagger, slip, fall, and groan. The true dregs of our earth, the ones who need their fates handed to them.

Dirty spic. When did he start a vendetta against the Spanish?

In front of Chris Owens' Club a fight breaks out. It's the wigger boy Sal tossed out, getting his head kicked in by a muscled up black guy wearing cream shorts and a sweater vest with nothing underneath. Sharp. The to-ken black in ads featuring golf foursomes. Sal gets close enough to see blood on his tan loafers. Without anyone's intention, Chris Owens' be-came the only real black club on Bourbon, something about the zebra stripe motif a call to plant a flag. Gunshots every couple months.

The sun peeks up as wigger boy rolls once again into the gutter, a mar-riage of justice and light. It appears you've called the wrong guy a nigger.

Moral satisfaction puts a spring in Sal's step, and soon he's at his apart-ment building. Moses, a staple of the French Quarter homeless scene, sleeps in the doorway. He delivered sandwiches for the Nelly Deli until he got shot in the shoulder. That was A. Him sleeping on the street with a greasy grey beard is Z. Sal could give a fuck about B through Y, but Moses is scary enough, even asleep, that he serves the function of a night watchman. Sal is careful as he steps over him and into the lobby. If Moses moves on, some-one worse will take his place, so Sal does what he can for him.

Right off the elevator he can hear Garnet dry heaving in the bathroom. She spent half her life forcing herself to puke and now it comes without effort.

Sal stands at the bathroom door. "I'm not taking you to get your stom-ach pumped."

"I just need ginger ale."

"Have you slept?"

"And chicken broth."

"In the cupboard. What time you due at work?"

"Breath mints. And Oksana needs to be walked."

"I'm not walking that fucking dog."

Oksana mistakes Sal's shout for a call and bounds out of the bedroom, a snooty little Shih Tzu Garnet found in a burned out car by Armstrong Park. It was Sal's idea to name her after Oksana Baiul, reckless driver, Olympic princess. He was busting balls but Garnet agreed. It's why they live together. He can leave his smile at work.

"She'll shit on the bed while you sleep."

"What am I going to do with her at the A&P?"

"There's a woman who walks her pig in the A&P. Take her inside with you."

So much of their shared life is conducted with Garnet's face in the toilet. Sal takes care of the day-to-day, an ex-military neat freak. He puts the right things in the refrigerator. It's all Garnet seems to require.

Sal hooks the leash to Oksana's collar, empties most of his cash on the nightstand, and starts back out. At the door to the street he tries to get Oksana to hurdle Moses, but instead she steps on his chest. His eyes flare open.

"Moses, you need anything at the A&P?"

"Get me a *Times-Picayune*. I bet the over/under on falling bullet deaths."

"You go over or under?"

"Under."

"Optimist. You're going to be disappointed, Moses. The guys who set the line are the same guys doing the shooting."

"Pessimist."

"My ass, pessimist. I lost fifty on a death bet. I thought your pal Chicken Man was gonna last out the year."

"I could have told you to lay off that one. Asshole had a liver of clay."

Sal doesn't drink. Anymore. Neither does Moses. Neither does Chicken Man. Anymore. Chicken Man was into voodoo medicine, an intangible Sal thought would carry his bet. It was the last time Sal put any stock in the mystical aura of the city.

"This year I'll put my money on you," Sal says.

"I don't like your chances."

"You're too unlucky to die."

Sal tugs at Oksana's collar and they move up Bienville Street. Sal's in no mood to take the dog down Bourbon, so he loops around to Dauphine.

Gambling. It's gotten Sal to where he is today, his A to Z a slinky down a staircase.

At Dauphine and St. Louis a couple of steroid motherfuckers in Florida State gear ask Sal for directions to The Dungeon.

"Down a block, left a block, right a block." Sal draws a map in the air. Half a Nazi symbol.

"You live here?" the shorter one asks.

"Yeah," Sal says. Oksana climbs up the side of his leg.

"What's with all the queers?"

Sal begins to answer that it's like San Francisco or Miami, they just exist, what the fuck can you do, but Oksana tugging at his pant leg makes him realize they don't want a real answer. Oksana is a first-class fag dog, and Sal is skinny and blonde. Sal doesn't see the first shot, but it knocks him down. Oksana breaks free and bolts.

This fucking life. I don't take enough shit every day, now I'm a fucking hate crime victim.

Moses, put ten dollars down on me, Sal thinks before the thinking stops.

This is where I say I'll see you around.

And leave me to wonder if you mean it.

Don't worry. I won't leave you wondering very long.

And then she's smiling, and then she's laughing, and then she's just enjoying herself. He's not breaking her down, he's not reaching a truth. He can't fuck the real her out of her.

And Matt can't come before he falls asleep. Some great reckoning.

"You caught yourself a pounding, nigger. This ain't about to be your millennium."

Ivory Anderson. Sal remembered the dude from the Cookhouse, his first Quarter bartending gig. Sal was a day away from quitting that shithole when Ivory piked the night's receipts right in front of his eyes.

Sal sits up, checks himself. Torn shirt and pants. One shoe off. "You're the second person today to call me nigger."

"Imagine how many think it and don't say it."

It hadn't even been a big money night at the Cookhouse. Maybe two grand. They stood in the kitchen, at the bottom of the stairs leading up to the main office. Kelso, the manager, had to let you out of the building, one of their fucked-up rules, and they were waiting for him to make his vodka and iced tea nightcap. Sharonda, the pregnant cashier, went up the stairs, earphones on, with the sack of money and a leopard print purse the size of a bowling bag.

Sal had just lit up a cigarette when he saw the money bag tumble down the top stairs and fall through the railing to the floor at Ivory's feet. He watched Ivory bend down to pick it up, then tuck it in his coat as casually as he might have handed it back to Sharonda.

Sal knew Ivory dealt something. Too many waiters gave him the time of day they wouldn't give to anyone else in the kitchen, and he was the only dishwasher who acted like he didn't need the job.

Sharonda came down the stairs a minute later. She looked confused but she always looked confused. Not a word as she walked out of the kitchen to the cashier's cage. Sal was alone with Ivory. They looked at each other. Sal had no idea what his face gave off, but it must have given Ivory the confidence to go through with his plan without issuing a threat or offering a cut.

Kelso stumbled into the kitchen. Sal had been mixing him drinks for the last three hours. He mumbled something about inventory as he opened the door to let Sal and Ivory out.

Sal had been through restaurant theft before. The owners huff and puff, stick a memo in your pay envelope; the crazy ones, like Ditta the Cookhouse owner, break out the polygraph, claim they're tight with D.A. Connick or whoever, but in the end no one ever gets caught. All you had to do was not disappear, which was the only thing Sal wanted to do.

They were going separate ways, of course, but now they shared the curb.

"I was going to quit tomorrow," Sal said.

Hands in his pockets, about two grand hidden in a fat crevice, Ivory said, "By all means do."

A week later Kelso passed out in the back dining room. When he got fired, he took the suspicion out the door with him. Ditta brought his nephew in as night manager, and Sal got the fuck out.

Sal makes a move to get up off the street, then decides against it. "Where am I bleeding?"

"Nose, mouth. You lucky your ass ain't bleeding, the way they was tearing at your clothes."

"You saw them."

"They saw me. Ran off."

"No shit." Ivory was the kind of black dude who had always scared Sal the most. You couldn't tell for a long while if he was a man or a woman. Heavy work outfit. Rolls of fat that could pass for tits. Two earrings. Afro thick but tight. Blacks like Ivory, growing up looking like that, wherever they grew up, you know they're battle-tested. Sal figured he probably indulged the style, dared the curious look of others.

"You should get your ass to Charity. You got a Troy Aikman look in your face, probably a concussion."

"Thanks for the advice. Always bet on the quarterback with the most concussions. That's my advice."

"Handle your own business. I ain't a EMT."

Sal gets up to his feet. "Not to say I don't appreciate."

"I had to get your back. You're good people. You didn't sweat the felony."

In the middle of a rush, "good people" would send Sal into a rage. But now he's determined to take things in stride. He feels banged up, but otherwise fine. And yet.

"You didn't see a dog running around?"

Ivory shrugs. "Me and dogs don't have a thing."

No way Sal was going home to Garnet now, not with Oksana running in traffic somewhere. His busted watch says 6:30. Time of assault, Sal guessed. With time to kill before Garnet leaves for work, he offers to buy Ivory breakfast, and regrets it immediately when he accepts.

Three hours of sleep, and Matt is up gathering his laundry. It doesn't take much to stink up a one-room, and Matt is unwilling to waste floor space on a hamper. He stuffs what he can into a pillowcase, throws on his Mets cap and starts down the back stairs.

Matt has never been much of a sleeper, dating back to when he was a preschooler. His parents were the hosts of the neighborhood and insisted on running Matt and Ron up to bed before commencing with card games and drinking. Aside from being sent to his room at a ridiculous hour, could they have honestly expected him to nod out with all the noise they were making? When he and his brother weren't fighting, Ron would drag out the Monopoly board and they'd have marathon games. Later, Ron taught him how to shoot craps, and the money became real. When Ron wasn't speaking to him, Matt would lie in bed and masturbate.

He likes living on Bourbon Street, the insistent noise a reminder that you're missing out on something. Plus mornings are his favorite time of the day, crazy for someone who works until sunrise, but while most people slurp coffee and suck down bagels like zombies on their way to work, Matt gets to read the paper, feast on pancakes, and even knock back a few beers afterward. Ron can run up his bank account as high as he wants, but he can't do that.

Bourbon is open to traffic, but Matt strolls right up the middle of the road, amidst the supply trucks and ambitious tourists. Everyone he works with loves to talk about how badly the Quarter stinks, as if it validates their suburban worldview, but even if Matt noticed it he wouldn't care. There's enough spotlessness in the world, enough antibacterial paranoia. Jesus, how many of his classmates at Tulane bitched about the "quality of life" down here? All the people he majored in business with, it's like they mutated right in front of him. All at once they rose above the simple joy of a nickel draft. No longer could he get a girl to fuck for the pure decadence of it. No one flirted. Instead they all wanted to complain, form a conspiracy based on resentment. The roads are so not smooth. The produce is gross. I'm way over the drinking thing. And off they went, girls, friends, virtually every college acquaintance, to Houston, Austin, New York, San Francisco. Law school, med school, bizarre internet start ups.

And business school. Matt has had enough of that. Senior year Matt was short on cash after chasing a spoiled local girl through her birthday, Christmas, and Valentine's Day. So he decided he'd make a dollar off of Mardi Gras. He walked up and down Bourbon looking to see who needed extra help. He landed at Kiwi Cruz, where he worked 100 hours over the six day blowout. He cleared about two grand. It was then Matt formulated his business plan, and he's been carrying it out faithfully going on a year. Now it takes a whole month to make two thousand, but that's after taxes. At a bitch job in a germ-controlled building Matt would have to pull down over thirty a year to earn the same cash. And that's five coffee and bagel mornings a week, and desperate Friday and Saturday nights when every pent-up suit in the world is out trying to get laid. How many years of that until you hang yourself? So Matt takes his cash, lives off half and hands the rest over to Merrill Lynch. He plans to be drunk for the next fifteen or twenty years, wake up one day and be a millionaire. To desire anything more, Matt feels, is an unattractive act of hubris, and God will certainly punish you for it.

It begins to occur to Moses that he's got to get his own *Times-Picayune*. Sal's not the worst white guy Moses has ever dealt with, but Moses knows his personal needs don't register high up in peoples' minds. Besides, he ought to get his circulation circulating. His left foot's been numb just a little bit too often lately, and he's seen gangrene run wild on a few of his street pals.

So here goes. Moses rolls himself off the lobby step and onto the sidewalk, where now he's got the leverage to get to his knees. From here it's a matter of pulling all the way upright, which isn't the problem so much as the head rush. It wouldn't be the first time Moses heaved up too quick and fell ass over into the street, a light show going off inside his eyelids.

Given this possibility, and his hollow stomach, Moses takes his time, and his patience pays off. A smooth morning rise and shine to start the day, the year, the century off right. Onward to the A&P.

Moses ambles down Bienville, left leg dragging, and turns onto Bourbon. The five blocks to the A&P is looking like a pilgrimage to Mecca, but it's that or raise fifty cents for the newspaper machine. A brother is hosing down the sidewalk in front of Arnaud's Rémoulade. Moses didn't need to be reminded of his current thirst. "I can use maybe a sip of that water," Moses says.

"I know you're not axin' me for no water," the brother spits back. His white undershirt is dirtier than anything Moses has on. Maybe Moses is ready to find employ again.

"I'm just stating a fact," Moses says. "But if I was axin' I know you'd help a poor brother out."

"I don't hear you axin'."

And here's Moses' problem. He's never been one to declare himself a charity case, which is peaches when you're self-reliant but can lead to unneeded struggles when your ass is on the street. Pride becomes foolish pride when it's your last asset, but Moses aims to keep a reputation around here. Too many no-legged, one-eyed people in the area to play the helpless card, so Moses tries to portray himself as a sound investment, a man not far at all in spirit from the gainfully employed, someone who is one donation, one favor, one good deed away from joining his French Quarter friends and neighbors in the world of productive service.

JERI CAIN ROSSI

A Bus Named Cemeteries

THE SKY HAD THAT SAD LOOK. It had been depressed and close to tears for nearly a week. Finally, the sky broke down and cried. It wailed hard and long and wet like at a good funeral.

The river bloated and climbed up the levee, threatening to bleed over into the Quarter. The rain was a nuisance, but he was glad it washed away the sweltering July heat.

What is life? he thought, rolling another cigarette while staring out the window from his kitchenette. A good bottle of gin, he answered himself. He lit the cigarette and took a drag. The smoke appeared to float around the Beefeater bottle like a genie making an appearance. There's no wishes in this bottle here, he thought to himself. A fifth of gin and an occasional girl to have some laughs with, that's the best you can hope for.

He came to New Orleans seven years ago with the intention of becoming a professional drunk. You have to be good at something, and he figured it was destiny as he had three kidneys.

Try as he might he couldn't think of any one event in his life that was tragic. There was no dark shaded past, no lost love.

In fact, he grew up regular on a farm in Indiana. Nothing in particular pointed to that he would throw himself into a river of gin and tonics.

Around three in the afternoon the squall subsided and he wandered into a bar in the Marigny. He drank and played pool for an hour when a messy red-headed girl in white sunglasses stumbled into the bar and immediately tripped on herself. She sat loudly on a barstool and ordered a red wine. As she dug in her purse for money, the sunglasses slipped off her nose and fell on the floor. She lifted the glass of wine and immediately spilled it on herself, staining over the heart.

He watched her with interest and chuckled at her clumsiness. She wore only a slip, as many bohemian French Quarter girls did in the summer, and he admired her legs. She walked heavily in high heels to the jukebox and played Chet Baker. Nobody played Chet Baker in this bar except for him. She began dancing to herself drinking her wine.

He became transfixed with this girl right out of his dreams. He aimed and broke the rack of balls with a thunderclap. She looked out of her stupor and met his eyes and walked directly over to him.

"Can I use you?" she asked. Her eyebrows were penciled in dramatically and her large eyes gave her the appearance of a silent screen actress.

"Sure. What do you have in mind?" he said smiling, leaning on the pool cue.

"Let's get a bottle. Let's get lost."

They stopped at a deli on Decatur Street and bought a large bottle of red wine and a couple of shot bottles of gin and proceeded up the street toward Canal.

"Let's pretend this is turn-of-the-century New Orleans when there were still streetcars named Desire and I'm a Storyville whore and you are a criminal in exile," she said swigging the bottle of wine.

"I like that. What kind of criminal am I?" he said.

"A killer."

"You're a strange girl."

He held out his arm for her to hold on to. They cut up Toulouse to Bourbon Street. Drunkenly, they careened past strip clubs, sex and trinket shops and loud bar music.

"Now let's be weather. What's your favorite storm?" she asked.

"Twisters."

They became tornadoes and whirled up Bourbon, bumping into boring, annoying tourists and laughing hysterically.

At Canal, the Desire bus sped by, out of their reach. They boarded the very next bus, which read Cemeteries as the destination, and drank all the way to Metairie. The bus stopped at the complex of city cemeteries and they stumbled off.

They entered the closest cemetery across the street and staggered around giggling and kicking each other.

"So who are we now?" he inquired.

"We are Greek gods," she said passing by a pantheonesque tomb.

"Then I'm Dionysus, god of gin." He opened a shot bottle of gin and drank it down.

"And I am Melpomene, muse of tragedy," she said, then tripped, collapsing on the grass.

"What are you so tragic about?" he said, holding out his hand to pull her up.

She ignored the hand and looked at him. Her large, saturnine eyes welled up and reddened. He sat down next to her.

"I'm sorry. It's the wine," she drawled slowly.

"No it's not. Now tell me why it's so goddamn necessary to cry."

"To wash away the bad. But it just gets all bad again."

He sighed impatiently.

"You know everybody's got bad to deal with. You can't take it all so seriously. It's not worth it. When things get me down I take a swig and turn the page and forget it. That's how I stay on top. Girls, jobs, nothing is worth getting so down."

He pulled her to him and tried to kiss her. Her lips responded sluggishly. He looked at her and frowned.

"What's up with you? I thought you were my Storyville date."

Her eyes rolled in her head and her head jerked down.

"I'm tired right now." She leaned against him heavily.

"What's wrong with you? You passing out on me?"

"I took some pills," she mumbled, closing her eyes.

"Well, give me some."

"Sorry, I took them all."

"What do you mean?" He nudged her. "What do you mean you took them all?" he spoke loudly.

"I just get so tired of dying," she murmured.

He shook her, then patted her face strongly.

"I'm sorry I used you. I just didn't want to die alone." She fell forward into unconsciousness.

He stood up in horror and twisted around wildly. He ran out of the cemetery leaving her there, and entered into the world of sorrow and uncertainty.

GO TO HELL

MOST HATED WERE THE BIBLE THUMPERS Halloween night pacing between bone men and excess and silver faces, scaring us more than the spooks. Or the cross carriers who dragged their load through the swill and brine of Bourbon the Sundays before Mardi Gras. Those days, especially, they flocked in swarms, eager to clutch the raw corrupt flesh of our souls. As if anything could have saved us!

One night when the street was filled with us in costumes drinking, of course, and searching, all of us, for the next more more, filled with whiskey and paint and powders and the sweet parting of flesh, somewhere above the din of kiss and dance and drone of voices, the voice of the ranting preacher on the other side of the street rose above: "You are on the path to Hell—you must give yourself over to the Lord..." And we all looked at him with the unity of a strange congregation. Then one from the back began with a shout, and the word acquired weight as other voices joined it: a rumble with a rhythm shouting: "Sa-tan!" Satan. A many-throated chorus, we shouted "Satan" laughing, punching the air with our fists on the Ss and Ts. Villains and medusas and viny things, skeletons and hookers and aliens, we clapped and toasted as the chant grew, stopping only when the bus of Desire drove between us and him—thank goodness really because who knows where it would have ended?

When it passed, and we stood in the exhaust of Desire, everything wet and sooty, the Bible thumper was nowhere to be seen. It was then I saw the bartender: thick, burly, bumpy, looking at me with one bulgy eye, the other given over to droop and stupor, the slurp of his last meal still on his lips. A beast, double horned, he stared, and in answer to my unspoken question, belched his name or I would have spelled it out for you right here. But if you ask me, I swear he was the Devil himself.

APPEALING FOR THE TRUTH (A SAD JOKE)

AT FIRST THE LAWYER TOLD ME there was little likelihood I'd be convicted for it. Then he was amazed, as I was, when the judge handed down the highest possible sentence and called me a curse on society. Now I'm waiting for them to consider my appeal which may either turn over the conviction or reduce the sentence. Nothing seems too positive.

I say "my" appeal, but to call it mine would be akin to claiming the air in a leaky balloon was mine. I have no control over any of this ridiculous charade and even less input into the language and joke of what they call "the law." All I know is the truth. After two months I'm already sick of everyone in here, though I'm sure I'll get to know them all too well during the next twenty years. I still feel justified and never claimed to be innocent, before or after his death.

Midnight is usually a little too early to be at the Abbey, but after a stinking hot day and a hard week I didn't care and was into my third cold beer when Tina came over and asked me what I thought of a proposition she'd just received. I was instantly horrified, not only at the proposition but with the fact that she even wanted to buy some of his poison. She was mainly worried about it's purity.

He was selling real poison. We all know it's all poison. Alcohol will harden your heart, cocaine will explode it, heroin will stop it, crystal will burn it out while hamburgers will choke it in layers of fat. But this poison, simply labeled as poison, was there to kill it. The difference between dying and killing had been laid out in front of me so clearly I could barely think, let alone talk, so I asked her why she wanted any goddamn colorless, odorless, undetectable poison.

Tina talked in circles about never knowing when she might need some-thing like that to the joy of having the power to kill. We ended up discuss-ing the very tips of ten different issues concerning murder and death, none of which came close to explaining why Tina would need or even want a bag of killer poison.

I was sick of death. A week earlier a woman had disappeared from the French Quarter and had been so brutally tortured that a hardened homi-cide detective had been shown on TV choking on his bile at the scene. He had tears in his eyes and I knew the killer had been in a bar with me some-time that week. I was wishing I could have seen or remembered the bas-tard. Would he have averted his eyes when I looked at him? Was he loud or quiet? Did I know him? Was he a she? Now another killer was nonchalantly sitting at the end of the bar hoping to sell his effective, undetectable poison for $25 a soul.

"You really do want some of it, don't you Tina?"

"Yeah! I s'pose I do," she answered with a smile and a shrug.

"Well, I don't want any damn part of it! Why'd you even bother asking me if you're so determined to buy it anyway? I think you're stupid for even thinking about poison. Now if someone else dies around here I'll be think-ing 'Knew it! There goes little Miss Tina, slipping her poison pill into some poor lover again' or something like . . ." I was running off at the mouth but Tina was laughing too hard for me to continue.

"Mick," she said. "Mick, I'm only asking you because I thought you might have some idea whether it's a real deal or not. How do I know if he's selling me baking powder or something?"

"Easy. Put some on your gums as a test and just hope he's selling you some goddamn baking powder! Seriously, go ahead and buy your dream of 'the power to kill' for only $25. It's a bargain! That would be worth it and it could be baking powder for all you'd care because it doesn't matter, does it? It's impossible to get ripped off unless you're actually intending to use it."

"Nah," she drawled with no hesitation. "If I'm going to buy a little poi-son I want it to be real poison. Why should I get ripped off and give him the satisfaction of doing it!"

"Then, once again, I still can't see why you even bothered asking me. I wish you'd left me out of your poison fantasy."

Mister Poison looked over. The smarmy little bastard knew we were talking about him, poison and death, so he smiled. Even then I knew he was some rich college kid, but that doesn't mean a thing when it comes to morality or poison selling. He acted cool ("like I'm in a movie, dude!") as he tried to look mysteriously fantastic at the end of the bar. I thought baking powder and smiled back.

"Tina, I think that little turd is going to sell you baking powder anyway. You're wasting your money and you definitely don't need any poison. Don't be stupid and have another glass of wine."

"No Mick and don't talk to me like that! I need to borrow ten bucks."

"You what! Shit! You want me to lend you ten bucks to buy a gram of baking powder from young, smirking baby-cakes over there! You're kidding!"

"No I'm not. I've got money at home and I'll pay you back tonight. Give me ten."

"You really do want to pay $25 for a bag of baking powder, don't you! You're mad, you know that?!"

"Whatever, Mick. The ten?"

"Look, Tina. I'll tell you what I'll do. I've only got a twenty but you can borrow it. Go over, buy some of his damn death potion but slip some into his drink. As soon as he takes a drink tell him you put it all in and just watch his eyes. If it's real he'll panic and race off to get his stomach pumped as fast as hell and you'll still have the rest. If he doesn't, tell the whole bar as loud as you can and get your money back and we won't ever have to see his sorry little face again." I pulled a folded note from my shirt pocket and passed it to her.

I thought she'd have said something about that ridiculous plan but she didn't. I wasn't sure if she thought it was funny or part of my normal cynicism or too stupid to even comment on. She just grabbed that note and went over to Mr. Poison. From where I was I couldn't see much but she sat beside him for several minutes. I did see him bring his glass to his lips. A fraction of a second later his glass shattered on the floor and he keeled over, as dead as you can get. Tina's stunned face was whiter than ever as she rushed back.

"It works," she gasped on the way to the bathroom.

From then on it only got worse. The poison was potent and far from undetectable, as was the security video. It showed me passing her something from my pocket. It showed her tipping poison into his glass. It didn't show her buying the poison. He'd been too discreet. It did, however, show Tina leave his shuddering carcass, walk straight over to me and say "it works," as verified by no less than three independent, deaf experts, all of whom liked watching ice hockey on TV. Unfortunately, Mr. Poison was the son of wealthy parents. For some reason that seemed to be extremely important. It didn't matter that Mr. Poison was studying medicine and had purportedly poisoned a few dogs experimentally, nor did it matter that I knew absolutely nothing about poisons. It didn't seem to matter what we told the police or the judge or the jury. It was proven, beyond doubt, that I was well known for telling stories and therefore I had to be lying. They'll try Tina next week. I love the truth but it's difficult to appeal for. Have fun out there!!

hurricane

During prohibition Pat O'Brien operated a speakeasy. The password for entrance to "Mr. O'Brien's Club Tipperary" was "storm's brewin'." In 1933 he moved across the street and opened Pat O'Briens. During the Second World War whiskey became expensive but rum was in ample supply. With the help of a liquor salesman the Hurricane was born. He later moved the club to its present location at 718 St. Peter, where it is now purportedly the busiest bar in the world.

(traditional recipe)

juice of half a lime

$^3/_4$ oz. Rose's Lime Juice

$^1/_4$ oz. maracuja (passion fruit) syrup

$^3/_4$ oz. pineapple juice

$^3/_4$ oz. orange juice

$^3/_4$ oz. white rum

$1\,^1/_2$ oz. dark rum

lime

Shake over crushed ice in a shaker.

Strain into a large highball glass over crushed ice.

Add lime wedge.

ELLEN GILCHRIST

SUNDAY

I have come reeling out on Royal Street
at seven in the morning
strangely sober after hours
of wine and starlings.

I have danced alone
and with strangers
till the sun like a red rock
came sailing up from China.

Coming out of Lucky's having lost
my pocketbook, twenty dollars playing
bumper pool, and even my shoes
which I gave away to the jukebox.

Preacherman, sweet paid for confessor,
I tell you I am sorry
but I forgot to tell you
that I danced all night with starlings
and with bluejays.

I forgot to say that drinking
is a kind of prayer
when the world thunders.

TIM PARRISH

SUMMERTEETH
(for Wilco)

WE WERE FROG-SKINNED. The liquid air permeated us. Not toad-skinned, not bumpy and rough, but smooth and watery, a mix of flesh and beverage, the moistness of youth, the heavy summer passing through us and not us through it. Although we were. Passing through.

We were down from Baton Rouge and up for the evening, drunk and noisy to cover the anger and fear of the moves we were about to make: me to writing school and Shana with me; Don and Katie to lives without me. Not that I'm arrogant. They *were* moving to a life without me. Compared to them I was stable, employed in a bank, pseudo-godfather to their child. Don was sliding into his cups and cocaine, most nights careening toward shattering glasses or screwing somebody other than Katie, while Katie was realizing minute by minute she'd reeled in from north Louisiana to have a child with an unfaithful, alcoholic bartender. Sure, Shana and I had our own damage and bad behavior, but tonight we were knocking it all back. Summer 1985, a goddamned Reagan year, yet a year when you could still hit the Quarter and have it not knee-deep in frat boys and tourists, a night when Pat O's was the decadent patio of some French plantation owner who just happened to have a lot of friends and an eccentric taste for glass-ware.

Now we slouched and bobbed in a dive on Royal, waiting for the night to take its chemical turn. Don sniffled from the toot he'd just done in the bathroom and raised his full eyebrows in offer to me. I tried not to sneer as I shook my head, pissed off at the shit that was killing him, for making me party to it. Hell, when we'd been roomies he'd had me hide his coke so he couldn't do it all at once.

Shana laid her long fingers on my thigh and squeezed. I spread my legs a little more. She slid her hand up and inside and smiled, her almond eyes bright with booze, her fine close-cut auburn hair breaking in a cowlick over her forehead. I wanted to fuck her right there, fuck her like we'd done all spring and summer, after work leading her sun hot and slicked with suntan oil from her lounge chair to inside, peeling off her bikini, her body so small and hard it was barely finished, mouthing her tiny breasts, burying my face in her raucous bush, then fucking before we torqued into bitter fights without focus or finish.

"I'm so happy for y'all," Katie said. "We'll miss you."

"We'll miss y'all," Shana said. "Y'all have to come see us."

"Y'all have to come back," Katie said, "regularly."

"We will," I said.

"No you won't," Don said, and pinched at his nostrils.

"What?" Shana said.

"You won't," Don said. "How can you?"

"We drive," Shana said.

"Eight hours. You're shaking it off," Don said.

"We're not shaking it off," Shana said.

"It's not on you like it is him. He's shaking it off cause it's on him."

"What is?" I asked.

"It," Don said. "To shaking *it*."

"To *shaking* it?!" I laughed.

"To shaking *it*!" Don said. "Baton Rouge. Us and it."

"I'm not drinking to that," I said.

"Me either," said Shana.

Don smirked and nodded. "It's all right," he said, that rise in octave the little flag of patronizing he rose when the booze and blow got their hold. "To writing the truth, then," he said, and lifted his fresh shot of Absolut. I glanced at Shana, saw the flare in her eyes, then she, Don and I clinked shooters and threw back, the chilled liquid sliding into my chest and blossoming into my head. Katie smiled her big goofy smile and sipped her Shirley Temple, her restraint and offer to be our driver earlier having caused lots of abuse.

"Think you know it?" Don asked.

"Huh?" I asked.

"The truth."

"We'll see," I said, hoping Shana wouldn't throw in on him, the dark energy heaping up on her as my own throat tightened.

"Yeah," he said, "we will," and more shots I didn't even know he'd ordered arrived.

That night we'd done the tourist things I loved. Acme Oyster, Napoleon House, Lafitte's Blacksmith Shop. We'd stumbled, a week night in early August, the date for leaving lurking like a mugger or a pardon, the Quarter backstreets quiet in a way they don't seem quiet to me anymore even when they are; the aroma and architecture percolating mystery into the air; my senses seduced by the city with one foot in Europe, one foot in blight, and both feet fully in itself; neighborhood and street names succulent on the tongue like a lover's taste—Fauborg-Marigny, Chartres, Ursulines, Esplanade—exotic and familiar at once.

At Pat O's we'd been cases drinking colorful drinks. I'd sipped a Sky Lab, a blue drink with fruit like robust algae bloom, me a Baton Rouge refugee from my blue-collar roots, smartass post-punker who'd been driven or directed to New Orleans stoned and drunk so many times I might as well have been navigating Paris. Shana, my wolfen lover, angled and lean, gorgeous, loud in bed and a volatile drunk, she drank a Gin Fizz. Don dashing Don didn't like his vodka diluted, but he slurped Sea Breezes just to be festive, he so smooth it was easy to forget he'd lammed to Baton Rouge in '78 to avoid a bust in Monroe, easy to forget his liver was losing its war against him. And Katie, well, she'd gulped her hurricane, her only drink of the evening, her pale blonde voluptuosity and north Louisiana drawl as exaggerated as Betty Boop. We'd laughed too hard and floated on the first breeze of a buzz, the torches throwing crazy light on our outsides like what was being thrown on our insides. Hours ago. The torches flared more now.

"You might wanta slow down, Chief," Katie said to Don. Don gave her a look like the ones he gave before he went off on a customer he suddenly didn't like or a punk at a Black Flag show whose skinhead rubbed him wrong or somebody ethnic who raised the redneck in him. Then he plugged a cigarette in his mouth, lit it and tossed the shot back.

"Gotta drink to Baton Rouge," he said. "Hell, we all went there and met Tom, but Tom's got the sense to book. Can't be a big writer in a small town."

"Big writer. Bullshit," I said.

"Y'all gonna come visit *us?*" Shana asked toward Katie.

"Sure we are," she said.

"You ain't afraid we'll tear up your house?" Don said.

"Just you," Shana said. "But we'll hide the vodka before you come."

"Cause you sure don't drink," Don said.

"I drink. I don't slosh."

Don smirked.

Shana wasn't the boozer Don was, and she didn't drug besides a sliver of acid once in a while, but when she binged, the rot beneath her beautiful surface emerged, the swamp under the old city come frothing up. I'd met her Halloween at a friend's party out on River Road, she Ilsa She Wolf, me Your Tallest Nightmare. We'd gone home together but it was three weeks before hydraulics worked for coupling, three weeks after that before big battle number one, her slapping, me shoving, us already doomed.

"You oughta write again," I said to Don, who used to rattle out the funniest, sharpest, rifle-scope satire, used to before his barreling chaos landed him with child, cohabitant mother and time-consuming substance and sex habit. Don snorted.

"You *should*," Katie drawled.

Shana laughed. "That piece about the roaches living in the clock of your coffee maker still cracks me up."

"Yeah," I said, "and the one about the hierarchy of drunks scumming drinks at The Bayou. From top-shelf to bar-mat pour."

"I like the one about bumming rides from the 'rotating friend wheel,'" Katie said. "You had that great formula that figured in quality of car, amount of weed or booze needed for bribe, and sexual favors." She caressed the cushion of her lower lip. "Well, that sexual-favors-for-use-of-car hit a little close to home there when you were blowing me off."

Don blew a stream of smoke. "I'm all used up. Tom's the writer. I'm just the drunk clown holding the fort in the Chemical City."

"Right," I said. "They'll probably break all the pencils once I'm gone."

Don nodded and everybody tried to laugh with conviction. Earlier Katie had taken a photo of me, Shana and Don sprawled on the steps of The Cabildo like we'd been gunned down. Now I thought how I loved them, loved them because they believed I was something—intelligent, cool, sexy, talented, forgiving, wise even—that I didn't really believe. I didn't know yet that love wasn't all narcissism. Didn't know shit about New Orleans either, really, and I didn't want to know shit. I blew in for shows—The Clash at the Warehouse, Gang of Four at Jimmy's, Dead Kennedys at Jed's, King Sunny Ade at Tip's—staggered through the Quarter, then fled back to the glowing refinery sky of home. New Orleans was a shadowy temptation just down the road, and I felt cool in the shadow.

"So," Don said, "you think jetting to writing school's different from junking your band and taking that job at the bank?"

"I didn't junk the band," I said. "I got sick of being constipated in a van and getting ripped off by club owners. I'll start another one sometime."

"Yeah," he said, "but you think writing school's different?"

"The job at the bank fucking sucks, that's why I'm going back to school. What's your point?"

"You know his point," Shana said. "It's the same lame point—you don't have the integrity he has because he stays true to being a loud mouth at the bar."

"Was I talking to you?" Don said. "I look at people when I talk to them."

I said, "You think the band was so important, why don't you start one? I'm worn out."

"Hey, I was just asking."

"Right," Shana said. "You were just asking. You're like a little kid being left behind."

"Least I ain't just tagging along," Don said.

"Oh, I'm tagging along. I guess that's worse than fucking around."

"Hey!" I said. "Y'all chill."

"Yes," Katie said. "Chill. We're here to have fun. Let's have fun."

"To fun," Don said.

Don sipped his beer. Shana shook her head, bad vibe boiling off her, while Katie's face contorted with the effort of trying to find words to put us all on the happy party rail again. But that rail was already bent, as we all knew it would be, and that's when the real party started, the Baton Rouge party, Absolut mind erasers and flarestack skies, The Replacements and Husker Du chainsawing angst in the background.

Don had been there from my second start, the Kingfish Club 1978, the night the Sex Pistols steamrolled into Baton Rouge, both of us pounding shots at the bar as leathered creatures with safety-pinned faces scowled through. We mocked them, bonding, me a college boy with big fro, him coiffed and clean, beefy and ruddy like a leading man, in town a week on the run, mocked them until the Pistols unleashed their raggedy anger and unbuckled everything me and Don knew about music. We kept shoving each other, jaws dropped, grinning and fist pumping, the goddamn stale world ice-picked through the spot its heart was supposed to be. He was there through all my bands—punk, punk-pop, post-punk—thinking with the core of us we were fighting the righteous fight with renegade music and thrashing life, thinking the real things thrived only in the bars where the smoke and sound and chemicals roiled like mutant hormone stew. And he wasn't wrong, we weren't wrong, but that wasn't all there was, wasn't the only authenticity. I finished school, lost the stamina it took to be a fuck up, got tired of silly politics in music, got tired of being a Baton Rouge band when I played New Orleans, a Baton Rouge band in Houston, a Baton Rouge band in Atlanta, a Baton Rouge band in Baton Rouge. Hell, just tired.

"I love this town!" Don bellowed.

"I thought you loved Baton Rouge," Katie said.

"Yeah," Shana said, "you cheating on your town?"

"He's got enough love for two towns," Katie said, her inevitable sneer emerging like a knife from tender fruit.

"Maybe three," I said, flicking my own little blade.

Don tapped a cigarette on his chin. "None of 'em are my town anyway," he said to me. "I'm just a turn tail and run. Baton Rouge is Tom's town. Oops. Used to be."

"Moving isn't cheating," Shana said. "Cheating is cheating."

"You're the expert," Don said.

"What?"

"On moving."

"You're on her about moving?" Katie said.

"I'm not on anybody," Don said. "I'm being festive."

"Uh huh," Shana said. "You're real festive when you shut the bar down and don't head home."

"Shana," I said, "cool out."

Shana glared. "Cool out? *You* fucking cool out."

"You know what I mean."

"Yeah, I know."

"It might be our last night out with them."

"So what? I'm tired of this passive-aggressive shit pretending to be wit. He wants you alone, he can have you alone. I'll cool out in the bathroom."

"I'll go with you," Katie said.

The women whisked away from the table, Katie cutting Don a look, Shana implying menace in her stride.

Don smiled, the wedge bringing joy. "Another round," he yelled toward the bar.

"Why y'all gotta get into it?" I said.

"I'll miss you, man," he said, ignoring my words. The barstool shifted under me. Every step I'd taken—less drinking, steady job, writing school—

was to Don a sloughing off of authenticity. Like we'd ever had that much, smartass ex-jocks with special status in our small town scene by way of slinging drinks and band membership. Obnoxious, we hammer-and-anvilled skinny punks in skank pits, derided slower minds like sharks hitting chum. Me susceptible to Don's containment, Don's reserve, Don's detachment. Me forgiving and forgetful when all of the above cracked with booze and powder into abuse and self-destruction.

"You gotta take care, man," I said.

"You mad cause I made your woman mad?" he asked.

"No. Maybe. I guess."

"Uh huh. Well, y'all can work it out in the sack."

"Fuck you. I ain't moving to piss you off, you know," I said.

"I got no problem with you moving," he said.

"Right. You never got a problem, do you."

"Here we go."

"I'm not talking down. Don't start that shit."

"I didn't say anything," he said.

"No, you didn't say anything."

The waitress set three shots on the table. Don snatched one, tossed it off, shoved one toward me and lifted the third. I pressed against my eyes and toasted him. We drank.

"Give me a cigarette," I said.

Don lit me and I inhaled, the toxins rushing through me like rescuers. Sadness raked my insides, then I exhaled a slow cloud, tension and the bigger world leaving me stranded on a high drunk island.

"Shana's a mean bitch," Don said, and grinned. "Why you taking her?"

" 'Cause I love her, asshole. Don't you love Katie?"

He shrugged. "It's good when it's good."

"Y'all have a kid and that's the best you can do?"

"Hey, man, what you got? If you got something, why you taking off?"

I wanted to answer. Sure I had things, but I didn't know what they were, at least my tongue didn't know. I flicked the cigarette and braced against a drunken breaker that washed the sadness over me again.

Shana and Katie strode in and positioned themselves at the end edge of the tall table.

"Y'all get freshened up?" Don asked.

"It's late," Katie said.

"So it is," Don said.

"Give me a smoke," Shana said to Don.

"Yes, ma'am," Don said to her.

She took a pointed drag and blew a stream in Don's direction, the ember more in her eye than on the cigarette. We stumbled out the door into the darkness, the heat and humidity as dense as Jupiter's membrane. My drunk hit me fully, perforating my head, and the stench rolled in like the inside of an old garbage can stained with mildew and vomit, fried batter and beer. I pulled up short, lifted my arms and hooted, then filled my chest with the odor so undeniably real and organic, not the caustic burn of polymers and oil by-product of home, but the spew of human bellies and rot of spongy land. The Quarter.

The others smiled, looking at me. Shana swung round and round on a balcony-support pole like a musical was about to bust out. I blinked, the wall of buildings shouldered together completely unfamiliar. "Which way?" I said.

"This way," Shana said, and pointed. Don nodded. We walked.

The street was almost carless and nearly deserted except for straggling vampire punks and two tight-pants disco gay boys Don whistled at as we passed. "Come get it, stud," one said and we laughed. I took Shana's hand, then let go so our arms could slither around each other's waists. Katie slung a skinny white arm over Don's shoulders and he smiled and nodded as the four of us weaved and bumped into one another.

I was in lust with sweet decay, the decadent nectar of Louisiana, corruption, backwardness and bacchanalia. I reveled and guilted in the mess, I had that stripe of Louisiana in me. All of us did, uncentered and unhinged, steeped in chaos's luscious lack of commitment.

That night Shana and I made love, deep sex in sharing loss of beautiful times when the ringing in our bodies and the thrum in our heads were from celebration we'd made, when the bar squeezed us tight as lover's legs, when we watched the Baton Rouge sky burn like the signal fire of the apocalypse, sweet as juice. But no more love for me and Don. Six months later I came home to him a wild man, gone-native hair rioting halfway down his back, him wrestling his big woman co-bartender in a large puddle out front the Bayou. No love between us, not even reveling. Katie and the baby split by then, me and Shana on the rocks, Don wasted and betrayed by anyone he could name.

We turned onto some street and into red and blues slashing from the police car blocking the road. Two cops stood beyond the car, lights rolling over them and a body weirdly twisted at the waist. We gawked and puffed, all bunched together, our bodies already dampening from the air, the last time we'd be this close all at once.

"That's a bad spot to nap," Don said. We gave each other glances.

"Damn tourists," Shana said, and tittered.

"Holiday in Cambodia," I said, and then we were laughing, me, Shana and Don, laughing that hurt us and made us hug each other. The cops turned to us in that heavy darkness only French Quarter streets have.

Katie stepped away from us, her hand near her mouth.

"What's wrong with y'all?" she said. I hung on Don and Shana on me, all of us trying to suck in the laughter, but it wouldn't suck in. "That's a person," Katie said. "A dead person."

And so it was.

SUMMERTIME

SUMMERTIME, THE LITTLE GIRL ON THE LEVEE SANG, a small husky whisper too sorry for sexy, lost in the wind and the boat horns, the thick summer air. She sat crosslegged looking off nowhere, telling a sad story to no one in particular of stranded in New Orleans with not enough gas money to get home sweet home to Ohio or Iowa, wherever. A few off-season tourists might stop and listen, throw her some bills or change. She told them she was living in a Buick Skylark. I knew she had a place off Rampart, a shotgun opening onto the sidewalk, having followed her there one night from a bar in the Marigny where she was laughing and shooting pool with other kids like herself, pierced and tattooed, defiant and young, flush with quarters and dollar bills from her gig on the levee. I sat at the bar with the cold gin tonic sliding into my veins, sweat beading on my temples, my back, under my arms, running down my face and body like small cool fingers.

Summertime in this city the air gets thick and comes alive, wraps its sickly sweet self around you sticky and strong. We stay indoors or move from one shady doorway to the next like lizards, blinking. At night when the hazy sun has burned out, we come out into the dark heat and move slowly like underwater, which we are more or less, below the levee and the great unseen black river snaking its way around us silent and deep. The little girl worked the tourists every day, dawn to noon or so, then moving from the levee to a shaded step beneath a balcony off the square. I know. I walked the Quarter learning how to make myself invisible, fading into the heavy air, molecule by molecule until I was a seersucker ghost, a white blur wrinkling the air as I passed by. But she could always see me, a glimmer of recognition after weeks of nothing, not a look but an involuntary twitch, a hesitation in the deep beat of the bongo she wrapped her legs around, an awkward pause in the Joplin lyrics that changed each time she sang them. Your momma's a bitch, your daddy's still lookin'. I kept a distance, watched from behind dark glasses, sideways glanced as I glided by, disappearing, fading with the faint strains of her awful voice, her mournful story piercing me even though I saw its lie.

Summertime the ghosts appear, in the haze down the street, always turning the corner when I draw near, and at night in the blue glow between the streetlights, they waver and dance, unwilling to leave this decaying place. Nights like these the world closes in and the streets become crowded and I am glad to be invisible. A night like this the little girl with the drum between her legs and the awful ragged-throated voice disappeared into the strange shadows on Governor Nicholls, a block ahead. Deep faraway sounds like drumbeats, a pulse of breath and words drifted toward me as if in a trance. I steadily made my way to the place where she'd disappeared, a narrow alley, stopped at her drum where it had come to rest on the cobblestones against a battered downspout. I heard footsteps in my head like heartbeat, smelled something like fear and sex rising above the constant earthy funk. The little girl pulled herself back against the wall, into the shadow, a bare leg, a shoulder, a scraped and bleeding elbow all glowed in a light that came from nowhere. From the shadow her eyes appeared and I became visible in their light.

Summertime the river gives up bodies, ripe and bloated, bobbing along the shore, drifting slowly past the docks, the moored barges, the overgrown shore of the Bywater. A body decomposes in forty-eight hours in the summertime river, they say. I watched once, unseen in a murmuring crowd as uniformed men pulled from the river the body of a man in a white linen suit who had jumped from the Algiers ferry. He was wearing only one shoe, his one bare foot wrinkled and pale. The white coat and his shirt were pulled up over his head and face, his round belly exposed like an obscene moon. The men lifted him by his arms and legs and laid him onto a heavy black plastic bag and zipped it up. They loaded the black cocoon into a white truck, its lights flashing red and blue onto the dark river.

Summertime my loneliness grows heavy and settles onto me like a blanket. I walk slowly, wading towards her. The little girl in the shadows in the alley was the pale white of the man from the river, her belly a smaller round, exposed and pierced with a blue metal ring that I longed to feel between my teeth. I knelt beside her and placed my hand there, felt her warmth, a dampness, the small rising and falling between us. She made sounds, sounds from her throat, like words through a door, muffled, unclear, her sad music. I could only stare. I felt a great sadness then, something like a tear on my weathered cheek. We did not speak the same language, and her lies I realized had all been true.

Summertime lasts forever here. But then suddenly it is over and the world is visible again, edges defined, the air light and subtle. The night brings cool and the sky regains its color. As the streets grow crowded with the tourists, I stay more and more in my small room, up a narrow tilting stair, the tall screenless windows open, the ceiling fan turning slowly, its rhythmic groan hypnotic, each groaning revolution. I close my eyes and dream about the little girl, the heartbeat she beats between her legs, the hoarse cry of her voice, her painful tries to conjure up a dead woman's song. She struggled in the alley, and I held her. In the fear I felt her passion, and in the passion fear. She bit my lip and we tasted the blood between us, disappeared for a brief sweet time into the night of summer, became alive in our struggle, our pain and pleasure intermingling like blood and sweat on the damp bricks beneath us. She is gone now I know, Iowa, Ohio, or wherever. But she left here a part of her self, a smell that thickens in my mouth in the heat, a taste of summertime, the big sweet hush of the river, our decay.

Summertime but a memory, I make my way to the river. I dress in my best suit, my dark glasses, the practiced elegance of countless summers. Tonight I throw money to each mime, each busker, each young lost soul with outstretched hand. When I reach the landing, my pockets are empty. I wait in the shadows, unseen, apart from the chattering crowd, watch the ferry approach over the dark river and appear in the fog. And I hear her voice from somewhere neither near nor far, and she is singing horribly summertime, and I can taste the moment metallic and right. I move to board the ferry that will take me to the river, and into her deep dark beautiful night.

JASON WIESE

THE DIVE

IT WAS WAY OUT THERE, REALLY BEAUTIFUL. He'd snapped his legs together at just the right time and entered the river with hardly a splash. I was told later that his name was Quinn and he had been a championship swimmer. Even so, there's not a swimmer in the world who can tangle with the Mississippi in late April and live to brag about it. More than once I've seen entire trees rolling out in the channel, their stripped branches like crowds of skeletal hands reaching for the sun as the river carries them away, toward the Gulf.

I was right there when it happened because I work as a bartender on the *Evangeline*, and had picked up the afternoon shift that day. I was standing maybe fifty feet away, by the midship life-vest box, sneaking a quick cigarette with Amos the cook before cleaning up the bar. I don't think Berry was there, and Jeanette was inside, counting out the tips. Amos was throwing bits of andouille sausage over the rail for the catfish, really putting his arm into it, as if he meant to hurt them. We were wrapping up the day cruise, and I was just smoking with my eyes half closed and daydreaming about Vicky the hostess, the same old dream about an unlikely beach rendezvous, both of us frolicking in the briny surf and soothing each other's sand-chafed skin with lots of coconut oil.

I turned around when a girl screamed behind me, and there he was, standing on the rail like a carrot-topped Errol Flynn, his tie flapping. His face wasn't much like the one plastered on the walls and lamp posts around the Quarter in the months that followed, but it could be I just didn't look at him closely enough. He wasn't smiling, but he didn't seem to be unhappy either. He was just looking out at the river in a way that made me look, too, at all that angry water rushing by between us and the West Bank.

His fraternity brothers were laughing at him, chanting *jump, jump, jump,* and their girlfriends giggled behind their hands, and hid their eyes. They had rented the boat for some kind of theme party, and half of them looked liked extras from *Gone With the Wind.* A big guy in a Confederate officer's uniform looked around at everyone with a big guilty grin, shrugging as if to say "Isn't this just the craziest thing you ever saw?" There weren't any deckhands around. Dickhands, Amos called them, flinging the last of the sausage away. They were all down along the port side, getting ready to throw out the lines and tie us up to the dock. Amos took a step toward the Quinn kid and yelled at him to get his ass down from there and behave. That's when Quinn took a deep breath and launched himself. The metal rail hummed from the force of his legs.

The rest is always in slow motion. Everyone draws in their breath when he jumps and he seems to hang in the air for a long time, stretching out to reach for whatever secret he sees beneath the brown water. Then there is a slow blooming of bubbles where he went in, white on brown, that is soon torn apart by the current. I think someone has the presence of mind to throw out some life vests, orange ones with Evangeline *stenciled on them in sloppy black letters. They float on the water like toys, and the river pulls them away, too. We are shouting down at the water and the big red sternwheel is backslapping the river into a froth as Captain Charlie eases us up to the dock. I feel the bump under our feet when we touch the pilings. Amos' gold teeth flash in the sunlight, a sad smile, and when I see him shaking his head I know it's all over. One of the girls bawls in the arms of another girl, and their plantation-style dresses flare out like Christmas bells, shuddering in the breeze. Quinn never comes up. No one will see him again. Not alive, not dead, not ever.*

During the three months since it happened, I've lived through this scene over and over in my dreams. That moment of terror and elation when I realized that he was really going to do it. Where I once dreamt nightly about Vicky shaking out her long dark hair and pulling a lacy black strap off her shoulder, I see instead the cool concentration on Quinn's face, the thrilling, graceful arc of his dive. Jeanette says she doesn't know which is more sad: his drowning because of a stupid stunt, or his family's belief that he is still alive somewhere, wandering around New Orleans with a concussion, unable to remember who he is. They come down every weekend from Meridian, Mississippi, where Quinn was from, and have put up missing person posters and flyers from the Quarter all the way down to Belle Chasse. One afternoon I followed a man who I took to be Quinn's father, huge, and stoop-shouldered with reddish hair going gray. He had a canvas newspaper bag full of flyers, and rolls of duct tape. I watched him talk to policemen and bored waiters, tourist couples from Alabama and Texas, saw them all shake their heads one by one and move away, touched by the tragedy of it, probably thinking to themselves *poor bastard, glad it's not me*. I'd wanted to talk to him, but couldn't bring myself to do it; I had no idea what I would have said to him.

So the months go by, the Quinns keep their posters and hopes up, and the locals have ceased to notice them. I haven't, though. In fact, I am secretly on the Quinns' side, and hope they're right about their son. I'm glad for the mystery, in fact. I've taken to talking to him out loud when I'm by myself, confiding secrets in the dead of night. As long as he remains lost, I can imagine him wandering through the streets with me like a faithful shadow. Especially when I see those spooky posters fluttering on lamp posts and brick walls, faded by the sun and the rain. *John Allen Quinn. Will you please call home?* And his photocopied smiling face is like a gray ghost staring at me, following me down the sidewalk.

John Quinn is the least of my worries, though. My real problem is that I am becoming invisible. I'm not imagining this. In a way this has been an ongoing condition, but it seems to have gotten worse ever since that day in April, when Quinn took his dive. There are days now when it seems like no one can see or hear me. People crowd me off the sidewalks, close doors in my face, and step ahead of me in lines. I have a soft voice, and have to shout, sometimes, to be heard. Maybe it's my own fault. My friend Mark Wayne will listen to me, but I think he really seeks me out because I'm quiet, and a good audience. I almost never interrupt and I'm too polite to openly question his more fantastic stories. In short, I am as patient and faithful as an old hound, the kind that sleeps in the shade and is frequently tripped over.

I guess I just don't have what it takes to be noticed by people. I come from a very large family—good Catholics, you know—and I don't think my parents knew half the time whether I was there or not. I used to think this was an advantage, but now I know better. Nine times out of ten, my daddy calls me Michael if he sees me on the street. It's my older brother's name, but lately I've been letting it go because he doesn't like to be argued with. I've learned that whole days can pass without anyone speaking to me, beyond ordering a drink or begging my pardon. It makes me frantic. Last week I purposely held on to my rent money, just so Ruby, my landlady, would come knocking at my door, hollering my name for all the neighbors to hear.

But I'm still mostly invisible. The quiet guy in apartment 6, or a fixture behind the bar. A ghost. I thought about this when I woke up this morning. I looked around my apartment, which is small even by Vieux Carré standards, and it was like a stranger's place. I have very few possessions. Just a few books, and clothes that could belong to anybody. Some beads and doubloons from last year's Carnival. The walls are bare except for a small crucifix, which was a gift from my grandfather, and a Hibernia Bank calendar. I poked around my things for a while this morning, and it was like they were artifacts from another person's life. I discovered that I have a key on my keyring I never noticed before and can't account for, and that my library card has expired. I recited "Thomas Virgil Fontenot" (the name on my social security card) over and over again until it began to sound strange to me, a random grouping of sounds that had no connection to anything. I wondered, what if I really *did* disappear? Would anyone come looking for me? Would Amos smile his sad, golden smile? Would Vicky weep for me? Would my father paper the neighborhood with my picture for months, long after all hope had gone?

Mark Wayne and I are in Cecil's Washeteria on Esplanade Avenue. It's eleven in the morning, still a little early for Mark Wayne, but he says he can't stand waiting in line for a dryer, so we came early to beat the crowds. It's plenty warm, though, and we're sweating beneath the hum of the ceiling fans. There's no one else here but Hahn, the Vietnamese attendant, and a couple of drag queens. I've seen them around. One of them is wearing a pink silk blouse and tight jeans with pumps. He looks a lot like Dionne Warwick, but much taller, and with bigger hands. The other one, who has long hennaed hair, a halter top and short-shorts, has been talking on the phone for half an hour, and occasionally screeches "Oh my gawd, *really?*" at whoever's on the other end. I can tell this is getting on Mark Wayne's nerves. With every screech he blinks slowly and makes a big show of turning around to give the Telephone Queen a dirty look.

"It's like a police siren after a while," he says, wiping his brow and plugging another quarter into his dryer. "Not the kind of thing you wanna hear first thing in the morning, dawlin'." Mark Wayne likes to talk like he's a Ninth Ward yat because he's been living over there since he graduated high school, even though he's from Uptown, like me. He eats "ersters" and "berled" crawfish, and he'd probably put "erl" in his car, if he had one. He does a good fakey Cajun accent, too. Sounds just like Justin Wilson. "Gimme them dryer sheets, wouldya babe?" he says, tensing up as the Telephone

Queen lets off another volley of squeals and clacks his heels on the lino-
leum.

I try to toss him the box, but it sticks to my moist palm and drops to the
floor. I shrug and scoot it over to him with the toe of my shoe.

"You're not good for much, are you Tommy?" he says, bending over to
snatch it. There's a beard of lint hanging from it, and he picks it off, making
a face, and lets it float to the floor. The breeze from the fans catches it and
it goes slip-sliding along the bottoms of the dryers.

"A little lagniappe for you," I tell him.

"Uh huh." He peels off three sheets and tosses them in his dryer. "So
they'll be *extra* soft," he says. The Telephone Queen is just whispering now,
and Dionne Warwick has settled down with a magazine. There's a clatter-
ing in Mark Wayne's dryer like a loose quarter.

Cecil's Washeteria is actually one of my favorite places in the Quarter.
Hahn keeps it spic and span, and has recently put up some hand-lettered
signs above the dryers that say things like *"Ink pen in pocket leave stain forever!"*
and *"Donut feed dryer more than it can eat!"* These homey aphorisms are much
more useful and far-reaching than the mass-produced wisdom of fortune
cookies. And there's something about the whir of all these machines that
soothes my soul. Rows of washers and dryers doing their work without
complaint, asking only for a little spare change. It's deeply satisfying. I love
to listen to them and recite Hahn's wise little sayings to myself in my best
Hop Sing voice.

"Say, whatever happened to that girl you were interested in, the one on
the boat?" Mark Wayne asks suddenly. "What was her name?"

Farewell, Hop Sing. Mark Wayne has no use for washeteria wisdom. I
grab two of my tuxedo shirts out of my dryer and slip them on hangers. My
bartending uniform. I've got a couple pairs of black dress slacks tumbling
around in there, too. They're murder to wear on days like this, but shorts
and tee shirts aren't allowed behind the bar. "Vicky," I say at last. "Vicky
Delchamp." I don't really want to get him started on this.

"Like the grocery stores?"

"Yeah. Don't think there's a connection, though."

He hops up on top of one of the washers and dangles his feet. "So . . .
what happened?"

Mark Wayne has a relentless fascination for the sex lives of everyone he
knows, and makes no secret of his own, to the eternal shame of his family.
The Guidrys have a big house just off St. Charles Avenue, overlooking
Audubon Park, and I don't think they speak to Mark Wayne, or acknowl-

edge his existence. He knows, though, that my sex life is mostly theoretical, so I don't know if he's asking out of real curiosity, or if it's a polite segue into his own latest infatuation.

"All right," I say, wanting to beat him to it. "You know that poem I was writing for her? The one I wouldn't read to you?"

"Yeah?"

"Well, I finished it and mailed it to her a couple of weeks back. I got her address out of the phone book." I'm straightening out one of my hanging shirts, tugging down on the sleeves and shirttails to pull out the wrinkles. It never works, but I do it anyway.

"And . . . ?" he says. But when I look at him again I can see he's not really listening. He's looking over his shoulder at the Telephone Queen, who is aggressively scratching his behind with a red lacquered thumbnail and whispering "You're so *mean* to me. Why do you have to be so *mean?*" into the phone. Mark Wayne arches his eyebrows at me and pretends to gag. Dionne Warwick is watching him from over a folded *People* magazine. He's starting to sweat through his makeup a little, but otherwise he still looks pretty good. He'd fool you at a distance.

"I'm sorry," Mark Wayne says. "It's just I get distracted by such all. Tell me what she thought of the poem."

"I don't know," I say. I don't feel like talking about it now.

"Didn't she say anything to you? How do you know she got it?"

"I sent it anonymously," I tell him. "I don't know if she got it or not." This is a lie. Jeanette, the woman I work with on the *Evangeline*, passed on that Vicky told her last week she'd gotten something "creepy" in the mail. I didn't tell Jeanette that I was the one responsible, and I don't know if Vicky suspects me or not. One of the more prominent images is a lighthouse penetrating fog. Mulling over it now I can see how she could read it as being vaguely obscene. I've probably offended every particle of her debutante being.

"You didn't *sign* it?" Mark Wayne asks. "All that work and you didn't even scribble your little name at the bottom?" He sounds like I've told him I accidentally left a million dollars out in the middle of the street.

I don't answer, and in truth I'm feeling a little sick inside. What had seemed like a beautiful romantic gesture now seems ill-advised and doomed. Hahn should have put up another sign to warn me about this, something like *"Bad poet make good bachelor!"* Mark Wayne has got his dryer open and is rooting around in his clothes, clicking his tongue and shaking his head. I look across the room at the bulletin board next to the telephone. I hadn't noticed it before, but there's a copy of the John Quinn flyer, "Missing" printed across the top. The Telephone Queen has now removed one of his high-heeled pumps and is using it to scratch his back. It leaves red marks that stand out against the freckled white of his skin. Mark Wayne starts going on about how most of these goddamned queens have no taste at all, no sense of style or grace. But there's no real anger in it, and I get the feeling that he's mostly attentive to the sound and cadence of his own voice. I watch John Quinn rise and fall on the bulletin board under the fans. *Please call home.* "I wonder where *he* is right now," I say, hoping to make myself feel better.

Mark Wayne pauses in his tirade and looks at me, then over his shoulder at the bulletin board. "Sitting in the bellies of two hundred catfish, I expect," he says. "Fish food."

I don't reply, and I feel him looking at me.

"Say, you're not thinking he's still *alive*, are you? The Amnesia Poster Boy still at large? You were *there*, weren't you? You saw him go for his last swim."

I think to myself: *there, he's missed it.* He is immune to faith, to even the *possibility* of mystery. What's worse, he's ruining the magic of Cecil's Washeteria for me, now when I need it the most. What good are Hahn's pithy maxims and a six-foot-four Dionne Warwick in the face of this kind of skepticism and indifference? We might as well be blind, or in Shreveport.

"Excuse me," says a quiet voice. Dionne Warwick steps past us with a quick smile on his way to the ladies room. He holds his head high. It's the walk of someone who's used to being gawked at, who's always conscious of it. I stare, trying to regain the wonder, but the illusion has been dispelled.

"Don't forget to lift the seat, honey," Mark Wayne mutters under his breath. The quarter rattling in his dryer settles into a monotonous rhythm and neither of us speaks for a long time.

I have little tricks that I use on days like today to keep from slipping away completely. For example, if I can make it, without cheating, from my front gate on Royal Street through the carriageway and courtyard to my front door in exactly 21 evenly spaced steps (which is three times seven, both lucky numbers), I can feel better. When this fails, I go out in search of an omen, some singular sign that I can see and recognize. An unscripted moment. Something real. If I can see two nuns walking together from my front gate, that's a good sign. Sidewalk fights are doubly lucky; the last time I saw one of those I found a twenty dollar bill at my feet. I usually don't have to go far in the Quarter to find something. What I need is simply this: to feel, somehow, that I am alive in a particular place and time, and moreover, that I have a right to *exist* in this place and time. I need an anchor to keep me from floating away. Otherwise, the invisibility overwhelms me and I become detached from everything, a nobody, a lost and wandering shadow. It isn't enough to be attentive to the world around me, I've found. I must also be an integral part of it. If I can cross a 200-year-old courtyard in *exactly* 21 steps without trying, a courtyard that has gone mostly unnoticed and therefore unoccupied by generations of people, or both see and *recognize* the significance of nuns or midgets or bickering winos, I have validated my existence. My home town forms around me like a protective envelope, with all its sunshine and cockroaches and heartbreak. I have become a somebody somewhere, and I can go on about my business.

Today, though, it's no use. Royal Street is empty of nuns, and the 21 steps bring me to my apartment door and nothing else. Inside, I set my basket of clothes down and look around me. It is the same place I left this morning, silent and mostly bare. The calendar, the crucifix, the beads mean nothing. I lock the door, walk into the bedroom and lie on the bed sweating, watching the slow spin of the ceiling fan. "What are we going to do about this, Mr. Quinn?" I say. In my mind I again see the hump of Quinn's back before he straightens out, and the slow, mysterious blooming of bubbles he left behind. There was a message there, I'm sure, and I think that if I can just picture it in my mind clearly enough, I will know how to save myself.

Later, after dark, I'm working on the *Evangeline*. At nine o'clock the band is well into its second set of canned Dixieland, and Captain Charlie is turning us around in front of the Chalmette Tennaco refinery for the return trip upriver. It's a small crowd tonight, some trickle-over from the municipal utilities convention at the Marriott, so I don't have much to do but stand around and listen to Jeanette chomp her gum and bitch about her boyfriend back in New Iberia. Vicky is off somewhere else, probably up in the pilothouse. She'd asked me for a glass of ice water earlier, and when I gave it to her she smiled, but it was just politeness, the kind of smile that looks right through you. I had thought of my sonnet, wanting to look in her eyes and recite a few words, just enough to get a smile, a hint of recognition. But I could never do it. It's too easy to imagine her cold stare, a disgusted click of the tongue. So I did the usual thing and stood there like an idiot, pouring her water without a word. I could smell her perfume, it was like sweet olive blossoms, and see a tiny droplet of sweat run down the side of her neck. She looked through me at the mirror behind the call liquors and tucked her hair behind one ear with her fingertips. She might as well have stabbed me through the heart with one of the plastic cutlasses I use to spear martini olives and lemon wedges. After she left, I had to turn around and look, too, just to make sure I could be seen. My bow tie was crooked.

In the last hour I've set up some "Paddlewheeler Punch" and Hurricanes in souvenir glasses, and uncapped a few bottles of beer, but the drinking is slowing down. Nobody's dancing. The band goes through the motions anyway, nodding to themselves in that way old jazzmen have, like they're listening to a sermon hidden in the music. There's a big window behind the bandstand, and in the spotlights outside you can see the glittering arcs of water kicked up by the paddlewheel as it pushes us up the river. I can't listen to "Won't You Come Home, Bill Bailey" for the thousandth time, or I'll fade away completely. So I turn the bar over to Jeanette and walk back to the galley with a couple of cherry cokes. Amos usually comes out to the bar for them, but he got a peace sign shaved into the back of his head last week, and he's confined to the galley on Captain Charlie's orders until it grows out. He and Berry are back there cleaning up after the buffet.

As usual, Amos is doing the dishes. Berry's perched on the prep table doing one of his funny raps about Captain Charlie, swiveling his head back and forth, eyes as big as silver dollars. His chef's jacket is unbuttoned and I can see he's wearing a black silk shirt underneath, and a gold chain with a crucifix. "Mistah T," he says, when I hand him one of the cokes. I sit down on a stack of boxes and lean back against the wall, breathing in the steam and sweat and the smell of leftover gumbo and shrimp etouffée.

"Yo, Fame," Berry says, jerking his head up toward Amos at the sink. "Look alive over dere. Doncha know it's *pay* day?"

Amos flashes a gold-toothed smile over his shoulder at us. "I *been* knowin' it, Bee. An' tonight I goin' over by the St. Thomas an' buy me some *rocks*, and maybe some *wiggy*." He bends his knees and wiggles his head just thinking about it. He's talking about crack and ten dollar whores, the great loves of his life, and the reasons why he's always broke two days after payday. Jeanette says he's starting to act a little crazy, but I haven't noticed.

"Amos sho' do love dem rock stars," Berry says, chewing on an ice cube. "Look out."

"Amos," I say, pulling out a bent cigarette, "why do you wanna go messing with that stuff? You're just asking for trouble."

Amos doesn't say anything. I study the peace sign on the back of his head as he scrubs a bread pudding pan and rinses it out. Berry asks me if I've got another smoke, and I fish one out for him.

"I mean, half those guys are out there selling baking soda and mothballs, looking to burn somebody." I don't know if this is true. It's just something I heard somewhere. "And who knows what some of those girls have got," I tell him.

"Ain't nobody axed you nothin' about it," Amos says to the sink, hosing crab shells and rice out of a stainless steel pot. "Shit. I know *I* sho' din't."

I shrug and let it go. He's right. It's none of my business. What *could* I know about it? Berry starts his rap again, farting air out from between his lips to mark the beat, his face shining with sweat, and Amos bobs in time at the sink, drumming on it with a pair of forks. It's like they are the only two people in the room. After a while I get up and push through the door to the forward deck.

It's cooler out there, and quiet. I can hear the rush of riverwater under the bow as we glide by a Panamanian freighter tied up at the Piety Street Wharf. *La Luz.* The catwalk swings out in the breeze like a pendulum. I stand by the rail and smoke my cigarette down to the filter, thinking that I wouldn't mind going with Amos tonight, living a different kind of life for a change. There might be something to it, for all I know, spending all my money on crack and prostitutes. It could be a good, simple life, full of fellowship and good cheer. Maybe Amos and Berry could even teach me how to rap. This is so ridiculous that I have to grin, in spite of the queasiness I'm feeling inside. "What do you think, John?" I say to the darkness. "Could it work?" My voice sounds strange to me; maybe I just thought I said something. There's no answer, of course, and I glance around to make sure no one has seen me talking to myself. Then I flick the butt over the railing, watching its long arc out into the darkness until it hits the water and disappears.

After work, I don't go home right away like I usually do. Instead I walk over to the Spanish Plaza. I buy a strawberry snowball from the stand there and walk once around the fountain, looking at the tile mosaics. There are teenagers making out on the benches, shadows huddled together, and a few tourists walking arm in arm with their cameras and shopping bags. I feel like I'm hovering just off the pavement, like a strong gust of wind might blow me away forever. A gang of kids on skateboards almost runs me down as I make my way around the Canal Street ferry landing, heading toward the Aquarium and Woldenberg Park. Behind me, the downtown buildings glitter like jewels, hotel signs blinking, and the air has a creosote tang from the dock pilings. Usually these things hold me spellbound, but tonight I am immune to them. I feel as numb as a frozen fish.

I find a quiet spot on the Toulouse Street dock, overlooking the riverbend and Algiers Point beyond, and lean on the rail, resting my arms. I can hear laughter from the direction of the old Jax Brewery as I drink the dregs of my snowball and crush the white paper cone in my hand. I roll it around on my palm, and then pitch it out into the river. I can barely see it float away, a ghostlike speck in the darkness that is soon gone.

I've been spending a lot of time these past several days watching this river. The Mighty Mississippi. And here's the funny thing: I think I owe it all to John Quinn. He's the one who finally opened my eyes to it. I'd been out on this same river hundreds of times, riding the *Evangeline* seven miles down to Chalmette Battlefield and back. I'd flipped cigarette butts into it, poured leftover coffee into it, and tossed half-eaten dinner rolls in for the gulls and catfish to fight over. I'd walked along the river on the levee to and from work, and watched the fireworks explode over it every Fourth of July I can remember. But I don't think I ever really *saw* the river until that day last April. This river is an omen, maybe the most important one, and Quinn gave it to me with his dive. It's quite a bit lower now, and moving more slowly, but there's still a good current out in the middle of the channel, and in the darkness I can barely make out floating bits of junk going by. I can hear the water lapping against the pilings below me, and it sounds almost friendly. Hadn't I seen black kids swimming in this river summers ago, in the calm water below the Jackson Avenue ferry landing? What did they know that Quinn hadn't?

Pretty soon I'm standing on the very edge of the dock, next to a mooring cleat. I don't remember climbing over the rail a moment ago, though I must have done it. My mind is blank, and I feel a calmness that I haven't felt for a long time. Another moment goes by, and by the time I realize that I'd already made up my mind to do it, I've jumped out into the void.

Falling. It feels like a long time before I actually hit the surface, and then my knees suddenly buckle with an exploding sound, and water is closing over my head. It's colder than I expect, dark and very quiet. For a moment I don't fight it, and just drift in the darkness. Then I'm clawing and kicking my way to the surface, popping up like a cork. I've gulped some riverwater, though, bland and fishy-tasting, and the current is spinning me around so that I'm looking first at the underside of the Toulouse docks and then out across the river, which seems a lot wider now than it did a moment ago. My ears have filled up with water, but I seem to hear people shouting, as if from a great distance. The calmness is draining out of me now as I see the shore getting farther and farther away. I'm moving past the Jax Brewery now, and the end of St. Peter Street, heading around the bend. I start to swim, slowly at first, but then faster, harder. I keep getting mouthfuls of riverwater, gagging on it. My breath sounds ragged and panicky and I can feel my heart knocking. In my head I hear Mark Wayne's voice saying *You should've quit smoking a long time ago, dawlin'. Now you're in deep shit!* I'm measuring my life in breaths. After eight breaths I look up to make sure I'm not drifting farther out.

I'm kicking for all I'm worth now, flailing against the current, and when I look up again I think I'm making some progress toward the wooden walkways and lamps in front of Jackson Square, now drifting slowly by. Crowds of people are standing up there yelling and pointing at me, shadows backlit by moving traffic. Some are climbing down to the river's edge. I focus on their voices, and my arms slap the water like pieces of wood. Pretty soon my foot kicks something, and then I slam my knee into the shore revetment, sending a jolt clear down to my toes. I kick with my good leg and pretty soon I can reach down and feel the thick wire mesh that holds the big rocks in place against the current. I feel my finger snag something, some broken glass maybe, and then there's a searing warmth. I manage to crawl up the revetment a little farther, and I let myself be pulled out of the water by a couple of shirtless black men who smell strongly of beer and sweat.

"*Damn*," one of them is saying. "You gotta be *crazy*, be swimmin' out in dat nasty ass water! All dem chemicals an' shit." His fingers are digging painfully into my arm.

"I'm tellin' you," his friend says in my ear. My legs are weak and stumbling, but soon I'm falling into step with them, climbing up over the meshed-in rocks, mumbling about how it was an accident, how I'd been trying to reach a watch that I'd dropped. I can't think of anything else to say.

"You best let dem *fishes* have dat watch," the first man says. "Or dey gonna gobble *you* up, too!" And he laughs, a demented "*hee hee hee*" that I'll probably be hearing for the rest of my life. We get up to the Moonwalk, where there's a crowd gathered, and they turn me loose. I put my hands on my knees and cough, spitting to get the taste of riverwater out of my mouth. "Crazy ass fool," I hear someone say.

No one else approaches me, and after a few minutes of being gawked at I start walking toward the square. My shirt is transparent with water, clinging coldly to me, and my shoes are gurgling as I shift my weight from foot to foot. My hand is throbbing, bloody, and I don't want to look at it, so I clench it into a fist and jam it deep in a waterlogged trouser pocket. As I shuffle by the Café Du Monde, I can feel the stares of the people at the sidewalk tables. I don't feel bad about any of this, exactly. Something has happened to me, but I don't know what it is.

I'm halfway across Decatur Street when I notice a lemony sliver of moon hanging above the lit-up face of the cathedral. It's so beautiful and strange that I stop in the middle of the crosswalk, struck dumb. The mule carriages are lined up in a row in front of me, mules flicking their ears and stamping hooves, and the mounted statue of Andrew Jackson seems to be doffing its hat to the Pontalba buildings facing the square. The banana trees by the black cast-iron gate shudder in the breeze at the precise moment I look at them. Standing there, I feel all the streets in the city stretching out from this spot like a vast spider's web. Every one of them, and they're all mine. I'm lit up by headlights and the honking of the held-up taxis is like a hymn singing my presence to the world.

CHRIS ROSE

TIES

SOMETIMES IT SEEMS MY LIFE IS ONE LONG STRING of fetes, soirees, galas and doings. No one ever calls them parties. Parties are mundane, I guess. Parties are pedestrian. Regular people go to parties and shake hands and eat veggies and dip. My people air-kiss and eat *crudités*. I was 32 years old when I learned how to pronounce that word.

Rich people are strange, I admit. I'm learning how to be one of them. So I go to the Spring Fiesta, the Cavalcade of Homes, Opera Guild this, Junior League that, et-fucking-cetera.

Sometimes, I feel like a self-parody. Sometimes, what I'd really like to do is put on my jeans and cowboy boots and head across the river and down Fourth Street and play some George Jones on a juke box and just shoot pool and get liquor-store-robbing drunk. I never do that. Hell, I don't even have cowboy boots. And I guess I'm not very likely to win any clients over there at Rod's Rocket Inn, anyway. "Excuse me there, cowboy—could I interest you in a prospectus on a high-risk dot com IPO?" Not likely.

But it's not that bad, really. I can live this life in my sleep. I go to Samuel's on Wednesday nights and strike out with the paralegals, I go to lunch at Galatoire's Friday afternoons and suck it up while my boss makes fun of me and then pays the bill, then I kick same boss's ass in golf Saturday morning at English Turn and then, on Saturday nights, it's off to the fetes, soirees, galas and doings. That's my favorite, "doings."

All I have to remember in this life is to rotate my ties. Truly, that is all. One time, at some Preservation for Such-and-Such deal at the Pelican Club, my boss's fat-fuck partner, Phipps, reamed me in front of a group of chicks about how I'd worn the same tie to work the day before. I'm thinking A:

Who notices that kind of shit and B: I guess it's OK to be a fat fuck who wears stained ties—as long as it's not the same stained tie every day. I didn't say anything like that to him.

It's a good life, I guess, but sometimes I feel like Holden Caulfield all grownup. That's a strange thought. And you know what? I'm on the board of the Children's Museum and I don't even have any kids.

But I've strayed here. What I was starting to tell you about was what happened on my way to one of these doings one night.

I was meeting up for a party with Mickey and his new friend Angel and the night was full of possibility. I'd just met her the night before. We talked a little, laughed a little, yada, yada. It was just a quick chemistry thing, really. Eye contact, the brush against the arm, the flick of a wrist—all those body language hints that probably don't really exist but which we all cling to like life preservers.

The key to living, it often seems, is just the hint of possibility. I was very fond of Angel. Her skin was a little pasty, I admit, and truth be told, I hadn't really figured out if she was dumb, smart, artsy, racist, Buddhist, who knows, whatever. And that name. Please.

But her body was abso-fucking-lutely outrageous. Literally, I felt like her breasts were pointing at me like Uncle Sam: I WANT YOU to run your hands all over my body. Maybe it was just a push-up bra—I don't know—but I was completely unnerved by the confidence with which she pointed herself around.

I wasn't sure of the nature of her and Mickey's relationship, but with Mickey it was pretty safe to assume he was screwing her, was trying to screw her or had been screwing her. Whatever the circumstances, I knew he'd be rid of her in due time, double time usually, on to the next drama. We all have Mickeys in our lives, huh?

Anyway, we were walking past the old Tick Tock Stop on Royal Street, and there was the usual assortment of Quarter rats hanging out on the corner, smoking their generic menthols, drinking tall boys, stuff like that. Class A losers, basically.

As we walked by, one of them grabbed Angel's crotch. Honest to God. I could hardly believe it when she told us after we had crossed the street. I mean, we've all seen a million losers whistle or hoot or whatever at pretty girls, but—maybe I'm being naive here—I don't ever recall having someone tell me they had their crotch grabbed by a stranger. Well, perhaps Mardi Gras is an exception here, but that's another story.

I stopped in my tracks and turned to look back at the guy. Ugly was the first thing I noticed. Barefoot was the second. You gotta love guys who walk barefoot in the Quarter late at night, what with all those stinky curbside puddles that never seem to drain, even when it hasn't rained for weeks and the water starts smelling like dead oysters. Then there's the broken bottles and the dog shit and God knows what else. Or maybe it's just me—too much of a candy-ass to think barefootin' under the stars in the city is a relaxing lifestyle.

Anyway, one look at the guy and you could see he was an asshole. Greasy long hair, green homemade tattoos that said things like "Fuckin' A." He was wearing blue jean cut-offs and a wallet attached to a chain attached to his belt loop. He had some raggedy muscle shirt on and he was just looking at us with a drunken grin and that pissed me off.

But what pissed me off more was Mickey's reaction. Angel was ostensibly with him—at this juncture of the evening, at least—but he seemed perfectly content to shake it off and walk on. Forget about it.

Truth is, Angel wasn't even making that big a deal about it. She was shocked, I think, but maybe that kind of thing happens all the time, I don't know. She just didn't seem outraged enough and Mickey was downright pussyfooting, and meanwhile I'm cooking up a bucketful of indignation. I just don't think people should get away with that shit.

So, the incident began. And let me preface by saying I am not a fighter. I have never been a fighter. I threw maybe six punches between 6th grade and grad school put together and at least half of those were at my brother. I managed to avoid the rumble scene when I was younger. A: I think it's stupid and B: I'll tell you the truth here—I can be somewhat of a pussy. I just never thought getting my ass kicked was a valuable growing experience. What can I say? During football season, I ran cross-country.

Anyway, I walked up to the guy and I didn't really know what to do, so I said: Did you just grab her? He looked all wild-eyed at me and said: Yeah. Not a big yeah, just a "yeah" yeah, like "so fucking what?"

So we're standing nose to nose and I'm the first to give a big yeah, like YEAH? And he goes YEAH! And we trade Fuck You's and I tell you, I can imagine what this all looked like to the tourists walking by. Pathetic.

Well, he was scrawny but he had me by at least four inches and—just guessing here—he probably had a little more experience in these sorts of situations, conflict resolution not being an integral portion of his cultural portfolio. I only had a few beers before I left the house, so I was in full faculty and realized that I was out of my league here. I wimped out. I shook my head in one of those meaningful ways to communicate to him what an asshole I thought he was and how much smarter and more successful I was, and then I turned to walk away. And that's when the sumbitch jumped on my back.

He jumps on my back, banshee-style or something, and I start spinning around to shake him and Angel starts yelling "Police! Police!"—nice that she's finally getting involved—and then I shake the guy.

He gets off my back, reels around and cold cocks me in the side of the face, hits me so hard my glasses fly halfway across the street. This made me feel quite vulnerable and I'm pretty sure I went into low-grade shock.

There I had Mickey and Angel as my audience, two drunks in a doorway, a couple of tourists giving wide berth and this guy, this ridiculous crotch-grabbing man who had punched me very hard and was now crouching with his hands balled up like a street fighter in some old black and white movie.

Frankly, I was scared shitless. But when I sidestepped over to the curb and bent down to pick up my glasses, I noticed the blood on my tie, and my shirt, and realized my nose was bleeding pretty good and there I was: Committed to the act. The follow-through. Being born a male—and I hate this part—I had no choice. I had to hit him back.

Didn't I?

I'd like to tell you it was alpha male dignity that made me feel this way, or some other vestige of a boot-strap youth, but I'm pretty sure it was just Angel's tits, propping me up with a courage stronger than any shot of Jaegermeister that ever burned its way down my throat.

Also, it was my best fucking tie.

Laugh if you want to.

So anyway, it wasn't a great moment for me and I'll tell you something nobody else noticed that night: I think I was starting to cry. So I had to move fast.

The guy was just staring at me now, and I cocked my elbow and threw my balled fist between his hands and caught him square in the left eye. I was ecstatic. I simply hammered him. Honest to God, it felt like an orgasm. I hit this guy so fucking hard and I had never felt anything like it. I don't know if that sounds bad, but it's the truth.

He stumbled back three, four, five steps and I'm not sure whether the punch was that good or whether he was just so stunned that I was the one who threw it. I was so stoked by the feeling that I failed to follow through. I've yelled at enough boxers on TV to know you've got to be a closer in a situation like that, follow the punch with more punches, finish off your opponent. This clarity of thought was not with me at the time, though. I guess I'm not much of a closer in a situation like that. And that's when the situation went south.

He righted himself while I was just standing there frozen and several possible scenarios began running through my head on how this situation was going to conclude. None of them ended in my favor. And while this guy reckoned with my punch, I watched his eyes glaze over into the kind of look you might see on a man right before he mows down a schoolyard full of children with an M-16.

I turned to see Mickey and Angel pulling the door of a taxicab shut behind them and they drove off and I was thinking, I'm really fucked now. So I started running.

I ran up Royal Street, my tasseled loafers clicking like castanets, and didn't look back. I cut and weaved in and out of roaming clumps of fanny-pack-toting tourists with their red Hurricanes dribbling out of their cups and over their fat fingers. I caught one guy in the shoulder and I think I dropped him pretty hard on the sidewalk and I felt kinda bad but I wasn't about to stop and negotiate an apology.

I turned left on St. Philip and found myself in one of those cosmic French Quarter interludes—with 10,000 people roaming the Quarter at any one moment, not one of them was on this block. It was absolutely empty and still, except for an art gallery sign suspended from a balcony, waving back and forth on its thin chains, though there was no breeze whatsoever. I've seen that before and cannot explain it.

I walked gingerly down the sidewalk and came to a neon beer sign in a window and I opened the door and was in the Heartache Bar. A blast of arctic air-conditioning stung my nose which was still dripping blood, sort of welling up on the tips of my nostrils like snot when you have a bad cold. There was Mardi Gras music on the jukebox—in fucking July, can you stand it?—and a handful of folks hanging out at the bar and the pool table. I looked back out the door and down the street and didn't see the guy, so I walked up to the bar and sat on a stool, trying to look like I wasn't bleeding. I ordered a beer and the bartender brought me a cold one and a wet bar towel for my nose.

"Interesting night?" he asked me.

"Same-O, Same-O," I said, and we laughed.

He said he owned the place and his name was Denny and I told him mine and we talked a little. I drank my beer, and another, and another.

Denny asked me what happened and I told him—all except the running away part. I made it sound like the battle came to a draw and we parted ways like the dogs I see up on the levee by Audubon Park, they gnash and gnarl and nobody wins and then—what is it with dogs?—they just slink away. I made it sound like I just slinked away.

Well, Denny took this as his cue, and he went on a roll at this point, as bartenders sometimes do, I guess. He started railing on the junkies and the gutter punks and the meter maids and the niggers and the fags and basically everyone else that wasn't him, everyone who was screwing up the French Quarter and screwing up New Orleans and I've heard this rap so many times in bars and cabs and at the gym that I guess I stopped listening while he went on about it.

My loathing is compartmental. I didn't really care about the junkies and the gutter punks and the niggers and the fags; I got to stewing instead on the greaseball back at the Tick Tock. I suppose he had touches of junkie and gutter punk in him but those wouldn't be succinct descriptions. He was just an asshole, a street corner asshole, the kind you find from New Jersey to New Iberia, hanging out next to some corner store, bumming change and generally making people feel uncomfortable, usually right under the "No Loitering" sign.

And grabbing chicks in the crotch, for crissakes.

I hate these fuckers. At that very moment I realized Mickey was probably boning Angel and it could have been me riding that glory if Mr. Crotch-grabber hadn't stepped into our lives. I never did see her again. I mean, I REALLY HATE THESE FUCKERS.

I hate that guys like this can just walk into your life and mess your night up and then walk away to do it again to someone else. Over and over. This guy, this asshole, he ruined my shirt and favorite tie because you can't get dried blood out of cotton. Listen to me, a regular Martha fucking Stewart. I don't know why I know that, but I do.

And I'm sitting like some jackass in a French Quarter hole-in-the-wall listening to a dime store bigot—an honest to God Archie Bunker—and let me tell you: I AM GETTING ONE FUCKING SERIOUS PIECE OF HEADACHE HERE.

My wrist was beginning to ache, too. My brother broke his hand in a bar fight two nights before his wedding but didn't discover it until the honeymoon when it started throbbing. That's not what happened to me, but I started worrying about it.

At midnight, a relief bartender came on duty and Denny gave her the cash register keys and he turned to me and said "Take it easy" or "Don't take any wooden nickels" or something stupid like that. The bartender's name was Jill and we chatted a little. She was nice as can be but had a face like a roadmap with a lot of highway and not many rest stops along the way.

I got up the idea that I was still gonna go to the party that night, the doing-du-jour, all banged up and drunk, just to see how the society doyennes would react to a man with blood on his clothes. I would act like nothing was wrong. I'd love to see the look on fat-fuck Phipps' face when I showed up.

What the hell, I said, and paid the tab. I rolled out of the Heartache and headed for the Monteleone but turned right on Royal instead of left and I was walking in the wrong direction without really thinking about it. I went down Royal, down to the old Tick Tock.

There was a guy standing on the corner in a muscle shirt, darker than I remembered, smoking a cigarette and I was drunk and I started crying again. Why the hell do I tell you that part?

Anyway, I picked up a brick lying on the sidewalk and I walked up behind this guy and, though he seemed shorter and stockier than before, I hit him in the head with it. I hit him hard, but it didn't really carry the thrill of that punch from earlier and I had absolutely no inclination to close the deal.

The guy dropped straight to the sidewalk like a watermelon off the back of a pickup truck. I looked around and nobody was there so I turned and walked back up Royal Street to Canal, where I caught a cab home. My wrist hurt like hell and I was thinking: He deserved that. That guy ruined my night and a lot of other folks' as well, I'll bet.

At least, I think that was the guy.

On Sunday morning I got up late and my wrist felt fine, so after I read the paper I went to the gym for an hour. After that, I went to Saks to buy some new ties.

dripped absinthe française

The Old Absinthe House, on the corner of Boubon and Bienville streets, had a long cypress bar decorated with a pair of fountains adorned with brass faucets which dispensed water, drop by drop, into the emerald absinthe. The original bar moved to 400 Bourbon Street after Prohibtion where it remains along with the fountain, speckled with tiny pits from all the drops over all the years. Of course, absinthe substitutes today are free from the *Artemisia absinthium*, and the word "Absinthe" has been banished from bottle labels along with its oil of wormwood ingredient.

1 lump sugar

$1\,^1/_2$ oz. absinthe

1 glass cracked ice

Pour the absinthe over

a glass filled with cracked ice.

Place an absinthe glass or spoon over the

glass, add a lump of sugar, and slowly drip water

until the drink turns opalescent and the sugar is melted.

Stir with a spoon until frapped, then strain into another glass to serve.

TIDE OF THE SUN

"CAN YOU FEEL YOUR LEGS?"

"I don't know. I think. Well, I'm walking anyway. I am, right? I'm walking, right? Can't hardly feel too much at all but I'm walking." He carried his shadow through the green light coming out of the warehouse, back and forth, back and forth over Jim. "Dead. Feels dead as . . . Dead. Just dead. Dead as . . . Shit. Dead as shit out here, huh? The air. Even the air's dead still. But it's the humidity. It's cold and you don't even—you hear that?" He stopped. His shadow stopped. "A seagull. The lost cry of a seagull. Somewhere over there by the barge I think." His shorts began swishing behind Jim again. "Anyway, you don't even realize it's the humidity, but that's what it is. Drives it into the bone. The cold now, the emptiness too. Dead. Not like summer when there's everything in the air, like you're walking through your own piece of everything, and everything else is passing through you. Even when there's not a soul around there's still a piece of that life in the air—comfortable and warm and thick—filling your bones up. But now . . . now they just feel empty. Worse. Feels like there's this nothingness in my bones. Dead as shit."

"Are you certain you saw Leighton get out?"

"The bugs. That's part of it. Part of the emptiness in the air. They're not making their noises."

Jim's legs hung over the side of the dock, his bare chest hunched over his lap, his hair dry now. He scanned the water that separated them from the darkness of Algiers Point. He followed the business district's muted glow into the shivering lavender reflection of the sky. "You're certain you saw Leighton get out?" he asked.

"There's just the River. Its noise. That hum. Pure sound. Sounds like there's almost perfect silence out here but there's still that indescribable hum of the River. Just out of hearing's reach. Like you can almost touch it, you feel it there, but not quite. It's always there. Like air even when it's empty. I guess it doesn't matter what time of—"

"Colgan."

"What?" The swishing stopped. A tick of water dropped from the roof of the warehouse behind them. Then another. "I told you already."

"No. No, you didn't. At least you weren't making a lot of sense." He swung around into Colgan's shadow. "Let's walk. Tell me again." Jim stood. They left the two remaining pairs of shorts, crumpled and rolled, on the wharf log at the edge of the dock.

"Unless there was some guy," Colgan said, "some other guy big as a polar bear just going for a late night—or early morning, or whatever— dunk in the Mississippi, it was Leighton. He walked out up over there by the walkway."

"On the rocks? Right up to the Riverwalk? In the light and all?"

"Yup. Walked right up and just took off into the darkness. Didn't even look back."

They rounded the corner of the warehouse. A dozen large yellow disposal containers shielded them from the city to the left.

"He's probably just up at The Hole in the Wall. Why you worrying so much about him?"

"Don't you remember, Colgan? What he said last time? Right before we went back?"

"Not really. No. What? And Gillies? What about Gillies? We still don't know where Gillies is."

"Gillies didn't even go with us last time. Could be finished for all I know. Gillies doesn't worry me."

"Well, I suppose he'd make it to The Hole in the Wall. Might already be there. There. He was right over there by that nearest lamppost. I was just treading water, waiting until that skyline became familiar again. Hard to see, isn't it? Isn't it? All faded under the dark still like that. Even harder with the JAX sign all glowing in front of it, huh?"

Jim watched him. Colgan stood squinting towards the skyline. Colgan's shadow lay down behind him.

"Anyway, must have been about five minutes. Everything was still. I was just floating in a soft spot, just catching my breath, letting my eyes take it all in, and then I notice this big black blob rising out of the shadow on those rocks, like a different shadow forming up out of nothing, and it kept on coming up and up and up out of nothing until I could see it was shoulders and arms and then a head. And then he was up on the walkway, it was Leighton like a big moving piece of night. And then he came into the light, fully. No way it was Gillies. Too big. Like a polar bear. A flicker of flesh and then gone. Just vanished into the old neighborhood. *Bam*. Just walked right off . . . Listen . . .   You can just barely hear the waves below us . . . The River's sound, more than just sound, a rhythm, one you can *touch*, lapping below us . . ."

"Jesus, Colgan. Your legs. They're dark blue."

Colgan looked down, expressionless. "Huh. So they are."

Four train tracks. A parking lot. The arch of the empty French Market. Then the corner store. Jim told Colgan to stay put.

It was empty. A single rack filled with Zapp's Sweet Potato Chips stood in the center of the concrete floor. There was one silver Klondike Krunch lying on the bottom of the cooler to his right. Along the opposite wall were four shallow shelves holding just two of everything from diapers to cream corn, each item neatly placed a few inches from its partner.

"Does this look like some goddamn poolside bar at your country club?"

Jim swung around. She stood less than five feet tall behind the register. Her pink eyes flared out of her white face, haloed by thick white dreadlocks wrapped into a ponytail.

"I guess Lois is gone," he said.

"Boy, you can't be coming in here dressed—or *un*dressed—like that. What the hell is you thinking? *No* Lois don't work here no more. She don't own this place no more. No more since last summer. What the hell is you thinking?"

"I just want two of those pickled eggs and a fifth of Heaven Hill."

"Ever heard of no shirt, no shoes, no *shit*?"

Jim placed the crumpled bill on the counter. "Two eggs and a fifth—"

But she was already moving, still shaking her head. The bottle clanged against the others. A man's muffled laugh came from under the counter where she had appeared from.

She put the bottle next to the register, rolled up her left sleeve and stuck her arm down into the large pink jar. "Most people aren't gonna be so nice to you here, you know that? They're not gonna pay you any attention at all." She came up with two eggs, tremendous in her tiny fingers, just as white. Two drops of vinegar hit the counter.

Jim took the eggs. "That would be more than I could ask for," he said.

"Jesus. They're like big black mummies someone forgot to stick in a pyramid somewhere."

Jim turned, put his finger to his mouth even though Colgan was whispering.

They walked on. The long, shapeless, slowly shifting mounds were laid out in rows on either side of them. The River stretched out behind and below them, the red JAX Beer sign high above them, enormous. Ahead they could see an edge of the Upper Pontalba, the peaks of the Cathedral lit over the Square.

Two were sitting against the railing to their right. Jim held up a silent hand in greeting and then the bottle in the other, already a third empty. He could see the whites of their eyes, blinking, unmoving, as he walked towards them and crouched within arm's reach.

He swung the bottle like a gentle pendulum in front of them. "It's all cool," he whispered. "We're cool. Just came to make a little trade."

The two men stared through him, breathing consciously, blinking at the River and the darkness and the little cars passing high and far over the GNO Bridge.

"Hey man, I said it's all cool. We just need some clothes, that's all."

Then there was a quick, muffled whistle.

The last man in the row along the wall was propped up on an elbow, beckoning with his other hand. Jim and Colgan walked over.

"Don't you boys worry 'bout them. What you got there?" Jim showed him the bottle of Heaven Hill. The man took it, unscrewed the cap, sniffed, and handed it back to Jim. "That's liquid crack," he said. "Best motherfuckin' whiskey made. Won't drink none 'til it's light out though. Don't never drink 'less the sun's out."

"Look man, we just need some clothes. Two shirts, two pairs shoes," said Jim.

The man paused, eyed them. "Where the shit y'all come from? And what the shit you doing wearing no clothes but them trunks in this here cold-ass winter morning?" One of the dark mounds nearby shifted, let out a slurred groan. The man lowered his voice. "This might be the deepest deep south, but we still got the weather ya know."

"We came up from the bottom of the Mississippi. Just got in."

The man started laughing and then wheezing as he tried to muffle it. "Alright, that's your bullshit. Ain't gots to tell me if ya don't want." He propped himself up and then stood. "I pity the fool that messes with that River though." He walked about several paces over to a trash can, rummaged through it. He returned with a large yellow potato sack slung over his shoulder.

"You boys been good this year?" He wheezed some more. "Let us see here what we got here." He untied the knot and peered down into the darkness of his bag. "My-oh-my." He shifted through the contents, feeling through it all with one hand. "Nope. Nu-uh. Well. . ." He lifted out a black sweatshirt that said *Cape Cod*.

Jim took it and held it up. He tossed the sweatshirt to Colgan who put it on.

"Yup. That'll warm your freezing ass up a bit," said the man.

"Not like this bottle's gonna warm yours," Jim said.

The man plunged his hand back into the sack.

"Just a tee shirt," said Jim. "No holes. No stains."

"Hell man, you might be able to get that there bottle anytime of night here, but clothes? Good luck. I look like Wal-Mart? You can take your frigid ass out to Harahan if you want that. Closest place open now. Twenty-four hours too. Just catch the bus on—"

"Just give me something decent."

A smile lit on the man's face as he sifted through the contents. "You boys from back east, huh?"

"D.C. originally. He's from Pennsylvania."

"D.C.? Wherebouts?"

"Northeast."

"The city, huh. Most folks says they's from D.C. and actually they from Maryland or Virginia in one of them monster-ass suburbs they got over there. They's got suburbs bigger than most cities and enough to fill their own state too. Should call it the fifty-first state of 'Right Outside of DC.' All they's got here is river, lake, some swamp. Ain't gonna build no suburbs there." He stopped his hand, contemplated, but then continued, "Yeah I go up to D.C. once a year. Every summer nine years now. Just to go see that Vietnam Memorial."

"You were over there?"

"Vietnam? First Cav, Bravo Company. Bet your ass. I don't really see what so special 'bout that memorial though." He was no longer whispering, but spoke in a tone so low it was just barely audible. "Some girl comes up with this idea just to put our names on this slab of black rock. Hell, most of 'em already got their name on some gravestone back home any-

way. Just fifty-eight thousand, two hundred and twenty-six names. No statues. No nothing else. But they got many people going."

"*Our* names?"

"Yeah. Ain't gonna believe this shit but they got my name up there.
Merton Womack. No bullshit. Give me one hell of an ass kick first time I
seen it. They got me in there for that day we got hit on the way to Hue.
February tenth. That's how I found my name. Walked into an ambush, took
out the rest of the platoon. Matter of fact, them're most of the names on
the wall for that day. February ten, sixty-eight. Wasn't more than a couple
seconds and the other twelve were gone. Got hit too. See?" He lifted his
long plaid shirt, showed Jim a small tangle of flesh on the otherwise smooth
skin of his ribs. "I dropped belly down in that rice paddy, sure I was gonna
be dead. When finally I didn't hear no more I got up and I was Flash fuckin'
Gordon, the mofo with the lucky mojo that day, all the way back to camp.
They had to leave the bullet in me, least of my troubles though. And now
they got me engraved up there right along with all the rest."

His arm worked back and forth, deeper and deeper into the sack.

"So I tried writing them government people in the Park Service over
there. Told them I'm alive! I'm alive! Took a Polaroid of me with the newspaper date in it and signed this letter and everything. But then I go back the
next year and there it still is. Wrote 'em again, and again next year. Ain't
did no good. None at all. So now I given up. Guess they figure it would
mess the whole thing up if they went and scratched a name out. Hell, ain't
like it's actually a statue or big-ass fountain like a real monument or nothin'.
Just a big 'ol list of all us who dead. 'Cept me, of course."

Jim watched his arm, waiting. Colgan turned to look at the lights of the
GNO bridge sprawled out over the river. Somewhere off in the business
district birds chattered, hushed in their distance.

"But I tell you, I still feel it right here." He tapped that side of his chest
with a long yellow fingernail. "That bullet never let me forget how lucky I
was. Once in a while, gives me a taste of that burn I felt when I got hit.
Comes and goes."

He tapped his chest twice more, slow, then put his hand back on the
bag, holding it up as his other hand continued to sift.

"So anyways, I given up with them Park people. Now I go back there
once every summer, from no matter where I might be, just to see my name
carved up there, gives me one hell of an ass kick. Nice to jump on a freight,
tear through the summer for a thousand miles. But ain't nothin' better
than an ass kick."

He started wheezing again.

"Folks don't mind me no attention neither. Feels like they been ignoring me ever since I got back from over there. There I am laughing in front of that big 'ol black wall. They figure I'm one of them damned nutcase homeless bums they got up there in D.C. One of those dudes they had to let outta St. Elizabeth mental hospital 'cause it got so overpacked a while back. Sometimes I try to tell them that's my name there. Then they sure I's crazy as a loon and just keep on ignoring the hell outta me."

He was still wheezing when he finally tossed the crimson tee shirt to Jim who was within arm's reach. He put it on. When the man's shoulders quit jumping up and down and his breathing steadied, he gestured at Jim's feet. "What sizes?"

"Eleven and a half, ten." The man sat down, removed his shoes, and handed them up to Jim.

"There's twelve."

It was a pair of fairly new black Saucony sneakers.

"Can't complain about these," said Jim.

"Don't sweat it dude, I get those easy, have another pair in a couple hours. Want 'em red anyway."

He walked over to one of the sleeping men and unlaced the man's boots which protruded from his tarp, removed them one after the other, slow and quiet. He tossed them to Colgan who just barely caught the second one before it went over the railing. He walked back over to Jim. "Now what I don't get easy, least not without paying, is that stuff."

Jim handed him the bottle. "Jim. This is Colgan."

The man shook Jim's hand. "Alright. Alright, Colgan," he said, signaling. "Like I said, Merton Womack. Now you boys look like new men. Whole new men. And I guess that about concludes our business this morning."

And it was morning.

The lights from all the lampposts along the Riverwalk had shrunken back into their bulbs. The lights from the GNO Bridge were gone altogether, replaced by two dull, overlapping steel bridges. A blurred halo arched over the riverbend beyond Algiers Point.

And then there was the noises of the others—the shapeless masses that lined their path, groaning, growing into form, elbows, arms, bodies—stretching and yawning and sitting up, wriggling free of their blankets and bags, a sluggish chorus, their eyes aching into consciousness, the weight of day, blinking until they became relaxed. And they breathed in the light. And then the sun. A crimson yolk. Whole new men. Time to get going.

*   *   *

"Look." Colgan pointed up. "It's like a thousand little tiny pinpricks in that gray sky. You can't tell where they are—if they're just spots like atoms floating over your eyeballs or if they're all the way over there on the Westbank. Sparrows probably. There they go, look. Broke apart." He stopped. "Wow. Dissolved right up into the sky."

Jim turned down the stairs along the side of Jax Brewery. Colgan followed, still looking up.

"Man, Jim. You know that isn't really much of a sky up there. It's like… It's like it's so empty the sunlight can't even shine on it. The sun can't do nothing but burn that hole into it there at the riverbend like a blood blister under the sky's gray skin. Someone needs to let it out. The sky's just gray with a few of them gray-blue clouds tearing through it. Not like the summer when you got that deep, deep blue dawn sky, so deep it starts behind your eyes, and shoots out past the moon, through its little shreds of clouds, red then pink then orange then yellow then the final, clean, bone-white clouds of a day, naked in the day's full light. And that same blue air, it tears the colors out of everything. Makes the banana trees shine, fluorescent. But not now. Now they're just the color of banana trees."

They turned around the park, Colgan a pace behind Jim. "Now there's not even a breeze. There's just this skeletal light that balances between the gray stones of the Square and the soft khaki of the Cathedral. That's the problem, Jim, this December light, it's too weak, or maybe too greedy, it'll only fill the air that it shines through, up there at the top of the Cathedral, see. But there's not anything left over for its shadows, let alone this morning shadow of the curve of the world. Let's get our cards read, what do ya say?"

Jim looked over at her. She had a single small collapsible table in front of her, its top covered with a red paisley cloth. A wooden sign, waist-high, sat next to her. Her eyes seemed to be following behind them, searching for something there, but there was nothing. He kept walking.

"What do ya say, Jim? Won't be but twenty bucks for the both of us." They passed the Presbytere on the left. Pigeons flapped down into the square across their path. "Damnit Jim. Here she is, pretty name like Angelane, the only other living soul on Jackson Square this early in—What?"

Jim looked back ahead, still walking. "You should know. And we need to get over to The Hole in the Wall. Now. It's already late enough. Maybe too late. Did you notice she only had one leg under that dress?"

"Yeah, so?"

"She was just sitting there, all alone, one little table, that sign, and herself. No crutches, no wheelchair, no nothing."

"Maybe that's her one ability. You know how they say all real tarot readers have one special magical ability?"

"Sure. Hers is hopping."

Balconies and galleries framed Chartres Street and the shadow it was under.

"You see? Do you? See what I'm talking about," Colgan exclaimed, walking faster now, trying to keep up. "Look at the houses. Now if this was the summer and there was the blue morning light, that cobalt that sticks in the air all by itself with no need for weather, thick, thick like swimming in it, like swimming in everything the River is somewhere else, somewhere where it starts, where it's clean, then those houses would explode their colors, the reds and pinks and purples and blues. No room for white in that place, in the summer. Now we've just got this pallor, the white of the air up there at the tips of those houses with the sun, and then there's the black of the River underneath. That's what we have left now. And we walk through the gray between. But if August was here it would pull these colors out into itself, all the drastically different colors, as vibrant and different as their architectures. But now it's just this pale thin air and the colors—"

"—and the colors just sit their on their paint," Jim said. "They are the paint, only paint and not light. Just paint on the brick, wood and stone, as plain as the cars that dribble down the streets in the day."

Colgan looked down, searching for an expression, still a half pace behind him.

"Colgan, this is all I hear from you anymore. Again and again and again. The same things, the words even. All the same. Complaining about the winter in the air. And it's all you've even seen in eleven years." A bus shot up Decatur Street and Chartres trembled.

"I'd like the summer again, Jim. I'd like to stay here, have a place here long enough for change." He looked up again, now a full two paces behind Jim. "But I'll take this, because even this is still beautiful. I just have to tell it. Someone somewhere has to tell it or we fade, like we've already faded... The sky's gray skin. Someone needs to let it out." He closed his eyes tightly, shook his head, then looked at the back of Jim's crimson shirt.

"I am. Jim, I am. Like letters on paper, syllables' rhythm in air. We need to keep them tucked between the air. It's part of the little we have left of us. Without a voice sound is just a letter. I want to be more than another piece of sound moving through hollow December light along life's margins. But even if it has to be the margins, I want to make a place there, just small enough for me, and this is how I can. Even in this winter. Even here now, because it's all beautiful, Jim. Don't you see? Look at what we're walking through. The shallow shadow of this whole neighborhood, itself without shadows until the light up there falls down into it under our feet and everything's naked in the day's full light. Don't you see? It's all still so beautiful. As—"

"I know, Colgan, I know. *As all of everything.* I don't need to see it anymore."

The Cathedral bells rang twice. Quarter past seven.

"Motherfucker. Like clockwork. Santa must kick your asses out of his sleigh right over this place every year."

Tom Tamilio was a big man. His black-rimmed glasses, forever crooked, were held together with white tape at the bridge of his nose.

"Maybe one year he'll give you skinny fucks some decent shirts and shoes."

Jim slapped Tom Tamilio's hand from across the bar, catching it for an almost painful handshake.

Colgan shook his hand next. "Where y'at, Tom?"

"How's Gillies? Leighton around too?"

"Damnit man, you just answered *our* questions." Jim said as he sat at the bar. "This is no good."

"Well, good to see your shorts were still there anyway. One of these years you really oughtta think about putting some money into some shirts and shoes instead of getting that raggedy crap."

Jim glanced around the bar, as though expecting us to be there anyway. He cursed again under his breath, then looked back at Tom Tamilio. "No space. We only have about this much of a metal pipe to keep this stuff in. Besides, don't need them. Just shorts and some cash. A man can do just about anything if he starts off with his loincloth and a bag of coins."

Three snaps later Jim and Colgan and Tom Tamilio were holding Budweisers. Jim watched mist float out of the bottle mouth. "Least you're keeping them cold this year."

"As cold as you two dead sons of bitches." The three bottles clanged together. "To old friends who never get older!" They all pulled. Three shot glasses, tiny in Tom Tamilio's fingers, hit the bar. He filled them to the brim with Early Times. "To Santy Claus!"

"Forget Santa. Haven't done anything good anyway," said Jim. "Actually I haven't done anything. Here's to you getting some business today, Tom."

"Heck, *I'm* drinking to Santa Claus," said Colgan while Jim's then Tom Tamilio's glass thudded the dark wood bar.

Jim looked around the empty space again, the pool table alone in the center of the wide cement floor, the far wall covered in Miller High Life posters, the three obligatory video poker machines. There was the figure of an old man, almost completely transparent, sitting in front of the right machine about ten feet from the door, small, hunched, his head almost in the screen. He was constantly, monotonously jamming his thin forefinger onto the machine's monitor. He would pause to inhale his cigarette and put it back onto the ashtray between the machines which all displayed zero credits and flashed the different poker games they offered. "Residual?"

Tom Tamilio looked up. "Yeah, man. Been here about two, maybe three months. It's from this dude Alvin. Alvin or Albert or Alfred or something. Never talked much. Anyway, he used to play mornings. Tuesdays, Wednesdays, Fridays. Only that machine. All morning long, right through shift change. Eventually started asking us for money, a dollar or two, anything. Always sure he could get his money back. When he started bothering customers about it we eighty-sixed him. This thing started up a couple weeks later."

"Well, least he's not losing his money anymore."

"Wish he was, man. Those things make more than the bar."

There was a soft strip of gray morning light spilling from the doorway along the floor. Jim watched it eclipse into the bar's darkness under her footsteps. "Aww Christ," he groaned under his breath. "Here comes the poor man's psychiatrist." He swung back around to face his bottle.

She walked in, waved to Tom Tamilio, and stood at the bar to their right.

"Damnit Colgan, you shouldn't even have made eye contact with her," Jim mumbled.

"Where y'at, girl?" Tom Tamilio said, walking over to her.

"Where else would—" She paused. "Is that—Yes. Leningrad 1942."

They all looked up at the television.

"The Road of Life." She stood silently captivated, expressionless. "Lake Ladoga froze and they drove over it. It was their only connection to the mainland. They were able to get some supplies through the siege."

"Oh yeah. And when it thawed they tried to ferry people out. Open targets for the Luftwaffe," said Colgan. "But a lot of them still got out that way. Through the broken ice. Bet they were happy to be someplace where they didn't have to be lucky just to feed their kids pancakes made of paint and glue fried in engine oil. We've seen this one a few times." It was one of our favorites.

"Damnit," said Tom Tamilio. "What the hell kind of thing is this to show on Christmas? Glue pancakes ain't nothing. Here we are supposed to be thinking about roast turkey and dressing and potatoes and cranberry freeze when they were chopping their kids up for food. These History Channel sons of bitches trying to ruin my appetite?" Tom Tamilio flipped to the coverage of some church service. He walked over, leaned across the bar to Lane. "Anyway, how are ya sweetie?"

She kissed him on the cheek.

"Any luck last night?" he asked.

"Enough, I guess. The Square was pretty empty though, got lonely out there."

Tom Tamilio filled a plastic cup with a mix of cranberry and grapefruit juices, no ice.

"And you Tom?"

"Wouldn't do any good to complain. This here's some friends, from out of town you might say." He winked at her. "Jim and Colgan."

Colgan held his hand out. "Angelane, right?"

"Lane will be fine." She held her hand out to Jim. "Lane."

"Yeah." He looked across the bar, into the mirror. Colgan looked down.

She dropped her empty hand from midair. Her lips curled like a Cheshire with a joke all its own, yet she wasn't smiling. But Jim didn't see that.

The three of them sat in their silence. The soundless procession marched down the aisle of the church. Tom Tamilio walked by the television with two cases of Miller High Life. He stocked them and went to the back again, ducking under the low door frame, disappearing into the darkness. The day lay soft and straight out of the entrance along the concrete, brighter now, still blurred.

Lane walked over to Jim, whispered in his ear, "Can I show you something?"

"Look man, I don't know what your gig is, but I sure as hell am not interested. Save it for someone else. Someplace else."

"No gig. Just a little something. It's right back there. Won't take but two moments." She made a tiny cross over her heart with hardly a motion, a flicker of her fingers, the black nails. "Promise." The television screen faded into a stained glass window, the image of some bearded saint.

"Goddamnit. What is it with you people? I've never met a person who lived on the stones of that Square who didn't want to bother you. Carry a purse, at least pretend you have money."

"I think it's something you should see." Her tone remained gentle, indifferent. "Won't take but two moments."

Jim turned and looked towards the narrow corridor that led to the bathrooms and a small backroom, an entrance to the courtyard closed for winter.

"What is it?"

"Won't take but two moments. It's a special something."

"Look—"

"Two moments," and she started across the room towards that dim corridor.

Jim rolled his eyes at Colgan, sipped his Budweiser. He watched Lane's figure become a shadow in the corridor. He stood and followed. They passed the bathrooms on either side, a pay phone and then came out into the small back room. He saw something in the corner. There was one light bulb, hanging on by a wire from the stained ceiling, it flickered twice. There was a girl.

He stood next to Lane. "Annabel..." He started towards the girl. "Well what— We didn't know you were back here. How—" He stopped again. The light hung between himself and the girl, barely higher then her head, inches from his own. "What happened?"

"Last May," said Lane. "Car accident. They had been engaged for two months. I wanted to show you before you said something."

Annabel met his stare with oblivion, her eyes dry, unblinking. There was a single, hardly visible tear drop halfway down her left cheek. It was the one thing that shone light in the corner, a pinprick reflection, frozen.

"Annabel?" He spoke softly, leaning further towards the girl. "Christ. Why didn't he say anything?"

"He doesn't, to just about anybody. She was his heart."

"He knows she's here?"

"No. Tom can't see her. Like some people can't see you, just as you guys can't see all of them. She's not a residual or anything, but she's not really cognizant either. She's in-between. She comes and goes. She watches Tom. That's it. Every shift. She's here just before he gets on, disappears as soon as he leaves." Annabel's left pupil was blown, whole black against the white. A thin ring of her violet iris framed the other pupil, dilated under the small yellow bulb. "This is what goes on between your visits."

Jim reached out, touched the face, the skin, soft, cold. The tear was hard. Annabel looked into his eyes with her one, tilted her head slightly. "Why is she back here?"

"I don't know, she moves around the place. Could be because you guys came in, I know she knew you. She's my sister."

Annabel's eye shifted to Lane, then to the corridor.

"Your friend, Colgan, should he know? I realize she knew him but—"

"No. I don't think he'll even remember her. He knows very little anymore."

Lane looked to Jim, then behind him. "I hadn't noticed that. You don't even have a shadow."

Still gazing into Annabel's violet, he put his arm back to his side. "Maybe someday things will stop surprising us."

After a time, Lane said, "Look, you go back out. Tom will wonder what we're doing. Like I said, he doesn't know. I'm going to stay with her for a bit."

"What're you two up to?" asked Tom Tamilio.

"She's making a call."

"Anyway, like I was saying man," he continued, leaning across the bar towards Colgan, "it was just long enough to lull me into another goddamn sense of false security."

"And so who was it this last time?" asked Colgan as Jim sat next to him.

"Ooh man, it would make your ass cry, man. This little mulatto girl. Skin like a double mocha cappuccino." He took a last pull from his Budweiser and tossed it halfway down the bar. It smashed into a trash can. "But a red head, I mean a *real* red head!"

"No kidding."

"Wavy long red hair, down to about here. One dimple right here when she smiled. Quite a little box. Had an ass 'n tits that musta' missed Physics class the day they were teaching 'bout gravity. When she was walking up all those stairs 'head of me, I'm telling you, this bitch could kill your whole family with that butt. It was the third date, man. I finally get her up into that fourth story apartment of mine and *bam* they do it again. 'Nother round fellas? What I just don't get is why they gotta pull this stuff with the ones I really care about. Those I don't even give a damn about, the Thibodaux Trio are nowhere to be seen." He opened three bottles, put them on the bar, and tossed Jim's half-empty one into the trash can. "Hell, they would have been doing me a goddamn favor scaring some of 'em away—wouldn't have to see 'em in the daylight. But *no*, they wait 'til I get this perfect little box up there."

"So how'd it happen?" Colgan asked.

"Four a.m. I'm sound asleep," he took a long pull from his beer and rested his elbow back on the bar. "Hadn't slept that well in weeks. Next thing I know she's bent over me yelling at the top of her lungs '*Go away now! Go away now! Get out of here! Get out of here! Out! Out! Out!*' Scared the living crap out of me. There I am still half asleep, thinking she's yelling at me. Me! Thought I must have done something real crazy in my sleep and she's so upset she's trying to kick me out of my own goddamn bed. Thought maybe I'd lit up the mattress with all them beans I had eaten. But then I knew. Felt it in my bones. I looked up and sure enough there they were. Sons of bitches."

"All three?"

"All three. Right there, man. There's old Jambalaya Jimbo, standing right next to the bed. Just looking at us. No shirt, nothing. Great big nasty belly sticking out. Just staring, the fat son of a bitch."

"That's gotta be scary."

"Oh hell, Jimbo's just a big old black dude. He's even kind of jolly look-ing if ya know what I mean. No, well, I guess you don't. But his real prob-lem is he's got no manners. None. Son of a bitch doesn't even know to wear a goddamned shirt when he's never met someone before. Just that hat and those horizontal-striped pajama-looking pants. And personal space—hell, those gnarly, thick, black, belly button hairs of his were a goddamned inch from my nostrils. Thank the good Lord you can't smell them sweating, cotton-picking, chain-gang-working sons of bitches or I'd send their asses right back to Parchman Farm faster than . . . Let them roam around there for eternity all I care . . ."

Jim looked at the waves of grain in the bar.

"And the other two?" Colgan asked.

"That's what *really* got her—Jones and Pershing. Jones was kneeling down by the foot of the bed just laughing his ass off like you've never seen. He's blind, you know. Can't see a thing. Doesn't even have pupils, just big white eyeballs."

"All white?" asked Colgan.

"All white. It was maniacal. Just laughing so hard he had his hands on his head, mouth wide open, chest heaving. We couldn't hear him laughing of course, which just made it all the weirder. Then there's Pershing with his big old skull of a head standing on top of my damned bedside table. Those long crooked twisted-looking feet of his with those toe nails that are all green and ingrown right where my alarm clock should have been. Thick rusted chains 'round his ankles. I couldn't even see what time it is. He was leaning over us, looking down at us, completely still except for that head. He was moving it like this."

"Jesus," Colgan said, watching Tom Tamilio.

"Just like this. Back and forth. Back and forth. Each ear almost touching its shoulder. Over and over again. Back and forth. Completely steady. Like he was possessed of something awful."

"Would've scared the hell out of me too."

"Well, sure got her panties in a ruffle. Or would have if she had any on. She was trapped in bed—walls on two sides and dead chain-gang dudes on the other two, screaming all sweet fucking Jesus. I turned the light on and they disappeared and so did she after about thirty seconds. Why is it that women are always so damned good at seeing 'em in the first place? Just like kids. Most grown men don't even notice one when it's looking up their nostrils. 'Nother cran and grapefruit, Lane?"

"I'm fine. Thanks." She climbed onto the stool to the right of Jim.

"But ya see, I figure if I tried to get rid of them, and actually succeeded, it would just make way for some other house-spook or spooks—"

"Especially with all the history of the Almonaster."

"There's gotta be all kinds roaming through those big old apartments. And who knows what the hell I might get if I kicked these sons of bitches out. Janie, this other honey I was seeing a few months back, she used to say it wouldn't be so bad if it was just a little girl or an old lady or something. No way. Them dead little girls freak the living bejeezus outta me. There's always some demented story with them. My buddy Paul had this one that had been sexually molested by her mother and eventually shut up in the attic with nothing to drink but her own—You get the idea. Then she died. That's the story anyway."

"Jesus."

"So here's this little blonde girl wandering around his apartment with limbs skinnier than bone, eye sockets all sunken in. You think I want one of them hiding in the closet when I grab a pair of jeans first thing in the morning? Even the healthy-looking pretty little girls, there's still always some story behind them—disease, neglect, murder, freak accident. It's all sad and it's all scary. And the old women—the problem with them is that they're just like cats. They do what they want and half the time what they want is just to annoy the living hell out of you.

"I knew one chick who had this old bat that would move things around while this chick was at work. She was scared to all sweet Jesus the first time she came home and found her crucifixes hanging up in the kitchen instead of the living room. It wasn't until two days later when she was cooking up some noodles that she turned around and saw that old lady standing in the corner beside the refrigerator—scared her so bad she spilled the pot all down her leg. Third degree burns all down here. Now that's a pain in the ass. Or the crotch." He threw his head back in mock laughter, shot Jim a glance, then looked back at Colgan.

"But you see, the point is that at least you know where you stand with the Thibodaux Trio. Really they're quite harmless, maybe a little stupid, but harmless all the same. As far as house-spooks go, they aren't that bad. They can't be hiding in any closets or behind refrigerators or anything. Hell, Jambalaya Jimbo's bigger than any refrigerator I've ever seen anyway. And as soon as they're up to something you can hear the floor creaking below their big black asses immediately. No surprises. And surprise is just about the only thing they got to harm you."

Jim turned on his stool, looked over to the corner. Yellow flashes from a video poker machine bounced mute off the crumbling brick wall, making Annabel's figure into a staccato silhouette.

"What about last night?" Colgan asked.

"Yeah, I know, man. But that's really pretty rare. It's only 'cause I was sleeping so damn soundly that they managed to creep up like that. They just wanted to check out that little mulatto box—pardon me Lane. No doubt that's all it was. Now what the hell Pershing was doing with his head I just don't know. But it couldn't have been that big of a deal."

"You know Tom, it's no wonder you got no customers in here," said Jim. "You carry on like this, you should be paying *them* just to listen to *you*."

"Fuck *them*. Anyone who walks into a bar and thinks they can unload their day's, week's, life's sorrow onto some poor barkeep in exchange for a dollar tip can go to hell, far as I'm concerned. We can't be the bearers of the whole world's problems."

"If you could, you'd be a rich man at a dollar a pop," said Jim.

The phone rang in the hallway. Tom Tamilio went around to get it.

Lane bent over to Jim, whispered in his ear, "Your hand. It's not even cold. It feels like nothing."

Jim looked down. His fingers were tracing a steady line back and forth over her skirt, over the thigh that had been missing before, the stubborn firmness of the prosthetic.

Tom Tamilio came storming back around the bar. "Well, Leighton's up at the Babylon. Said he needed to take care of something, had some bones to pick. Said just to let you know and he'll come down here when he feels like it. I haven't seen the big son of a bitch in a year and he says he'll come down here when he *feels* like it."

"Gillies?" Jim asked.

"Didn't say anything about him."

"I'm going to have to go up there."

"Wait a bit. Have another." Tom Tamilio cracked the tops off three more bottles, refilled the shot glasses. "Still want nothing, Lane?"

"Nothing is fine. Thanks, Tom."

"Can't do it. Put it on ice, Tom." Jim stood. "Colgan, you stay here. Just in case Gillies shows, keep him here until I'm back."

"Bad luck to be the last man to leave the bar anyway," said Colgan. "It's warmer in here too and I guess I'll do your shot for you."

"I'll come with you." Lane stood up. "I need to walk." She waved to Tom Tamilio and then followed Jim through the soft light across the floor and out of the bar into the day.

They turned left. She walked steadily, naturally, perfectly. The tips of the roofs across the street glowed sunlight. "It's even quieter than Ash Wednesday," she said. Her fingers hooked themselves through Jim's, her pulse into his palm. "His legs are blue, you know."

"Sure. And you don't even have a leg. Where was that thing earlier?"

"The prosthetic? Away. It's more comfortable to sit without it. But sometimes I need it so people have something to see."

There was a man on the opposite corner coiling a long hose. Water rolled around his feet, over the curve, into the sloped street. The sidewalk beneath him was freckled with light even though the sun was not there yet.

"Maybe someday things will stop surprising us," she said. They crossed the street diagonally and stepped underneath a balcony that slanted sharply to the sloped curb below them. "No, my leg's baking in a family tomb, above ground, out in Old Metarie. Until May six next year. One year and one day, just like a body. On May sixth they'll open it up, sweep out the dust, and put it in the lower compartment with our mother and father and Annabel and all the rest."

"What is it they call that? How you could feel my fingers? Feeling as though you still have a leg attached?"

"Phantom sensation."

"Like in Moby Dick."

"Yup. It wasn't until the Civil War that they started to take it seriously. Dr. Weir Mitchell documented cases of soldiers still able to feel their amputated limbs—feel *with* their amputated limbs—like they were still there, like they could move them, even tried to stand on them."

He looked at her profile—her upper lip protruding, unbalanced faintly over the lower one. The slight chin ascending into a sharp jawline. The tall, close nose hanging below a hazel eye. The full dark eyebrow.

"We were walking through the Saint Thomas Housing Project on our way here," she continued to look straight ahead, far away. "Three in the morning. There was nothing, no one there. It was after they had torn down the whole development and were rebuilding it, the roads supposedly shut off. No nothing but a little crescent moon through the clouds and Annabel and I dancing back and forth across the street, dancing to that little crescent moon. There was a concrete barrier to the left. I heard it coming fast, loud, and got over to the side along the barrier. I heard Annabel behind me. A thump. I turned and then there was only a scratching, his fender scratching a little path along the concrete barrier right below me. I saw the driver move by me, someone in the passenger seat too, a flickering instant, frozen, his mouth yelling, cheering, his eyes smiling into my own and then they were past and the scraping had passed from below me. I remember seeing them drive away. Straight and steady as an arrow. Then I fell."

A bronze-colored man, not more than four feet tall, was scrubbing the sidewalk in front of some generic Cajun/Creole restaurant with a long broom. They walked into the street to avoid him and turned left on Royal.

"When I woke there was light. There was blood. There was a whole pool of it. I had been sleeping in it. I couldn't understand where Annabel had gone and why I was in this pool of blood. I felt fine, fine as nothing at all. It was warm too, the blood. Maybe it was just that I was so cold, but it felt warm and comfortable. All I could really think about was getting some water, I had never been that thirsty before. I walked up to Magazine Street. It was almost like floating, like flying very slowly. And when I got there all the cars stopped and people came to me and I looked down and fell, again."

"Then?"

"Then there was the styrofoam ceiling of Charity hospital falling up and away from me. And then there was Annabel at my side the next day, the leg gone. I remember it was still there when I was on Magazine because I saw it before I fell, hanging behind me out of my skirt. They said everything in that part of my thigh, in the part the fender scraped along, was destroyed. The bone was hardly dust they said. Annabel stayed with me the whole three weeks in there, past her funeral and all. I brought her to The Hole in the Wall and that's where she stays now. Hey Ronald!"

A white-haired, rail-thin man, dressed in a starched white shirt and black slacks, looked up and waved to her from across the street while he hosed the sidewalk. "How's my baby? Sure missed a fine revillion last night baby! Come on over after lunch."

"Thanks Ronald." Lane flashed a smile, then looked back ahead.

"Gonna be a bright and beautiful Christmas day today baby!" Ronald watched her for a second and then turned his face down to the stream of water as he guided it over the sidewalk.

"Turns out it was not enough blood to kill me. They said I left about four pints on the street. It was as though my body had to let go of just enough of itself to keep me warm in the dark and the cold, the night, and then it kept the rest inside of it. Inside of me. Just enough to keep me *me*."

Her hand trembled as they stopped. The Babylon Club was across the street. The entrance was erased into black against the bright pink walls of its building.

"I don't want to go in there," she said.

"It'll just be a couple minutes. I just need to—"

"No. No, it's my leg. This happens. I need to walk some more. I'll meet you back here in a bit." She let go of Jim's hand, leaving it warm and damp.

He watched her walk away, the black dress swaying behind her, betraying only the heels of her boots. He crossed the street. A large woman with a stretched black tank top that read BABYLON 'N ON 'N ON walked slowly out of the bar past him in a daze. He stepped up into the bar and let his eyes breathe in the darkness. "So hell froze over after all," he said.

There were frozen bodies stacked in a snow-filled street. Passers-by went about their business.

"Kinda' like hunched shadows in their black trench coats, huh," said Leighton. He did not turn or look up, but just kept his eyes fixed on the small silent television at the opposite end of the bar. His legs were up on the next stool, bare feet crossed. "Shadows floating over the blank white streets. Silhouettes against a relief of stone wreckage—their city shattered into inestimable broken and scattered tombstones. Yeah, it froze over alright. For eight hundred seventy-two days anyway."

Jim walked over and stood to his back, along the bar.

"Talk about casual death," Leighton continued. "Couldn't figure out what to do with them. No one had the strength to dig any more graves. The Leningrad air defense groups themselves had to blast holes in the ground to make pits for mass burials. They were just showing that park they got over there built as a memorial to the two hundred thirty thousand, something like that, they finally cremated in the brick factory. Ashes scattered every which way, dust on the ground like the skin they had shed every day. Must be one of my favorite things about this town—drinking a beer in the morning, watching the History Channel in some empty bar." Leighton turned his head, meeting Jim's eyes in the mirror behind the bar. He was wearing black jeans, too large for even him, and a white shirt with the words *Babylon Club* stitched over his breast. "Guess you had no luck either, huh? Gotta mope about another day. Colgan still got his shadow?"

"Sure. Everything's new to him," said Jim. "Like a broken record on one more revolution."

"Never gonna get out of here, is he? Needs to stop looking up is what it is. Gillies?"

"Haven't seen him."

"I knew it. Lucky bastard. We would have, you know that. You would have seen him over at The Hole in the Wall if he came up this time. I knew he'd be the next. He's finished. Just the three of us now. Lucky bastard."

"What is it? What's wrong, Leighton?"

"Sometimes I feel like we drove the wrong way over that Lake Ladoga." He looked down at his plastic pint cup, a third full, and rotated it in his right hand. "Why won't these soft parts go away, Jim? They're supposed to go away."

"Why come here? Why couldn't you have just waited for us?"

"I was too damned tired to even wait for myself and I've been waiting for myself for eleven years. That's enough for me right now. I'm done waiting for you." He lifted the beer slowly to his mouth, sipped, and returned it to its place. "Just needed to get the hell away from that thing, like a goddamn monster that River, a goddamn muddy, hungry bastard of a monster that keeps chewing on us and then spitting our asses right back out."

And on the television still more dark corpses like frozen statues, clothed, stacked, waiting. Vertical black scratches rained down the film. Jim looked around the bar. No bartender, nothing.

"One day to recover from a year of it. And then—in what? twenty-one, twenty-two hours—we'll be making our way back there. No choice, right? Gotta lie with our bones, clothe our bones once again. For me, this last year was the worst. For me, Jim, it only gets worse. I've gotten so tired now that the instant I go back in I get thrown down into this heavy, heavy and deep nightmare so quick. And yet it's only my body there. No rest up here." He tapped the side of his head. "Up here I know, I know I feel my body, all its movements, the movements of the water, sounds, all amplified, ringing, echoing through my body into my head, where I know and feel the nightmare of it all. Makes it like being buried alive, my body helpless down there. And knowing I'm feeling, I want only to tear myself out of it and I do. I can. I've learned to. And this, Jim, is the part that exhausts me—wrenching myself out of the nightmare of all this weight and rhythm echoing through my body, the echo of every drop of snow changing to water rolling down through gravity, cutting its path along a mountainside in Montana, sliding through ground, sediment, river, into the final River and down the backbone, the spinal cord of our great nation, here to its tail, down over us on its way to excretion into the Gulf and on into all the water of the world—

"And then, then for a moment, there is me. Me for a moment there. The flesh and the bones lying down there together, alone. Me until the exhaustion of having gotten myself out of it throws me back down into it again, dizzy, dark and heavy and deep until I can tear myself out of it again only to drop back into it again and again and again and again and again, an infinity of collapsing nightmares in a year until that final one when I feel the old pull. Up.

"Boom. Gravity yanks us up for a day. Up for air. Right where we died, same day we died. This is what we have. Christmas in the historic old square. And me too tired to even wait for myself. I can't fathom who the hell thought this one up." He smirked at his fingers, slowly turning his cup. "I'd give my life to be weightless, painless." Leighton grunted at his own joke.

Jim was silent.

"See, way I see it, you gotta be free of the flesh to stop the pain of gravity. No more rotting, just bones, just stillness. If only we could have been as lucky as that snow up there in Montana. Us like a drop of snow. There's a thought. The way it's supposed to be, right? In the beginning whole, one piece of energy, a body and spirit held together with flesh. Impregnated with the unique snowflake. Then our crash into the world. Born into movement from a crystalline womb, put into aching movement by heat, light, into light, to cut its own path to the River, to die with its dispersion there, to dissolve into the tremendous, indomitable flow of total energy. But instead it remains, not whole but in some fraction, a piece of the original, still together, this residue." He looked down at his chest, his legs, and gestured over his body with his left hand. "An impossibly frozen tear drop separated from the rest of ourselves, still shackled to a piece of the Earth.

"It was kind of convenient for a while, I guess. How in life this flesh kept our body and spirit all wrapped up in one. Kept it from spilling out, getting lost. Kept it in like blood. Things just got messy when the two separated. And now we've got this residue, and it's for *nothing*. That idea of tormented spirits roaming this world in agony until they finish some sort of business is the stuff of bad books.

"This isn't me. This is shit. Me, I'm in the mud down there. I'm talking to you from down there. Why can't our damned bones just get on without this stuff? Why can't they forget it? We died. Froze. Drowned. Forget about it. Move on for Christ's sake.

"But instead, just like all the rest of the poor bastards dragging themselves around and around the earth, moving through their slight existence here, we have to drag ourselves along, chained in gravity, decomposing us, still pulling our dust down to the earth. Pleasure, pain, the whole package. Who knows why? I don't and I'm not going to worry myself with all that. I just know that with bone there is nothing left to rot, only a slow fade into the anonymous fossil sleeping in the River's sediment. Where it can't pull me down any more. Sleeping in sediment, absorbing the water's minerals, turning to stone, my skeleton my own tomb."

Jim turned away from Leighton whose head was still hunched over the bar. He saw Lane standing across the street. "Leighton . . ."

"The Piskariovskoye Memorial."

Jim turned back to the television. It showed a walkway of cracked stone blocks, the width of a wide alley. A thin, shallow strip of flowers ran down its center. Large grass-covered mounds lined the walkway to either side, each marked with a single stone. The first two read *1942*. The others were illegible as they stretched on and on into the distance, endlessly up the small television screen until its top cropped them off.

"They think there's almost three thousand under every one of those," said Leighton. "In death as in their struggle. They say the rest of them are spread all around the city in other mass graves. Don't even know where some of them are." Now there was a shot of Mother Russia, immense, elevated on a stone block, her long black dress falling underneath her as she swayed towards the grass mounds before her with open arms, a wreath draped across her cupped palms. Leighton looked back to his cup, took the last sip and returned it to that same spot. He watched his fingers rotate the cup from its bottom. He shook his head, chuckled to his fingers. "So how many people you think can see you anyway, Jimmy?"

"I haven't taken a survey yet."

"Well, I'm guessing it's about one in four, maybe five. Colgan probably more. Me less, I think. Can't figure any explanation for it." Sirens rose and faded and rose again in the distance.

"Guess we're still relatively new at all this. But I'm figuring—trying to figure—a lot out. See, at one end someone's residue might just be a single sense, a smell, pipe smoke or something, maybe a goose bump on your shoulder blade, or those creaks people try to dismiss as natural, things falling just because it was their time to fall. Taste? Well, I've never seen that one yet, but I'm sure it's out there—hell, that might explain why Sara never liked a damn thing when I'd try to take her out some place nice. I always thought it was just women, but maybe it was shades all along. Shades sitting in the soup, making it a little too peppery, the pasta a little too cold, blah, blah, bitch, bitch, bitch." He leaned back, looked into the bottles behind the bar, at Jim's reflection behind the bottles.

"Anyhow, some leave nothing but a monotonous video playback, more a reminder than a remainder, like residuals, repeating endlessly on and on. And then there are those who have no idea they're even dead they got it so strong. Like a lot of them swimming the streets of this aquarium of a neighborhood. Their residue's strong enough for every cop, Wisconsin tourist, and even themselves to see and ignore. I bet you at any given time the holding cells over at Parish Prison are half full of shades with fingerprints and photos, the whole package.

"Seems with some, their residue sits here until the end of all, with some it comes and goes, and with some, most, it fades into nothing over time. Maybe this residue," he again gestured to himself, "is still rotting, aging, fading as it did in life. Maybe we're one day older every time we come up for air. Maybe in three, four hundred years we'll notice some change." He looked past them in the mirror. "Four hundred years. I don't even want to think about that."

A police officer was staring at The Babylon Club sign that hung over the sidewalk. Lane still stood on the opposite side of the street, watching something just outside the entrance now. The officer walked up the three stairs and paused. His partner came up the steps, bumped into him. "Goddamnit. Sorry Doug. Darker than—"

Doug scanned the interior. "I knew this was bullshit."

"Did they say boys or girls?"

"Don't remember."

Doug walked to the back and opened the door to the men's restroom, glanced inside, let it shut. He walked over to the women's restroom and opened the door.

"Shit . . ."

"Whatta ya got there Doug?"

"Shit. Oh shit."

His partner walked over and glanced into the restroom over Doug's shoulder. He swung around, buried his mouth in his sleeve, his eyes closed shut.

They stood that way for almost a minute until Doug shut the door slowly and walked back past Leighton and Jim and then outside. There were muffled radio dispatches. Red lights began to bounce off The Babylon Club sign and slant through the doorway. Doug returned with a roll of yellow police tape. His partner stood motionless by the restroom, his mouth still in his sleeve, his eyes now watching Doug seal off the front of the bar.

"What the hell is this, Leighton?" asked Jim.

Two more officers ducked under the yellow tape and came up into the bar. They stood there, absorbing the darkness.

"All this fussing about and only two hundred ten and change in the till," said Leighton.

"Leighton, what the hell's going on in here?"

The two new police walked back and peered into the bathroom over Doug's partner, who had dropped his arm back to his side now and stood just looking at the floor.

"I feel like going to a restaurant," said Leighton. "Remember when we used to do that? Just go eat at some restaurant? Most of the tourists, the few here over Christmas, would stare all crazy and confused, watching our forks and knives working away at the food disappearing bite by bite like they were in some silly movie. Remember Gillies? Bet we got booted from a dozen places. Remember the time he took a big forkful of spaghetti, musta' been half a plate of spaghetti on that fork, all dripping with marinara sauce, and then he shoved it in that poor kid's mouth. Served him right eating spaghetti on Christmas."

"Leighton, what the hell's going on here? Who called the cops?"

"Me. You have to understand, I needed to do something that mattered. I thought maybe if someone cared, it would matter, because I sure as hell don't. That's part of the deal, right? Leave that up to someone else. Someone somewhere that'll make it all matter. If someone somewhere cares about this, then I've made a dent in this whole goddamn thing we got going on here. I'm having another beer, you?"

They had propped open the cracked wooden door with a brick. Dim apricot light spilled from within. The two new police had plastic gloves on. They too stood motionless now, just outside the doorway. The first pointed to something inside the bathroom. "I think just one," he said.

The other whispered something.

"Female. See there," said the first.

Leighton stood, reached over the bar, grabbed a plastic pint cup and held it under the Bud tap as he turned it on. "There you are." He placed it on the bar and filled his own then sat back down. The tap was still running. "To things that matter." He held up his cup.

Jim stared at him.

Leighton drank. He gazed through the doorway, across the street where Lane stood on the opposite sidewalk, behind the police, the police lights, the growing commotion.

"I just want to—We— *I* have to get away from all this gravity, whether it's the movement and the weight and the pull of the River or it's these filthy sidewalks, cracked, torn, paved over like long quilts of scraps stitched together in every shade of shit. I want to run away from it, run away like we used to run away from all those towns, flitting about the country, train-hopping, hitchhiking, whenever something caught up with us. But we can't do that anymore can we? I knew we should never have slept down there. I know, I know—no fucking point . . .

"But, you see, Jim, it's a metamorphosis." He took a long sip. Jim watched beer flow from the open tap behind the bar in front of them. "It's just taking us a little while longer than most people." Leighton replaced his cup carefully on the bar. "A little longer to get out of this cocoon. Every time we get thrown up from the River we've shed a layer of our skin, not in growing into something realer, something larger like a snake does but in shedding ourselves, our residue. At least the River does *that*, grinds away our residue. It does with us anyway, did with Gillies. Colgan, hell, he still hasn't even shed his shadow, still makes a dent in light all over the ground wherever he brings himself like a goddamn mess, a goddamn walking tomb. But we've got to wait it out. Wait it out until we fade out.

"It's all so goddamn foul, this stuff, this body, the blood, the mucus, the painted flesh glossing over the breathing broken machine, the meat, the old shadow in the light. I want to be clean, clean of the juices of the womb. I want to be naked and final bone. Just bone frozen in the void of the River, deathless, dead."

With another gulp Leighton finished his beer. He put the cup down next to Jim's which was still full, untouched.

"No worries, Jim. There won't be any others. I don't think so, anyway. I'm hungry. Look, Jim, I'm going up to the corner store on St. Philip. No messing around with tourists, no funny stuff. I promise. Just get me a sausage sandwich and take it over to The Hole in the Wall. Meet you there. You said Colgan's still over there, right?" He stood, walked to the door, ducked under the yellow tape, and turned left.

Jim stared at the ensuing chaos outside. Lane was the only piece that stood still. Another officer, this one in plain clothes, a sleeveless collar shirt, his badge on his belt, walked into the bar. He had a small black case in his hand. "Ho-ho-ho, merry fucking Christmas, guys," he said as he walked past the bar. Then Jim saw the television.

It was the Piskariovskoye Memorial again. It's large grass-covered mounds still stretched along the walkway endlessly into the distance. But they were more than the gray grass of their mounds now. They were thousands, stretching up the screen until they faded into flickering white spots in the black and gray film. He could see the ones in the foreground clearly, fat and naked. He could see the bread, fish, meat, fruit, wine, all the food scattered amongst the children of Piskariovskoye, dancing, singing silently though the flickering film, the adults, parents, grandparents, all watching, cheering, clapping, laughing, eating. All shining their own light, the light of themselves, and the light of all of them together, whole, over their own mounds of earth, their own mass graves. And I could see them too.

He watched them all until his eyes fixed on a single boy. Sitting atop the stone marker on the right side, his bloated stomach over his lap, the boy was chewing a piece of the dark loaf in his hands when he turned and looked into the screen, into the bar, Jim's eyes. He kept chewing slowly, swallowed, then took another bite, chewing still more slowly, staring through the television. He raised his eyebrows and held the bread out towards Jim.

"What the hell?!" Doug's partner came running around the other side of the bar. He knocked the tap off, perplexed for a few moments while he stared at the two pint cups on the bar, one empty and one full. Then he went back towards the others who had congregated by the bathroom. Jim followed him. Two camera flashes went off from inside it.

And another siren came crying into the block behind them, moaning, falling away to a whimper as they turned right on Royal Street.

"Don't. I don't want it. I don't want to know." Lane spoke in soft monotone. "I felt some of it already. That's all I can hold right now."

"Felt?"

She put her hand in Jim's. It was cold and damp now. Something rose in her throat and she swallowed it. They walked, drifted along the high black rails of a fence protecting an old inn. The sunlight peeled the inn's second floor out of shadow, leaving the white of the paint, shining.

"These phantom sensations are strange creatures," she said. "Science can explain almost every other affliction experienced by patients." Again, there was only her profile, her looking ahead into the line of some other horizon. "It's very common though. Something goes wrong with the nerves when they're cut. Their messages get confused, contorted into the wrong places in the brain, the places that should not be working anymore because there's no body part left for them."

They turned in the shadow of the buildings to their left, walking in the middle of the empty street unbalanced now by the sunlight that fell across the buildings and onto the sidewalk to their right. Jesus Christ, life-size in stone, stood ahead in the garden behind the Cathedral. His patient arms were spread high and wide, welcoming, cautioning, parting the street, the Cathedral, the neighborhood down its center, along their path.

"No one can even figure out what function it serves, especially the chronic pain that's so often part of the phantoms. And there's still no cure. We manage our conditions. Each to their own. All there is to do." Light slanted across the garden to Christ's right, Himself tiny in the Cathedral's shadow. "I suppose if they could go to high school and perform symphonies in Leningrad during the siege, we can get by with our phantoms."

"And if you can't?"

"Well, as Weir Mitchell said, nothing breaks a man like phantom pain. It can turn any strength a person has into pitiful weakness. Makes them go bad."

"Dr. Mitchell," said Jim, "the Civil War guy."

"Uh-huh."

The street ended. They stopped in front of the closed gate to the garden. Within it, on the right side, was a sycamore tree as high and white as the Cathedral itself, shooting from the ground like a contorted antler, mostly skinned of the bark that still clung to its base. To the left was a slender elm just as tall, its body dripping with the weight of ivy down into the shadow of the Rectory. A blue tabby cat skulked about the banana trees around the elm's roots. The cat's ears stayed turned towards the two of them. Yet its eyes observed them with as little care as for the nineteen French sailors' memorial just inside the fence, marking the vault of their exhumed remains, built with seven hundred dollars raised by the crew of their ship and the town's citizens long ago; as little care as for Christ, paid for by and built in memory of a banker and his wife; as little care as its footsteps reserved for the three centuries of unnamed bones laced through the elm's roots.

"Mitchell, Melville," Jim said as he watched Lane facing the garden, again her throat constricting faintly and relaxing. "I've got Homer and still not a goddamn inkling of any real understanding. They can't even prove our condition exists." Jim watched the cat move through the azaleas. He looked at Christ, the four of them in the Cathedral's shadow. "Which way?" he asked.

She turned and their legs moved through the sun that passed below the elm, leaked through the iron fence, split into strips along the sidewalk like an egg perfectly sliced and frozen in the instant before collapsing over its slicer, around her shadow, underneath him. Jim let her lead him into the wide alley to their right, to Christ's right, beside the garden. The cat followed their path along the side fence. Barely above their heads, ivy sagged from the elm. A thin, shallow gully ran down the alley's center, dark with the memory of water all the way to Jackson Square at its end.

The garden ended with the walls of the Cathedral alongside them. The cat stopped, its ears followed their footsteps upon the empty air. There was another black iron fence to their right which started at their waists, rising from a short white wall a few feet out from the wall of the Cathedral itself, between its buttresses. The Rectory stood parallel to their left and merged into the Presbytere, both stone, immense until the end of the alley.

A woman turned into the alley from the Square ahead. She was holding her elbows, heading straight towards them, her skin the color of gray ash. Her nose was bent and bleeding. Lane eventually stopped and had to step aside to let her pass. The woman bounced into the buttress next to them. "Nuts to you," she said. Then she turned and began another diagonal path to the other side of the alley. There was a security tab hanging behind the neck of her black sweater. She zigzagged from one side to the other, only turning when she had bounced her face into a wall or fence pole, until she disappeared out of that piece of Royal Street still visible at the end from which they had come.

Jim realized the alley was completely empty, that on any other day there would be people at least passing by its ends, that this is the way it was for him now. Lane stood motionless, her back to the Cathedral, her face watching him as he turned away from the end of the alley and into her eyes.

She blinked. A tear rolled out of each eye. Two tears, tiny and slow, equal with each other in their paths.

"I know," he said. "But I can't even do that anymore. Did you know her?"

"No. I never knew anyone at The Babylon Club. But I suppose that doesn't really matter, does it?"

Jim looked into the lines down her face, twin reflections of the sharp blue sky above him. "No. But I told you, I've lost that." He put his left hand to her left cheek, wiping the tear away, smudging its warmth over his palm. "This." His arm fell back down to his side and he brought his other hand up towards her face, the other tear, but she met it there in the space between them.

"Just one," she said.

He folded three fingers around her thumb in his palm, knowing a pulse there, knowing her warm fingers on the back of his hand. She brought his forefinger through the air until another prickle of warmth shot through its tip, resting on the top of her jawbone now, barely in front of her ear. The left side of her lower lip quivered, a shudder of the instant, then nothing.

"Like that." She held his finger there, the skin thin over the hardness. "Like that I can feel the toes. It almost tickles."

There was nothing in her face, her eyes no longer wet. She guided his hand faintly, steadily inward, across the damp memory of her tear, onto her cheekbone.

"My ankle."

Her Cheshire lips curled, not smiling but growing, their ends winding like roots into her face. Jim realized she was as tall as he was.

"It's just the brain. Cortical remapping. It's very rare, but at least that's one thing the doctors can explain. It's the motor cortex homunculus. The region for my right cheek is right next to the one that corresponded to my leg. They became confused after the accident."

She let his finger fall down over the curve of her cheekbone until that curve went away into her and he stopped there, where hardness yielded to the soft flesh of her cheek.

"Back of the knee. It flickers now. It all used to be much stronger. I think my brain's figuring it out."

He floated his finger back and forth below the ball of her cheekbone until he felt the weight of her hand, and his fingertip dropped into the cushion of her cheek.

"Thigh."

Light faded down the Cathedral wall to its bottom behind the smaller outer wall, slanting sharply down the side of the buttress next to them, prickling the crest of her black hair with white. His finger went down, down until the flesh rose from her cheek and over the long, thin jaw. And then nothing. And then the warmth of her fingers gone too.

A siren rose into the space around them and fell back again into its distance. He opened his eyes. His hand hung empty in the air. His finger was still extended. There was only the plain white of the Cathedral's wall splintered with the flame-like shadow of the top of the iron fence that had been behind her. Stripped of shadow itself now, the iron's rust lay bare as scars.

Her back against the low wall, Lane sat on the broken stone floor of the alley below him, its cracks stitched with small brown leaves, themselves broken. There were footsteps. Jim turned to see an old man pushing an old woman in her wheelchair across the sliver of Jackson Square exposed at the end of the alley. Both wore black. Jim watched them pass, and the footsteps with them. Only now did he notice the murmur in the air, an impalpable whisper, echo of an unfelt wind. He crouched beside Lane.

Her face hidden, her straight black hair spilled into threaded waves glimmering white and black across the single whole gleam of the satin dress in her lap. She was reaching to her ankle. Her hair slid away as the dress came up, leaving a crimson underskirt, revealing the tops of her black boots. She pulled the underskirt also up to the top of her right thigh. There was only the prosthetic now.

Jim reached to the rubber, colored, wrinkled, soft like the skin of a thigh, shaped like the skin of a thigh. It felt so much more real than it had through her dress in the bar. The calf was the same, its size matching her other one still under her dress. Only where it bent at the knee did the bare metal pole of the prosthetic's frame expose itself.

"I'm still not used to it—knowing I can feel my fingers with my leg, but not my leg with my fingers."

Jim watched her hand move to the inside of the thigh, her fingers floating over the myriad tiny rivulets there, the imitation of flesh, until her hand held his, the three pieces together, motionless in a reflection from her eyes to those pieces, still motionless as she looked up above him, above the Rectory, into the nothing blue horizon there.

"Those of us who are more sensitive to visual information, rather than motion and touch, are more receptive to these phantoms. Optic rather than kinesthetic," she said.

"Not seeing is believing?"

"Believing in something that's not even there. Motion, however, doesn't lie so easily." She moved her hand away from Jim's, down to the end of the rubber thigh. She pushed in a thin metal button where the leg bent, where her knee had once been.

Jim felt the leg come loose and then the prosthetic went away and there was only a large white sock, filled with the little that was left of her leg, resting at a small angle from the ground. A thin silver screw protruded about three inches from its tip.

She placed the prosthetic along the wall. She put her hands on the sock, its top hidden under her dress which now sprawled over the ground next to her like spilt black water, frozen in motion. His elbow on his knee, Jim let his hand hang into the space where the prosthetic had been.

"Of course, it's different for everyone. My orthopedist says he wakes in the middle of the night screaming. He lost his arm in Vietnam." She hooked her fingers in the top of the sock barely underneath her dress. "He says it's like he's still clenching the grenade the instant it went off, his hand frozen in a fire of explosion for minutes sometimes. Some people, they have nothing after the operation, only an emptiness, and for others the pain echoes from the severed nerves for the rest of their lives. It varies amazingly—the intensity, duration, severity, chronicity, pain, pleasure—" The Cathedral bells rang high and heavy above them and down through its wall into the ground below.

"Eight thirty," she said. "Half an hour to mass." She slid the sock down and it turned inside out over the metal screw as she pulled it free with her left hand. Now there was only a thick yellow liner the same size as the sock protecting the stump.

"And you?" Jim asked.

"Well, we'll see, won't we."

Two pigeons flapped down into the alley. A family walked across their view of the Square towards the Cathedral. She handed him the soft white sock.

"Fabraloc. It helps numb the sensations, keeps the nerves locked up, their messages trapped in the stump. Keeps you from knowing what you feel. Sometimes. Sometimes nothing can stop the knowing."

Jim ran his fingers over the thin green band around its top, thick and hard, the whole thing harder than a normal sock.

"It's hard to explain. It's something I can't even understand enough to tell a doctor."

She inched her skirt up and hooked the tip of her finger under the liner's top. "Silicon." She rolled the liner down and down, little by little, delicately replacing it with white-pink skin. She stopped about two inches from the bottom where the metal screw attached to it and put her hands to her side.

"It's knowing others like a canvas knows the painter through the cool wet touch of his paints until the dried stain of an end is left. I realize how this sounds. Like I said—hard to explain. I guess all people have a bit of this. Empathy's what makes us people. But sometimes I feel so much down here, it's as though I know for the whole world."

"The weight of the world's paint?" Jim said. "I'd sooner chew my leg off."

And then there was a smile. Slow, fine lines shined from each corner of her eyes. With a flick of her thumb the silicon liner, and its screw, came away from the bare flesh of her stump. It was the cleanest thing Jim had ever seen.

Only a tiny purple circle broke the pale rose color of the roundness, smoothness, wholeness of the piece of her leg. He reached out, touched the circle.

"That's where they drained the fluid after the swelling," she said.

He ran his finger around its coldness, the white ring that outlined the scar, the lavender tautness inside.

A thin, bearded man in a black suit passed her in the alley, his footsteps suddenly there. He carried a small baby, bundled in white, sleeping. He looked down at Lane, not knowing what to say and so said nothing. He turned the corner towards the Cathedral.

"When everything else is gone away," she said, "I have this, this ability here."

"Well?"

She looked down at what was left of her thigh, to his hand, his finger, the small lavender circle of dead skin. The smile left her eyes and sunlight took its place, its line across the bridge of her nose. Not long now. "Tell me Jim, why do you keep coming up?"

"I used to think there was no choice. But now I think it's because we still want."

"Fuel of every living thing."

"Sure. I think that's it. Anyhow, I got rid of what it is to be human a while ago." He touched the real skin, felt along its rose hue just outside of the scar. "I left this in the bottom of the River. Now I'm just living."

She looked up to him. She was squinting slightly. "And what do you want, Jim?"

"To be forgotten."

Behind her, on the low white wall, thin rust stains streaked down from the iron fence above, fading before they reached the ground.

"What does it feel like?" she asked. "Being down there for a year, every year?"

"Like nothing at all anymore."

"Always?"

He couldn't find himself in her eyes. "I suppose it was very cold those first years after eighty-nine. And the weight too, there was all that slow weight pressing over, immense, more than the weight of the world even, it seemed."

Lane waited, watched his face turn back to her under the soft silent whisper of air around them, my whisper, myself nothing more than a whisper between the light, through the air of this time. Myself remembering now the cold weight of one's world, sleeping under the Governor Nicholls wharf, freezing gently under sleep, an early morning tide rising the inches to take us under that piece of the world.

"It was like sleeping on a cold night with very, very heavy dreams," he said, "but so cold that you are never far from waking from the coldness itself, no matter how heavy those dreams get you still know your body is there, cold, a thread away from being awoken, but you want to stay asleep, stay in the dream, not because it is happy or good, but because it is sleep and you are tired, and so you stay there, holding onto that thread. And then later, after years went by, it just became like plain old sleeping. Like a very deep sleep, no dreams, no motion or weight, just a restfulness, like the thread's just lying there, coiled loosely around me."

"And now, not even like sleeping?"

"Nothing."

He saw she was no longer squinting, as though her eyes had become adjusted to the sun itself. The left side of her lower lip shuddered and relaxed again. "There's more . . . more than wanting. There's still that thread. The gravity of it all's just different up here. It keeps, is keeping, you hanging from this piece of the world. Once it snaps you won't have to worry about wanting, it'll come. You'll fall into a place where it is, an empty place large enough for just you."

She looked down to his finger still tracing tiny paths that radiated from the scar. "The only sure thing in life," she said, "is that we die alone. All of us, we wander, drag ourselves around until we find an empty space to fit into, where we are alone, whole—a tomb for what's left after the skeleton. He found it a year ago." She looked down, through me, to her leg. "Gillies."

Jim stopped. His finger stopped. He looked at her, then to each end of the empty alley. "Gillies?"

"Here." She held her hand in the air, just below the slant of the Rectory's shadow, and a piece of me fell onto her hand, onto the pastel skin like the skin itself over the branched olive tints of her veins. "And on here." She moved her hand behind her towards the wall, below the blurred line of sunlight descending. The muted shadow of her hand, under the Rectory's shadow, swam grayer and darker until it grew into the shape of her fingertips, those pieces becoming black with her touch to the wall, squeezing me from those pieces of the wall, touch the only true shadow. On the wall, around her fingers, on her fingers, were places you could see the light I lay between, and places inside me.

Me.

"It was the loneliness of one, unalone, surrounded by so much he chooses not to feel or know, knowing only the gap of feeling inside, hollowed into a sadness that made me hold myself and shiver and weep for all the tiny hollow places one never realized were there, and then suddenly knowing them they burn. Annabel I could see. But Gillies was the first thing I felt. And that's how he came to me. In the light. He stays with me there on the Square at night. It's very hard for him. He is new at this and he is still very tiny in the night. There's not much space for him there. Not as much light as there is in the morning, even before the sun has fallen down into this place. Now he is more, and still more when the day is more."

He looked into her left eye, her right one, her left again, her irises, black points inside hazel starbursts, glossed over with that line of sky cut with the horizontal darkness of the Rectory's wall behind him. "Gillies is light?"

"He's a small piece in the nothing between the light, something nestled between its waved blankets, flowing between the photons. A little consciousness in the tiny hollow spaces of light, anywhere there is light for him to be.

"In the night he sees what he can, hears what he can, no more than a movie camera records. He was lonely, as I said. Now he stays with me. The hollowness he is, filling the hollowness I have. Small and happy and alone. Alone together here, watching, seeing, hearing." Alone with her through the Cathedral's silence. "Alone with me every night except last. He was with you two when you passed this morning."

"With us?"

"He can be over your shoulder sometimes. Sometimes practically in your head, behind your eyes. He watches. Follows you. I think he has been. I think he's been telling your story since you climbed out of the River this morning."

I am.

"He is now. It's a wonderful place to be, Jim. A final place. Light. To rest there fluidly, weightlessly. There are many there. I wish Annabel was there. I wish I . . ." She waved her left hand over her head in a quick, willowy figure eight. She brought her palm down in front of her, cupping the sunlight there. Then she brought her other hand also in front of her, slightly lower, below the slanting sunlight across the inside of her elbow now, the shadow light there cupping that hand.

"Most float themselves around and around the Earth with the sun's direct light." She flattened her left palm, letting the sunlight fall through her fingers. "Easiest to follow the tide of light through the Earth's atmosphere. They wash over me, an indiscernible ocean of things that once were. Atoms.

"Some, like Gillies, they avoid being swept along with the rest. They crawl about the overflow, the echoes of the current, the lighted shadows of this place. And there is plenty in the day." She separated the fingers of her right hand, stretched them out into the shadowless, shadowed air, me. "Here he becomes. And becomes more. In the leftovers of the sun's rays. The brighter the shadows become the more he is, the more he knows he feels. But without dragging himself around the Earth. Away from the flow of things." She held her right hand there, but dropped the other.

"But it must be shadows of place. Living things move too easily. Like I said, he's new at this. I suppose he has until the universe expands into dust and coal to grow."

The sun had now washed down, steep, white, over Lane, the wall behind her, into the narrow gap of the alley like salt water into an open wound. It sunk to the line where the low wall behind her met the ground in that crease of broken brown leaves. She placed her hand, her outstretched fingers, through me and onto Jim's hand, Jim's hand inside hers inside of me, inside the space where the leg had been, barely inside of me now, being ebbed away with the burn of the sun's edges.

"So he flits about, avoiding the drag of the sun around and around our world, but at the same time he needs its light, or the spaces that lie between its light, to fill them, to be where he fits. There are others like him. And there are places where some of them can stay always, avoiding the tide. Through night. Places that have light always, like a neighborhood where bars never close. A neighborhood of lighted shadows where one can be small and happy and alone."

And then the end was where I was—the slightest curve cut away from the sun's line. The beginning of a shadow, the sun arching over the top of Jim's head. His shadow.

"That's everything," she said. "That's all I know. And I don't understand any of it."

He saw it in her eyes. Whole. The sky's white hole in pinprick points shining out of her eyes. He did not squint. He looked. "Maybe someday things will stop surprising us," he said and the sun's reflections came behind his eyes. He blinked and the points were gone, her eyes again hazel starbursts shining alone, broken only at their contracted black cores. He did not know the burn down his left cheek.

She looked at the curved silhouette of his head that had begun to take form around her leg, their hands, me. The ephemeral stain of an eclipsed epiphany. "I don't think they ever have," she said.

She let go of his hand and brought her own out of me and into the sunlit space between them, to his left cheek. Then she drew away her hand in order to show him the tear that had fallen from his eye. There was light in it, warmth. She watched its tiny whiteness roll down her finger towards her palm. Not a reflection. Light. And then she looked ahead at the stone wall, squinting, and felt the sun on the exposed skin of her leg, its shallow burn broken only by the unfeeling lavender circle.

She rested her palm on that piece of her leg, shielding it, cooling it with her warmth, the Rectory's unbroken shadow barely touching it. She was falling out of me. She looked across the alley at the white plaster shaped into blocks covering the building's brick structure, up to a statue of Louis the Ninth over the entryway across from her. A sparrow flew onto his left hand, settled on the stone crown of thorns he held there. But Lane could not see the thorns, nor could she see the sparrow now. She could only see what appeared from below to be some sort of pillow in the Saint's hand and she could only hear the sparrow's call like the gentle wail of a blade slicing the brittle air. Her whole life she had wondered what was so important that Saint Louis would hold it on a pillow.

The tear stretched a thin white path back down her finger, fluid through the final edge of me, between wave after wave after last wave of shadow light. She did not notice it drop, whole, from her finger into that space where her leg had once been and onto the ground, into a gap between two stones on the alley floor.

She watched the wall in front of her as the light peeled away the alley's shadow into the plainness of itself, of day, her. She did not realize that it was warm, not the air but the sunlight, the stones still cool under her, the wall behind her. The enormous vines, flaming sea green now against the bare sky, dangled inconsequential over the dark frame of the elm's body and swayed through the sun, another whisper upon the air into her ear. The space in front of her hung empty, unbalanced between the sharply patched gray of the ground and the muted, shadowed, shadowless white of the Rectory and the shining egg-white of the Cathedral and its bells rang, six times, signaling three quarters past the hour, heavy and high, and then low, a delicate vibration into its outer wall, into the gray of the alley's floor.

She stood, ran both hands through her hair once, squinted into the sky, the sun, a long thin cloud stretching like gauze below it. She leaned down and picked up the silicon liner and the Fabraloc sock, rolled them together and placed them into a pocket in her outer skirt. She picked up the prosthetic, lifted it through the iron fence and lowered it until she felt its place. She laid it down into the small indent on the inside of the outer wall facing the Cathedral, a nook none remembered left long ago for a reason none knew. A place just large enough for it, a place sheltered from the elements, a place where at one time I too stayed, lonely through the days and the ocean of the sun, waiting for it to fade out. It was one of so many nooks that exist in such a neighborhood, if one knows to feel for them, and this is a place she felt long ago and had always wondered what it was for until she had something to put there.

Her black dress sparkled as people began walking quietly by her, and the sparrows sliced though that whisper in the air. She turned, walked parallel with the thin gully to her left and disappeared around the corner, into the flow of people, towards the Saint Louis Cathedral's entrance.

The white tear rolled through the break in the alley's slanted floor, a miniscule tributary, alone, into the gully where it hung against the dry stain of water. Hidden under pale sunlight against that dark memory, it was too tiny for the few people who walked by it that day to notice.

Too small to notice even for a man who sat on the steps underneath Louis the Ninth for most of an hour. The stones had been warmed with day by this time. The man sat alone in that whisper in the alley until the first drop tapped his knee, and then another and another. He had already capped the bottle of whiskey, almost empty now. Even the garden's trees seemed to have withdrawn into a shade of gray. He walked over to the feather he had watched for most of his time there. It was lying on the ground by the Cathedral's outer wall. It was of typical size and seemed to be of typical texture. He would not have noticed the feather at all had it alone not shined with the cobalt afterglow of a summer day inside that black and white and gray scene.

"Well now," he said, running a finger up its edge, the feather's silk-like barbs separating, falling back together, "ain't that an ass kick."

The man dropped it into his yellowed sack, slung it over his shoulder, picked up the bottle, and walked off. The steps of his new red sneakers were soundless as the sky collapsed into cloud.

That evening, as the alley began its final fall away from me, as its shadow slipped under the shadow of the Earth, and I waited for the lanterns, a thin rain fell. It would lift the white tear, slide it along the gully, along the whispers in the air, and bring it below the city, through its aqueducts echoing the faint murmur of the rain's quick pulse. And out into the River, a shimmering reflection of the last sunlight bleeding onto the last broken clouds, drenching their whiteness.

There Jim would fall apart under the opaque flow of River, slither through its sound forever heard on empty nights along empty docks in the empty spaces between the life in the air. On until these pieces would fade into negligible grains in the waves of the world for all times, too small for remembering.

*   *   *

"Odd, isn't it? How those few stars shine like that. As bright as back home over the mountains. And yet there's only those few. One, two . . .   Eleven. There's eleven of them. I think that's right. Eleven. Makes no sense. All the rest, the millions of other stars that would speckle the night back home almost into daylight, they get erased into that lavender reflection of the city here. Erased behind the lights of the city bouncing off the sky. But still, there's those eleven."

It was the last one in the warehouse still alive and it flickered once. When the small green light came back, Colgan's shadow was still there and so was Colgan.

"And still, no moon. Is it possible to have two nights in a row with no moon? Maybe that's gone too. Gone too behind the lights of the city painted into the air, mixed together across the blank night sky into lavender. Every one of those pinprick lights, Christmas lights after Christmas is over, up and up into the sky, all the individual lights by themselves, tiny by themselves all across

by themselves, tiny by themselves all across the city, all
                    the city, all swirled against

                                        swirled against the sky, all
                              the sky, all into lavender, the
sum total
into lavender, the sum total of the city's lights.
                    of the city's lights…That's all." Colgan stood with his neck arched back, his eyes squinting, studying. "No. I'm not doing it. No. I'm not going back in this time. I want to be here in this place. I want to stay."

Leighton carried himself past him. "Shut up, Colgan. Shut the fuck up," he said. "Just shut the fuck up." He stepped onto the wharf log, where his shorts still lay rolled tightly next to mine, and then walked off. There was a splash, heavy as Leighton's weight, and then waves under the dock, and then they relaxed into a gentle lapping, and finally only the voiceless hum of the River again. The green light flickered once. Twice.

"Leighton… Leighton? My legs. My legs are cold. They're so cold they burn they cold so They're cold are legs My legs My… Leighton?" *Still there, his shadow carried him, back and forth, back and forth through the little green flickering that would soon not be.* "Lavender into sky against the one night painted
painted lights erased into daylight speckle stars millions eleven two one

stars warmer anyway   leave
man Jesus me hell.   scared…
all time last time
oil engine in fried glue and paint thawed everything as day falls until shadow
    without itself whole shadow shallow see?

    *And then the light left, as Colgan had not, left only with sound pierced occasionally
with the thin tick of water left behind, falling to the concrete into a space where his shadow had
once been and still was, now left with nothing but the enormity of the night sky's light, too little for a
shadow to have anything but itself, nothing but sound.*
                                            winter will remember me
through us letters around margins along sound
life's a long li ght hollow soun d betweenn air
syllable's letters am I fade d a lready
  be tween gray under nneath River   the bl ack and sunpallor
unseenwhitecobalt colors explode swimming in light   living
shadow shines everything out of colo r
    white boneeyescloudsskinblood burnnnnnothing   shine
e mpty sky dis solved a part over eyeballs float inng atomspinnnn npricks
little thousan ndforgot mummies they tou ch s o unnd waves listennn n…
nn nnnight moving head annn d arm s and nnnno thing forming
shadowrisinng black breath glowinng dark faded
    And so it went.
pure hum R iver nnn no ises their makinn ng emptinn ness .   nnnn nno
t They're air.   Feels. Feels.Feels.Worse. em
empty too empti nnness, nn n nnno w cold. the bonnn n n n nne
                col d so me where   cry   los t
as d e ad Feel s. rig h   t? walk in nng
I'm righ t?   I am n.   annn yway walkinng I'm Well. thin
nnnnnnnnnnnnnnnk I kn no w donnnn n nn n n   't I . n nn nn n   n
n n nnn   n n   nnnnn no   n n   nnn

nnnnnnn   nnnnnnnnnn n nnnnnnnnnnnnnnnnnnnnnnnnnnnnnnnnnnnnnnnnnnnnnnnnnn

nnnnnnnnnnnnnnnnnnnnnnnnnnnnnnnnnnnnnnnnnnnnnnnnnnnnnnnnnnnnnnnnnnnnnnnnnnnnnnnn

 innnnnnnnnnnnnnnnnnnnnnnnnnnnnnnnnnnnnnnnnnnnnnnnnnnnnnnnnnnnnnnnnnnnnnnnnnnnnnn

innnnnnnnnnnnnnnnnnnnnnnnnnnnnnnnnnnnnnnnnnnnnnnnnnnnnnnnnnnnnnnnnnnnnnnnnnnnnnnn

M.O. WALSH

PENNY PITCHING

A BLACK T-SHIRT ON A TEENAGE TOURIST READS "NO WAY OUT" and there's a pink electronic device on her belt. Carl sits with his elbows on his kneecaps, slouched over, sucking ice out of a clear, plastic cup. Long fingers and skinny. His light brown uniform is getting damp and dark down the middle of his back and a stiff, brown cap lays on the table beside him.

Barges move sluggishly in the background, their towers visible behind the levee. They go one way slowly and then the other, completely absorbed into the scene. A deckhand casts off the barge and towards the levee, the line heavy with bait.

Carl's waitress hasn't been back with Coke refills and hopes he'll get the hint and leave. It's already hot outside, the middle of February, and he's been sitting there, alone, for an hour and a half, his head angled down from cursing himself and his now former fiancée.

Darius, he thought, *why did it have to be Darius?*

D, as he's called, is bigger than Carl is, he's blacker than Carl is. He is a man with huge biceps and rough hands made to carry boxes. He's one of Carl's fellow delivery drivers and has been fucking Carl's petite fiancée for the last month. And she has been fucking him.

"*At least* once a day for a month," she confessed with D still in their bedroom, pulling up his pants and tucking in his work shirt. He didn't say a word and left the quick scent of an undershirt.

Then came Denice's long, abstract attempt to justify her actions. She pined about *cold feet* and *wild oats* and Carl knew she wasn't sorry. At least not once a day.

Carl said goodbye, told her to fuck herself, and hopped back in his truck. Then he drove out of the neighborhood right behind D's identical UPS truck, and they both pulled carefully into traffic.

That was about two hours ago, and now Carl is just sucking ice cubes, sweating, and watching people walk by.

His truck is, undoubtedly, still running in front of Jackson Square, nearly out of gas. It was full of packages when he left it, boxes and envelopes, money orders and computer disks, and he can't remember if he locked it. He's already so far behind schedule that he'll lose his job regardless of what happens to the cargo. The fate of the truck and the boxes now seems to him more like a suspenseful narrative than anything else; a strange situation that he has distance from.

So he's been sitting at the Café Du Monde, about two blocks from the truck, damning his own situation and watching the lovesick street performers set up shop. Palm readers, musicians, magicians, and tired mimes.

Carl is perpetually struck by the weight of it all, the stretchy flesh of the woman he trusted. He can do nothing but speculate sex scenes and torture himself with B-movie dialogues. He thinks of a "special delivery" and can't believe that there is no love in the world.

He sees thin lips on thick skin, and small hands on huge shoulders. It is, he wants to think, a sick repetition of the modern love story.

Carl's head is clean-shaven and burning in the sun. Swirling the remaining cube around the bottom of the cup he leans back and takes a heavy breath, sliding the ice into his mouth. He smells the sweat under his shirt and spits the cube into his palm. He moves it to his fingertips and eyes it like a diamond, trying to feel it on his skin.

A stream of cold water runs down his forearm as the ice starts melting. Leaning back in the plastic café chair and looking at the cobblestone street in front of him, Carl picks a corner stone on the far side of the street, by the park. It's large and gray. *Three-two-one*, he counts, and lobs the cube.

The pitch is magnificent, pouring sharply through the thick air, making a defined arch, well aimed, but stopping a bit too abruptly, falling on to the hot street. The cube sits on the concrete and twists back and forth on its own body, melting and shifting from underneath.

A few yards beyond the melting cube is a small, square park. Reclining fully, with the empty cup in hand, Carl stares deeply. In his mind, he is a man without woman, friend or job. In the park, there is grass, an oak tree, and a mime in a box.

(An acorn falls from the tree limb above the man, bouncing off the invisible box, not making the sound you would expect, like a pebble to glass. It's more of a rubbery sound, subtle, like tapping a balloon. **The Man Inside The Box** *looks disappointed each time an acorn falls, thinking it should be a much crisper noise. He's a ruffled man, but distinguished, crouched and sitting on his shins with his white palms pressed out in front of him. He appears to be a mime without paint. He woke up in the park, in a box surrounded by shells of people, setting up tables and handmade signs. His clothes aren't dirty, but are wrinkled and stretched. His apparent rendition of "a man in a box" elicits a few nickels and quarters from the tourists, especially when he leans his back against the invisible wall. The grass in the park is thick, waxy, and smells of a recent cutting.)*

During the first few hours the man was awake, when dawn was breaking, he screamed and pounded. He seems to realize now, however, that his situation could be worse. He still finds it peculiar of course, but knows New Orleans can offer a much harsher condition than this grassy square: a block of green with an oak tree in it, in a triangle with the smell of Café Du Monde's fried beignets and La Madeleine's French bread.

It's coming upon noon and the foot traffic is picking up. More and more people are displaying their wares and the clear heat rises from the concrete in waves, obscuring the man's vision.

The box, as far as he knows, works in accordance with its own rules. A woman tossed a coin at him earlier that hit the man from the side. However, any time he tries to stand up or crawl, the walls of the box are there to block him.

He quickly realized it was useless to try explaining his situation. The first man that saw him thought his plea for help was simply part of the mime act and so he doled out more coins. Others gave awkward smiles and backed away politely.

A box as a symbol, the man thought, *is too obvious*. He could be trapped in his life perhaps, or trapped with a wife and without love, or maybe he's trapped in capitalism.

All of these metaphors interested him for a short time, but after noticing the squirrel, perched motionlessly on the root of the oak tree, they faded from his mind.

It is just so odd, he thinks, *that it hasn't moved*.

(Frequently glancing at his bare wrist, the man seems bothered without his watch, so he looks at the sun and squints, wishing he had a real skill. He wants the ability to determine the time by the position of his shadow. The square isn't completely

*congested this early in the year, but is still full of consumer activity: women with
sneakers and fanny packs and men with cameras and directions. Most of the
people are constantly eating, walking on cobblestones, and buying postcards. Some
others, however, are walking right by the tree not noticing a thing. No one has
tried to feed that particular squirrel, or pet that particular squirrel, not the one
the man's looking at.*

*A couple of hippie-looking teenagers with bare feet and rubber sandals in their
hands sit on the grass to the left of* **The Man Inside The Box**, "MITB."
*Barges silently forge down the river behind the levee and the breeze slides the
smell of beignets and bitter sweat into the audience like liquid.* **MITB** *sits up
quick upon seeing a man,* "**Grady**," *walking close to the tree.*)

MITB- Eh, excuse me. Could you do me a favor? Hello? Please don't
walk over there. *(louder)* Sir.

Grady- *(stopping and looking towards MITB)* Me? Sorry 'bout that. You
taking a picture?

MITB- No, just please, if you wouldn't mind.

Grady- No, sure, I was looking for a place to sit anyway. Can I sit here?
Is that all right?

MITB- Yes, yes. You can do wherever, whatever, I'd just rather you not
walk by the tree.

Grady- *(sitting down and taking a cellophane wrapped sandwich out of his
knapsack)* So, any particular reason, or just a rule of thumb? Don't walk by
trees. It's a beauty though isn't it? So majestic looking in the middle of all
the concrete, it looks like a commercial for something. Grey concrete,
Green grass and The Big Grey Tree. Like A Rock, I suppose. *(he takes a bite
of his sandwich, chews quietly for a moment and then turns towards MITB)* Want
some of this sandwich? It's not McDonald's or anything, just butter and
honey.

MITB- That actually sounds pretty damn good. The smell of those
beignets has been driving me crazy.

Grady- Yeah, smells'll do that. They say it's the most memorable sense
in the body, the real treasure.

MITB- What does that mean, most memorable one? Scientists say that?

Grady- *(leaning over towards the man, offering half of the sandwich)* I don't
really know. I've just always thought it was an interesting fact. A factoid.

MITB- *(reaches hand towards the sandwich only to have it stopped by the
invisible wall)* I hate to sound rude, but can you come closer, or maybe just
toss it to me, I can't reach it.

Grady- *(tossing the sandwich)* My name is Grady by the way.

MITB- Grady? I know a Charles Grady in St. Louis. But, no relation I guess. It's nice to meet you, thanks for the food and all. I'm just a bit out of sorts today, having apparently gone to bed last night and then lost my fucking mind. It's been a strange day, Grady.

Grady- *(looking at the assortment of coins on the ground around **MITB**)* Every day is a strange day, my friend, no apologies necessary. You at least making some money?

MITB- *(savoring the sandwich and swallowing slowly)* What, the coins? I'm not a beggar, I'm an attorney. It's a long story about the coins, but before you ask me anyway, I want to ask *you* a question.

Grady- Anything in the world.

MITB- Do you see the squirrel on the root of that tree?

Grady- *(looking at the variety of squirrels spiraling around the oak tree)* Which one?

MITB- *(pointing towards the particular squirrel with the remainder of his sandwich)* The one on the root there, the still one. Grady, I'm telling you, I've either gone crazy or I've spotted a fake. Look at it. It's perfectly still. That's why I don't want you to disturb it. I've been watching that damn thing for what has to be a full hour now, and it hasn't moved an inch. Literally.

Grady- Maybe it's scared or spooked. *(looking intently)* You're right though, it doesn't look like it's sleeping or dead, just being still.

MITB- That's what I thought for the first ten minutes after I saw it. Maybe it was sleeping sitting up or something. But an hour? A god damn hour that squirrel has been still. Seems like that would be eons in squirrel time, since they move so fast. But I'm telling you, Grady, I can't see why it should be so still.

Grady- And you want to see how long it can stay still.

MITB- That's not really it, I want it to move on its own. If it just responds to you invading its space, like a robot or something, that wouldn't prove anything. It could have all sorts of sensors and programs to respond to you coming towards it. Does that make sense? It's gotta be just me and him. I should be able to tell if a damn squirrel is real or not. It could have sensors for stimuli in its fur, or tail, or something. I'll be here until I can tell for sure. *(they look at each other and smile)* But I assure you Grady, this is my first day of lunacy.

Grady- *(finishing his sandwich and wiping his hands clean)* Well, friend, I don't know if you are familiar with this area, or even this whole city, but you have to be more disturbing than that for me to get up and move after I already sat down. Besides, who cares about the squirrel, it's the lawyering part that's crazy. What kind of lawyering do you do?

MITB- *(looking intense)* Patent. Can I try again?

Grady- To make me leave? Sure.

MITB- Alright, are you also aware, Grady, that I'm trapped in an invisible box? Completely solid and invisible. Watch. *(he leans toward **Grady** and presses his forehead to the wall, flattening out the flesh and skewing his hair)* How about this Grady? Qualify for crazy time?

Grady- *(studying the situation briefly)* Yeah, I think that will do it.

MITB- Any ideas on what the deal with this is? It just happened today. I woke up here. I have no idea why.

Grady- I think I'd probably have to start by looking at the box as a symbol if I were you. But, boxes as symbols seem too easy. *(pondering the question)* But, that explains the sandwich tossing at least. You can't stand up or move, can you?

MITB- No, I can't. *Hence* the sandwich tossing.

Grady- But this is kind of nice for me though, you see, I have a captive audience. Hypothetically, I could just sit here and talk to you for hours.

MITB- *(smiling)* Hypothetically.

Grady- Well, my lunatic friend, since I know for a fact that you aren't going anywhere anytime soon, I'll get something off my chest that you might find a bit peculiar. Maybe you can relate.

MITB- *(leaning back against the invisible wall)* Speak to me.

Grady- Seven years ago I got hit by a streetcar on St. Charles.

MITB- In your car?

Grady- No, just me.

MITB- Damn. Life flashing before your eyes type of thing?

Grady- Yeah, but that wasn't the interesting part, that was just like a montage or something in a movie, but I can't remember the soundtrack. The crazy thing about getting hit is that, ever since then, I've been able to travel exactly one minute into the future. Sixty seconds ahead.

MITB- *(smiles and peers uncertainly at Grady, then towards the squirrel, then quickly back to Grady, in a jolt, as if startled)* What was that? You cold or something?

Grady- Are you kidding? I'm hot like an Amish mule. *(smiling)* Whatever that means.

MITB- I thought you just shivered, just now. *(mimicking a shiver)* Like a quick shake.

Grady- Sorry, don't think so.

MITB- *(jovially)* Well then, my man, as soon as I get out of my invisible box here, you can go ahead and sign me up for the loony bin. Or maybe we could team up and join a freak show. Box Man and Future Man! Damn, Grady. Traveling into the future, huh? We could be kings in a day. Why aren't you on some tropical island, rich from gambling winnings or the lottery or something?

Grady- Because, like I told you, one minute is all I get. You don't think I tried getting rich? You don't think I tried for steak and lobster instead of butter and honey? For seven years I've been able to do this, and all I've learned is that it's a completely worthless talent. There's not enough time to make bets or buy lottery tickets or trade stocks or anything like that. Not enough time to save lives, change history or find true love. But it *is* real, nevertheless, I *can* do it.

MITB- Then prove it to me. I'd be interested to see it. I can prove my box, can't I? Look at me lean. If you can prove it, it's real. But hey, if you see that squirrel moving a minute from now, don't tell me, I'll wait.

Grady- I already did it, I flicked your ear just now. I have to do it quickly or else I disappear for a minute and it hurts like hell when I catch back up to myself, like an elbow to the solarplexis. *(**Grady** abruptly leans over and flicks **MITB**'s ear sharply, his middle finger shooting against the cartilage)*

MITB- Damn. Shit, Grady. That hurt. I haven't had my ears flicked since I was at Jesuit.

Grady- I told you I could do it. See, actually, I really flicked it exactly one minute ago, and now we are here in that minute. We caught up.

MITB- *(rubbing his ear, beginning to smirk)* No offense Grady, but that's the most unconvincing, bullshit display of time travel I've ever seen, ever. Star Trek teleporters and Schwarzenegger movies at least *try* to seem real. All you did was lean over and flick my ear and tell me that you did it a minute ago. *(laughing)* Time traveling ear flicker.

Grady- Alright then, so you see my point. It's an absolutely worthless, empty talent. Pointless. If we had a television here, you'd believe me. I could tell you every single commercial before it even came on. That would convince you wouldn't it?

MITB- *(thinking for a moment)* Yeah, I guess it would.

*(Sitting in silence, both men look back at the squirrel. It seems to shudder slightly but they might just be inventing the movement. Frustrated, **MITB** picks up one of the coins and brings it to his nose, inhaling deeply. He tosses it through the invisible*

wall and towards the tree in a purposeful and glimmering arch. Flying heavy, the coin falls just short of the root and sparkles instantly. The squirrel doesn't budge.)

Barges move sluggishly in the background, their towers visible behind the levee. They go one way slowly and then the other, completely absorbed into the scene. A deckhand casts off the barge and towards the levee, his line heavy with bait.

After putting his tip on the table, Carl squints from the sunlight bouncing off the change. Quarters, nickels, and dimes. He's now sitting at a table of mirrors, spraying sharp beams of light at the people taking and the people making, all walking in circles around the grass square. Shivering and stopping abruptly.

He picks up a quarter and tries to find his reflection in it, searching for something to resonate back to him in a deep tone. The mirror-image of a deep tone. *But a mirror as a symbol*, Carl thinks, *is too obvious.*

He rolls the bright quarter up and down between his knuckles with nowhere to go, using his thumb like a magician or a cashier. The bright silver shines against the light brown fingers. A gentle, hot brown, like the smell of coffee.

UTAHNA FAITH

TRACKING THE DOUBLE YES

CORA WALKS ON CHARTRES STREET, alone in the crowd, cool in the sunshine. She looks in the windows. She doesn't know the meaning of art or antiques, but she watches them. She crosses Jackson Square, past the street bands and jugglers. She turns to face Saint Louis Cathedral. Bells toll.

Turning on Saint Ann, Cora buys an ice cream. She eats it in three bites. French vanilla, chocolate fudge, waffle cone, and then nothing. She wipes her mouth on a napkin, drops the napkin in the gutter. She passes the street artists, the fortune tellers, the mime.

Cora walks to the river and watches it flow. She watches the people who are watching the river. She walks down the bank, amidst stray cups and broken beads. A river boat docks, its red paddle wheel slowing. Calliope music fills the thick air with transparent colors. Cora walks into the river. The tourists don't notice. She disappears beneath the muddy water. Her shoes stick in the primordial muck, and she walks out of them. Cora walks the bottom of the muddy Mississippi, to the bottom of the Nile, to the bottom of the Euphrates. She walks across the sky, to an imploding star.

In the void of maximum density, Cora has a lover. She lets him fill her up; her space takes his shape.

"Oh Cora," he gasps, voice rasping in ecstasy. Her body receives his heat, accepts his desire, but her fingers are bloodless as she presses them to his lips.

"Hush," she says. "Cora does not exist."

POPPY Z. BRITE

MUSSOLINI AND THE AXEMAN'S JAZZ

Sarajevo, 1914

STONE TURRETS AND CRENELATED COLUMNS LOOMED on either side of the Archduke's motorcade. The crowd parted before the open carriages, an indistinct blur of faces. Francis Ferdinand swallowed some of the unease that had been plaguing him all day: a bitter bile, a constant burn at the back of his throat.

It was his fourteenth wedding anniversary. Sophie sat beside him, a bouquet of scarlet roses at her bosom. These Serbs and Croats were a friendly crowd; as the heir apparent of Austria-Hungary, Francis Ferdinand stood to give them an equal voice in his empire. Besides, Sophie was a Slav, the daughter of a noble Czech family. Surely his marriage to a northern Slav had earned him the sympathy of these southern ones.

Yet the Archduke could not divest himself of the notion that there was a menacing edge to the throng. The occasional vivid detail—a sobbing baby, a flower tucked behind the ear of a beautiful woman—was lost before his eyes could fully register it. He glanced at Sophie. In the summer heat he could smell her sweat mingling with the *eau de parfum* she had dabbed on this morning.

She met his gaze and smiled faintly. Beneath her veil, her sweet face shone with perspiration. Back in Vienna, Sophie was snubbed by his court because she had been a lady in waiting when she met the Archduke, little better than a servant in their eyes. Francis Ferdinand's uncle, the old Emperor Francis Joseph, forbade the marriage. When the couple married anyway, Sophie was ostracized in a hundred ways. Francis Ferdinand knew it was sometimes a painful life for her, but she remained a steadfast wife, an exemplary mother.

For this reason he had brought her on the trip to Sarajevo. It was a routine army inspection for him, but for her it was a chance to be treated with the royal honors she deserved. On this anniversary of their blessed union, Sophie would endure no subtle slights, no calculated cruelties.

The Archduke had never loved another human being. His parents were hazy memories, his uncle a shambling old man whose time had come and gone. Even his three children brought him more distraction than joy. The first time he laid eyes on Sophie, he discerned in her an empathy such as he had never seen before. Her features, her mannerisms, her soft ample body— all bespoke a comfort Francis Ferdinand had never formerly craved, but suddenly could not live without.

The four cars approached the Cumuria Bridge. A pall of humidity hung over the water. The Archduke felt his skin steaming inside his heavy uniform, and his uneasiness intensified. He knew how defenseless they must look in the raised carriage, in the Serbian sun, the green feathers on his helmet drooping, Sophie's red roses beginning to wilt.

As they passed over the bridge, he saw an object arc out of the crowd and come hurtling toward him. In an instant his eye marked it as a crude hand bomb.

Francis Ferdinand raised his arm to protect Sophie and felt hot metal graze his flesh.

Gavrilo Princip's pistol left a smell on his palm like greasy coins, metallic and sour. It was a cheap thing from Belgium, as likely to blow his hand off as anything else. Still, it was all Gavrilo had, and he was the only one left to murder the villainous fool whose good intentions would crush Serbia.

He had known the other six would fail him. They were a young and earnest lot, always ready to sing the praises of a greater Serbia, but reluctant to look a man in the face and kill him. They spoke of the sanctity of human life, a short-sighted sentiment in Gavrilo's opinion. Human life was a fleeting thing, an expendable thing. The glory of a nation could endure through the ages. What his comrades failed to fully comprehend was that it must be oiled with human blood.

He raked his dirty hair back from his face and stared along the motorcade route. It looked as if the cars were finally coming. He took a deep breath. As the wet, sooty air entered his lungs, Gavrilo was seized with a racking cough that lasted a full minute. He had no handkerchief, so he cupped his hand over his mouth. When he pulled it away, his fingers were speckled with fresh blood. He and his six comrades were all tubercular, and none of them expected to live past thirty. The fevers, the lassitude, the night sweats, the constant tickling itch deep in the chest—all these made the cyanide capsules they carried in their pockets a source of comfort rather than of dread.

Now the task was left to him. Mohammed and Nedjelko, the first two along the route, were carrying hand bombs. One of them had heaved his bomb—Gavrilo had seen it go flying—but the motorcade had continued toward City Hall with no apparent damage. His comrades between Cumuria Bridge and City Hall—Vasco, Cvijetko, Danilo, Trifko—had done nothing.

The Archduke's carriage moved slowly through the crowd, then braked and came to a standstill less than five feet from Gavrilo. This struck him as nothing short of a miracle, God telling him to murder the villains for the glory of Serbia.

He fired twice. The pistol did not blow his hand off. He saw Countess Sophie sag against her husband, saw blood on the Archduke's neck. The deed was done as well as he could do it. Gavrilo turned the pistol on himself, but before he could fire, it was knocked out of his hand. The crowd surged over him.

Gavrilo got his hand into his pocket, found the cyanide capsule and brought it to his mouth. Hundreds of hands were ripping at him, pummeling him. His teeth cracked the capsule open. The foul taste of bitter almonds flooded his mouth. He retched, swallowed, vomited, convulsed. The crowd would surely pull him to pieces. He felt his guts unmooring, his bones coming loose from their sockets, and still he could not die.

Sophie stood on the steps of City Hall between her husband and Fehim Effendi Curcic, the burgomaster of Sarajevo. Though Sophie and several of her attendants were bleeding from superficial cuts obtained from splinters of the bomb casing, and twelve spectators had been taken to hospital, Curcic obviously had no idea that the motorcade had come close to being blown up. He was surveying the crowd, a pleased look on his fat face. "Our hearts are filled with happiness—" he began.

Francis Ferdinand was white with anger. He grabbed the burgomaster's arm and shouted into his face. "One comes here for a visit and is received with bombs! Mr. Mayor, what do you say?"

Curcic still didn't understand. He smiled blandly at the Archduke and launched into his welcome speech again. The Archduke let him continue this time, looking disgusted. Never once did Curcic mention the bombing attempt.

Sophie gripped her husband's hand. She could see Francis Ferdinand gradually pulling himself together. He was a man of inflexible opinions and sudden rages, painfully thin-skinned, capable of holding a grudge for eternity. He was like a spoiled child, bragging that he had shot five thousand stags, darkly hinting that he had brought down as many political enemies. But Sophie loved him. Not even her children fulfilled her vast need to be needed. This man did.

There was a delay while Francis Ferdinand sent a wire to the Emperor, who would have heard about the bomb. The Army wanted to continue with the day's events, but the Archduke insisted upon first visiting the wounded spectators in the hospital.

He turned to Sophie. "You must not come. The risk is too great; there could be another attack."

Fear clutched at her heart: of dying, of losing him. "No, I must go with you," she told him, and Francis Ferdinand did not argue. When they entered their carriage again, Oskar Potiorek, the military governor, climbed in with them. His presence made Sophie feel a little safer.

The motorcade rolled back through the thronged streets. When they turned a corner, Sophie saw a sign marking Francis Joseph Street. Just as she noticed this, Potiorek sat up straighter and cried, "What's this? We've taken the wrong way!"

The driver braked. The motorcade ground to a halt. Sophie felt something graze the top of her head, a sharp stinging sensation. The Archduke's head snapped to one side. At the same time, Sophie felt something like a white-hot fist punch into her belly.

Through a haze of agony she reached for her husband. He leaned toward her, and a torrent of blood gushed from his mouth. She crumpled into his arms. Attendants swarmed around them, asked Francis Ferdinand if he was suffering. The last thing Sophie heard was her husband replying in a wet whisper, "It is nothing. . .it is nothing."

They were both dead before the sun had reached its apex in the blazing sky.

New Orleans, 1918

New Orleans is commonly thought of as a French and Spanish town. "Creole," a word now used to describe rich food of a certain seasoning and humans of a certain shade, first referred to the inevitable mixture of French and Spanish blood that began appearing several years after the city's founding. The buildings of the Vieux Carré were certainly shaped and adorned by the ancestry of their builders: the Spanish courtyards and ironwork, the French cottages with their carved wooden shutters and pastel paint, the wholly European edifice of St. Louis Cathedral.

But, block by sagging block, the Vieux Carré was abandoned by these upwardly mobile people. By the turn of the century it had become a slum. A wave of Sicilian immigrants moved in. Many of them opened groceries, imported and sold the necessities of life. Some were honest businessmen, some were criminals; most made no such clear distinction. The *onorata società* offered them a certain amount of protection from the hoodlums who roamed the French Quarter. Naturally they required a payment for this service, and if a man found himself in a position to do them a favor— legal or otherwise—he had no choice but to oblige.

The Italians gradually branched out of the Quarter into every part of the city, and New Orleans became as fully an Italian town as a French or Spanish one.

Joseph D'Antonio, formerly Detective of the New Orleans Police Department, had been drinking on the balcony of his second-story hovel since late this afternoon. Bittersweet red wine, one bottle before the sun went down, another two since. His cells soaked it up like bread.

Two weeks in, this hot and sticky May portended a hellish summer. Even late at night, his balcony was the only place he could catch an occasional breath of air, usually tinged with the fetor of the Basin Canal nearby. Most nights, he had to force himself not to pass out here. These days, few things in his life were worse than waking up with a red-wine hangover and the morning sun in his eyes.

D'Antonio was forty-three. The circumstances of his early retirement had been as randomly cruel as the violence that presaged it. A crazed beat cop named Mullen walked into headquarters one afternoon and gunned down Chief Inspector Jimmy Reynolds. In the confusion that followed, an innocent captain also named Mullen was shot dead. Someone had come charging in and asked what happened, and someone else was heard to yell, "Mullen killed Reynolds!"

The yeller was Joe D'Antonio. Unfortunately, the dead Mullen had been widely known to harbor a strong dislike for Italians in general and D'Antonio in particular. No one accused him directly, but everyone wondered. His life became a hell of suspicious looks and nasty innuendo. Six months later, the new chief persuaded him to take early retirement.

D'Antonio leaned on the rickety railing and stared at the empty street. Until last year he had lived on the fringes of Storyville, the red light district. In the confusion of wartime patriotism, somebody had decided Storyville was a bad influence on Navy boys, and all the whorehouses were shut down. Now the buildings were dark and shabby, broken windows covered with boards or gaping like hungry mouths, lacework balconies sagging, opulent fixtures sold away or crumbling to dust.

D'Antonio could live without the whores, though some of them had been good enough gals. But he missed the music that had drifted up from Storyville every night, often drawing him out to some smoky little dive where he could drink and jazz away the hours till dawn. Players like Jelly Roll Morton, King Oliver, and some new kid named Armstrong kept him sane throughout the bad months just after he left the force. He got to know some of the musicians, smoked reefer with them from time to time, warned them when undercover presence indicated a bust might be imminent.

Now they were gone. There were still jazz clubs in the city, but many of the players D'Antonio knew had moved to Chicago when Storyville closed down. They could record in Chicago, make money. And in Chicago they didn't have to sleep, drink, eat, and piss according to signs posted by white men.

Pissing sounded like a fine idea. He stood, steadied himself on the railing, and walked inside. The place had none of this modern indoor plumbing, and the odor of the slop jar filled the two airless rooms. Still, he'd never stooped so low as to piss off the balcony as some of his neighbors did, at least not that he could remember.

D'Antonio unbuttoned his fly and aimed into the jar. Behind him, the shutters on the French doors slammed shut with a report loud as a double-barreled shotgun in the airless night. His hand jerked. Urine sprayed the dingy wall.

When he'd finished pissing and cursing the freak wind, he wiped the wall with a dirty sock, then went back to the balcony doors. It was too hot in here with the shutters closed, and too dark. D'Antonio pushed them open again.

There was a man standing on the balcony, and the shutters passed right through him.

Francis Ferdinand scowled in annoyance. The first flesh-and-blood creature he'd met since his inglorious exit from this plane, and of course the fellow had to be stinking drunk.

Perhaps his drunkenness would make Francis Ferdinand's job easier. Who could know? When one had to put himself together from whatever stray wisps of ectoplasm he could snatch out of the ether, it became increasingly difficult to fathom the minds of living men and women.

Joseph D'Antonio had a shock of black hair streaked with silver and a pale complexion that had gone florid from the wine. His dark eyes were comically wide, seeming to start from their sockets. "Hell, man, you're a *ghost*! You're a goddamned *ghost*, ain'tcha?"

English had never been one of his better languages, but Francis Ferdinand was able to understand D'Antonio perfectly. Even the drunken slur and the slight accent did not hinder him. He winced at the term. "A *wraith*, sir, if you please."

D'Antonio waved a dismissive hand. The resulting current of air nearly wafted the Archduke off the balcony. "Wraith, ghost, whatever. S'all the same to me. Means I'll be goin' headfirst offa that balcony if I don't get to bed soon. By accident . . . or on purpose? I dunno . . ."

Francis Ferdinand realized he would have to speak his piece at once, before the man slipped into maudlin incoherence. "Mr. D'Antonio, I do not come to you entirely by choice. You might say I have been dispatched. I died in the service of my country. I saw my beloved wife die, and pass into the Beyond. Yet I remain trapped in a sort of half-life. To follow her, I must do one more thing, and I must request your help."

Francis Ferdinand paused, but D'Antonio remained silent. His eyes were alert, his aspect somewhat more sober than before.

"I must kill a man," the Archduke said at last.

D'Antonio's face twitched. Then he burst into sudden laughter. "That's a good one! You gotta kill somebody, but you can't, 'cause you're a goddamn ghost!"

"Please, sir, I am a *wraith*! There are *class structures* involved here!"

"Sure. Whatever. Well, sorry, Duke. I handed over my gun when I left the force. Can't help you."

"You addressed me as 'Duke' just now, Mr. D'Antonio."

"Yeah, so? You're the Archduke, ain'tcha? The one who got shot at the beginning of the war?"

Francis Ferdinand was stunned. He had expected to have to explain everything to the man: his own useless assassination; the ensuing bedlam into which Europe had tumbled, country after country; the dubious relevance of these events to others in New Orleans. He was glad to discover that, at least in one respect, he had underestimated D'Antonio.

"Yeah, I know who you are. I might look like an ignorant wop, but I read the papers. Besides, there's a big old bullet hole in your neck."

Startled, the Archduke quickly patched the wound.

"Then, sir, that is one less thing I must explain to you. You have undoubtedly heard that I was murdered by Serbs. This is the first lie. I was murdered by Sicilians."

"But the men they caught—"

"Were Serbs, yes. They were also dupes. The plot was set in motion by your countrymen; specifically, by a man called Cagliostro. Perhaps you've heard of him."

"Some kind of magician?"

"A mage, yes. Also a doctor, a swindler, a forger, and a murderer. He is more than a century old, yet retains the appearance of a man of thirty. A wicked, dangerous man.

"He was born Giuseppe Balsamo in Palermo, 1743. By the time he began his scourge of Europe, he had dubbed himself Cagliostro, an old family name. He traveled the continent selling charms, potions, elixirs of youth. Some of these may have been genuine, as he himself ceased to age at this time.

"He also became a Freemason. Are you familiar with them as well?"

"Not particularly."

"They are a group of powerful mages hell-bent on controlling the world. They erect heathen temples in which they worship themselves and their accomplishments. Cagliostro formed his own 'Egyptian Order' and claimed to be thousands of years old already, reminiscing about his dalliances with Christ and various Pharaohs. It was power he sought, of course, though he claimed to work only for the 'Brotherhood of Man.'

"At the peak of his European success, he became entangled in the famous scandal of Marie Antoinette's diamond necklace. It nearly brought him down. He was locked in the Bastille, then forced to leave Paris in disgrace. He wandered back through the European cities that had once welcomed him, finding scant comfort. It has been rumored that he died in a dungeon in Rome, imprisoned for practices offensive to the Christian church.

"This is not so. His Masonic 'brothers' failed him for a time, but ultimately they removed him from the dungeon, whisked him out from under the noses of the French revolutionary armies who wished to make him a hero, and smuggled him off to Egypt.

"The practices he perfected there are unspeakable.

"Fifty years later, still appearing a young and vital man, he returned to Italy. He spent the next half century assembling a new 'Egyptian Order' of the most brilliant men he could find. With a select few, he shared his elixirs.

"Just after the turn of the century, he met a young journalist named Benito Mussolini, who called himself an 'apostle of violence' but had no direction. Cagliostro has guided Mussolini's career since then. In 1915, Mussolini's newspaper helped urge Italy into war."

D'Antonio started violently. "Aw, come on! You're not gonna tell me these Egyptian-Dago-Freemasons started the war."

"Sir, that is exactly what I am going to tell you. They also ordered my wife's death, and my own, and that of my empire."

"Why in hell would they do that?"

"I cannot tell you. They are evil men. My uncle, the Emperor Francis Joseph, discovered all this inadvertently. He was a cowardly old fool who would have been afraid to tell anyone. Nevertheless, they hounded him into virtual retirement, where he died."

"And told you all this?"

"He had no one else to talk to. Nor did I."

"Where's your wife?"

"Sophie was not required to linger here. We were."

"Why?"

"I cannot tell you."

"You keep saying that. Does it mean you don't know, or you aren't *allowed* to tell me?"

Francis Ferdinand paused. After a moment, D'Antonio nodded. "I see how it is. So I'm supposed to dance for you like Mussolini does for Cagliostro?"

The Archduke did not understand the question. He waited to see if D'Antonio would rephrase it, but the man remained silent. Finally Francis Ferdinand said, "Cagliostro still controls Mussolini, and means to shape him into the most vicious ruler Europe has ever known. But Cagliostro is no longer in Italy. He is here in New Orleans."

"Oh-ho. And you want me to kill him for you, is that it?"

"Yes, but I haven't finished. Cagliostro is in New Orleans—*but we don't know who he is*."

"*We*? Who's *we*?"

"Myself, my uncle."

"No one else?"

"No one else you would care to know about, sir."

D'Antonio sagged in his chair. "Yeah, well, forget it. I'm not killin' anybody. Find some other poor dupe."

"Are you certain, Mr. D'Antonio?"

"Very certain."

"Very well." Francis Ferdinand drifted backward through the balcony railing and vanished in midair.

"Wait!" D'Antonio was halfway out of his chair by the time he realized the wraith was gone. He sank back, his brain seasick in his skull from all the talk of mages and murders, elixirs and dungeons, and the famous scandal of Marie Antoinette's diamond necklace—whatever the hell that was.

"Why me?" he murmured into the hot night. But the night made no reply.

Cagliostro stood behind his counter and waited on the last customer of the day, an old lady buying half a pound of salt cod. When she had gone, he locked the door and had his supper: a small loaf of bread, a thick wedge of provolone, a few olives chopped with garlic. He no longer ate the flesh of creatures, though he sold it to maintain the appearance of a proper Italian grocery.

Above his head hung glossy loops of sausage and salami, rafters of wind-dried ham and pancetta, luminous globes of caciocavallo cheese. In the glass case were pots of creamy ricotta, stuffed artichokes, orbs of mozzarella in milk, bowls of shining olives and capers preserved in brine. On the neat wooden shelves were jars of candied fruit, almonds, pine nuts, aniseed, and a rainbow of assorted sweets. There were tall wheels of parmesan coated in funereal black wax, cruets of olive oil and vinegar, pickled cucumbers and mushrooms, flat tins containing anchovies, calamari, octopus. Enormous burlap sacks of red beans, fava beans, chickpeas, rice, couscous, and coffee threatened to spill their bounty onto the spotless tile floor. Pastas of every shape, size, and color were arranged in an elaborate display of bins facing the counter.

The aroma of the place was a balm to Cagliostro's ancient soul. He carried the world's weight on his back every day; he had pledged his very life to the furthering of the Brotherhood of Man; still, that did not mean he could shirk small duties. He fed the families of his neighborhood. When they could not pay, he fed them on credit, and when there was no hope of recovering the credit, he fed them for free.

He had caused death, to be sure. He had caused the deaths of the Arch-duke and his wife for several reasons, most importantly the malignant forces that hung over Europe like black clouds heavy with rain. Such a rain could mean the death of millions, hundreds of millions. The longer it was al-lowed to stagnate, the more virulent it would grow. It had needed some spark to release it, some event whose full significance was hidden at first, then gradually revealed. The assassination in Sarajevo had been that event, easy enough to arrange by providing the dim-witted Serbian anarchists with encouragement and weapons.

His name was synonymous with elaborate deception, and not undeservedly so. But some of his talents were genuine. In his cards and scrying-bowl Cagliostro could read the future, and the future looked very dark.

He, of course, would change all that.

This war was nearly over. It had drained some of the poison from those low-hanging clouds, allowed Europe to shatter and purge itself. But it had not purged enough; there would be another great war inside of two de-cades. In that one, his boy Benito would send thousands of innocent men to their useless deaths. But that was not as bad as what could be.

Though he had never killed a man with his own hands, Cagliostro bit-terly felt the loss of the human beings who died as a result of his machina-tions. They were his brothers and sisters; he mourned each one as he would a lovely temple he had never seen, upon hearing it had been demolished. He could not accept that their sacrifice was a natural thing, but he had come to understand that it was necessary.

Mussolini was more than a puppet; he was a powerful orator and propa-gandist who would learn to yank his followers in any direction that pleased him. But he was unbalanced, ultimately no better than a fool, ignorant of the Mysteries, incapable of seeing them when a few of the topmost veils were pulled aside. He would make an excellent pawn, and he would die believing he had engineered his own destiny.

The only reason he could be allowed into power was to prevent something far worse.

Cagliostro had seen another European tyrant in his cards and his bowl, a man who made Mussolini look like a painted tin soldier. Mussolini was motivated exclusively by power, and that was bad enough; but this other creature was a bottomless well of hatred. Given the chance, he would saturate all creation with his vitriol. Millions would die like vermin, and their corpses would choke the world. The scrying-water had shown terrifying factories built especially for disposal of the dead, ovens hot enough to reduce bone to ash, black smokestacks belching greasy smoke into a charred orange sky. Cagliostro did not yet know this tyrant's precise identity, but he believed that the man would come from Austria and rule Germany. Another good reasons for the Archduke's death: Francis Ferdinand would have made a powerful ally for such a man.

Cagliostro did not think he could altogether stop this tyrant. He had not foreseen it in time; he had been occupied with other matters. It was always thus when a man wished to save the world: he never knew where to look first, let alone where to begin.

Still, he believed he could stop the tyrant short of global domination, and he believed Mussolini was his key. Members of the Order in Italy were grooming him for Prime Minister. The title would unlock every door in Europe. If they could arrange for Mussolini to become the tyrant's ally, perhaps they could also ensure that Mussolini would in some way cause the tyrant's downfall.

Cagliostro finished his simple supper, collected the day's receipts, and turned off the lights. In the half-darkness he felt his way back to the small living quarters behind the store, where he sat up reading obscure volumes and writing long letters in a florid hand until nearly dawn. Over the past century, he had learned to thrive on very little sleep.

D'Antonio was sitting up in bed, back propped against the wooden headboard, bare legs sprawled atop the sweat-rumpled coverlet, bottle nestled between his thighs. The Archduke appeared near the sink. D'Antonio jumped, slopped wine onto the coverlet, cursed. "You gotta make me stain something every time you show up?"

"You need have no fear of me."

"No, you just want me to murder somebody for you. Why should that scare me?"

"It should not, sir. What should scare you is the prospect of a world ruled by Cagliostro and his Order."

"That guy again. Find him yet?"

"We know he came to New Orleans before 1910. We know he is living as an Italian grocer. But he has covered his tracks so successfully that we cannot determine his precise identity. We have a number of candidates."

"That's good." D'Antonio nodded, pretended to look thoughtful. "So you just gonna kill all of 'em, or what?"

"I cannot kill anyone, sir. I cannot even lift a handkerchief. That is why I require your help."

"I thought I told you last time, Duke. My services are unavailable. Now kindly fuck off."

"I feared you would say that. You will not change your mind?"

"Not a chance."

"Very well."

D'Antonio expected the wraith to vanish as it had last time. Instead, Francis Ferdinand seemed to break apart before his eyes. The face dissolved into a blur, the fingers elongated into smoke-swirls; then there was only a man-shaped shimmer of gossamer strands where the Archduke had been.

When D'Antonio breathed in, they all came rushing toward him.

He felt clammy filaments sliding up his nose, into his mouth, into the lubricated crevices of his eyesockets. They filled his lungs, his stomach; he felt exploratory tendrils venturing into his intestines. A profound nausea gripped him. It was like being devoured alive by grave-worms. The wraith's consciousness was saturating his own, blotting him out like ink spilled on a letter.

"*I offered you the chance to act of your own free will,*" Francis Ferdinand said. The voice was a hideous papery whisper inside his skull now. "*Since you declined, I am given no choice but to help you along.*"

Joseph Maggio awoke to the sound of his wife choking on her own blood. Great hot spurts of it bathed his face. A tall figure stood by the bed, instrument of death in his upraised hand. Maggio recognized it as the axe from his own backyard woodpile, gleaming with fresh gore. It fell again with a sound like a cleaver going into a beef neckbone, and his wife was silent.

Maggio struggled to sit up as the killer circled to his side of the bed. He did not recognize the man. For a moment their eyes locked, and Maggio thought, *That man is already dead.*

"Cagliostro?" It was a raspy whisper, possibly German-accented, though the man looked Italian.

Wildly, Maggio shook his head. "No, no sir, my name's Joseph Maggio, I just run a little grocery and I never heard of no Cagli-whoever . . . oh Jesus-Mary-and-Joseph please don't hit me with that thing—"

The blade glittered in a deadly arc. Maggio sprawled halfway off the bed, blinded by a sudden wash of his own blood. The axe fell again and he heard his own skull crunching, felt blade squeak against bone as the killer wrenched it out. Another searing cut, then another, until a merciful blow severed his jugular and he died in a red haze.

It was found that the killer had gained access to the Maggios' home by chiseling out a panel in the back door. The chisel had belonged to Joseph Maggio, as had the axe, which was found in a pool of blood on the steps. People all over New Orleans searched their yards for axes and chisels, and locked away these potential implements of Hell.

A strange phrase was found chalked on the pavement a block from the Maggios' house: "Mrs. Maggio is going to sit up tonight, just like Mrs. Tony." Its significance has not been discovered to this day.

Maggio's two brothers were arrested on the grounds that the Maggios were Sicilians, and Sicilians were prone to die in family vendettas. They were released by virtue of public drunkenness—they had been out celebrating the younger one's draft notice on the night of the murders, and had staggered home scarcely able to move, let alone lift an axe.

The detective in charge of the case was shot to death by a burglar one week after the murders. The investigation languished. News of the Romanov family's murder by Bolsheviks in Russia eclipsed the Maggio tragedy. The temperature climbed as June wore on.

"*I detect Cagliostro's influences still at work on this plane,*" the Archduke said. "*We must move on to the next candidate.*"

Deep inside his own ectoplasm-snared brain, which the wraith kept docile with wine except when he needed to use the body, D'Antonio could only manage a feeble moan of protest.

A clear tropical dawn broke over New Orleans as John Zanca parked his wagon of fresh breads and cakes in front of Luigi Donatello's grocery. He could not tell whether the grocer and his wife were awake yet, so he decided to take their order around to the back door. He gathered up a fragrant armful of baked goods still warm from the oven and carried them down the narrow alley that led to the Donatellos' living quarters.

When he saw the back door with its lower left panel neatly chiseled out, his arms went limp. Cakes and loaves rained on the grass at his feet.

After a moment, Zanca stepped forward—careful not to crush any of the baked goods—and knocked softly on the door. He did not want to do so, but there seemed nothing else to do. When it swung open, he nearly screamed.

Before him stood Luigi Donatello, his face crusted with blood, his hair and moustache matted with it. Zanca could see three big gashes in his skull, white edges of bone, wet gray tissue swelling through the cracks. How could the man still be standing?

"My God," moaned Donatello. "My God."

Behind him, Zanca saw Mrs. Donatello sprawled on the floor. The top of her head was a gory porridge. The slender stem of her neck was nearly cleaved in two.

"My God. My God. My God."

John Zanca closed his eyes and said a silent prayer for the Donatellos' souls and his own.

The newspapers competed with one another for the wildest theory regarding the Axeman, as the killer came to be known. He was a Mafia executioner, and the victims were fugitives from outlaw justice in Sicily. He was a vigilante patriot, and the victims were German spies masquerading as Italian grocers. He was an evil spirit. He was a voodoo priest. He was a woman. He was a policeman.

The Italian families of New Orleans, particularly those in the grocery business, barricaded their doors and fed their dogs raw meat to make them bloodthirsty. These precautions did not stop them from lying awake in the small hours, clutching a rosary or perhaps a revolver, listening for the scrape of the Axeman's chisel.

In high summer, when the city stank of oyster shells and ancient sewers, the killer returned. Two teenage sisters, Mary and Pauline Romano, saw their uncle butchered in his own bed. They could only describe the man as "dark, tall, wearing a dark suit and a black slouch hat."

Italian families with enemies began finding axes and chisels dropped in their yards, more like cruel taunts than actual threats. Some accused their enemies. Some accused other members of their families. Some said the families had brought it upon themselves. Tempers flared in the sodden August heat, and many killings were done with weapons other than axes. Men with shotguns sat guard over their sleeping families, nodding off, jerking awake at the slightest noise. A grocer shot his own dog; another nearly shot his own wife.

The city simmered in its own prejudice and terror, a piquant gumbo.

But the Axeman would not strike again that year.

D'Antonio came awake with a sensation like rising through cool water into sunlight. He tried to move his hands: they moved. He tried to open his eyes: the ceiling appeared, cracked and water-stained. Was it possible? Was the fucking monster really *gone*?

"Duke?" he whispered aloud into the empty room. His lips were dry, wine-parched. "Hey, Duke? You in there?"

To his own ears he sounded plaintive, as if he missed the parasitic murdering creature. But the silence in his head confirmed it. The wraith was gone.

He stared at his hands, remembering everything he had seen them do. How ordinary they looked, how incapable of swinging a sharp blade and destroying a man's brain, a woman's brain. For a long time he sat on the edge of the bed studying the beds of his nails and the creases in his palms, vaguely surprised that they were not caked with blood.

Eventually he looked down at himself and found that he was wearing only a filthy pair of trousers. He stripped them off, sponged himself to a semblance of cleanliness with the stale water in the basin, slicked his hair back and dressed in fresh clothes. He left his apartment without locking the door and set off in a random direction.

D'Antonio wandered hatless in the August sun for an hour or more. When he arrived at the *States* newspaper office, his face was streaming with sweat, red as a boiled crawfish. He introduced himself to the editor as a retired police detective, an expert on both Italians and murderers, and gave the following statement:

"The Axeman is a modern Doctor Jekyll and Mr. Hyde. A criminal of this type may be a respectable, law-abiding citizen when he is his normal self. Compelled by an impulse to kill, he must obey this urge. Like Jack the Ripper, this sadist may go on with his periodic outbreaks until his death. For months, even for years, he may be normal, then go on another rampage. It is a mistake to blame the Mafia. The Mafia never attacks women as this murderer has done."

He left the *States* office with several people staring bemusedly after him, but they printed the interview in its entirety.

After that, he lived his life much as he had before the wraith's first visit. Armistice Day brought throngs of joyous revelers into the streets, as well as a blessed wave of cool weather; it had stayed sweltering through October. The war was over, and surely the wraith would never come back and make him do those things again.

He could not forget the organic vibration that ran up his arms as blade buried itself in bone.

In fact, he dreamed about it almost every night.

Francis Ferdinand returned in the spring of 1919.

He did not muck about with appearances this time, but simply materialized inside D'Antonio's head. D'Antonio collapsed, clawing at his temples.

"*He deceived me for a time, but now I know he still walks this earth,*" said the wraith. "*We will find him.*"

D'Antonio lay curled on his side, blinded by tears of agony, wishing for the comforts of the womb or the grave.

Giacomo Lastanza was a powerful man, but he had been no match for the fiend in his bedroom. Now he lay on the floor with his head split as cleanly as a melon, and his wife Rosalia cowered in a corner of the room clutching her two-year-old daughter, Mary. Mary was screaming, clutching at her mother's long black hair. As the Axeman turned away from her husband's body, Rosalia began to scream too.

"Not my baby! Please, Holy Mother of God, not my baby!"

The axe fell. Mary's little face seemed to crack open like an egg. Rosalia was unconscious before her skull felt the blade's first kiss.

D'Antonio lay naked on the floor. The apartment was a wasteland of dirty clothes and empty wine bottles. But his body was relatively sober for once—they'd run out of money—and as a result he was sharp enough to be carrying on an argument with the wraith.

"Why in hell do we have to kill the women? You can't be worried one of *them* is Cagliostro."

"He has consorted with a number of dangerous women. When we find him, his wife will bear killing also."

"And until then, you don't mind killing a few innocent ones?"

"It is necessary."

286

"What about that little baby?"

"If it had been Cagliostro's daughter, he would have raised her to be as wicked as himself."

D'Antonio got control of one fist and weakly pounded the floor with it.

"You goddamn monster—you're just gonna keep wasting people, and sooner or later I'll get caught and rot in prison. Or fry in the chair. And you'll go on your merry way and find some other poor sap to chase down that shadow of yours."

"The next one must be him! He is the last one on the list!"

"Fuck the list."

A bolt of excruciating pain shot through D'Antonio's head, and he decided to drop the argument.

Cagliostro was reading by candlelight when he heard the chisel scraping at his door. He smiled and turned a page.

The creature crept into his room, saw him in his chair with his head bent over a book. When it was ten feet away, Cagliostro looked up. When it was five feet away, it froze in mid-motion, restrained by the protective circle he had drawn.

By looking into its eyes, he knew everything about Joseph D'Antonio and the Archduke Francis Ferdinand. But the creature upon which he gazed now was neither D'Antonio nor the Archduke; this was a twisted amalgamation of the two, and it could only be called the Axeman.

He smiled at the creature, though its eyes blazed with murderous rage. "Yes, poor Archduke, it is I. And you will not harm me. In fact, I fear I must harm you yet again. If only you had accepted the necessity of your death the first time, you would be Beyond with your beloved Sophie now.

"No, don't think you can desert your stolen body as it lies dying. You'll stay in there, my boy. My magic circle will see to that!" Cagliostro beamed; he was enjoying this immensely. "Yes, yes, I know about unfortunate ex-Detective D'Antonio trapped in there. But why do you think it was so easy for the Duke to take hold of your body, Mr. D'Antonio, and make it do the terrible things it did? Perhaps because you care not at all for your fellow human beings? 'When they came for the Jews, I did nothing, for I was not a Jew' . . . ah, forgive me. An obscure reference to a future that may never be. And you will both die to help prevent it."

He reached beneath the cushion of his armchair, removed a silver revolver with elaborate engraving on the butt and barrel, aimed it carefully, and put a ball in the Axeman's tortured brain.

Then he put his book aside, went to his desk, and took up his pen.

The letter was published in *The Times-Picayune* the next day.

Hell, March 13, 1919

Editor of The Times-Picayune
New Orleans, La.

Esteemed Mortal:

They have never caught me and they never will. They have never seen me, for I am invisible, even as the ether that surrounds your earth. I am not a human being, but a spirit and a fell demon from the hottest hell. I am what you Orleanians and your foolish police call the Axeman.

When I see fit, I shall come again and claim other victims. I alone know whom they shall be. I shall leave no clue except my bloody axe, besmeared with the blood and brains of he who I have sent below to keep me company.

If you wish, you may tell the police to be careful not to rile me. Of course, I am a reasonable spirit. I take no offense at the way they have conducted their investigations in the past. In fact, they have been so utterly stupid as to amuse not only me, but His Satanic Majesty, Francis Joseph, etc. But tell them to beware. Let them not try to discover what I am, for it were better that they were never born than to incur the wrath of the Axeman. I don't think there is any need for such a warning, for I feel sure the police will always dodge me, as they have in the past. They are wise and know how to keep away from all harm.

Undoubtedly, you Orleanians think of me as a most horrible murderer, which I am, but I could be much worse if I wanted to. If I wished, I could pay a visit to your city every night. At will I could slay thousands of your best citizens, for I am in close relationship with the Angel of Death.

Now, to be exact, at 12:15 (earthly time) on next Tuesday night, I am going to pass over New Orleans. In my infinite mercy, I am going to make a little proposition to you people. Here it is:

I am very fond of jazz music, and I swear by all the devils in the nether region that every person shall be spared in whose home a jazz band is in full swing at the time I have just mentioned. If everyone has a jazz band going, well, then, so much the better for you people. One thing is certain and that is that some of those people who do not jazz it on Tuesday night (if there be any) will get the axe.

Well, I am cold and crave the warmth of my native Tartarus, and as it is about time that I leave your earthly home, I will cease my discourse. Hoping that thou wilt publish this, that it may go well with thee, I have been, am, and will be the worst spirit that ever existed either in fact or realm of fancy.

-THE AXEMAN

Tuesday was St. Joseph's Night, always a time of great excitement among Italians in New Orleans. This year it reached a fever pitch. The traditional altars made of a hundred or more kinds of food were built, admired, dismantled, and distributed to the poor; lucky fava beans were handed out by the fistful; the saint was petitioned and praised. Still, St. Joseph's Night of 1919 would remain indelibly fixed in New Orleans memory as The Axeman's Jazz Night.

Cafés and mansions on St. Charles blazed with the melodies of live jazz bands. Those who could not afford to pay musicians fed pennies into player pianos. A popular composer had written a song called "The Mysterious Axeman's Jazz, or, Don't Scare Me, Papa." Banjo, guitar, and mandolin players gathered on the levees to send jazz music into the sky, so the Axeman would be sure to hear it as he passed over. By midnight, New Orleans was a cacophony of sounds, all of them swinging.

Cagliostro walked the streets for most of the night, marveling (if not actively congratulating himself) at how completely he had brought the city together, and how gay he had made it in the process. No one so much as glanced at him: few people were on the streets, and Cagliostro had a talent for making himself invisible.

He had left the Axeman's corpse locked in the back of the house where it wouldn't spoil the groceries. First, of course, he had bludgeoned the face into unrecognizable mush with the Axeman's own axe. Everything that suggested the murdered man might be someone other than "Mike Pepitone," simple Italian grocer, was in the satchel Cagliostro carried with him.

On the turntable of his phonograph, as a final touch, he had left a recording of "Nearer My God To Thee."

When the jazz finally began to die down, he walked to the docks and signed onto a freighter headed for Egypt. There were any number of wonderful things he hadn't gotten around to learning last time.

Italy, 1945

Toward the end, Mussolini lived in an elaborate fantasy world constructed by the loyal sycophants who still surrounded him. Whole cities in Italy were sanitized for his inspection, the cheering crowds along his parade routes supplemented by paid extras. When Hitler visited Rome, he too was deceived by the coat of sparkle on the decay, the hand-picked Aryan soldiers, the sheer bravado of *Il Duce*.

He believed he had cost Hitler the war. Germany lost its crucial Russian campaign after stopping to rescue the incompetent Italian army in Albania. Hitler had believed in the power and glory of Italy, and Mussolini had failed him.

Now he had been forced into exile on Lake Garda. He was a failure, his brilliant regime was a failure, and there were no more flunkies to hide these painful truths. He kept voluminous diaries in which he fantasized that his position in history would be comparable to Napoleon or Christ. His mistress Claretta lived nearby in a little villa, his only comfort.

On April 25, Germany caved in to the Allies. The Italian people, the ones he had counted on to save him with their loyalty, turned against him. Mussolini and Claretta fled, making for Switzerland.

A few last fanatical companions attempted to help them escape by subterfuge, but they were arrested by partisans on the north shore of Lake Como, discovered hiding in a German truck, cringing inside German coats and helmets. They were shot against the iron gate of an exquisite villa, and their bodies were taken to Milan and strung up by the heels to demonstrate the evils of Fascism.

All in service of the brotherhood of man.

CONJURE ME

AN OPERATING TABLE. A SCALPEL. This was Josephine's dream. The Good Doctor was carving her up. Each incision released a torrent of blood. His grinning face was splattered, his apron drenched. She screamed and screamed. Suddenly it was over, the straps removed, the blood gone, and he handed her a bouquet of red roses. "I'm sorry," he said, tears running down his face. "But these instruments are useless." His eyes rolled back, his body began to convulse, and she watched in horror as a black cottonmouth emerged from the roses and crawled against her thigh.

In the morning she walked through the courtyard behind her quarters. She removed her robe and stepped into the laundry basin. The charcoal was still glowing; the water was warm. She lathered a rag and scrubbed her neck and arms. Afterward she put on her new white dress and slippers. She pulled back her hair and tied it with a red ribbon, twisting strands of her hair into curls that hung before each cheek. She fastened the gold earrings the Good Doctor had given her. She was proud as she examined herself in the fractured mirror above the sink. Then she went into the house to prepare the Good Doctor's breakfast.

She made a spoon bread and veal hash. She brought out silk napkins and the finest silver and placed a bowl of fig preserves in the center of the table. She took a moment to think of their future together, and the prospect of a wedding breakfast bloomed in her imagination. But her fantasy was soon spoiled by a noise upstairs. It was the Good Doctor's wife, Celeste, moaning again. Josephine listened for his voice. Usually the Good Doctor would soothe Celeste with gentle words, then call for Josephine to bring the calomel and a little wine. Right now he remained quiet, most likely using a cold wet cloth to wipe perspiration from the dying woman's brow.

A few blocks away the cathedral bells tolled the hour. As if provoked by the clanging, the cannon in the Place d'Armes fired. The powder blasts were intended to purify the disease-ridden air and stave off the bayou's fetid vapors. Inside the Good Doctor's home, the windows shook and the china cups vibrated on their saucers. Accustomed to the sudden explosions, Josephine did not flinch but continued cooking. She had just started the coffee when he came downstairs. She could not remember him ever having looked so fatigued, and yet despite his rumpled clothes and sallow complexion, he was handsome beyond measure.

"You need rest," she told him.

He placed his hands on a chair and leaned forward. "She must go to the hospital."

Josephine repressed the urge to kiss him. She didn't know anyone who had left the Charity Hospital alive.

"Is she that ill?"

He nodded and sat down wearily at the table. "I gave her something to make her sleep."

The water in the kettle was boiling. She poured it over the coffee grounds. She cut a slice of bread and scooped hash on top of it. When he was done, she approached, stroking his wispy, blonde hair. Determined, she let her hands linger against his cheek.

He petted her arm and said, chokingly, "I'll never forgive myself for allowing her to stay."

When the epidemic had begun to spread, he stayed behind out of a sense of duty. On her part, Celeste would not leave her husband's side. Now it was summer, and everyone in the quarantined city was dying. Victims lay on the floors of the Charity Hospital, where the Good Doctor had volunteered before his wife contracted the fever. Ever since the Sorceress had announced colored people were immune, Josephine stopped worrying about getting sick.

"I forgive you," she said, pressing her mouth to his throat.

At first, he remained impassive; he did not succumb. But she was certain his defenses were ruined from exhaustion, so she removed her dress and untied her hair.

He took her on the parlor table.

As he dozed on the sofa, she went upstairs to retrieve the *gris-gris* from under the wife's mattress. It was a small chamois bag that contained strands of hair plaited together; scrapings of dried blood, hers obtained from a menstrual napkin, the Good Doctor's from a towel he'd used to dab a shaving cut; a tiny heart of red wax. The room smelled terrible. Surrounded by mosquito netting, the dying woman lay asleep in her great mahogany bed, drawing ragged breaths. Standing naked over her, Josephine reached inside herself to smear the Good Doctor's seed on the *gris-gris* She returned the charm to the mattress. Briefly, she considered pressing a pillow to the bleached face. But direct intervention was unnecessary. The spell had been improved; the woman would be dead by nightfall. She would never make it to the hospital.

Josephine bathed in the porcelain tub, using the expensive, sweet-smelling soaps. It was her second bath today, and she felt a sumptuous delight in drying herself with her lover's inscribed towel. She redressed and walked out into the yard to gather sprays of jasmine that grew upon the trellis and carried them inside. She placed them in a vase atop the mantelpiece. Throughout the morning, she sat quietly in the parlor and worked on her sewing, rocking back and forth in her chair. She filed her nails with the dying woman's emoryboard. All the while the cannon boomed and the dogs howled and the death carts clattered. Finally, there was a muffled whimper from the sofa. It was the Good Doctor, having just awakened, his face buried in a cushion, weeping. She put her arm around him and felt his body shudder.

"Hush," she said. "It's almost over."

In the afternoon, they received a visitor, Dr. Tallant, the Health Warden in charge of the Fourth District and, confronted with the spectacle of mass death, an unrepentant drunk. He prescribed whiskey for medicinal as well as inspirational purposes, and at dusk he could be found hovering near the chain-ganged slaves in the cemetery, letting them swig mightily from one of his many bottles, keeping them at their grim task of digging trenches for the growing piles of corpses.

"Liberal and frequent," he said. "Liberal and frequent potations of whiskey will rescue us from the Black Angel." He was pouring himself another drink in the Good Doctor's study. The Good Doctor refrained, as liquor made him tired and careless. Instead, he sat numbly in his leather chair, checking his pulse against the clock on his desk, waiting for the cocaine to do its work.

"More rumors," Tallant continued, spilling whiskey on his vest. "There's a shortage of gravediggers, and the people are fearful. They suspect we're burning bodies."

"Well, are we?"

"Of course not. The stench would be hellish. Even worse than the tar."

"Still. Perhaps the Roman custom isn't such a bad idea."

Tallant snorted. "Nero's human lamps. No, what we need are more niggers. Big, strong, stupid, fever-resistant, liquor-prone niggers. Give me just twenty, and we could bury the entire city."

"Be careful what you wish for." The Good Doctor was about to go upstairs. He was gradually achieving clinical detachment. He no longer saw the dying woman as his wife, but as yet another condemned patient mutilated by absurd treatments. He felt detached from his own actions, from the world that was collapsing around him. He was burdened with the awful knowledge that nothing he did mattered. His abilities to heal had been all along a mirage. Would everything be taken from him? He wanted to get down on his knees and plead for Celeste's recovery. Or else demand a speedier oblivion. Either way he was running out of tears.

Tallant pulled out tobacco and rolled a cigarette.

The Good Doctor shook his head. "I'm taking Celeste to the hospital."

"I would not recommend it."

"The Sisters of Charity might help."

Tallant sighed, struck a match.

"Nothing works," insisted the Good Doctor. "I've tried everything. Bleeding. Blistering. Quinine."

"Calomel?"

"It ulcerated her gums and tongue. Her teeth fell out."

"The fever spares no one, not even the Sisters. Better she passes away here, where it's clean and quiet and sane."

The Good Doctor swallowed and said, "Yesterday three fever victims walked out of the hospital. In sound health."

"Easily explained. They were not fever victims, but individuals with minor complaints who assumed they were stricken. No miracle, sir."

"I'm killing her." He removed his glasses and pinched the bridge of his nose.

"What?"

"That damnable opium. I'm killing her with it."

Again the cannon discharged. It seemed, at least to the Good Doctor, that Death himself was bombarding the city.

Tallant silently raised his glass, as if saluting the noise.

"Let it come down," muttered the Good Doctor to no one in particular. He shuffled the papers on his desk in search of an editorial from the *Crescent*.

"Another rumor," he said. "The witch-woman plans to resurrect the dead." He handed over the clipping.

"I've heard," said Tallant, waving it away.

Josephine knocked and entered the study. "She's awake, sir."

"All right," said the Good Doctor. His voice thickened. He was hesitant to say anything more, fearing Tallant might discern their secret.

When she left, the Good Doctor wanted to ask Tallant if he thought Josephine was beautiful, but the question was foolish. Her wide hips and round breasts, her dark hair and green eyes. At seventeen, she was already a vision. Indeed, the single flaw in her beauty was that she was aware of it.

"Tomorrow night," Tallant continued, "there will be a ceremony in the bayou."

"Will it be stopped?"

"No. The authorities are too busy. Let the niggers have their little party. Soon we'll all be food for worms."

"Josephine said the strangest thing the other day. She said the fever doesn't attack colored people."

"She's in for a shock," said Tallant, laughing.

"I'm a doctor. This is a doctor's house. Where does she get an idea like that?"

The opium was wearing off. Celeste drifted in and out of consciousness. During the day, the window was kept closed, but now, at night, the burning had lessened and the cannon had stopped, so Josephine threw the shutters open. She lit a lantern and pulled a chair to the bed. With the bowl in her lap, she wrung the excess water from the rags. Her hands shook badly as she bathed the dying woman's forehead. She set the rags down for a moment to collect herself. She wanted very much to strangle the Good Doctor's wife.

She brought to mind the afternoon she and the Good Doctor rode through the city in his carriage, from one clothes shop to the next. He never considered his own attire, always settling for old shirts and shabby coats. He was only meticulous when it came to choosing for Josephine dresses that were elegant and simple. He bought shoes for her and an expensive pair of green-silk gloves. She wore the gloves in the coach on the way back. "Do you like them?" he said. That week his wife had displayed the early symptoms of the fever. Josephine hoped the Good Doctor would soon be hers.

"Oh yes," she said.

*   *   *

The next evening, when the Good Doctor's wife refused to die, Josephine went to see the Sorceress, Queen of the Voodoo. Some people said the Sorceress consorted with Satan, who sometimes appeared to her in the form of a snake called Zombi and protected her from the whites. Other people said she was a thief and a blackmailer. The mistress of a legion of men. That she had committed murder. So it had seemed likely that she possessed the means to realizing Josephine's desires—the magic a slave girl needed to conquer a white doctor. But now the slave girl's heart was filled with anger and disappointment. The charm the Sorceress had promised would bind the Good Doctor to her had failed.

She stepped out into Canal Street. The air was a scourge of buzzing, biting mosquitoes. The tar barrels positioned on every corner palled the city with smoke. For weeks people had been pouring out of New Orleans, breaking the rules of quarantine. Everywhere porters were securing trunks atop carriages as waiting passengers—the plague clearly visible in their mottled features—coughed into stained handkerchiefs. The poor hurried along the sidewalks, luggage and children in tow, out of breath, on the verge of collapse. Josephine had no idea how these doomed souls expected to evade the armed sentries patrolling the bayous. The streets also swarmed with packs of stray dogs. Josephine watched a street cleaner carefully proffer a poisoned sausage to a mutt, its mouth flecked with foam. She passed a thin, bespectacled white man, wearing a heavy black coat, clean-shaven, plugs in his nostrils, who tipped his hat and smiled at her. In his mouth was a piece of orange peel.

Josephine drew her shawl around her and pushed on.

She went to the edge of the city, where the cobblestones abruptly ended. Gripping the pole of a gaslight, she stopped to rest and survey her surroundings as bits of afternoon light faded from the sky. Beyond stretched a dank, swamplike region spotted with grassy places. Along the riverbank, a servant was ruthlessly beating a carpet with a stick. Josephine made the mistake of drawing a big breath and inhaled an insect. The coughing fit was severe. She applied some more camphor to her skin. After dabbing her slick forehead with a handkerchief, she plunged into the bayou's darkness.

The moon was full, lighting up the moss that hung from the oak branches, reflecting off the waters of St. John's Bayou, but the stars remained invisible, as though the moon had siphoned their energies. Lightning flashed;

thunder rumbled in the distance. Fireflies flickered among the palmetto leaves. A frog croaked so obscenely that Josephine felt a chill run through her body.

She reached the clearing in time. The Sorceress was still reclining on her throne, a wicker chair with a high back atop a wooden platform. She wore a short garment made of scarlet handkerchiefs sewn together. Around her waist was a heavy blue cord, and about her shoulders a red shawl with black fringe. Her hair was bound in a *tignon*, its gray-streaked knots standing above her head. Her scrawny feet were bare and on each leg was an anklet ornamented with tiny bells. Her bead necklace hung to her waist, and gold bracelets covered her arms from wrists to elbows. Shiny rings adorned her fingers. The Sorceress sat, motionless, eyes wide open and staring at the fire in the center of the clearing. Her followers were nowhere in sight, but Josephine could sense them moving around, stalking the perimeter of shadows.

A black rooster strutted from behind the throne. The Sorceress limped towards it. She picked it up by its feet, a knife glinting in her hand. She placed her foot on the rooster's neck, and yanked. She cut off the head and tossed it into the fire. The body went on flapping, and when she released it, it scampered recklessly around the platform, blood spurting with every beat of its dying heart. The old woman returned to her throne, and, finally, leveled her intense gaze at Josephine.

"Girl, come here. No need to hide in the bushes like a rat. Remove your clothes and speak your troubles."

Josephine stepped warily into the firelight. She stripped off her silt-streaked dress and muddy shoes. Standing before the Sorceress, she wore only her white camisole, as was the rule. Years ago, the old woman had barely survived a knife attack by the agent of a rival priestess. Soon after she decreed that whoever sought her help must approach in their undergarments so that no weapon was concealed. Josephine ascended the stairs and knelt before the Sorceress, beside whom the headless rooster twitched and flapped its life away.

"Closer."

Josephine scooted forward until she was inches from the old woman's face. Her cheeks were marked with grotesque scars, her breath foul.

"Does your man belong to you?"

"No," said Josephine.

"Then someone has discovered us. Has he another woman? Is he impotent with you?"

"No."

"Perfume. Sprinkle some of your perfume on the *gris-gris*."

"Sorceress, yesterday I made the *gris-gris* stronger."

The old woman looked at her in surprise. "What have you done, child? Tell me."

"The charm is marked with his seed. It lies under his dying wife's mattress."

For this, Josephine was brutally slapped.

"Stupid girl, that *gris-gris* was a love spell. Now you've made it a dagger. And why did you not say the man was married? Oh, the *loa* are angry and will require a sacrifice."

Still on her knees, Josephine rubbed the sting from her cheek. She set her lips tightly together and said, "His wife must die. He cannot love me otherwise."

The old woman held up a gnarled finger. "If she's not dead, then he has found the charm and removed it. He knows!"

"He knows nothing."

The Sorceress stood and stretched out her arms, bracelets jangling. "Walk the land for a thousand miles. O, devil-o, you are a swamp thing. Black ghost. Whore of Dambalah. You will walk and walk, the dead among the living. You will walk and have no peace. Not until your death is avenged." Then she cocked her fist.

Josephine jumped down from the platform, gathered her clothes, and ran, tripping over the roots of cypress trees. She looked back once, relieved that no one followed.

Tallant was playing a minuet in the parlor. The Good Doctor's eyes hurt from lack of sleep. He fought against the numbness in his heart. He wanted to feel pain, but there was nothing. Fine, then. He resolved to leave grief behind and not know it anymore. It was replaced by an entirely different sensation—cold curiosity. Curiosity as to whether he would come out of this epidemic alive to see sunlight fall across a young woman's face as she walked among the squirrels in Congo Square. He struggled to raise himself and swung his legs to the side of the bed. He glanced at the mirror. A picture of absolute wretchedness. He left the guest room and entered the kitchen. He drank several cups of strong coffee. He was in his shirt-sleeves, and his trouser legs were thrust into the tops of his boots. He saw Tallant standing awkwardly by the piano. The Good Doctor took his coat from the rack and slipped it on. "I'm ready," he said.

Tallant cleared his throat. "Josephine is gone. Her obedience is questionable, I think."

The Good Doctor looked away, then back at Tallant. He shrugged. "It's just as well."

Together they went upstairs, where Celeste's body lay peacefully in bed.

"Let's wrap her in the sheets," Tallant suggested.

They pulled the sheets from the bed. The Good Doctor heard something hit the floor.

"What is that?" said Tallant.

The Good Doctor stooped to pick it up and answered, "*Gris-gris.*"

"Well, what's it doing here?"

"That little whore."

She ran until she was exhausted, famished. Then she walked. On the banks of the river an old man gave her chunks of salted fish. She continued eastward until she reached the port, at which point she left the riverside and meandered back up through Esplanade. There were noises everywhere. The tolling of bells. The slow clumping of hooves. The rattling of wheels on cobblestones. The moans of the dying. She saw two men cramming a woman's corpse into an undersized coffin. The men jammed the lid shut, mangling her lifeless face and crushing her skull so that the flies swirled in agitation.

It was midnight when she reached the house. On the porch was a filthy gray dog, who raised its head to growl at her. From the front yard she seized a fallen tree limb, keeping it between her and the dog. She paused at the door, afraid to enter because of her disheveled appearance. She was thirsty. She would do anything now for a glass of water. She stood at the door of the house, her ear pressed close to it. Silence.

"Hello?" she called out. There was no answer.

She walked through the house and into the courtyard, where she removed her soiled clothes and took a bath. Inside her quarters, she put on her sleeping gown and got in bed. A few minutes later, her door creaked open. "Is that you?" she murmured sleepily. The breathing she heard was unfamiliar. Her heart beat frantically. A ringing filled her ears. She lay completely still with her face in the pillow. She could not turn to look at the stranger looming above her.

Tallant threw the blankets to the floor. He took hold of her gown by the neck and yanked it. She heard it tear, and she was naked, scrambling to the other side of the bed. He grabbed her by the arm and pulled her to him and used rope to tie her wrists to the bedpost. "No," she said, but his grip was unbreakable. In a panic she tried to bolt, but he punched her until she tasted her own blood. He was behind her now, pulling her hips toward him so that she was on her knees. He took her long black hair in his fist. He pressed the pillow to her face, muffling her screams. When he was through, he flipped her over.

She felt the knife cutting into her.

In the Fourth District Cemetery, the fires were always burning. As the cart drew closer, Tallant dropped the reins for a moment so he could pull on his gloves. He took the flask from his coat. Then he lit a cigarette and picked up the reins. He had been going to the cemetery every day for the last six weeks, and it had always made him happy. Tonight, things were different. He saw that the slaves were being directed by Dr. Matheson, an elderly physician with a penchant for clubbing negroes with the butt of his rifle. Dr. Matheson was waving his rifle now, signaling to Tallant that the proceedings were without flaw.

Tallant brought the cart to a halt and jumped out, anxious to get the task over with quickly. He threw the catch and jerked down the rear gate. He pulled out one of the sheet-wrapped bodies and dragged it to the edge of the shallow pit. There he stood it on its feet and shoved. The body rolled down the incline until it settled on the pile of lime-dusted corpses. Drawing harsh breaths, he hurried back to the cart. He didn't mind the sight of so many dead things. Rather, it was the terrible smell that constricted his lungs. A rank odor hung above the cemetery—*mephitisme*, the French called it, the smell of death. It was believed to cause milk to curdle and wine to turn to vinegar. Now he dragged the second body to the edge and pushed it over. After emptying a sack of lime over the pile, he went back to the cart again and closed the gate. Then he walked to the edge of the cemetery, drawn by nothing more than the chaotic flames of a tar barrel. He lit a cigarette, suffused with the satisfaction of his crimes.

A slave by the name of Robert approached, leg shackles clanking.

"Mr. Tallant, sir!"

"Yes, Robert, what is it?"

"One of those dead bodies you brung. Body ain't dead!"

"Of course it's dead. You don't suppose I'd bury a living person, do you?"

"Sir, I swear I saw it crawl off somewheres."

"How could it crawl if it was wrapped in a sheet? Goddamn it, give me back my whiskey!"

"It got loose," Robert continued, handing over the bottle. "A dead girl, I think."

"Shut up, Robert. You're drunk."

"Hard to say because of all the blood."

Tallant drew his revolver and fired it, obliterating Robert's lower jaw.

As the mortally wounded slave writhed in the dirt, the other slaves stopped their digging and stared at Tallant. The cemetery was silent. Then he watched as his murderous behavior incited Dr. Matheson, who, whooping with delight, raised his rifle and executed another slave standing beside him with a point-blank bullet to the chest.

"Please, Dr. Matheson," Tallant said calmly, putting his own gun away. "There's much work to be done."

She regained consciousness, the light of the distant stars reminding her that she was lying on muddy ground. She tried to stand, but fell back down. She succeeded in getting up on her elbows. She was too weak to cry for help. Who would hear? Who would care? The whole city was crying for help. With a tremendous effort, she finally rose, staggering. Her knees trembled, her feet were like lead. Now the stars grew in intensity, rolling in the sky, and she had to look away because of the nausea the sight induced. She reeled, and each step caused her wounds to throb with pain. She wiped her mouth where the blood still flowed. She followed the sound of beating drums and chanting voices.

Hands outstretched, she felt her way through the darkness. She toppled into a ditch. She clawed at the thistles and weeds with her fingernails. She felt the clammy touch of the dead. The harsh smell of lime filled her nostrils. It dawned on her that she had fallen into a mass grave on the bayou's edge. Desperate, she managed to pull herself out, but she couldn't find the strength to stand. She vomited something thick, something clotted, and her legs went numb. The path wavered before her like a stream in the moonlight. There was so much blood, perhaps there *was* a stream. A stream of her own blood running into the void ahead. Her blood had turned to water. She wept and prayed. But what good are prayers when the last hour has arrived? A dog approached and licked her face with its rough tongue before vanishing into the trees. She crawled on her belly, dragging her dead legs.

The drums were loud now, the singing was fierce. When she reached the clearing, black faces huddled around her.

"Who is this?" someone said.

"It's the Zombi," said another.

"No," said the Sorceress. "Her name is Josephine."

They carried her to the altar and examined her by torchlight. They washed and bandaged her wounds and lighted a white candle at her head and another at her feet. She could feel the old woman's bony hand in her own. Someone was applying dirt to her face. Someone placed a heavy instrument in her other hand—a machete? Somewhere nearby a hen was cackling.

She breathed with shallow gulps, trying hard to shut out the noises around her, the words spoken so fast and so loud until they were garbled, until they buzzed against her chest like giant insects, but it was no use. The ceremonial words triggered a thing that had been inside her all along, a monster that had known her ever since she'd come to the city to live with the Good Doctor.

It was larger than anything, larger than the darkness that had enveloped her, forever removing her from the solace of light. She would not get better, and she would never return. If she returned, it would be as something unrecognizable to her.

So she said to those gathered around her: "Conjure me."

After Tallant left to dispose of Celeste's corpse, the Good Doctor threw away the vase of jasmine that his slave had placed on the mantel. He knew little of voodoo, but he understood that a charm like the one placed under his wife's bed was evil. It was meant to cause serious harm. His slave had betrayed him. No doubt she had worsened Celeste's condition. Perhaps the girl had even tortured his wife during her final days. Where had Josephine gone? If she returned, he would sell her. Put her back on the auction block where he had found her.

In the silence of the library, he sat with his arms hanging off the chair. He drew in a breath. A mosquito buzzed his ear. He swatted it; blood spotted his palm. If I could die now, he thought. Peacefully, gently, without a tremor or a crying out. If I could be with her. If I could believe I would be with her. His fingers tightened slowly and his head sank forward on his chest. He sprang suddenly forward and grabbed the gun, putting it into his mouth. The taste was vile.

Celeste. Take me where you are.

He stared at the portrait of his mother, a beautiful Spaniard, whose long red hair flowed down over her milk-white bosom.

He had no idea how long he'd been there. After a while, though, his deepest sorrow had faltered. The most penetrating despair of his life had lost its edge. The flagellant's curse, he thought, to grow accustomed to the whip.

He straightened up and stood. Still alive. His heart pumped senselessly, his blood churned without purpose. Bones and muscles and tissue—all functioning, but for what reason? He looked at the gun on his desk. He picked it up again, put it back down. Then he turned away with a sigh and left, closing the door behind him quietly. He was on his way to the Charity Hospital, where he would do his best to placate the dying. He would do his job and hope to find some meaning in it.

On his way home, Tallant smashed the bottle against the wheel of an incinerated carriage. New Orleans smelled of death and useless remedies and, above all else, naked fear. For the first time since the epidemic began, Tallant felt at one with the city. He remembered the night, years ago, when the sky was lighted by the fires of a slave revolt. An angry crowd had ignited ten thousand bales of cotton on the levee. Ships were cut from their moorings and sent floating down the river in flames. Warehouses were raided, and molasses and sugar were poured onto the burning cotton. Great clouds of black smoke shut out the warm spring sunlight. A night of complete terror. It was the same kind of pleasure he felt now, an exhilaration in the promise of further unrest and suffering. Only now the gutters ran with blood and decomposing animals. Indeed, he felt at peace in a doomed world.

At his front door, he stomped the crud from his boots before taking them off. Inside, the house was quiet, and, socks on his feet, he padded upstairs. Miles away in the bayou, the Sorceress and her followers continued to practice their heathen religion. Tallant heard the drums going; the ceremony was reaching its climax. Raising the dead. Sacrificing the goat. Fondling the snake called Zombi. Tallant laughed and shook his head and took a light from the kitchen. He proceeded into his darkened bedroom.

The lantern seemed to dim; was the kerosene low? He fumbled in his pockets for a match, but there was none. He would have to go back downstairs to get more kerosene and some matches. He stumbled in an effort to locate the bedside lamp. Beneath the sound of the drums, he heard a floorboard creak. He stood stock-still for a moment, then swung his fading lantern left then right. The sound of something sharp whistled through the air. He felt the blade catch him in the neck.

JOHN BIGUENET

GREGORY'S FATE

IT WAS IN LATE ADOLESCENCE that my childhood friend Gregory first gave evidence of the unique talent that would doom him to the most pathetic of fates.

A shy and self-conscious young man, Greg must have discovered the earliest manifestations of his strange gift in the privacy of his room or, perhaps, in the steaming waters of his tub. I am sure that these signs—what we would later call "symptoms"—were so slight as to barely attract his attention. There may have been a certain slackness to his thigh, an inexplicably enlarged knuckle, a pattern of bright pigments emerging on the pale skin stretched across his breastbone, but nothing so extraordinary as to frighten him into the waiting room of a physician. Too, whatever happened to trouble his drowsing bath or daydreaming solitude would have waned in a few hours, leaving him unsure that he had really seen anything at all in the dresser mirror or beneath the cloudy water.

Eventually, curiosity and vague anxiety would have impelled Gregory to rub the erupting pores or poke the knob of bone protruding on the back of his hand. He would have been startled to see his manipulations affect the physical changes he was witnessing. Mesmerized as he watched himself attenuate his arm into a wing and twist his toes into talons, Gregory would not have noticed his fear yield to wonder. Hours later, turning his feathered face to the mirror, how he must have marveled at his miraculous transformation.

The change was not, as in literature or even as in film, instantaneous. Flesh and bone had to be worked into fresh relationships. Each piece had to be tooled. The latent memory of each ligament and tendon had to be massaged into oblivion. Then each aching new joint had to be rotated into each raw new socket. Bones had to be bent, the skull deformed, the skin hardened. It could take hours.

Once, after he had revealed to me his secret, I walked in on my friend in the process of changing into a dog. He seemed horribly disfigured and turned to me with the most pitiful and suppliant gaze I had ever encountered. I put my arms around his furry nape as he convulsed with the changes that wracked his body.

At the time, I thought it mere impulse that Greg had divulged the marvel of his transformations to me. But looking back, I see now that he intended to confess everything. Unwilling to confide in his parents, he really had no one else but me with whom to share his secret. Surely the urge to tell someone of the incredible things that were happening to his body must have nearly equaled the overwhelming urge to continue the strange experiments he was performing on himself.

At the same time, I sensed that his astounding gift was a source of shame for him. Gregory thought of his ability as simply a bad habit—one that he ought to overcome. He associated it, somehow, with his virginity. He confided to me his certainty that only a woman could cure him of the malleability that so afflicted his flesh and bones.

On the other hand, Greg lacked the malleability of imagination that might have allowed him to become what he appeared. No matter how extreme the transformation, he remained Gregory, a man, stuffed into a sack stitched in feathers or stretched over the long skeleton of a giraffe.

As summer progressed into the darker nights of autumn, the consequences of his adventures became increasingly worrisome. They were exactly the results anyone might engender by walking down the street in a gorilla costume. One might try to explain that it was just a joke, but to the terrified child whom the gorilla was attempting to calm, only a mumbled growl would seem to issue from the fierce, hairy mask. There was an enormous sense of the ridiculous surrounding these episodes—and a growing danger.

Regaining his original form took longer and longer. The flesh lacked its former resiliency. It sagged where it had been distended. It chafed where it had turned to scales. It erupted into boils where horns had sprouted.

Now the transformations lingered, at least in isolated patches on his body, beyond the weekends. For some days afterwards, feathers would rustle beneath the wool of his slacks whenever he crossed his legs, or the ridges of a serrated spine would spoil the line of his blazer.

Gregory began to refer to the restoration of his true form as recuperation: "I'm still healing from the last attack," he confessed to me one Friday over the phone. I was no doctor, but I fell into the same terminology. I found myself calling Greg's unique talent a "condition." But neither of us could imagine what therapy or surgery might alleviate his disease.

It was in these low days of worry and suffering that Gregory first pointed out Esperanza to me. We were in a café on Royal Street, sharing a newspaper and sipping coffee after classes at the university, when a tiny young woman, encumbered by swollen shopping bags and immense packages, lumbered through the narrow carriageway to the patio where we sat. Disgorging her purchases onto a table next to ours, she collapsed into an ancient wrought-iron chair. The bags, I noticed, were emblazoned with the crests of the most expensive boutiques in the French Quarter and the huge packages were bound in the delicate ribbons of the city's most exclusive shops. Taking a quarter from her change purse, she tapped on the edge of her table till a waiter scurried over to take her order.

Greg seemed to take no notice of the hubbub. Slowly turning the pages of *The Times-Picayune*, he was engrossed, it appeared, in the small type of the stock exchange reports. It should have occurred to me that, having never played the market, my friend had no reason to peruse the financial section. In fact, the newspaper was merely a blind behind which Gregory savored the good fortune of our chance encounter with the woman he adored.

Though he had never met her, Gregory had somehow ferreted out her name and her family's history from those mutual acquaintances that so complicate life in a small city. Esperanza Obliga was the youngest of four daughters of a wealthy Nicaraguan family who had escaped their country after the Sandinista rebellion. Though reduced in circumstances, the family survived on their vast holdings in Brazil and in the Yucatan as well as on their accounts in Switzerland and Miami. Señor Obliga had been an intimate of the recently assassinated dictator, Anastasio Somoza, and therefore kept a low profile in the émigré community. "Despite her father's position in the government, Esperanza's heart, of course, was with the revolutionaries who overthrew the detested tyrant," Gregory assured me, though how he might have glimpsed the workings of her heart—having never so much as spoken to her—was beyond my powers of comprehension.

Personally, once we did meet her, I found Señorita Obliga a rather odd girl with an annoying habit of lapsing into trances in the middle of conversations. Gregory furiously defended her: "What do you expect, Francis, when you insist upon such tedious arguments? Even I find them a bit bor-ing." Her pinched face with its huge black eyes and her small, tubercular frame reminded me, I suppose, of an albino bat. But Gregory worshiped her.

The slightest departure from the indifference with which Esperanza usually responded to my friend's embarrassing flattery would thrill him for days. Her smallest, patronizing gesture of gratitude for the costly pre-sents he laid at her feet would send him back to the stores on another shopping spree that left him yet more deeply in debt. At last, though, even the love-besotted eyes of poor Greg began to see that Esperanza's tiny heart remained closed to him.

In a desperate final bid for her tenderness, he determined to employ the full resources of his metamorphic powers. He imagined over emptied mugs of beer—in which he more and more indulged—how he might dazzle the object of his affection with his transformations, and thus woo her.

I counseled my friend to find another way. If his desire insisted upon Esperanza Obliga, then he should write poems to her, join her church, go to work for her father. Over the last months, the transformations had grown steadily more debilitating; I worried about the medical consequences if Greg, in his fevered state of mind, should undertake a program of these dangerous changes.

Gregory took my advice—in part. When I next saw him, he clutched the catechism of the Obligas' church. Not only was he preparing for bap-tism, but he proudly announced that a friend of his family had secured a part-time position for him as personal secretary to Esperanza's father. Unfortunately, though, Gregory had no talent for poetry. He was grateful for my advice, but he remained convinced that only his special gift could reveal to the woman he loved the depth of his affection. When I tried to remind him of the dangers, he grew testy with me.

Seeing that it was pointless to continue my efforts at dissuasion, I agreed to assist my friend in the elaborate sequence of transformations he had planned. (I thought, if something went wrong, at least I could get him to a hospital.) To assuage my concern, he assured me that, once he had com-pleted the first metamorphosis, his body would yield easily to the others. "It's just getting back to being human that's difficult," he admitted.

Gregory had prepared a script for me. I was to serve as a kind of narra-tor for Esperanza as my friend metamorphosed from eagle to gazelle to dolphin to pony and then back to Gregory. He had penned a rather awk-ward introduction and series of interludes in which he suggested, employing the hoariest of clichés, the relationship of these creatures to the emotions he felt for the young lady. "My heart soars like an eagle," he had written, "whenever I see you." A literature major at the university, I offered to revise his narrative, but Gregory declined. He trusted Esperanza to see his love for what it truly was.

Though of course I did not say so, I was terribly concerned about Greg's wounded pride and broken heart when Esperanza, if she even agreed to attend the little performance, reacted to his ridiculous sideshow act—as I had no doubt she would—with the condescending laugh she seemed to reserve for him. I felt certain no good could come of revealing his secret to Señorita Obliga.

Gregory had chosen to start the performance as an eagle because it required the most preparation; in fact, he thought it might take him three or four hours. That afternoon I locked him in the small campus theater we had reserved from the drama department; I had overcome the objections of the departmental secretary by assuring her that we were rehearsing scenes to be performed in an English class on the theater of the Middle Ages. Then at seven o'clock, as Greg had previously arranged, I picked up Esperanza and drove her to the university. It was obvious from our conversation in the car that she had agreed to come only out of curiosity. Gregory had given her no hint as to what she might expect, but he promised her a spectacle that would remain unmatched in her lifetime. I assured her that he had not exaggerated.

Having shown Esperanza to the specific seat that Greg had chosen for her, I climbed the steps to the stage and peeked behind the mangy velvet curtain. Gregory, beautifully transformed into a magnificent bird, nested on the floor. I crossed to the edge of the stage, and, standing on its apron where I could reach the curtain's drawlines, I took the script from my pocket and began to read aloud.

When I had reached the end of Gregory's cliché-ridden introduction, I hauled on the rope in my hand and parted the curtain. Waddling forward on claws that scrabbled along the wooden planks of the stage, the eagle squawked a contorted call into the darkened auditorium where Esperanza sat. I think the feathered throat was trying to say, "It's me—Gregory." But, to be honest, it sounded more like the rasping caw of a crow. I squinted into the spotlights, which I had turned on before we began, trying to see Esperanza's reaction. I could barely make out her form in the silent hall. Dragging his wings behind him, Gregory retreated, and I closed the curtain.

A bit nervous, I read the next passage too quickly. The grace of the gazelle, to which Gregory alluded in the narration as an image of Esperanza's beauty, was absent from the hairy beast with twisted horns that pawed the stage when, a few minutes later, I parted the curtain for the second transformation. Obviously rushed in its creation, the animal seemed a crude approximation of so lithe a creature. Greg had needed more time; in fact, a few feathers still clung to his hindquarters.

I knew that the third transformation was the simplest, so I hurriedly closed the curtain on the crude gazelle and began to recite a homage to the idyllic life of the dolphin, a life of love beneath the waves. I must admit that I embroidered Gregory's prose with some of my own rhetorical inventions. Hearing my revisions, Greg interrupted me with a string of high-pitched barks. I drew open the curtain to reveal a pair of intelligent eyes regarding me above a silver snout. Dragging himself forward on his pectoral fins and slapping his flat tail against the stage, Gregory seemed on the verge of speaking, but the squeals that issued from his ridged jaws explained nothing. Once again, I closed the curtain.

Esperanza, infuriated at having wasted half an hour on such a ridiculous menagerie, made clear her utter lack of belief that these creatures could be manifestations of the awkward boy who plagued her with his incessant fawning.

Storming up the aisle, Esperanza interrupted my speech about the relationship of horses to love. Pushing past my feeble efforts to stop her, she tore open the curtain. Over her scrawny shoulder, I saw Gregory trying to cover his nakedness with his still-webbed hands. Pitiful under the harsh light of the single bulb that illuminated the backstage, he recklessly tugged upon his arms and legs, grasped his jaw in both hands to elongate his chin, flicked the top of his ears into points. Before the amazed and dumbstruck Esperanza, Gregory completed his performance, finally turning his long, sleek neck to the tiny girl and licking her outstretched palm.

Clapping her hands and giggling furiously, Esperanza leapt upon the dappled back of the little pony and, driving her heels into its haunches, whipped it round the bare stage with her belt. The pathetic whinnying at each lash punctuated the clopping of its unshod hooves against the worn wooden flooring.

A month later, the young couple was married in one of the most extravagant ceremonies the city had ever witnessed. That evening, while the reception roared on in the ballroom below, the new Mr. and Mrs. Gregory

Kunstler ascended in an ornate elevator, whose carpet had been littered with red rose petals, to the bridal suite atop the hotel.

And what became of Gregory, my friend? He prays in Esperanza's church, which forbids divorce. He works for his father-in-law, shamefully funneling arms and money to right-wing regimes in Central America. And late into the night, his wife makes him sit on the bathroom floor, where she pulls his fingers and rubs his flesh raw in the vain hope of reawakening the marvelous talent that disappeared—as Gregory had once guessed that it might—in her bony arms on their wedding night.

sazerac

The most credible claim to the origin of the word cocktail comes from Antoine Amedee Peychaud's concoction in New Orleans towards the beginning of the 19th century. The inventor of Peychaud Bitters, he opened his pharmacy at 437 Royal Street, where he often mixed his bitters with cognac in a French egg cup known as a coquetier (ko-k-tay´). Mispronounced in English, the drink became the first "cocktail." Rye whiskey was substituted for *Sazerac-du-Forge et fils* cognac after 1870, and absinthe was added. In 1949 the Hotel Roosevelt bought exclusive rights to what had become known as the "Sazerac Cocktail." The Sazerac Bar stands in the lobby of what is now The Fairmount Hotel.

1 sugar cube

dashes Peychaud bitters

$1\,^{1}/_{2}$ oz. rye whiskey

$^{1}/_{4}$ oz. Pernod

Swirl Pernod in a chilled Old Fashioned glass to coat.

Dissolve sugar.

Add a couple dashes of bitters to taste.

Fill with Whiskey & Garnish with a twist.

Serve neat.

LEONARD EARL JOHNSON

SEX IN THE SUMMER OF DISCONTENT

I READ TO AIDS PATIENTS. IT IS A TENDER EXPERIENCE. When I told this to an out of town editor her response was a bland, "Nice."

We were having this conversation on the telephone. Outside the open window I heard a tourist buggy passing, the driver telling a version of French Quarter history never heard in university. After hanging up I thought, "tender" and "nice."

One day I read "Riverday, the Day the Man Jumps in the River." It is about a suicide on The Moon Walk thwarted by friends from a homeless camp under the bridge. When I finished a man in a wheelchair asked, "Have you ever been depressed?"

When first I came to read I was introduced to a modern Catholic Nun. She wore street clothes and earrings and smiled warmly. She told me, "We demystify death here." I had asked, "What will happen if I cry?"

"You might give someone else a chance to cry." She paused, then added, "They think anything you might think."

"Yes," I told the man, "I have been depressed."

He said he had been terribly depressed. "I know I will never walk again, and I know I have to live here." He moved one arm around overhead and back down to his lap. We were on a balcony over a pleasant street, under a huge magnolia tree. He rolled his chair back and turned towards the tree. After a moment he said, "I don't think you could live in a hobo camp with AIDS." In the story I had just read, a sixteen-year-old white boy and a black man lived in such a camp.

He rocked his chair and said, "Did you see somebody? For your depression, I mean, or just get over it?"

"I see a woman still," I told my new friend. "When I started getting better, I said to her, 'I had hardly known how depressed I had been.'"

Visitors arrived and I left the balcony to them and went below. Through kitchen windows I saw my bicycle chained near a huge fig tree. The tree bulged with fruit. A black woman carrying laundry passed and said, "They sweet, too." She gave me a small plastic bag.

A beige-suited white woman touched my arm and asked if I would co-witness AIDS Law documents for two new people.

In one room beside an open window sat a silent boy of about nineteen, twenty, twenty-one.

In another room a boy of similar years sat up in his new bed and greeted us. He was from Big Mamou, drawn to New Orleans when he was thirteen. He told us of the Creole custom he learned here of dropping first names when speaking. "You would be 'Earl,' not 'Leonard,' not 'Leonard Earl,'" he said.

I carried my end of the conversation wishing we were not here, doing what we were doing. "Do they drop first names in Acadia, too?" I asked. I shifted my weight and kicked a pair of gargantuan tennis shoes sitting on the floor near his bed. It was a set-up for a conversation repeated in damn near every male's life. I wanted to say, should have said, "You got feet big enough to fill those shoes?" but I didn't. I feared it sounded sexy. I'd never before thought much about that, but sexy seemed out of place now.

We said goodbye and I went outside. Standing beside my bike, I looked at the big fig tree and started filling the plastic bag. The leaves were thick and scratchy. I closed my eyes and felt my tears on the backs of my hands.

MAKING GROCERIES

SHE BEGAN TO CRY WHILE STANDING IN AISLE THREE of the A&P looking for Fat-Free Sugar-Frosted Mini-Wheats. She was just standing there staring at the stacks of cereal boxes and thinking, damn it, where are they, they must be here someplace, when her eyes began to fill up with tears. They came on so quickly that to keep them from overflowing, she tilted her head back and regarded the shelves of cereal through half-lowered eyelids.

The bright colors swayed and wavered and floated hypnotically behind the blurred bars of her eyelashes. An underwater reef of cereal boxes, and I'm a shark cruising for diet food. The thought made her smile, and she gulped air trying to clear the lump in her throat.

I can't make a fool of myself in here, she told herself. These people know me. Their Saturday night is bizarre enough without having a weeping, wailing woman on their hands.

But she wanted to tell somebody—anybody. She wanted someone to hold and comfort her while she cried out loud her frustration and grief and anger. Where the hell are those Mini-Wheats? She went on scanning the cereal shelves, barely registering the fact that the thin young man squeezing by in the narrow aisle accessorized his tight jeans with a wide red patent-leather belt and red high-heeled sandals.

"This damn place never keeps enough of what I want," she finally murmured to herself in exasperation. "So it's the smallest A&P in the world. Big deal. I want my Fat-Free Sugar-Frosted Mini-Wheats." And she sighed heavily as she bent down to pick up a box of Shredded Wheat 'n Bran and read the list of vitamins and calories. Resigned, she dropped it into her basket between the three bananas and a carton of skim milk.

She walked the few steps to wait in line at the check-out counter and glance at the magazine covers lying in wait for last-minute readers. "BABY BORN WITH DOG'S FACE," she read. Sure enough, the accompanying photo did resemble a baldheaded dog. Or a pig, she thought, a baby born with pig's face. She stared at the baby's tender bald head, and for an instant the photo was real.

My God, I'm going crazy, she thought. How am I ever going to get through the night? I'd leave right now, but the train doesn't go until morning.

She unloaded her basket on the counter, resisting the urge to fall weeping into the arms of the cashier, whose huge black eyes gazed at her with infinite mercy. She paid for her groceries and walked outside to buy an early edition of the Sunday *Times-Picayune*. She tipped the stooped old newsman more than usual.

She walked slowly up Royal Street toward her apartment, deliberately dawdling among the window-shoppers, not wanting to be alone. Underneath her feet, pale crushed flowerets of Sweet Olive lifted their perfume to mingle with a ripe whiff of garbage. From around the corner came the faint rhythmic beat of tap dancing.

Her eyes found details now, details she had scarcely noticed before, piercingly beautiful, bittersweet. Tall buildings in the business district fading headless into fog. A balcony still twinkling with left-over Christmas decorations, a single red light blinking on and off like a pinprick warning. Hazy halos of streetlamps glittering against wet pavement. The shadow of Touchdown Jesus arching its giant finger over a couple walking arms entwined along Pirate's Alley. A pigeon huddled within the precise geometrical turn of a cornice. The glint of light on silver bangles behind glass. A dress of lace delicate as a spider's web. A doll whose huge black dead eyes stabbed directly into her own—a doll with Linda's hair.

Her heart bounced when she saw those tumbled blonde curls so like Linda's before. A red bow teetered there, Linda's favorite color. She pictured the doll egg-bald and wearing Linda's defiant substitute for a wig: a red velvet baseball cap. Too young, too soon, she thought. And I am going home too late. Reflected over the window's perfect, rigid tableaux, her tears rolled down the doll's face like drops of rain.

From *A RECENT MARTYR*

I CAME DOWN WITH A MYSTERIOUS ILLNESS that lasted four days. I ran a high fever and was so weak at times I found it difficult to walk. On the first day I was better, I determined to take Chris out of the dark, air-conditioned rooms in which she and I had been confined. She was as reluctant about it as I. We both knew we should get out, but one had only to open the front door and be greeted by the glare of the sidewalk to reconsider all options. We waited until three, in the hope of a shower. There were clouds, had been clouds in the afternoon for days, but by five or six they cleared off, leaving not a breath of moisture behind. I hadn't the strength to ride a bicycle, so we agreed to take a bus to the Square, where there would be shade for me, ice cream to eat, and pigeons to feed for my solitary daughter. I left a note for my husband and set out.

We took the bus to Esplanade and changed to another that brought us to the steps of the Square. Chris was serious, afraid we were on the wrong bus, as we had been once before. When the doors opened and she saw the trees, the cool stones, the fountain, the pale facade of the Cathedral, she broke free of my hand and ran. It was a relief to me to let her run. I had a clear view of her and she could go as far as the church with impunity. I followed her to the ice cream store, where we purchased a bag of corn for the birds. Then we crossed to the Square and she began tearing at her bag, jabbing her fingertips with the staples.

I sat on a bench nearby and watched her. Then I looked around myself. On the next bench an old man was pretending to be awake. On the bench next to his, turned slightly in my direction, her head bent so that she could read the small black book in her hand, was a woman I recognized. She looked up, not meeting my eyes, apparently unaware of being watched, then down again. The top button of her blouse was open and I noted the small black cross at her throat. It was Claire. Chris had a pigeon on her arm and began shouting at me, "Look, Mama, look, look!"

"That's fine," I said. "He's a big one." Then, because I had spoken, Claire looked at me, recognized me, and in the next moment our eyes met. She smiled uncomfortably. Would I speak to her? Her book fell closed in her lap.

I was condemned to stay. Chris would never leave the park until the last kernel of her corn had been consumed by the birds. She was for them, and for herself, at the very center of interest. I watched her abstractly, aware that Claire was standing up and moving, not, as I expected, toward the safety of the church, but directly toward me. I looked up to find her standing in front of me, clutching her purse in one hand, her black book in the other.

"We've met," she said. "In the garden. I wonder if you remember."

"Of course I remember," I said. "You're Claire."

She gave me a confused look so that I understood she didn't know why she had decided to have the conversation she evidently sought.

"Will you sit with me?" I asked.

She took my offer and found herself looking at Chris. "Is she your daughter?" she asked.

"Yes," I said. Chris was flat on her stomach, and three birds fought for a seat on her outstretched hand.

"She's very beautiful," Claire said.

I agreed with this observation but I didn't add what I felt to be the proper corollary, that the beauty of my child was the consolation of my life. Every night before I went off to my own troubled, guilty sleep beside my husband, I stood next to Chris's bed and watched, with renewed wonder, her innocent, beautiful sleep, her fair skin, the long, dark shadow of her eyelashes, the delicate pink flesh of her earlobes; this sight never failed to refresh me. Now she looked up at her mother, her face smudged with dirt, her hair awry, and then, attentive to her birds, she looked away.

"She looks like her father," I said.

Claire glanced at the wedding band on my finger. Disconcerted by the conclusions she was forced to draw, she looked down at her own hands folded over the book in her lap.

"How do you come to know Pascal?" I asked, though I knew the answer as well as she did.

"I don't know him really," she said. "His father is a friend of the priest at Saint Mark's. I used to run the catechism classes there, but I've moved here now"—she looked up quickly at the Cathedral spires—"so I never see him."

"Are you teaching catechism here?"

"A little. I'm doing a little of everything. The night I saw you I had been learning how to keep accounts."

"You like it better here?"

"Oh, yes," she said quickly, then, regretting what she had revealed, "I like it for all the wrong reasons."

I smiled, thinking for the first time that she was probably ten years younger than I. "I think that's always the case where preference is concerned," I said.

She gave me a wondering look. "I wish I had no preferences," she said. "Of any kind."

I thought of Pascal, of my husband, and found I agreed with her. "I don't think there's any way to avoid it," I said.

"No. It's a matter of always preferring the good. But sometimes I'm not even sure which is the good."

"I'm never sure of that," I said. She gave me a quick sidelong look in which I felt myself as she had first seen me, disheveled from Pascal's embrace. She was, I thought, as uncomfortable with that memory as I was.

"Though I am certain," I added, "that it's not Pascal."

"He's an aggressive man," she said, excusing me.

"Interestingly enough, he doesn't know it."

"I don't know him at all," she said. "And I've no interest in him." Her remark suggested that we change the subject.

"Is there a man who interests you?" I inquired.

She looked annoyed. "No," she said. "None."

"It seems inevitable," I said, "for someone as young and attractive as you are."

She gave me a dry smile, "Does it?"

"It was for me."

"I can't see how an affection for a man could help me, unless he was a very good man and interested in the ultimate fate of my soul."

"That would be unusual," I admitted.

"I know it." She looked around the Square as if to indicate the absence of such a man. "It seems to me that for any person inspired with a love of God, persons of the opposite sex represent a real danger for the soul. Which accounts, I suppose, for religious orders."

"Is that the life you intend for yourself?"

"Yes," she said. "It's useless for me to consider anything else, though now I'm under orders to do just that."

"Orders from whom?" I inquired.

"From people who are older and wiser and who have good intentions toward me. They do it on the best authority and I have no choice but to believe there's some wisdom in it that's beyond me."

"They want you to have some knowledge of what you turn your back on."

"I know it," she said. "It's not my will that resists, it's my ignorance."

"The world isn't so bad," I said, though I had told myself the night before, as I lay awake beside my sleeping husband, that the world wasn't worth living in. "It's a good thing to have a child." I looked at my daughter, who held her bag upside down now, spilling the last of the seeds on the bobbing heads of her admirers. "In fact," I said, "having a child is a miracle. It makes everything else narrow and trivial."

Claire gave me a surprised look. "Do you think so?" she said. "Doesn't it make life awfully complicated?"

Chris came running up to us, waving her empty bag. One of her shoe-laces was untied and I bent down to redo it. She put her arms about my neck, nearly pulling me down onto the pavement and shouting in my ear, "They ate from my hand! It didn't hurt. I thought it would hurt, but it didn't."

"You're very brave," I said, freeing my neck from her grip. "Can you say hello to Claire?"

She looked at Claire quickly and said hello, her eyes fixed on the seat next to me.

Claire returned her greeting, then, addressing me, said, "How old is she?"

"I'm five," Chris told her.

"I beg your pardon," Claire said. "Of course you know how old you are."

"I know my house number too, and my street."

"In case she gets lost," I added.

"If I get lost," Chris said, excited now and looking intently at Claire to make sure she understood, "I'll find a policeman and tell him where I live and then he'll bring me home."

"Have you ever been lost?" Claire asked.

"No." Chris was disappointed. "But I might be someday."

"Would you be afraid?"

"No. I'm never afraid," she said. Then, "Sometimes I'm afraid."

"Me too," I said.

Claire slapped a mosquito on her knee. Her hand, I noticed, was very white, her fingers long and slender, the nails trimmed in perfect ovals. She raised her hand to brush back a wisp of her hair, smiling at Chris, who, I could see, was interested, though still shy of her. "I think what frightens me," Claire said, "is not knowing what I can do for myself." Chris could make no sense of this, but her curiosity got the better of her and she put her hand out to touch Claire's skirt. A dog passing in front of us veered suddenly into a bush, flushing out a thrashing cloud of pigeons. Claire and Chris looked up with expressions of matched wonder and watched the birds rising furiously in the air, stretching out into a long formation and circling the park once to come down gracefully, easily, only a few feet from where they had ascended.

I took the opportunity to observe Claire at close range and I could see what Pascal saw in her. She was not a natural beauty—her features were good though ordinary—but she possessed something more: real spiritual beauty. Seeing this, I couldn't seriously resent her. She was a sensitive young woman, that was clear, but she didn't have the special sense I have spent so long developing in myself, and to such futile ends; that is, the ability to tell when something is going on because of me. Yet she had the ability, which I don't possess, fortunately for myself, of causing people simply by her presence to want to do something. Often, as was the case with Pascal, people felt that she was in need of some instruction, that she was intelligent enough to be weaned from her dependence on religion. What most people failed to see was that she was indifferent to all such entreaties, nor did she bother herself about why anyone would want to change her. It amused her that they tried. And this amusement was usually mistaken for acquiescence, so that she might appear to wish to be parted from her faith.

As we sat there I thought that perhaps we had something in common. When a girl, I too had nurtured a great love of God. I communicated my thoughts to Him regularly and asked for His help in forming good resolutions. I hadn't the courage for more than that, I fancied that He was always with me, though I didn't make the necessary extrapolation of looking for Him within myself. I knew my interior was not a habitation anyone would choose. I had, among the general run of souls, I thought, something decayed, something riddled with unpleasantness. I could feel the thing within me, my soul, and the genuine disorder of the place, its potential for havoc, made me reticent to expose it to any light.

I knew I was handicapped by this dark spiritual landscape and that without light no healthy growth was possible. I remembered once throwing myself on the cold tile floor in the chapel where I prayed, alone and at the close of day. I had watched the sunlight failing to illuminate the stained glass windows (how each figure faded from the heart outward), and it seemed to me that I was next in the great withdrawal of light. Struck by this, I threw myself over the last rays upon the floor, but no sooner had I touched the spot where they fell than they were gone.

Nor was I ever enlightened.

As I watched Claire I hoped she would meet a better fate than mine. Chris took off after the dog, and we sat in silence for a few moments.

"It's very hot," she said.

"Perhaps we could walk down to the river," I suggested. "It might be cooler."

She agreed. We got up and, catching Chris up in the midst of her chase, walked across the Square. We crossed Decatur Street while Chris tugged at my arm and climbed the glaring white stairs that led to the river. At the top was a wide flagstone platform, littered with benches and shaded by carefully spaced crepe myrtle trees, the trunks of which look so like twisted human limbs. The effect at night was eerie but in the daytime it was a pleasant spot; one could walk down the steps on the other side right to the water's edge. Chris broke free and ran across the platform, then stopped abruptly and took one nervous step backward. She saw something that both frightened and fascinated her; I could tell by the way she stood, poised to run, and by the way her hands were clenched into fists at her sides. I hurried toward her and, seeing what she saw, stopped in awe. Claire came up beside us without speaking. I knelt down beside Chris and took her hand in my own.

Before us the river flowed sleepily, but between us and the dark water was a sight that would disturb our sleep for nights to come. There were great piles of stones, broken bits of cement, and, here and there, driftwood sticking up at mysterious angles, lodged by the continuous rise and fall of the brown tide. Upon these rocks, as far as we could see in either direction, were strewn the dead and dying bodies of thousands of rats. They lay in every possible contortion of an agonizing death, and some, still living, writhed among the stones or clawed frantically at the bodies of their companions. Their bodies were clotted with blood, particularly about the face. As I watched, one dying animal convulsed on the still bleeding body of another. He bit at his dead companion, then turned and dug his teeth into his own hind leg. Frantic with pain, he lifted his head and issued a little scream, but he had scarcely got the sound out when blood poured forth from his nostrils and his mouth as if he had been shot. In the next moment he was another among the dead.

Amid this carnage men walked. They wore city uniforms and they carried large plastic bags and shovels. Some worked alone, but many found it easier to work in pairs, one holding the bag open wide while the other shoveled in the bodies, dead and alive. They didn't look up at the few people who watched them from the platform, and the sight of their grisly work was too unnerving to allow any free exchange of conversation. As we stood there one man clambered over the stones and spoke to another, who stood on the platform. This man then turned to the growing crowd and said, "It's not a good idea to stay around here. We don't know what killed them."

People began to move away, as we did, and encountering others on their way down, discouraged them from the view. More city workers were chaining off the stairs that led to the platform. Within five minutes it was impossible for local citizens to see what we had seen.

We fairly staggered back to the Square and none of us spoke. Chris held my hand fiercely in her own and when we sat down again on a bench, she threw her arms around my neck and began sobbing into my shoulder. Claire was deathly pale, and she leaned forward, dropping her head down between her knees, her eyes closed, breathing deeply. "Are you all right?" I asked.

She sat up, sucking in a long breath through her nostrils and smiling weakly at me. "Sometimes," she said, "I think I see things. I think I know things. I think I knew that."

Though there was not a great deal of reason in this remark, I thought I understood it. "Why was it so hard to look away?" I said.

Claire nodded and touched Chris's shoulder, who only looked up quickly, then returned to her weeping. "It's all right, baby," I said. "I feel like crying myself."

"What does it mean?" Claire spoke softly, nor did she address this question to me.

"Maybe they've come up with a really effective pesticide," I suggested. This idea, though I didn't believe it for a moment, lifted my spirits a little. There might be an inoffensive explanation for this mass death. But the man had said, I recalled, that they didn't know what had killed the rats.

I couldn't explain to myself the nature of my shock at the sight. I was appalled first to think that there had been that many rats alive. To see them dying in such agony aroused a series of emotions: pity to see such suffering even in creatures one can't help despising, a sense of horror at the ugliness of the animals, and a suspicion that I understood more than I wanted to understand and that this dark, convulsing underside of our rotting city would soon cause an upheaval that we could not ignore. Claire and I exchanged a look I was to see many times that summer. On doorsteps, in buses, on street corners, in groceries, everywhere they went, our citizens began to eye one another. Is something going irreversibly wrong? that look said. Is this going to be the big crunch? Will I survive it? Will you get out with me? Will you try to stop me?

Chris's tears subsided and she relaxed in my arms.

"I'm glad I wasn't alone," Claire said with a shudder.

That night I looked in the paper and watched the news reports on television for some further explanation of what we had seen. But there was no mention of it. It had not been, I gathered, of more import than a small fire at a plant five miles west of the city, or a shooting at a bar, or the breakdown of three pumping stations, which, for reasons no one could adequately explain, had stopped pumping out the filthy water beneath whose natural level our city, for hundreds of years, has prospered. There was also an in-depth report on a recent political battle that had at long last been resolved by the smallest election turnout in the history of our state. I had not, I thought guiltily, voted myself.

JAMES NOLAN

LA VIE EN ROSE CONSTRUCTION CO.

"NEW ORLEANS A CITY BUILT ON TOP A SWAMP," the airport shuttle driver recited as the Garden of Memories loomed to the right. "Bodies are sealed above ground in them little white houses. You can't put 'em in the ground account of the water table."

The haggard man winced behind dark glasses as the driver's spiel worked its magic on the rowdy conventioneers in the van, who began to sing off-key choruses of "When the Saints Go Marching In." Every time he flew in or out of New Orleans, this information was there to greet him like a gargoyle at the gate. He had just bid goodbye to a friend dying of breast cancer, and now he was coming home to his ailing mother. This gargoyle and he were old friends, but he had hoped this once to be spared acknowledging it.

The pirate Dominican taxi had been by at five that morning to pick him up for LaGuardia and, still flush with Cuba Libres and goodbyes, he had maintained an animated discussion with the driver about—what else?—how the hell can anyone live in New York. He had been gone the whole month of August, hadn't slept in two nights, and all he wanted was to sip a glass of wine in his courtyard and crawl asleep between the sheets.

Over the past three years, he had gradually been moving back to New Orleans, and in his suitcases was the last load of rugs, papers, and photographs. This time he had even taken the silverware. He was hanging up his freelance photography business in New York, capitulating to origins. He had won every battle, but had lost the war for independence from this place. And as the shuttle turned onto a narrow street of wrought-iron balconies spilling over with begonias, he was relieved to admit it.

With his last burst of strength, he trundled the bulging suitcases from the van and threw them against a green gate, behind which was a serene rose-colored courtyard. He identified with this aspect of Mediterranean architecture, nondescript on the outside, like this shabby fence, but with a luxuriant interior landscape hidden behind walls. He couldn't wait to slam the gate shut onto the world, with its incurable diseases, honking horns, and aggrieved parties.

Unlocking the wooden gate, he was met by the glare of eight men in purple T-shirts, black pants, and gold baseball caps. Slouching on patio chairs in the shade of the live oak that dominated the courtyard, they were sitting around a battered blue water cooler set on his grandmother's oak table, leisurely chipping mortar from bricks heaped in piles at their feet. In the shock of intrusion, he and the men just stared at each other, as once, washing dishes at his sink on West 14th St., he'd locked eyes with a cat-burglar passing along the fire escape. His own resentment wilted in the waves of misgiving he felt coming at him. Lowering his eyes, he began to wheel his suitcases one by one across wobbly bridges scattered over dank trenches of corroded pipes. The purple t-shirts read, in flowery script, LA VIE EN ROSE CONSTRUCTION CO.

"How's it going? You Mr. Weems in apartment B, that right?" a portly man growled.

"Yes I am, and I'm real tired. You all doing a little work out here?" Mr. Weems ventured, defying the obvious.

"All these pipes in the courtyard gotta come up. They a gas leak here, big time. We been at it for a month, be at it for another one to come. Just got the toe-mice out your kitchen. Had to tear down a coupla walls."

Hoisting the largest suitcase over the apartment threshold, the wheels popped off. He bent down to scoop them up with pale shaking hands while the eight men studied him. Then he walked inside, choking on the fine white dust that covered everything. All the family antiques he had so carefully restored were stacked in one corner under a shroud of cement chips. His table lamp squatted on the floor with the shade ripped off, an outdoor spotlight beaming into his eyes.

He kicked the door closed and sat down on a suitcase to survey the damage as, on the other side of the green storm shutter, an electric saw blade cut into a length of pipe.

Derwood Weems didn't even begin to unpack his suitcases for three days. Most of that time he spent in bed in chili pepper boxer shorts eating fudge-ripple ice cream with ear plugs in.

Half-heartedly he studied the "for rent" classifieds in *The Times-Picayune* but, in the end, didn't make a single call. He hauled the construction debris out of his bedroom, swabbed the floor three times, then closed off the rest of the apartment. He kept the jalousied shutters shut and the bedroom air conditioner running, sealing himself inside like an eggplant forgotten at the bottom of the refrigerator. He cancelled his photographic shoots, and didn't return calls.

Beep. "Hello, Woody honey, Mama. Guess you decided to stay longer in New York, because I been ringing you forever. Your number up there's been disconnected, so I don't know where in the world you are. Everything's fine here. That new medicine is working real good, and I don't have so much fluid. Now you ring me soon as you get in, hear?" *Beep.*

He let the message erase.

Like people enduring a siege, his neighbors only emerged at dusk to scamper to the corner store or dry cleaners, then bolted themselves inside, away from clanging pipes, jackhammers, and crashing loads of bricks. On the second evening home, when Derwood at last stumbled outside after the workers had packed up, he ran into his neighbor, Irene Guidry. Fingering the leaves of her shriveled bougainvillea, she reminded him of a photo he printed last spring of a Bosnian woman who had endured the shelling in Sarajevo by hiding for two years in a crawl space.

"Guess the dust smothered these," she was murmuring to herself. "I see you're back, Derwood. Bet you wish you weren't."

"Irene, when are they going to turn the water and gas back on? How long is this going to last? I'm definitely moving."

"That's all I thought of . . . for the first month," she snorted. "That's when I asked the workers about their progress and tried to reason with Eustice LaRose."

Conchita's light-skinned handyman had been in and out of the courtyard flashing his gold tooth and dusting off his chinos ever since Derwood moved in. He was the kind of fast-talking man his father had taught him to avoid at the racetrack.

"The day after you left," she began with a deep breath, already exhausted by the litany of disasters she was about to recount, "Eustice found what he calls 'toe-mice' in your kitchen wall, and proceeded to call the termite man. The termite man drilled into the courtyard to bury bug poison and proceeded to hit a gas pipe. The gas man came and proceeded to impound the meter, and Eustice sweet-talked Conchita into replacing all the service pipes in the courtyard and the woodwork in our kitchens, though most of this doesn't need to be done. He started his own company and will be a millionaire by Christmas."

"By Christmas?"

"You know Eustice. Every night he probably runs home to study the *Time-Life* books on plumbing and carpentry so he can tell his crew what to do the next day. Now I just accept it as Allah's will, and hide upstairs all day while they tear out my kitchen floor, looking for Formosan termites. I haven't had a bath in ten days. Yesterday at Mass they offered me literature on the parish homeless shelter."

"Isn't this an awful mess? Hi, Woody, welcome home, sugar." They were joined by Conchita Charbonnet, who was tiptoeing in stiletto heels along the plywood over the trenches with her blind Llasa Apsa waddling behind. "Over here, hon. Come on, Choo-Choo."

Conchita Claret Charbonnet, from Hammond, was accustomed to tour the courtyard at dusk every evening with a highball in hand, surveying her kingdom. She was a sixtyish former Strawberry Queen whose hair got bigger and bigger as it turned blacker and blacker. Conchita had been a secretary who retired to marry her boss and lover, Monsieur Charbonnet. The elderly Parisian dressed up every day in a loop bow tie and double-breasted brown suit, as if he were about to promenade along the Champs Elysées, although he never moved from his glass of Johnny Walker Red in front of the blaring TV set. Nobody knew how old he was but, if it's any indication, he claimed Edith Piaf as an early conquest. "After she make sex with me," he told Derwood last Mardi Gras, "her voice it really improve."

An engineer, Monsieur Charbonnet had been invited by Governor Huey P. Long to teach Louisiana how to drill for oil. During that era he bought this creole cottage, built in the 1820s, and fixed up the slave-quarters behind it into apartments. His first wife, an artist, had made the complex beautiful, and it appeared in several Vieux Carré patio books. Conchita had made it interesting for herself, filling it with the handsomest young men she could lay her hands on, including Eustice LaRose.

"That fat one, the minister, thought I was flirting with him," she confided hoarsely to Derwood and Irene. "He said 'I do believe you flirting with me, Miss Conchita. You and me should step out some time. I like white women.' The nerve. I told him, 'Look, Reverend, I'm a married lady and, besides, I don't date nigras.' " She furrowed her clown-white brow to whisper in mock horror, "You think I want to get Ebola?"

Sniffing among the rubble, the Llasa Apsa almost slid into a ditch. Conchita screamed, "Choo-Choo, remember you've had your bath!"

Derwood yanked the yelping animal by its collar back onto the bricks as Monsieur Charbonnet appeared through the shutters, grasping a cane in each hand.

"Stop this sheeet!"

"Sweetheart, Choo-Choo almost fell in a ditch. His cataracts won't let him see where he's going to make peepee."

"I bet he can still smell pussy," Monsieur Charbonnet remarked. "I am so tired of this sheeet. All day long, boom boom boom. If they are not finish by Friday, I fire them all." And swiveling his toothpick body around on two canes, he faced Conchita. "And you, too!"

Derwood led the dog by its collar across the courtyard to the Charbonnet's door. Irene scurried into her kitchen, and Derwood let the gate slam behind him as he burst onto Burgundy Street, where the gay bars were hosting a weekend celebration called Southern Decadence.

The devil sure is flexing the biceps in his left arm tonight, Derwood thought, stepping out of the gate into a group of balding men in black leather chaps and bare butts with hardware dangling from every crevice and joint of their bodies. They were carrying go-cups of beer toward a corner bar called The Rough House, where a crowd of identical creatures milled under a canopy of white and baby-blue helium balloons. Derwood decided he might as well stroll in that direction toward the A&P.

Once, while fixing the kitchen sink drain, Eustice LaRose told Derwood his vision about homosexuals. Eustice was not only an ordained Pentecostal minister, but also considered himself a prophet. "When homosexuals die," he explained, loosening a socket with a wrench and looking straight at Derwood, "they go straight into the left arm of the devil down in hell." Then he tightened the socket with a grimace.

"Now a while back, I had me a woman who was mighty fine in bed," Eustice continued, cleaning the drain trap, "best I ever did have. But I gave her up to please the Lord, and to marry a woman who'd be a good mother to my children." Derwood thought about what unhappy people plumbers always are, mucking around in other people's waste all day. And he suspected, trying to make sense of this conversation, that the woman who was so mighty fine in bed probably wasn't a woman at all.

Derwood's trip to the A&P on Royal Street was waylaid into an all-night drunk on dollar-fifty well drinks at a bar called Your Little Red Wagon on North Rampart. That night the club featured an ancient drag queen who looked like a tax auditor and sang "We're in the Money" in pig Latin in front of a gold lamé backdrop tacked across the storefront window. You can lead a whore to water but you can't make her drown, Derwood chuckled to himself as he fell into the hairy arms of a handsome man from the West Bank named Earl. Earl's keys jangled when he walked, and his slow smile exposed rotten front teeth. "Duke, Duke, Duke," he kept singing, "Duke of Earl," a song that Derwood hadn't heard since high school.

"I'd love to invite you home for a drink, Earl," Derwood protested, coming to his senses, "but they're tearing the damn courtyard apart to put in new plumbing and didn't even have the decency to turn my water back on before they split this evening. I won't have water all weekend."

"For true? Who's doing the job?" the Duke of Earl asked, with a sudden professional interest.

"Some outfit Eustice LaRose put together called La Vie En Rose."

"That Vie En Rose don't know shit. I'm a plumber, hear, and it ain't nothing to turn someone's water back on if the pipes is laid right while you working on them. Lemme go by my brother-in-law's in Marrero," he said, shooting Derwood a sweetly rotten smile as he massaged his thigh, "and get my wrench, know what I mean, Woody? Gimme your address on this napkin."

My God, what have I gone and done? Of all things, a plumber! Derwood's head was spinning as he lay stretched out on his crummy sheets, hoping the doorbell wouldn't ring. But it did. He stumbled barefoot in his shorts across the plywood bridges toward the gate, ready to make any excuse. When he opened it, there stood an enormous woman with a cascade of curly red locks in a kelly-green dress, hand on her hip.

"Woody, where y'at? It's me. So whatcha think, cher? Pretty foxy?" the figure gushed, doing a runway twirl and voguing in through the gate.

"Man, look at this mess. Them guys don't know they ass from a hole in the ground," Earl mumbled in disgust, swaggering bowlegged in beige half-heel pumps that went tap-tap-tap across the plywood bridges. Yanking a wrench out of his beaded handbag, he hiked his slip up to his crotch and squatted like a bull frog to inspect the water main.

"Piece of cake," Earl said.

Leaning over too far, his thin soles slipped on the mucky plywood and he skidded feet-first into a sinkhole under the pipes, up to his knees in fetid water. With a sucking sound, he step-kicked one meaty calf over the pipes to strike a vampish pose with one bare foot resting demurely on his knee.

"I'll get you out. Here, grab my hand."

"Whoa, not so fast. Where my shoe at? Don't rip them twenty-dollar panty hose, hear?"

As Derwood and Earl grappled over the ditch, Conchita's pale yellow kimono appeared framed in the French door of the Charbonnet's apartment. "Woody, is that you, honey? Who's that lady in the ditch? She with you?"

Conchita padded out in velour slippers to get a better look.

"It's the plumber, Conchita. Everything's all right," Derwood boomed in a business-like baritone. "We're just trying to turn my water on."

"Turn who on? At this hour of the morning? Hey, she's a redhead. She's a red-headed plumber! I never seen such a red-headed plumber before." Conchita thought this a hilarious observation, and insisted on helping to hoist Earl out of the ditch, her mascara-smudged eyes widening as she grabbed hold of his thick tattooed forearm. "How would you and the plumber like to come in for a teeny-weeny nightcap?" she slurred. "My husband's gone beddy-bye."

Heavy-lidded, she gave the mud-splattered Duchess of Earl a slow up-and-down. "You sure you a plumber?"

Earl was furious. He'd lost a new Dillard's pump in the sinkhole, and wanted to go straight home to change his dress. The offer of a shower tempted Derwood, but when he considered the Duchess' other charms, he declined. They exchanged phone numbers, and for the next few days—during which Derwood was on the phone to New York every minute of the day and night telling everybody he was moving back—Earl didn't call.

"Mama, I've tried everything to come home, but it isn't working out . . . No, I don't want to own a house here anymore . . . because my expectations have changed. I expect things to work, and for things to work people have got to. It takes more than a pound of crawfish, a couple of beers, and a carnival parade to make me happy these days. I guess New York has changed me . . . Thanks, but you don't need to remind me this is where I'm from—it's a great place to be *from*. And a great place to come *back to*, once in a while. In the meantime . . . Permanently? Inside that tomb with you. That's where I'll end up permanently. Then I'll settle down for a century or two. But right now, to find another apartment and move again, I might as well move to Paris for all the trouble. I don't know. Something tells me I may never get out of here. How you feeling? . . . Well, why did he change the medication if the other one was working so well? Try it for awhile, I guess

. . . Yeah, I'll be out to see you this weekend. First thing I'll do is check out your hot water . . . I love you, too."

He always knew New Orleans would be his undoing, Derwood thought as he hung up. It had taken him twenty years to get out, and another twenty to get back, transformed from a blond catalog model into a mature photographer. Unlike most New Yorkers, who thought they could take the slow, sensual Crescent City by storm, Derwood understood the value of lifelong contacts. No, here he wouldn't edit and print for the World News Service, but at least he could shoot the right weddings and Mardi Gras courts. And this would leave him time for his own projects, like the photo essay on New Orleans cemeteries. The creative possibilities here seemed endless.

And so did the destructive.

At night he could feel the city sinking back into the swamp it rose from, a miasma of hereditary alcoholism, violence, and dementia. He could sense hideous tumors blooming like bayou orchids inside the lethargic bodies that sleepwalked the streets. Swatting at mosquitoes on his balcony, he stared down into the Venice of trenches in the moon-lit courtyard below, examining for signs and portents the brackish entrails that lay two feet beneath the surface of a city that so charmed visitors. Just below the pipes floated a soggy bed of cypress logs placed by French settlers and their slaves on top of a snake-infested marsh.

I know where I'm from, he thought.

Mosquitoes already had begun to breed in the stagnant ditches, and Formosan termites were devouring the city alive. The termites could only be stopped here and there, a bathroom or kitchen at a time, by endless restorations like this one. Sixty percent of the primordial live oaks shading the city were already being hollowed out from below by these insects brought over from Taiwan aboard World War II freighters. This species only swarmed during three or four evenings in July, ferocious to fuck each other and then nest before their double wings fell off at 10 PM, like a Darwinian Last Call.

The wrought-iron courtyard furniture had been abandoned to the August rains, and in a matter of weeks was as barnacled with rust as the heaps of corroded pipes that lay next to it. The spongy night drove him back into the air conditioning, where he slipped into a deep sleep. He dreamed of a dark reservoir filled with naked swimmers. They were clamoring for him to "jump in, jump in" but he knew the tank was bottomless, stretching into the bowels of the earth. He hesitated at the edge of the water that wound deeper and deeper down into nowhere, and woke with a start at the first low rumblings of thunder.

It was about to storm.

For two nights Derwood Weems was held prisoner in his slave-quarter. All lines to the outside world were cut—electricity, gas, water, and telephone. He survived on sardine sandwiches and brushed his teeth with Dr. Pepper. The hurricane had passed yesterday, but still the shutters were locked tightly from the outside. Through the louvers, he could see the courtyard was nothing but flooded moats with pipes sticking out at jagged angles.

All of his neighbors had escaped days ago, when the workers from La Vie En Rose Construction Co. got into a violent argument with Eustice. After they had done the most back-breaking part of the job, digging ditches and pulling up old pipes, Eustice wanted to lower their wages, or he would fire them to bring in even cheaper workers. That was their side. Eustice, on the other hand, admitted these guys were just preachers and homeless men he'd recruited at the Vision of Zion soup kitchen on Perdido Street. Now that he had to connect new pipes, he needed trained plumbers and electricians, and these other men could continue working as assistants. Derwood didn't know whom to believe.

For several mornings leading up to the blow-out, Derwood was woken up by the stentorian voice of a minister gesturing in the shade under the live oak, preaching about Joshua. "Now Jericho was an old city, and Jericho was an evil city, eaten up by weevils and sin. And Joshua had him a trumpet, and stood outside them gates, blowing to let a little LIGHT in, blowing to let a little JUSTICE in, blowing to let a little bro-ther-ly LOVE in . . . ."

"And the wall come tumbling down," was the uproarious response of the men, who stood listening with shovels and pipes in hand.

This was not a good sign.

Work came to a standstill, and within a few days, Eustice fired the crew. But without a week's severance, they refused to allow new workers in. They camped out in the courtyard overnight, when Derwood heard more about corrupt Jericho, Joshua, and his golden horn. He let them keep beer in his refrigerator and call home from his phone, and stopped short of offering them space on the floor.

That evening Conchita waltzed in from Arnaud's in a lilac mother-of-the-bride's dress, and marched around and around the courtyard with a tumbler of scotch in her hand screeching "Go home and go to bed, you naughty boys, before I call the cops." At three in the morning Eustice brought over the sheriff to evict them for trespassing. Conchita told him that the takeover had driven off all her tenants, which was almost true, although Derwood didn't know how much longer he could have taken it. So early the next morning, when hurricane Diane unexpectly veered west from Pensacola and headed toward southeastern Louisiana, Eustice came by to test the storm shutters. He double-latched all door and window shutters from the outside while Derwood was upstairs sleeping off the battle of Jericho.

By the time Derwood got up and stumbled to a balcony door, the hurricane was already starting to hit. He noticed a broken wire flapping in the wind outside. When he tried to call Conchita, his line was dead. The last time he saw her, from between the louvers, she was trying to fold M. Charbonnet's palsied limbs into the Buick in the driveway. A suitcase had blown open, and undergarments were twirling furiously around the courtyard. Conchita was screaming "Choo-Choo, Choo-Choo," trying to find the Llasa Apsa. Later he heard the car start up and, after ramming every shutter in the apartment with a solid brass coat stand, he curled up in bed to listen to stinging sheets of rain whip across the house, bombarding the roof with tiny green acorns.

The bloated Llasa Apsa with a rhinestone barrette was floating belly-up in a trench, next to a beige pump. A mandarin silk pajama top, an alarming red, dangled from the top branch of the fig tree.

The waters had receded, coating everything with a primal gray slime.

Derwood kicked through the acorns and branches that matted the slick courtyard, his blue eyes blinded by morning glare. He'd lept up to embrace the flashing grin of his jailer and liberator when Eustice arrived to unfasten the storm shutters the second morning after Diane hit. Like a trapped animal, Derwood had almost destroyed the apartment trying to gnaw his way out. In one particular hole, over the stove, he had burrowed with a butcher knife as far as the original brick wall of the slave-quarter.

Eustice apologized for his terrible mistake, but otherwise was all business.

"Yes sirree, it's a new day for me," he kept repeating, as he tossed tools into canvas sacks. "Lucky the Charbonnets asked me to come by to look for they pooch," he said, glancing at the dead dog floating in the trench, "or you could've been locked in there till kingdom come. They staying out by her sister's house across the lake till Thanksgiving. Mr. Charbonnet ailing and Miss Conchita ain't about to drag him back to this holeful of toe-mice."

"When will the work start up again?" Derwood wanted to know, calculating how long it would take to haul his things out.

"Not for a long time now. I'm bailing out of this town and following the storm down the coast. La Vie En Rose got a brand new bag, and we gonna be cleaning up after the hurricane. We're talking exclusive home reconstruction and insurance megabucks, get me? You should see Biloxi. It a mess. By the way, babe, got a plumber gonna work with us name of Earl who says if I see Woody over by Miss Conchita, be sure to tell him 'way to go!'"

A flock of sparrows, driven off by the construction project, had returned to the live oak, now split to one side. Morning birdsong joined the high whine of an air conditioner in allegro accompaniment to the Creole Queen's calliope on the levee, belting out "Do You Know What It Means to Miss New Orleans?" The worse part of his incarceration was Derwood had run out of cigarettes, so he and Eustice sat smoking on the rusted patio chairs under the tree, Derwood plotting how to revive his career in New York, Eustice flush with plans to make a killing on the devastated Gulf Coast.

Suddenly the sparrows surged all at once from the tree top into a black funnel of wings shrieking to a nearby roof. The sound almost tore the top of Derwood's head off. The two men jerked backward, gazing up into the quivering branches, but before either knew what was happening, the quivering became a massive sway.

And then a splintering.

The tree trunk split open like papier-mâché, tumbling down on top of the two natives smoking together after the storm. Derwood could feel the warmth of Eustice's limbs entwined with his own, but couldn't lift either his arms or legs as a salty syrup that tasted like blood seeped into his mouth. He thrashed his head in the struggle to free himself, finally surrendering his panic to a familiar comfort that closed over his head like dark water.

A group of early-morning revelers with sausage balloons tied around their heads stopped to marvel. The top of a huge live oak had just come crashing to Burgundy Street through a green wooden fence exposing the radiant pink flesh of a French Quarter courtyard. "Whoa, did you see that?" they asked each other, as a parked car smacked by a gnarled limb let out its supersonic wail. Then checking their map, they ambled toward the Mississippi, looking for the blackjack tables and another cold one.

JOHN VERLENDEN

LOST TEXT: HOTEL ST. PIERRE

From a group of papers whose authenticity could not be established by Mr. Reynard Estes nor by Dr. Floriana Gascard of the Historic Preservation Foundation-New Orleans. That is, papers which could not meet the requirement that they were produced in New Orleans and not in Europe or the southerly Americas. Mysterious also is whether the papers were originally written as sober, though misguided attempts at personal history, or as entertainments, or, as some have suggested, by the mind of a disturbed person, possibly even a slave. They are made available as part of a private collection owned by a New Orleans restaurant family who wishes to remain anonymous.

THE TEXT

THE HOTEL LOOKED LIKE A COTTAGE HIGH IN BAVARIA, a place where alpine travelers might recover what vigor they'd lost to snow and ice. I came upon it in the tropical slave port of New Orleans during the new Spanish reign.

But then this New World—all of it—is a hopeless hodge-podge. From our first stops among the Gulf islands containing yards of moaning Africans to the long, low benches beneath shade trees where native aboriginals lounged in front of ponderous Spanish bureaucrats, the place seemed to be waiting for an element lost, an ingredient yet discovered, to congeal its mismatched parts.

I am such a part.

Yet I knew immediately that the little viridian blue cottage, with its lone, high, peaked gable, with its white boards making fastidious angles across its washed front, was a place where I might not feel completely estranged. And it's the St. Pierre—not especially the muddy grid known as New Orleans, nor the gaping, torpid wilderness of Louisiana—which I make haste to chronicle. I know now that my fate has been lying here all along, that a confused idea of adventure led me on, that I will never emerge from this place as the man I once observed in the mirrors of Europe. On the contrary, I must now grow rhapsodic about that most abhorred condition: mental clarity. For it's all I have left.

But first . . . a final look backwards, over the course of these wonderful if exceedingly painful first weeks. To that end I offer:

A Tale of Hearts in this New World,
an unimportant yet curious history
by Your Newest Servant

Feb. 19, 178_

Carriage wheels do not so much roll as slide through the mud of Calle Real. The sharp pace of horse hooves sends tiny droplets of earth and feces to the sidewalks where gentlemen and ladies, if they must be about, turn their faces aside and grimace. I watch these things from within the lone, gabled dormer of Hotel St. Pierre—the one room I had wanted, for this precise view; the one room untaken in a hotel which, according to Madame Hartnett, is always full.

"Just who was the last lodger here, may I inquire?" I said to Madame Hartnett, when she first showed me these rooms.

"Oh"—she laughed—"you can be quite sure I observe the strictest confidence about our guests, Monsieur _____."

"Then perhaps, as a matter of record, you'll tell me whether the letting party departed on good terms with Madame?"

Standing near the door, she said, "The room is yours if you want it."

I knew I'd take the room, but I remained silent. There was something not quite right with the place, though I couldn't place it. Just as I was stepping back into the hallway—a narrow space, only one gas lamp lighting its wallpaper of interlocking triangles—I saw a fair-sized smudge on the floorboards. The spot lay just within the doorway, a bit to one side. "What exactly is that?" I said and pointed to it.

"A maid will wash it out," Madame Hartnett said. "Perhaps if you would be our guest at dinner, the work can be done without impeding you in the least."

She quoted a price for board, payable on the Monday of each week, in advance. The food, she said, was quite good and, in any event, plentiful.

Just as I was assessing the light flickering upon her green eyes—a pair of old emeralds scored a thousand times each—the door across the hallway swept open.

I began my bow, though I couldn't have glimpsed any part of a dress nor seen the deep rouge of her cheek—not then, not yet. Perhaps a delicate scent preceded? Nevertheless, she flew from her door—a peculiar, upsetting vision. Over her shoulders flowed a long, white lace mantilla. But what tiny shoulders they were! I fought to restrain myself from staring at her crimson skirts rustling against the floor. The place was that well kept, a bit like a castle or a government chamber where deputies make decisions—clean, polished. But, my god, what a bewilderingly shrunken gem. Miniature is the word. She couldn't have been as high as my vest's second button.

I frowned at Madame Hartnett.

"Sir—" she said, pressing her lips tightly. The locking key was in her hand.

"Yes," I said. "Agreed, all around."

A passage of weeks . . .

The smudge, worked on over and over, resists banishment. It has even pushed itself through a coat of new varnish. I cannot worry about it unless, of course, I begin coughing or wheezing. Its presence mimics that of molds, which, for me, are especially vicious. One sees such black stains everywhere in the New World, even on the great oaks in town.

But so far: no bodily reactions.

What's more to the point is Señora Alvarez, who lives across the hall. An exquisite tormentor, she's become, within my soul: the Hotel St. Pierre itself.

She concocted a novel explanation for the smudge.

"Monsieur_____," she began, standing just beside the spot's cloudy blackness, her dwarf hands folded together, the fingers so small, pink and tender that her fists formed a whorl no larger than a camellia blossom. "That spot will not subside for some time. However, nothing about it will affect your person in the least."

"Fine, Señora," I said, "but how can you know?"

"Because," she said, "this smudge is none other than the remains of a Mr. D'Arcy Thoroughgood. He too began his New World adventures at the St. Pierre."

I contorted my face into a parlor mask which says, 'May two can play this game?'

She continued to stare at the shapeless blot.

"Mr. Thoroughgood," I said, "enjoys the room enough to excuse the occasional bootsole I place upon his person, I hope?"

"Mr. Thoroughgood feels nothing," Señora Alvarez said. "He's gone, more so than all the citizens whose coffins keep floating to the surface just outside of town."

"Please sit, dear lady," I said. "And deliver the rest of this fantastic tale!"

She said nothing, but when I stepped toward the table which stands just within the fierce white light of the dormer, she came in behind me. I felt her hand brush against my sleeve and I turned around.

"You don't understand," she said. The door behind her had shut. "Mr. Thoroughgood began shrinking, as I have, until he . . . fell away. He seeped into these boards. No doubt he was trying to open the doors of this room one last time—but couldn't reach the knob."

I looked at the smudge, considered these extraordinary words, yet felt a tug in my heart which disarmed my tongue's ready lash.

"Joke if you must about this Mr. D'Arcy," I said, "but don't joke about yourself. No princess in the Old World can match your exquisite charm."

"Really?" she said. "I think if I were the size I was when I first came here, you wouldn't find my features quite so entertaining."

Her words had a damnable effect. For a moment, I saw another person, her of course, but of average height, of normal fullness.

"Bravo," I said. "Stellar performance. You must surely be the most famous stage actress in all the New World and I, its newest, most impressionable fool."

She kept to role—not even a glance to let me in on her masquerade. Instead, she gazed upon me with the same flat expression she had leveled on the smudge itself.

"You mock my intelligence," I said. "Just look at your dress, your rings, your pearls, those sapphires winking in your ears, why, everything about you is in perfect harmony. If matters were as you say—"

"No, no. Everything attached to your immediate person—even your most personal possessions, sir—shrink along with you. If you have heirs, I suggest—"

"I do not."

She swiveled her immaculate jaw from left to right, closed her eyes briefly. "I knew that already."

"Why ask then?"

"As a test." Her brow formed a tiny yet lengthy wrinkle. "Though I'm not sure a mistake's possible here. Anyway, you're real enough—certainly one of us. May I tell you something? As you let your eyes adjust to the dimensions of this place—and there are always two sets of dimensions: then and now—may I say that your reference to the princesses of the Old World cut right to my heart, also to the center of our insignificant drama here in New Orleans?"

"You flabbergast me," I said. "What can you possibly say next?"

She shook her head. "I do come from the Old World, Monsieur. Therefore, there's no need to inflate my status by comparing me to princesses whom, I suspect, you've never quite been given to know anyway?"

I opened my mouth.

"It doesn't matter," she said. "The point is, you're in the presence of Princess Eugenia Alvarez y D'oro."

She walked directly from my room. A sweetness hung upon the air: rotting magnolias.

Things have not turned out well. It began with the auction. I had heard of these spectacles and wondered whether my next enterprise should demand sufficient overhead of labor—nearly every New World enterprise did—and whether, therefore, I should embark upon holding slaves myself. I knew nothing of the trade. In fact, I'd been avoiding the issue, maintaining that I—nevermind the others—would enter a business wherein I was sole agent of my fortunes.

However, as I walked down Calle Real, an overpowering sensation assailed me: my funds were dwindling. I had no idea where investments might be safely made. I told myself that I'd best learn all the factors of this new society, or face ruin.

Gentlemen in saturated waistjackets and cravats, in fine, water-pasted leggings and polished-heeled shoes stood in heavily trampled slime. Already once that morning the rains had opened up, as if from a sealed envelope. One young man with a huge supply of tousled, sandy hair was coursing his fingers through its wet ends. I took him for a rugged up-and-comer, one who deemed it necessary to have stood out in the cloudburst. Was he preserving a particularly clear view of the auction block? Not at all. He and the others who stood at that particular corner, milling, waiting, were merely sweating, like mules, in the soft, watery air that steamed from the mud beneath their boots. Soon I was among them, my neck immediately damp, trickles of perspiration causing the flesh beneath my shirt and jacket to crawl, to develop pockets of feverish heat, at last to itch. In a few moments I was as soaked as the others.

None of us could stand like sober citizens. The sun, though obscured by an enormous silvery cloud, cooked us like pork skins in a skillet. Our constant shifting, stirring, had nothing of choice about it. Nor did the ceaseless conversation, the same phrases over and over:

"Seen this lot yet?"

"No. You?"

"No."

I exchanged these exact words with a short, stocky middle-aged gentleman who wore a tall tophat. His cream-colored vest had been sweated through. He stamped his boots like a horse, seemed offended that I had nothing more to offer, then stalked off.

At last, a man whose peculiar French accent seemed absolutely unidentifiable, mounted a mortar slab of considerable size. He informed us that the auction would soon begin. He sped through a list of rules to do with the bidding procedures, with when a sale was final; he then supplied a short disquisition on currencies. The franc was preferred to the peso. The American dollar would be accepted. He barked out the exchange rate and, in any event, demanded cash or a banker's letter of credit. Another man followed him, yielding the same information in Spanish. No one listened. When he stepped down from the grey, pebbly slab, his face had achieved the color of my cravat, a dark red, a dye which only the Neapolitans have mastered.

My fingers curled, my breath drew short when I heard a bell announce the first human property. This low, dolorous knell, I realized, emanated from a set of long shackles around both ankles which allowed an almost complete stride—a long one, actually, fully required for the first slave to mount himself on the block.

I recognized a third man, local to my own street. I'd seen him striding with dispatch, roughly polished cane in hand, shoulders tipped forward as if encountering a stiff alpine breeze. He stood upon the slab next to the African beast. A most terrible thing then happened. As soon as our auctioneer raised his voice to that pitch which legitimizes frenzy among buyers, another voice rose up garbling his words.

It was, of course, the property. I don't know why I hadn't expected it. Surely I knew—or did I?—that these brutes possessed language?

Another voice, from my neighbor on Calle Real, ejaculated a loud command. Nevermind I'd never heard the word in my life. This one word— inherent in its very sounds—meant 'stop, desist.' The slave fell silent. His pinched grimace, the partial sucking of the lower lip, the protuberance of the upper lip, the clouded but focused gaze—within himself, you see— told me all I'd ever suspected. The beast was strategizing. His cares lay beyond himself. Family?

At that moment—I dare say my mouth had opened—the voice from my neighbor barked out yet another single word, again, no mystery to anyone. Something along the order of "Behave!" or "Look smart!" Then, as by formula, I heard—didn't see—the whack-whack of his rod, that rough polished cane, falling in measured rhythm on the slave's back. A wince, the smallest propulsion forward at each blow, these were his sole reactions. At once, his face became clear, blank. His brow opened to a dark, glistening expanse. Sweat poured. His mouth fell slack. Incredibly, as if on celestial command, the entire street corner glowed suddenly with whiteness. The heavens chose this moment to unmask their centerpiece: the sun itself. As if I'd inhaled cinders or a terrible tiny seed cushioned in filaments riding the wind, I coughed out a string of words:

"My god, it's too much!"

Boots around me began to stamp the popping mud. Coats, hats shifted as if invisible fleas had taken hold. A voice beside me said, "What is too much, sir?"

I turned, frightened, aware I'd said something, already forgetting its sense. I went numb in my chest, felt I should pitch over, expiring on the spot. The short, tophatted man who'd questioned me earlier stood within a cleared circle. His mouth, like mine, had fallen open. He was in a state of perturbation. His attention rested not on the slave, but on me.

"I'm ill," I said.

It was too late.

"'Too much'? 'Too much'?" This polished stump of a man looked around him. "Why, I'd say not nearly enough. No, sir. Not if you know 'em. Man's got to know 'em. Don't buy, otherwise. You'll leave this place more penniless than when you came!" By 'place,' he meant the entire New World.

A small roar took up. I thought I should be knocked down, beaten perhaps. On the contrary, amid the laughter, I felt hands placing themselves gently upon my shoulders, upon my arms, clapping me warmly here and there. You'd have thought I was heading to a platform in assembly, to accept an award for superior citizenship.

Like a mule now myself, I picked my feet up, dodging the people who seemed to position themselves suddenly in my way, weaving slowly around their blurs. I remember my hand, the sense of thanks I experienced when it had as its duty the unlocking of the low, white picket gate which opened onto the St. Pierre's small, gardened courtyard. I raced inside its hallway, its shadows only slightly cooler than the street corner where men sold human flesh.

Madame Hartnett emerged from the drawing room. "Dinner in forty-five minutes, Monsieur_____."

The day's provender was lean: a thin soup of indeterminate stock with the frailest squares of green onion rolling in its watery midst like small flags. I was bedeviled the entire time by the thought that they represented the countries of us all, the diners, I mean, including Señora Alvarez, all of us who called this hotel our home. There the squares spun, green and uniform, with little spunk left in their flaccid tissues, all alike now, boiled and on the verge of their fibers beginning to fleck apart. Oh, I was courteous; never a reason for boorishness. I managed to inject a comment or two, incumbent on the polite diner, designed to settle spirits as an aid to digestion.

"No end of sunlight here, thank goodness," I said. "Hardly like France this time of year."

"Nor," said Señora Alvarez, "even like Spain."

No one seized upon these comments right away, as per usual, but during the lengthy course of the meal we received lone, dangling comments from everyone.

"One certainly wastes no time here waiting for the banker to open his doors!"

Later: "A planter from Mandeville has sold all his property and it seems that laborers will have their houses built upon it. Thank goodness it's in the swamp."

Finally, toward meal's end, Madame Hartnett had this to offer: "May we all pass an agreeable Thursday afternoon."

Rents were due on Friday.

I climbed the staircase like a worm inching up a twig. My left hand pulled hard on the bannister, my head plunged itself down, in a gloom. So much intensity of gravity seemed a danger to the very structure of the whole creaking house. Once I got to my door I hung my weight upon it, as if upon a hook, my right hand turning the wrought iron key in the lock's black rectangle.

"Monsieur_____."

The Señora stood at her door behind me. Her exquisite beauty, riven by her implacable madness, knifed open my heart. God, what suffering all around! What thoroughly dishonorable and, to my eye, unearned fates filled this new land.

"Yes, kind lady?" I said, bowing, my door slightly ajar.

"I am interested," she said in a flat voice, her brow gathering against the crest of her facial powders, "in knowing your progress."

"I'm well enough," I said. "Thank you."

"No," she said. "That won't do. Not at all."

She stood there, her mouth tightened into a bud.

It was plain she was used to having her pleasure accommodated. I would have counted myself cruel to insist that she observe the facts of our new surroundings, to recall how, in this country, none of us warranted any particular attention, especially as regarded the province of whim. But then, for this particular day, I felt utterly crushed, beyond repair.

"At your service, Señora." I opened my door. She wafted in ahead of me, like a tiny breeze.

"You've lost your composure," she said, taking the chair I offered. The two of us had an unimpeded view down upon the muddy thoroughfare in front of the hotel.

"Is it so stunningly obvious?" I said. I crossed my legs and observed her from across a small slice of the round-top table. The air gushed in through the open window with metered regularity. In it was the fetid muck, the sweating backs of horses or mules, the destruction—by immobile water—of leaves and limbs in the swamps behind our city. The Señora sat in the face of this torrent, at ease, glowing like a polished diadem set into a plain wooden box.

The curl of her mouth insinuated a universe of superior knowledge.

"You wish to hear of matters that have torn me down? I'd have thought you might refer to me a gentleman or lady eager to meet a newcomer fresh with the spirit of enterprise," I said.

"You are not that person." Her eyelids did not descend.

"Come now. I know myself."

"What you know, and what you're in the process of becoming, and therefore knowing, form two separate worlds."

"Do they?"

"You've encountered elements of your new homeland which, frankly, you cannot live with, Monsieur. That much is obvious."

"Be that as it may, Señora. I am still quite as lively a factor as any who ply that street." I pointed out the window, but looked at her face, without wavering.

She lowered her eyes. In the line that crossed her cheek—a loveless indentation of sheer age, also, to some extent, deprivation—I saw a sign of defeat. Yet also, an unaffectedly deep sympathy.

"Forgive me," I said. "I've been boorish, defensive." I smiled. "I happened to go to the slave auctions today."

She slumped forward so abruptly I thought I'd have to catch her.

With her shoulders only inches from my ready hands, she said, "I know."

"You were there?" I found the news fantastic.

"Sickened," she said. "That first day, to hear your absolutely correct intonation—I mean, the exact calibration of lilt, of resonance—in the French you used."

"You—"

"Yes, I was listening. Of course. A new voice in this place . . ." She raised up finally and presented a mask of bottomless sorrow. I reached for her hands.

A mistake.

At once, a wire—heretofore carefully coiled, hidden behind an impenetrable front—sprang loose. How long had I been in the hotel? Two, three weeks? Yet it had been nearly unendurable. The silence, the brusque manners, the wretchedly thin conversation—never a word from Europe. My arms encircled her fragile back. I brought my lips to her small bud, that mobile flame, which she pressed against me.

I was as if a lightning stroke had melted two inferior metals into a single mass, her mind and my own fused. Her limbs, the extremities, the denser centers of her body—all our parts at once were finding, winding, becoming more completely of one sympathy . . . her garments, herself the mistress of their vents and angles, came to rustle against my own while I was yet seated in my chair.

Her feet, I realized, now free of their small black boots, had never touched the floor. She'd swung from her chair to mine, clinging to my neck like an arachnid. With one set of hands or another on buttons, freeing painful screenings and chainings of various levels of cloth, we were now aflame. Oiled chambers rose in circular tiers within confines that only blood and flesh could hope to seek out.

I locked one eye upon the road below. Its carriages, its foot traffic, its terrible mud that kept everyone on the alert—no one could hazard an upward gaze. In this crude, barbarous world, we'd found, ironically, an utterly safe vantage.

The Señora's wax makeup had melted. Beneath her royally high cheekbones a matching pair of raw, chaffed hollows were exposed. Long creases traversed these hollows, one on each side, the sorts of markings which ennoble a field battery captain, adding virility to cold, dashing eyes. Contrasted to her luscious dark irises, these creases seemed, however, especially cruel.

I wondered what I looked like—then shivered.

Her eyes opened, immediately fastened on the window. Blue sky filled with puffy Gulf clouds poured in upon us. We lay on the hotel's large if spottily bolstered bed.

"That was not my intention at all," she said. Her gaze was strangely focused, as if fixed upon the untrue glass panels of the window's frame, not on the clouds beyond.

"I must apologize then," I said.

"Don't."

"But if—"

"Let me tell you," she said, her Spanish voice grown weary, "when you seized me, your hands, your breath against my neck, the scent of the sun's furious energy within your coat and shirt, my mind dissolved. But it was D'Arcy Thoroughgood, not you, who placed his hands around my waist."

"You and Monsieur D'Arcy . . ."

She didn't answer.

"I confess my mind was on yourself only," I said.

"Stop," she said. "You could almost substitute the word anyone, though that is not quite true either. My qualities—my tininess, my sympathy, my brutal honesty, my physical aliveness—these things you did desire, perhaps still desire—"

"I do—"

"Quiet. Let me say these things. I cannot possibly allow any other moment to occur . . . I . . . who climbed on you like a beast—"

"I refuse to—"

"—atop you in the same way as I mounted and dealt with Mr. D'Arcy. Can't you see it? How completely I dominated him?"

Her words had the effect of a medicinal draft—from a strange cabinet. I pushed her back, pinned her hands beneath mine, rolled atop her with all the gentlest strength I could muster. She gave way to me soon enough, a releasing of the tension at body's center. My mind was sucked down into that vortex, that endless releasing. Soon she was touching my elbows with her knees, clinging with her arms around my back, saying, "And now it is me for you. For you, Monsieur."

The day's light cast its strength into a corner of the room, far from the bed where we lay. Of all things, here at day's close, I felt ready for encountering strangers about the subject of business—so long as it avoided that awful institution of slavery.

"You're restored, Monsieur. I feel it. As for me, I've been diminished," the Señora said.

She rose, seized her boots in one hand, then let herself out of the door.

At supper she didn't show—thank god. I wasn't ready for it. Afterward, I smoked in the parlor. I tried absorbing myself in the papers, which, at last, I tossed upon a table. I'd not found the smallest idea as to how my fortune was to be pursued. At precisely that moment, Madame Hartnett passed by in the hallway with the most smug expression imaginable. I couldn't fathom what business she had been attending to. A moment later, as I mounted the staircase I realized her expression had been cast into her interior—even then, without particular focus. I thought, 'Here is the New Worlder. She knows some certainty; moreover, that certainty is guaranteed to render dividends.'

What a fool I'd been! Why had I waited so long to come to here—the one place where I had any future at all?

"I am not so hungry anymore, you'll understand," the Señora said. We sat at my table, late, taking spiced tea. It had been prepared in those islands of the Gulf which lay nearer the headland of that other continent.

Prepared by slaves, I thought idly. What wasn't? On the other hand, at the Hotel St. Pierre, we at least enjoyed tea on demand.

. . . strange refuge.

"You're not well?" I said. After the day's dionysian activities, after such surfeits of ecstasy—if not hysteric release of troubling, ruminative ideas born of this fantastic landscape—I desired nothing so much as a period of reflection. But she had knocked within minutes of my closing the door. Now the drug of her presence again filled the room and myself.

"Of course I'm not well," she said.

I looked away, eager to avoid these particular fields of her mind.

On the spur, I said, "Have you seen a slave auction?"

"Never."

"They are most peculiar."

"You speak like a powdered wig. We're out of court here, you know."

"I mean, they are detestable, repugnant."

"That's better."

"They expect men like myself to watch their own kind—differing in but a few superficial characteristics—be treated like stock animals. Why, I've never felt so degraded in my life."

" 'Degraded.' I should have left without finishing my tea, had you not driven straight to that word."

My god, the smile she opened over those tiny teeth. So chill she'd been the one moment, so cozy the next—what kind of person sought excitement in such precisions of the truth?

Then I remembered: royalty. Of course. The truth had always been one of their dispensations, another territory denied to those whose positions were less than secure.

A terrible idea stole over me—a game. I'd seek the utmost honesty in my next comments, then see if she abandoned herself to me once again— for the third time that day.

My larger concerns of course evaporated.

"This one particular chap—" I began.

"Chap?" she said. "Chap?"

"This man—a complete man, like myself—"

She pulled a small fan from her bodice, raked it open. On its rice paper backing a picture had been painted: yawning, almost suppurant mouths of flowers. Yellow, white, vermilion. Behind this effulgent display I located, however, the presence of two painted eyes.

"Mocked!" I said. "I felt mocked by the proceedings. Never mind what the man looked like."

The flowers, the eyes above them, swept back and forth.

"Stripped," I said. "I felt stripped, humiliated—in public."

"Why?"

"Because . . ." I spewed out my recollections of the short, stout man. "I tell you, he had made himself monstrous by the addition of that tophat, don't you know, as if conferring upon himself a stature he knew he didn't possess."

I laughed, on the verge of the performer's hysteria.

"Go on." The fan continued its sweep.

"'My god, it's too much,' I said while standing right in their midst. 'It's just too much.'"

She closed her mouth. Her nostrils flared suddenly. "Liar!"

I sprang from my chair, hammered my boots across the small floor. "I spoke those exact words. Strike me dead if I didn't!"

"Liar!"

"How dare you throw that word at me! You, who fairly live——" I caught myself.

"——in lies?"

I couldn't speak. Behaving like a royal competitor in an afternoon's badminton game. Hotheaded, oblivious—a fool.

"Listen to me, Monsieur," she said coolly. "It's not my lies—if in fact that's what they are—which need concern you. The point is, you have been lying since that very moment early this morning. The lie occurred just prior to when you spoke at the auction. Listen back, if you can, inside yourself, Monsieur. It's your own words, even though they were spoken, that composed the lie."

I was stunned. My cheeks flushed. My mind was tumbling in search of some firmness in this small, crazy room. Yet I did hear now another set of words.

I nodded—to myself—held up a finger, an old schoolboy habit when giving back rote. I opened my mouth, waited upon memory, upon instinct to come again. The Señora stretched far forward in her seat. Her eyes flickered with the heat of a late tropical cloudburst in the making. She'd collapsed the fan into an upright wooden rod which she held in her lap.

"'Free That Man!' That's what I wanted to say. I wanted to turn the whole mob onto the auctioneer. Rather, no, onto the short, stout man. I wanted to see them parade that tophatted monster onto the slave block. Once there, with his hat exaggerating the very notion that his head owned any capacity for thought at all, I wanted to see—not to perform myself, but to see, for my own benefit, my very own deep pleasure—his head be taken off. Nothing less would have satisfied."

She pitched to her knees, wringing her hands. Her fingers began pinching the button heads out of their tightly sewn clefts on the front of my trousers.

"I was terrified—absolutely terrified—that they'd parade me onto the block and wrench my head off."

"We have a moral repugnance—you and I," she said in a single wind, "to all this so-called New World."

One of the room's three brass lamps flickered on the bedside table. We stowed our bodies beneath the coverlet; night hung in the air like a damp sheet; we'd been losing one degree of heat per hour.

"The land of equality, of freedom," she said.

"You're speaking of the States, dear lady. This is Spain."

"The idea's here already," she said, resting her head on one hand, her elbow plunged into my dewy, feather-filled pillow. She looked past me toward the wall. "No one will truly enjoy these things, even if they come to pass. It's not what the stronger half of us wants."

The hour was well in advance of two a.m. We'd slept fitfully, there being the confusing sensation that a pact was in the making. The Señora said:

"Sleep is not upon me, Monsieur. And you need to hear what I need to say."

"Speak then." Though I felt abused.

"When I was granting Mr. D'Arcy my affections—drawn, ineluctably, as I am now to you—" her voice flat, the words emerging at precise meter, "he was my size, perhaps a bit larger. I was nearer the height of your shoulder."

If she were as tall as my shoulder, she would have been a foot taller than D'Arcy. I myself was almost two feet taller than she was. I could easily imagine her as a larger woman. As I say, no lack of proportion; no shortening, say, of legs, no over-largeness of skull. She constituted a marvel. As for D'Arcy's diminution, my mind reeled. The woman was disturbed, like an orphan, to find herself so abjectly alone in this foreign world.

"Imagine, if you will," she said, "how very completely I dominated that tiny, perfect gentleman?"

My eyes begged her, my voice lost itself in my chest. "Why are you saying these things?"

She laughed. "We can't get away from our state of affairs, can we?"

"State of affairs?"

"One of us will dominate the other."

"Intolerable idea!"

She raised her eyes to mine, then laid back, exhaling deeply. "You and I have come to the one place left to us." She drifted her hand toward the darkened window. "Unfortunately, it's the one place we can't enter."

In the morning, a vast whiteness—that of the magnolia, with its New World flower, or else the lily, that decorant of local graves—covered my room's objects: table, chairs, the shelf of the dormer where one could sit or place a potted plant (I had yet to do so). At the end of my bed with its piled-back coverlets, this same whiteness—the morning's gigantic sunlight—showed me she was gone.

I got up, tried the door—locked. Hardly a surprise. The Señora had maintained that D'Arcy had given her his key on his last night in this room— my room now.

After breakfast—she failed to show, a wise decision, I thought—I went to the front porches to smoke a narrow cigar which I'd purchased at the open-air river stands. The tobacco had been grown—so the concessionaire assured me—at the oldest plantation of the Carolinas. 'The Darkies and the tobacco have become as one at that plantation, governor,' he'd told me. I stood on the pale blue Bavarian boards, stared at our alley's traffic stirring mud and dung into a primordial muck. The deeply cured, sugary leaves of tobacco suddenly seemed so monstrous that I slung the object into a short stand of azaleas. While I wondered where I might find relief—the fantastical shores of California? perhaps the frozen forests of the north—Madame Hartnett came to stand at the front door behind me.

I wheeled upon her. "Not that you shouldn't protect your lodgers, Madame, myself among them, but can you say how, or if, over time, your clientele has changed?"

"Why, what a question!" she said, and shut her mouth. I walked over, nevertheless, and stood beside her.

"I'm an interested observer of history at this moment, Madame Hartnett. I'm aware that in this still young enterprise—"

"Young enterprise? This hotel has been operating since 1761!"

"No, no, Madame. This New World—that enterprise."

"Oh." She closed her mouth. Her twitching lips, her heavily caked eyelids fairly danced with the whiff of innuendo.

"I meant merely to inquire how this city and its fortunes have"—I chose my words carefully—"developed from the point of view of someone, like yourself, who's seen a period of grandeur which has done nothing but grow." I smiled largely.

She was unmoved, as dreary as a penitent beneath flails. "My lot, Monsieur, is one of meeting demands. I'm afraid that history's a luxury."

I took charge. "Yes, it's true that some of us here sprang from lines of nobility whose ends have been cauterized by the fires of revolution, but—"

"You and the Señora. That is all," she said. "I now rent to Americans only."

She looked at the churning street, its fare of mules clopping, gentlemen marching in high boots en route to or from market.

"There's nothing personal in my decision," she said. "It's simply that when Americans check in, they stay. Over time, this business becomes quite laborious, you know. Excuse me, Monsieur."

She turned to leave but I followed her inside where she said, "I've been telling everyone that we shall be renovating the St. Pierre. Workmen are due any minute. No hammering or sawing after five p.m., however."

"Improvements," I said. "There you are—the New World spirit." I spoke with an overly bright voice, to hide my sense that this lady was somehow bent on destroying a unique refuge.

"Yes, the facade and its hideous blue color will change. As will the name."

"The name?"

"We're the Hartnett Inn now."

"The Hartnett?"

"Yes. Hotel St. Pierre, as you probably guessed, was erected by one of your kind, an ex-noble or something. He wanted to serve immigrants who came here sick of heart."

"What?!"

"I mean, homesick."

She walked to her rooms. I trudged to the staircase.

In the darkness of our hallway, all doors looked shut. The hotel felt empty.

Desolate, I knocked at the door of Señora Alvarez. No answer. I knocked again, but when another door began to rattle open down the hallway, I turned and hastily unlocked my own quarters. I half expected to find the Señora at the table—or in my bed.

I've learned the following things. Señora Alvarez had been an émigré for two decades, living in Geneva, then Rome. The province in Spain where she was born had been ruled by her father's family for over three hundred years. There had then occurred a revolution—by the people. Under the influence of a democratic firebrand named Juan Martin (known as Juan the Revealer), this popular movement most immediately led to mass executions—of the nobility. Alvarez the old Grandee was first to be placed upon a raised platform. A traveler in the region—nameless, bearing no trade or product—volunteered when the executioners asked the throng for a booted foot. The service for which he earned a single real was just this: he clamped his bootsole against Señor Alvarez's side-turned face—this, though the Señor swore he would accept all the crowd's outrages without need for bonds or coercion. While this stranger pinioned the old man's head thusly against weathered boards, a second, masked hombre proceeded to knife it off.

Twenty-three days later, the cavalry from the neighboring province of Luz entered the city. Under the Capitan's orders, they began a fresh round of executions, by firing squad, until the square streamed crimson with the blood of commoners. At least one brick wall fell beneath the ceaseless impact of lead slugs. Juan the Revealer was caught and scalded alive. The skin was peeled from his body, which was then hung, by grappling hook through the anus, from a butcher's storefront.

In the face of these examples, the remaining male citizens offered themselves as slaves. Their offer once accepted was transmuted into the somewhat darkly famous Luz Document for New Citizenship. Under its provisions, the people were, in fact, freed of many former obligations to the Alvarez nobles—most notably, from excessive taxation. In return, they submitted all written documents: letters, books, including Bibles. These writings were taken for 'safekeeping' to the neighboring regent's castle. Within ten years, the people had become a docile, mule-like workforce whose occasional interludes of riot were marked, without exception, by mass murder entirely self-directed.

I recognized the name of this neighboring principality: Luz. It was, in fact, the sole link to that tincture of royalty which coursed through my own blood. The greatest Catalan poets of that time had emerged from this city of my forefathers, that is, on my mother's side.

What else did the maids and Madame Hartnett find in the Señora's room? I have no idea. Madame Hartnett gave me these papers, because, as she put it, 'You have the leisure for histories, I don't.'

I kept as distant from the proceedings as possible. I had sensed—all along—that the Señora might disappear, without notice, for reasons I'd never know. She'd certainly succeeded in inventing a monstrously amusing chapter—call it our love affair—for her life's book. I reckoned my name was now afloat on the Gulf's warm waters, borne along as a memory toward shores where she might speak, in all its tripping, vowel-rhyming vocables, her native tongue. Perhaps, I thought, she might meet the man whose worldly position was worthy of a princess—though a fiery, unrepentant, thoroughly unreliable princess.

Over the days that followed, I found myself pacing my own floors, talking aloud to myself, chanting gibberish concerning business. It was all a gigantic folly, the product of an agitated imagination. This talk was intended only to drown out the rough palaver of American wenches hired to eradicate a spot left beside the Señora's door.

After six days, an itinerant banker, if there is such a thing, took the room, easing his card one night beneath my door. To see this white rectangle appear suddenly, with a noise like mice feet, into my lamplit quarters was to experience the deepest revulsion and self-recrimination. This sort of naked self-advertisement constituted exactly the bold, artless behavior which I should have seized on for myself, long ago. No doubt he'd tucked his card under everyone's door, including Madame Hartnett's.

I will make myself anew—on the morrow. I swear it.

Until then, however, I turn in reverie to the Señora, to the world we'd departed so recently. That Old World—how quickly it disappears. Its peculiar brutalities, its exquisite refinements have sunken beneath the muck of the Calle Real.

TOM PIAZZA

BROWNSVILLE

I'VE BEEN TRYING TO GET TO BROWNSVILLE, Texas, for weeks. Right now it's a hundred degrees in New Orleans and the gays are running down Chartres Street with no shirts on, trying to stay young. I'm not running anymore. When I get to Brownsville I'm going to sit down in the middle of the street, and that will be the end of the line.

Ten in the morning and they're playing a Schubert piano trio on the tape and the breeze is blowing in from the street and I'm sobbing into a napkin. "L.G.," she used to say, "you think I'm a mess? You're a mess, too, L.G." That was a consolation to her.

The walls in this café have been stained by patches of seeping water that will never dry, and the plaster has fallen away in swatches that look like silhouettes of countries nobody's ever heard of. Pictures of Napoleon are all over the place: Napoleon blowing it at Waterloo, Napoleon holding his dick on St. Helena, Napoleon sitting in some subtropical café thinking about the past, getting drunk, plotting revenge.

I picture Brownsville as a place under a merciless sun, where one-eyed dogs stand in the middle of dusty, empty streets staring at you and hot breeze blows inside your shirt and there's nowhere to go. It's always noon, and there are no explanations required. I'm going to Brownsville exactly because I've got no reason to go there. Anybody asks me why Brownsville— there's no fucking answer. That's why I'm going there.

Last night I slept with a woman who had hair down to her ankles and a shotgun in her bathtub and all the mirrors in her room rattled when she laughed. She was good to me; I'll never say a bad word about her. There's always a history, though; her daughter was sleeping on a blanket in the dining room. It would have been perfect except for that.

The past keeps rising up here; the water table is too high. All around the Quarter groups of tourists float like clumps of sewage. The black carriage drivers pull their fringed carts full of white people from nowhere up to the corner outside and tell them how Jean Lafitte and Andrew Jackson plotted things out, as if the driver knew them personally. The conventioneers sit under the carriage awning, looking around with the crazed, vacant stare of babies, shaded by history, then move on.

The sun is getting higher, the shadows are shortening, the moisture is steaming off the sidewalks. The Schubert, or Debussy, or whatever it is, has turned into an oboe rhapsody, with French horns and bassoons quacking and palmetto bugs crawling across the tile floor, making clicking sounds that I can't hear because the music is too loud. If she didn't love me, why didn't she just tell me so? I asked her why she lied to me and she said she was afraid to tell me the truth. In other words it was my fault. She doesn't even have a friend named Debbie.

I keep trying to look at what's right in front of me. I want to stop trying to mess with the past. The last thing she said to me was, "I have to get this other call." But I'm not going to think about her.

One cloth napkin.

One butter knife.

One fork.

One frosted glass containing partly melted ice and a slice of cucumber. Another frosted glass with similar contents. Where's the waiter? A small menu, marked with coffee along one edge. Breeze from a ceiling fan. Three Germans at the next table. The pictures of Napoleon must make them nervous. A waiter on a stool, leaning back against the wall by the ice chest, hair already pasted to his forehead with sweat.

A white Cadillac just backed into a car parked right outside, making a loud noise and partly caving in the wooden column supporting the balcony above the sidewalk. People are getting up and walking to the door, looking. The driver is black and is wearing a full Indian costume, plumes mushrooming as he gets out to look. He is about seventy years old; a five-year-old boy waits in the front seat. The driver gets back into the Cadillac and drives off.

One coffee mug at the next table. One crumpled pack of Winstons.

Hopeless.

I saw a sign once, on a building outside Albuquerque, that read ALL AMERICAN SELF-STORAGE. If you could just pay a fee somewhere and put yourself in a warehouse, just for a night.

Brownsville.

I picture a little booth at the edge of town, with a bored-looking woman sitting in it. You pay fifty cents and leave everything you can remember in a box with her. You walk down Main Street at high noon, wearing a leather vest, on the balls of your feet. The one-eyed dogs bark and shy away, walking sideways, eyeing you. You walk into the saloon, which is cool and dark, and order a bourbon. You look in the mirror behind the bar and talk to yourself in the second person. Maybe it would be better to stay outside in the sun.

Here is what morning is like in New Orleans. Just before the sky starts getting light, the last freight train inches its way through Ville Platte and the stars have drifted off to sleep. Slowly, the sky exhales its darkness and the trees look black against the deep blue over Gentilly. The houses along Felicity Street, and farther out toward Audubon Park, are cool to the touch, and dew covers the flower beds. A taxi pulls up to a traffic light, looks, goes through. The smell of buttered toast disappears around the corner and televisions are going in the kitchens of the black section. The St. Charles trolley, as unbelievable as it was yesterday, shuttles its first serious load toward the business district. Later, the men will have taken their jackets off and folded them in their laps, staring out the streetcar windows, caught in that dream. Already the first shoeshine boys are out hustling on Bourbon Street, and the first dixieland band is playing for the after-breakfast tourists, and the first conventioneers are climbing into carriages at Jackson Square, and the Vietnamese waitresses at the Café Du Monde are getting off their all-night shifts, and luggage is lined up on the sidewalk outside the Hyatt.

If there was just some way to stay in it, to be there and see it without starting in. If there was just some way to wipe the slate clean. As soon as I can, I'm going to pay my tab and step outside. I'm closing my accounts and going to Brownsville. I'll leave everything at the edge of town. I'm going to walk in and take it from there.

NANCY LEMANN

Adapted from *MALAISE*

THE SLEAZE GAVE A NEGATIVE PRESSURE that was darkly beguiling, like the French Quarter in New Orleans, which is the type of place where people are drinking beer at ten o'clock in the morning, and the trash has not been picked up from the night before, and the whole place basically has the air of a bordello, and the view from your hotel room is to the brick wall of the Holiday Inn next door. But it is home, of course, and that makes all the difference, for in that there is redemption. So you're picking your way among the tourists and the trash and yet if it's home, then anything could happen, and every situation is a stage set, every bar or lounge. All the ghosts of those you most have loved are there, and it is overpowering. The whole place peopled with ghosts, and maybe one or two who accompany you everywhere you go.

It was home, although I did not know that at the time. I only know it now. And I know now that there was never elsewhere such a home.

obituary cocktail

Jean Lafitte, famed pirate and hero of the Battle of Orleans, reputedly lived on Bourbon Street above his blacksmith shop which functioned as a front for his smuggling trade. In 1850 it became a bar. Around the turn of the 20th century America saw the creation of the martini, and Lafitte's Blacksmith Shop, which still lays claim to being the oldest bar in the United States, augmented the martini with a splash of absinthe, labeling it the Obituary Cocktail.

$1\,^1/_2$ oz. dry gin

dash dry vermouth

$^1/_4$ oz. absinthe

Chill in a shaker and strain.

CLARENCE JOHN LAUGHLIN

THE LAND OF THE POPPIES

I Myself am Heav'n and Hell…
　　　-The Rubaiyat.

IN A REALM UNTROD OF MAN and of the cruel disastrous feet of the Years lies spread the land of the poppies.

Poppies there sway and swoon, innominate and numberless, flushed with their own secretive essence, bright with the treasures they have cunningly distilled from the earth, the air, and the sun. The fingers of the wind strive to support them when they reel in floreal intoxication.

An undulating encrimsoned ocean, they stir in vast and vivid, waterless waves. And the waves shift and deepen through all the tones of red as shadows darken and dissolve in swirling water. But not only do they mimic the sea. Sometime they are like raiment. Then the gently curving valleys are covered as though a billowy vermilion cloak were thrown over the land. But our connotations of apparel do not seem to fit, as they should, this marvelous living color and its movements, that together appear, at once, attire and sentient nudity. For the massed poppies on the rounded knolls often heave and bulge forth. Then they seem part of a huge recumbent creature—an earth elemental perhaps—with pulsing scarlet flesh, who is softly and widely breathing.

Here it is ever quiet; peace and a sleepy delight imbue all the land. The violent soundless explosions of color in which the countless tiny stalks of the poppies culminate seem only to accentuate the quietude. Mayhap accuracy of hearing is dulled somewhat by the spell in which the subtle play of tint binds the eyes which behold. A gleaming road, untraveled, swings softly into the distance. While the sea-farthest border of this domain is bounded by the sinuous and somnolent flow or a slow stream whose shining glissade of water holds reflections that are like dreams of dreams. When a petal falls toward its image in the water it seems serenely flitting from the world of materiality to a far heaven; toward a second more perfect self immured in another dimension. But it finds its other self only to shatter it and the water twinkles derisively.

Truly, it is a blessed realm; noises are never known, all metallic activity is dispensed with, the wandering feet and the rough crude hands of men are not present to despoil. Oblivion's calm and stately figure rules impassively for aye.

Trees throw sensitive and turbulent shadows here, shadows that quiver and retreat shyly at the approach of the sun.

The shadows seem to render the body of the poppies more alive, so that they press about the trees in circles that contract and widen, darkly flaming their energies against them.

And the endless strands of the wind's hair when they are cast swirling over the fields net the poppies in an intangible web of scarcely audible murmurs. No sound more human than this is heard, excepting the voluptuous sighs of trees under the caresses of the wind and the multi-tongued monotone of the rain. In little open-eyed pools the wind washes its hair. You could glimpse, were you there to see, the unseen filaments making delicate enlargening whorls on the smooth waters. And a twin world immersed and marvelous lies imprisoned in the clear pure glass. How wholly perfect that world is! In it, blue and crimson and gold tint all there is. In it, all is noiseless and clear and secret.

In the blue immeasurable ocean of the skies of this land float clouds that are the huge disengaged dreams of demiurges. Some of the dreams are like falling feathers of strange great birds, and some the foamy flashing crests of the sky-ocean's waves. Others seem indeed frail crystallizations of evaporated superhuman ecstasies, for whose forms there are no earthly parallels.

The great fields of the poppies possess an endemic atmosphere that clings closely about their hosts. The merged multitude of their odorous aureoles is at once delightful and deadening, poignant and languorous. At times even the wind seems drugged, yet still in this slumber of the air, long rows of the poppies will ripple suddenly. Their features, which are suffused with smoldering blood, appear to be almost somatically alive. And they become cernuous as with the wisdom that holds the ultimate secret of happiness within its power. Which in reality they do, perhaps, as we shall see . . .

At other times the blazing tide of flower fires shudder convulsively as the rain falls to assuage the lovely torture of their need for moisture. Incarcerated in flames that are hues their petals tremble beneath the soothing element. For a while they seem extinguished and cool, but brightening up, the scarlet splendor of their armies once more shines flamboyant. Secretly, strangely, burning they are unquenchable.

Turbid with aerial gold the days slip quietly by, while the nights glisten with fluid silver. With dark dream eyes the poppies nod myriadly under a lustrous moon that is like a congealed bubble of golden hued gas.

Time has no triumph here. For as fast as the poppies wither, new ones, exactly like the dead in every particular, spring up in their stead. So minutely similar are they that one cannot be sure that they are not the recrudescence of the dead. The leap of flower from dead flower seems only the rhythm of an unvarying pulsation. And the sun and moon and wind are unchanging.

The swift birds of the Hours fly lightly by; in truth, the whir of their wings is unmarked since there are none to notice or to care; none to split Life in the dead analysis of minutes, and to raise the dreadful phantom of the Future with its dark pre-visions of Life's end.

If a common man was to appear here he would be so extraneous as to seem no more than a crude and impossible shade thrown by the candle of the sun in a grotesque shadow-show. And of the fate of any man who dares to enter herein I shall tell presently. For the gods have insured the eternal tranquility of this far kingdom.

In the inexplicable way in which all things come to pass it is related that in after years the radiant road gradually disclosed two human figures. Among the few (so the old tale runs) whose ambiguous fortune it was—because, perhaps, of the perfection of his life or the keenness of his senses—to find this domain was one who in those days humbly and joyously practiced his craft of verse. Let us look at that one with true eyes of poesy, one of the few available means we have of penetrating the dust of Time, of seeing that which cannot directly be seen. We peer, therefore, at these two figures, and with the strangest emotion of recognition . . .

Can it be our beloved Omar who journeys hither or is it his phantasmal double? As the figures approach we see that it is he indeed and no other. And his companion is a sloe-eyed red-lipped Persian maiden, unknown to us, round whose supple waist his arm is clasped. She wears wide silk pantaloons embroidered with vivid arabesques and her raven hair is bound in the manner that is the custom of her country.

And he, famed poet, presents quite a spectacle: silken turban, peaked slippers, a figure slightly stout, and a brown bearded face. His countenance betokens a subtle combination of thinker and sensualist. He strides along right joyfully and in his smoldering eyes is something as bright and dancing as the flowers. Nor is she devoid of flower-delight in the sun and the efflorescence of her body.

His rich voice mounts in song. At intervals her tender voice joins his. And the sum of all their song is to make merry while we may, before age destroys Life's sweetness; to seek, above all, forgetfulness of the dark curse laid upon the race of men.

Presently they come to a cool grove of trees washed by the waves of poppies. Near the border of these, beneath the restful shade, they seat themselves. They fall to converse. "The poppies flame so fiercely," she says pensively, "as though to burn themselves the sooner away."

To which he returns: "And why should they not? Must we hoard our moments, thinking they will give us longer life? Age will come and take them nathless, and we want then the brightness which we denied ourselves, and the warmth we did not have."

"Ah Time! Do the poppies know time, I wonder, in their abandon, in their vivid intoxication?"

"It is doubtful," he responds gravely. "They harbor none of our accursed conceptions of Time. They think not of the future and so do not dread it. They look not back at the Past and do not shudder. Living and delight with them are one. They seize without hesitation, without fear, the momentary span Life allots them, implicitly knowing it eternal. And that living knowledge—better than all our crumbs—renders them intoxicated and superb. We reach intoxication more hardly, and it never lasts." He smiles, somewhat bitterly.

She melts, touches his lips tenderly with her hand. "Yet are we not wiser than most men?"

"Perhaps," he concedes, "but not wise enough. Enough, perhaps, to see that he who scoffs at the wisdom is himself most wise. Enough to see, in part, how we are all corrupted by our ideas of time, by the tiny segments into which we have divided reality—but not enough to see as we should, the vast panorama of the Present as something endless, incapable of division, something in which all cessation is only apparent. Let us endeavor, however, to be wise enough to trust implicitly, even as the flowers do, to the expansion, the strength, of the Life force; and to accept, in an acceptance uncontaminated by our warped views of Time, our deaths with being continuous with the drawing of breath."

To which she breathes a soft assent.

Then he exclaims fervently: "And when I sleep let my sleep be deep, so deep as to last eternally. Let me not ponder awakening or have any foreknowledge of my sleep! With the dawn let there be dawn in our minds, and with the shadow let us sink softly to rest. All that shall befall me already exists being so existent in time, why then should my worries or my fancies avail me any?"

From the girdle at his side he draws a leathern bottle filled with the time-dispelling juice of the grape. They both drink. He holds the bottle on high and questions: "Ah wine! Would Life be possible without it? Would Life be endurable? Does it not alone redeem us from Time and make us akin to the flowers?"

Each in turn, and lovingly, they slowly imbibe the regal fluid. In it they know again the light of the sun and the shadowy blood-leap that holds the secret of growth. They grow amorous and lie with their heads near the poppies. The contact with the earth and the impassioned perfume of the flowers act as a precipitant factor for that which is in their blood. They begin to fondle one another and like the stalks of the poppies in a sensuous wind their limbs are shaken with desire. Her bared breasts with their nipples poppy-dark, her mouth like an opened flower-pit, place them in a world of immediate living reality—divorced from all abstractions, all divisionings and countings. Knowing the fire of the sun, the secret, mindless and unfearful urge of flower-growth, they become timeless. They journey to Love's furthest realm and taste the utmost delight, to descend then into a drugged slumber, remaining still in the transitional agent of their embrace. The crimson flowers wave gaily and significantly above their dark heads. Jet and scarlet, how well they match, how well do they seem to imply a relationship other than chromatic!

And the lovers never awaken.

For the spell of the poppies upon them descends and imperceptibly they drift from the land of Love to the land of Dreams and thence to a land far darker . . .

It is this that is the fate the gods prepare for all men who enter here and this the method by which death comes, softly and by stealth, in this slumberous land. The fiery red petals are his strange instruments which he uses for his own grim purpose. That is why, the old chroniclers say, that poppies blush for very shame, knowing what their power may be. Yet, it seems, this is the most merciful of all possible deaths. Meditate upon this—O ye who are among the living!—to slip easily and without any previous knowledge thereof, just as you would fall asleep, into the deep dark grave . . .

Let us, however, pick up the broken thread of our tale.

When it was learned that such a gentle poet was dead the gods bethought themselves of his fate and repented of their design in allowing the land of the poppies to give unto all who journeyed thither the priceless gift of Joy and Death made into one. It was known that only those of rare intelligence could find this land and so few were these that it was best that they should not be killed off before the fullness of their powers. They say, too, that at that time the gods were wroth with men and angry with their pettiness, so that if all the best of men were to vanish, there would be none left to alleviate the wrath of the gods.

The old tales differ on this, and as to what happened thereafter. Some say that the tears of the gods hastened the end. The gods, they say, wept for Omar. Now the tears of the gods, though relatively small when compared with their shedders, would be, when contrasted with those of men, most huge. So that the celestial lacrimations formed a terrific downpour. The rain fell in unprecedented torrents. Gusts of wind whipped the rain into nameless shapes elusively outlined with wavering water. Strange beings of a moment, these forms of wind and water swept ambiguously through the air. These sorrow-beings moaned most sadly. Flurries of rain scurried and frisked fearfully on the shifting floors of the winds. Drops striking the flood ricocheted in countless white watery flames, the cool fire of a supernal lament. The sea began to surmount the land . . .

There are those who do not wholly agree with this interpretation and who insist that it is anomalous for the gods to weep and that they do but laugh at, when they do not ignore, the dull antics of men. The gods (they say) desired the transformation of the land of the poppies for reasons unknown. In carrying out their divine design the waves alone were commanded. The sea, unaccompanied by rain, crept in inch by inch and yard by yard until it had thinly overflown all the land and gulped the blood of the last of the poppies. Poppies however deadly and sweet were impotent to drug its inexorable advance or lull to sleep its ruthless waters.

In these versions, as in others, we may not unlikely see some trace of the smallness of vision which Omar himself bewailed. But in some such wise was the land of the poppies submerged.

Palustrine and delitescent it became. Blackness grew out of the blue of its skies. Its shadows now had lost their sensitivity, becoming crude and sluggish, losing their delicate distinctions, clinging alike, and tenaciously, to its leafless and decayed trees, its slime-gripped poppy stalks, its unreflective and windless waters. It receded from the minds of men and went unrecorded in the matter-of-fact annals of history; living now only in the nostalgia of poets.

Subsequent to this a joyful death among the races of men has not been known . . .

TENNESSEE WILLIAMS

THE NIGHT WAS FULL OF HOURS

Somebody had once called him 'the loneliest man on God's green earth,' and though there exists no instrument subtile enough to determine the degree of that affliction in one individual for comparison with degrees of it in others,

the man so defined had accepted the definition as one of remarkable acuity to have come from someone unknown, encountered briefly in a foreign hotel-room.

This observer and interviewer had also mentioned in print the curiously intense quality of the subject's eyes, and was probably intimating that this 'loneliest man,' now perched nervously over London's Cadogan Square of green earth

(fronted also by the charming little hotel in which Saint Oscar of Our Sorrows had awaited arrest and two years at hard labor in preference to his friends' advice of flight to Calais)

was habituated to (prescribed) drugs, and again the guess, the published inference, not unkindly intended,

shot not wide of the mark.

*   *   *

The taking of drugs is lonely enough in itself without complications. It indicates an instinct to withdraw, and there are few instincts among humankind that are satisfied with more ease.

But there were complications in the case of this 'loneliest man,' ensnared for interrogation too soon after work, for

shallowly hidden beneath the pale, cackling apparition which he presented to public view,

was panic, a chronic state of it, and panic is incalculable in its degree as
loneliness is.

No modification of the condition seems particularly worth noting these
three years later.

(Cry out 'self-pity': unleash the hounds of derision.)

*   *   *

Tonight this titular possessor of leadership in the company of the lonely
on God's earth, whatever its color, subject to place and season, is no longer
under the scrutiny of anyone but himself, which is more than sufficient, an
inescapable thing. He has looked about for a bit of oblivion as a parched
mouth for water: he has looked everywhere but into the limitless, timeless
blankness of self-destruction which somehow frightens him still.

He has gone through his usual ritual of preparation for sleep, which
usually evades him till near daybreak. He has taken the little pale yellow
circular disk called Aldomet, whose function is said to be to pacify somewhat

the riotous dark red torrents whose turmoil, immanent ever, witlessly
threatens

to break through the corridors that protect the man and themselves
from spilling into extinction.

He has then curled up in bed, the memorial brass one, somewhere between single and double,

in which he'd once slept with a horse, oh, yes, with a lover affection-
ately known as The Horse.

He has taken two other pharmaceutical items: a green valium tablet
(ten milligrams) and a capsule of nembutal.

Still sleep evades him.

Two hours later, at midnight, he has dared to indulge himself in a second 'yellow-jacket':

The result of this indulgence is not the desired one, for only a short
while after he's begun to have muscular spasms, first in one leg, then the
other, and finally engaging his entire frame.

He gets up, then: fills the bath-tub with hot water, as hot as he can stand
it, a practice that usually numbs his muscular system long enough to sub-

due the spasms for a while that may be sufficient for him to sleep before daybreak.

This night it doesn't, the spasms recurring shortly after he's hauled himself back to bed.

And so what is next on 'the loneliest man's' agenda of coming attractions? Now this is a laugh, a legitimate laugh, I would say.

Up he rises again, from the memorial bed of brass, no longer kept polished, neglected, now, as a casket long interred. From it he does rise not as a rose and goes back to the little kitchen tucked away in his New Orleans pad, in his progress passing the eyes of his terrier, Gigi, sleepless as he, past Victor's clothes thrown over a living-room chair but no sign of Victor except the thermos of chicory coffee which he always prepares before retiring to his separate bedroom or changing to an outfit more suitable for cruising the all-night streets of the Quarter.

(Dear Victor, relinquished as lover because more needed as friend.)

After a slightly tepid cup from the thermos, what is our protagonist's next move?

Let slip again your howls of derision.

He then goes to the work-desk in his bedroom, sits down before his enemy and lover, his Smith-Corona electric portable, and with nothing to write about but what you read here, an account of his passage through a tunnel of night, he sits there and writes about that . . .

It is written for you, some of whom may also be among the loneliest ones on God's green earth.

Shouldn't one of you be with him, comforting him, offering him your loneliness as companion to his? Isn't it possible that some solace might be shared in that way?

The embarrassing problem is that he is still addicted to the beautiful and young: and he is a man past sixty, struggling to retain a remnant of younger days and nights but knowing that it is a losing battle, indeed one already lost . . .

He considers a bit the question of getting dressed, now, and adventuring out upon the streets of the *Vieux Carré*. A miracle might occur: he might encounter a lovely youth that could be induced to return home with him at a price within negotiable limits.

But, no, he won't go out now. He is fiercely restless but at the same time exhausted. To get into his clothes would be too much of an effort, let alone the prowling of streets that are hazardous at this hour, especially to an old *solitaire* in a narcotized condition.

His life stretches behind him, not before: full of adventures it was and yet tonight he is famished for still more.

It would be sufficient for him now, possibly even then, five years ago, to unclothe the vagrant youth and simply to lie beside him, to run his finger-tips over a smooth, warm body that was lulled toward slumber by the comfort of the brass bed, ignorant of the memories buried in it: for the *solitaire* no longer desires penetration: he needs very little, now, but quiet-ing companionship and this bit of tactile comfort.

It is twenty minutes of five. The night is full of hours. And the loneliest man may cease to exist before daybreak, not by a simple act of self-de-struction, consciously performed, but rather by folly and whatever is burn-ing his house down.

He believes in God. Who else is left? And maybe that steadfast mystery accepted as in childhood,

will send him some emissary upon an errand of mercy, quietly as the pink-shaded lamp is turned off, if he now returns quietly to bed.

Ask any dog in the street: 'What about this man?' and if the dog under-stood, it would either slink away, admitting it had no answer, or it would howl like a coon-dog at the base of a night-time tree.

And now having already set words on several pages of corrasable bond, the 'loneliest man on God's green earth' will retreat to the loneliest space on that earth which is that of a bed once warmly shared but now occupied alone.

Tennessee Williams
New Orleans, 1973
(Revised in Key West, 1978.)

Remy Benoit is the author of *Letty*, *Island Quilts*, and *Peace, Now*, among others. She is a writer and historian honored with a Presidential Award for Literary Excellence for her poem, "Out of the Mess and Smoke." Originally from Philadelphia, and now living in the New Orleans area, she is a spokeswoman for the rights of both our youth and our veterans. She is also webmistress of www.welcomehomesoldier.com (where she invites you to join her in The Niquahanam Project: Healing the World).

John Biguenet's fiction has appeared in such publications as *Book, Esquire, Granta, Playboy, Story*, and *Zoetrope*. The winner of an O. Henry Award for short fiction, he teaches at Loyola University New Orleans. His books *The Torturer's Apprentice*, a collection of stories, and *Oyster*, a novel, were published by Ecco/HarperCollins.

Poppy Z. Brite has published four novels, *Lost Souls, Drawing Blood, Exquisite Corpse*, and *The Lazarus Heart*; two short story collections, *Wormwood* and *Are You Loathesome Tonight?*; and a collection of nonfiction, *Guilty But Insane*. She has two novels forthcoming, *The Value of X* and *Liquor*. She lives in New Orleans with her husband Christopher, a chef. Find out more about her at www.poppyzbrite.com.

A native of Laurel, Mississippi, hometown of Blanche and Stella Dubois, **Marda Burton** lives, writes and hosts salons in a balconied apartment on Royal Street. An award-winning non-fiction writer/photographer specializing in travel and the arts, she writes fiction in her spare time. She is an editor for *Veranda Magazine*.

Robert Olen Butler has published ten novels and two volumes of short fiction. His stories have been included in four editions of *The Best American Short Stories* and seven editions of *New Stories from the South*. His was the only work of fiction in the 2001 edition of *The Best American Magazine Writing*. He is the recipient of a Pulitzer Prize, the National Magazine

Award, a Guggenheim Fellowship (all three in fiction), a National Endowment for the Arts grant, and the Richard and Hinda Rosenthal Foundation Award from the American Academy of Arts and Letters. His most recent novel is *Fair Warning*. He teaches creative writing at Florida State University in Tallahassee where he lives with his wife, the novelist and playwright Elizabeth Dewberry.

Christopher Chambers was born in Madison, Wisconsin, and has since lived in North Carolina, Michigan, Minnesota, Florida, and Alabama. He's settled in New Orleans where he writes, teaches, edits, and works on an old shotgun house. His work has appeared in *Gettysburg Review*, *Exquisite Corpse*, *BOMB Magazine*, *Carolina Quarterly*, *Quarterly West*, and *Lit*.

Maker Clark is a bartender, photographer, writer, editor, and filmmaker. He fell in love with the Big Sleazy just like everyone else and eventually came up with a good excuse to stay here a bit longer.

Andrei Codrescu (www.codrescu.com) is the author of *Casanova in Bohemia*, a novel. He writes regularly for National Public Radio and *Gambit Weekly* in New Orleans. He is the editor of *Exquisite Corpse: a Journal of Letters and Life*, at www.corpse.org.

Utahna Faith lives and writes in the French Quarter. Her work appears in *Exquisite Corpse*, *The Missing Fez*, *Night Train*, *Clean Sheets*, *flashquake*, *The Cafe Irreal* and other journals. She is flash fiction editor for *3am Magazine*.

The author of five novels and two collections of stories, **Richard Ford** was awarded the Pulitzer Prize and the PEN/Faulkner Award for *Independence Day*, the first book to win both prizes. In 2001 he received the PEN/Malamud Award for excellence in fiction.

Mary Elizabeth Gehman is a resident of New Orleans since 1970 and a native Pennsylvanian. She is assistant professor of English at Delgado Community College and has authored two books, *Women and New Orleans* (1988) and *The Free People of Color of New Orleans* (1994). She is also a licensed tour guide specializing in women's and Creole history tours.

Barry Gifford's recent books include the novel, *Wyoming*, *Out of the Past*, *Essays on Film*, and *American Falls: The Collected Stories of Barry*

Gifford. He also co-wrote the film, *City of Ghosts*, with director Matt Dillon.

Ellen Gilchrist is the author of seventeen works of fiction, including the short story collection, *Victory Over Japan*, which won the National Book Award, and most recently, *The Cabal and Other Stories*, and *I, Rhoda Manning Go Hunting with My Daddy*. She lives in Fayetteville, Arkansas.

Lee Meitzen Grue's works include *Trains and Other Intrusions: Poems*; *French Quarter Poems*; *In The Sweet Balance of The Flesh*; *Goodbye, Silver, Silver Cloud*, a collection of New Orleans stories; and *Live! On Frenchmen Street*, a spoken word CD. The recipient of an NEA Fellowship, prizes in poetry and fiction from Deep South Writers, The Associated Writing Programs, and a PEN Syndicated Fiction Prize, Grue has taught at Tulane, Westminster, and Xavier universities. She is the former Director of The New Orleans Poetry Forum and The First Backyard Poetry Theater and editor of *The New Laurel Review*

Bruce Henricksen's creative writing has appeared in *The Briar Cliff Review*, *The Edge City Review*, *Folio*, *North Dakota Quarterly*, *New Orleans Review*, *Pacific Review*, and *Southern Humanities Review*. His book on Joseph Conrad, *Nomadic Voices*, was published by University of Illinois Press. Bruce taught at Loyola University New Orleans for many years before returning to his home state of Minnesota, where he lives by Lake Superior with his wonderful wife.

Christine P. Horn lives in New Orleans.

Leonard Earl Johnson moved to New Orleans after a week's Carnival visit turned into six. He lives in a Faubourg Marigny garret named "Squalor Heights" and writes the column "Yours Truly in a Swamp," for *Les Amis de Marigny*. He has received numerous awards, including the Key to The City of New Orleans, the pen used by Louisiana Governor Mike Fosterwhen signing the South's first hate crimes bill, and a New Orleans Press Club Award For Excellence. His web site is www.LEJ.org

Jarret Keene, the son of a Tampa firefighter, was born in 1973. He received his Ph.D. in English from Florida State University, where he served for a number of years as the editor of *Sundog: The Southeast Review*. As well as being a music writer for the Las Vegas Mercury, he teaches creative writing and literature at the University of Nevada, Las Vegas.

"The mystery of time, the magic of light, the enigma of reality, and their interrelationships are my constant themes and preoccupations." **Clarence John Laughlin**, a remarkably prolific surrealist, produced several photography books, including *Ghosts Along the Mississippi* which he also wrote, reprinted 20 times. He lectured throughout the country on photographic aesthetics and American Victorian architecture. His photographs appeared in *Harper's Bazaar, American Heritage, Vogue, Architectural Review, Life, Du, Aperture, Look*, and *Art News* among other publications. Laughlin, who lived most of his life since 1910 in New Orleans, has been the subject of an Aperture monograph, and over 200 one-man shows. He died in 1985.

Nancy Lemann is the author of four novels, *Lives of the Saints, Sportsman's Paradise, The Fiery Pantheon*, and *Malaise*, and a nonfiction book, *The Ritz of the Bayou*. She has contributed to many publications, including *Esquire, The New Republic*, and *Paris Review*. A native of New Orleans, Lemann lives with her husband and daughters in Washington, DC.

Joe Longo was born in Providence, Rhode Island, and graduated from Rhode Island College and the University of New Orleans. His unpublished novel, *This Side of Providence*, was a semi-finalist in the novel competition of the William Faulkner Society Creative Writing Awards, and a portion, "Date Rape Anthems," was excerpted in *PRISM: international*. "S.I.N.ners" is taken from a novel-in-progress, tentatively titled *S.I.N.*

A native of Knoxville, Tennessee, **David Madden** has taught at LSU since 1968. As writer in residence, then Director of Creative Writing Program, then Founding Director of The United States Civil War Center, he has written and published more than 40 books, including nine novels, the last of which was *Sharpshooter: A Novel of the Civil War*, and two collections of stories, the last of which was *The New Orleans of Possibilities*. His work-in-progress is *London Bridge Is Falling Down*.

Valerie Martin is the author of six novels, including *Mary Reilly* and *Italian Fever*, two collections of short fiction, and a biography of St. Francis of Assisi. Her most recent novel, set in ante-bellum New Orleans, is *Property*.

Nick Moschovakis, who edited "The Night Was Full of Hours," is a co-editor of *The Collected Poems of Tennessee Williams* (NY: New Directions, 2002), and of other writings by Williams, including a previously unpublished short play set in New Orleans. Titled "And Tell Sad Stories of The Deaths of Queens," it is now available in *Political Stages: An Anthology of Drama*, ed. Emily Mann and David Roessel (NY: Applause Books, 2002).

James Nolan is a widely published poet, fiction writer, essayist, and translator. His two collections of poetry are *Why I Live in the Forest* and *What Moves Is Not the Wind* (both with Wesleyan), and he has translated Pablo Neruda (*Stones of the Sky*, Copper Canyon Press) and Jaime Gil de Biedma (*Longing*, City Lights Books). Recently he has been writer-in-residence at both Tulane and Loyola universities in his native New Orleans.

Lorin Oberweger is an award-winning author whose articles, short stories and poetry have appeared in dozens of periodicals, including *StoryQuarterly, Amelia, The Montserrat Review, Woman of Power, Journal of the Arts, The Sarasota Arts Review*. For the last six years, Lorin has worked as an independent editor and has produced writing seminars through her company, Free Expressions (www.free-expressions.com). She has taught poetry online, is an instructor for the Tampa Bay Writer's Voice program, and gives talks on fiction writing and the publishing industry.

Tim Parrish is the author of *Red Stick Men*, stories set in and near his hometown of Baton Rouge, Louisiana. Parrish was nominated by Tim O'Brien for *Best New American Voices 2002*, was the 2001 Walter E. Dakin Fellow at Sewanee Writers' Conference, and received a 2001 Connecticut Artists Grant. He teaches creative writing at Southern Connecticut State University.

Tom Piazza is a graduate of the Iowa Writers' Workshop. His books include the short-story collection *Blues And Trouble* (James Michener Award for Fiction), *The Guide to Classic Recorded Jazz* (ASCAP-Deems Taylor Award for Music Writing), and *True Adventures with the King of Bluegrass*, a portrait of Jimmy Martin. His first novel, *My Cold War*, is due to be released fall 2003 (HarperCollins). He has been a Professor at Millsaps College and the Visiting Writer in Residence at Loyola University in New Orleans. He is a regular contributor to *The New York Times* and *The Oxford American*. He may be reached at www.tompiazza.com.

Chris Rose is a staff writer for *The Times-Picayune* newspaper in New Orleans, a collector of sad stories, an inveterate barfly and a pool player of rapidly diminishing capacity.

Jeri Cain Rossi, born and raised up-river from the city of New Orleans in which she now resides. Her writing credits include *RedWine Moan* (Manic D Press, 2000), and *Angel with a Criminal Kiss* (Creation Books, 1996). She has written two plays. "The best gal you'd ever want to belly up to the bar with."

Josh Russell's novel is *Yellow Jack* (W.W. Norton). His fiction has appeared in *Epoch*, *New Stories from the South*, and in the limited edition *Winter on Fifth Avenue, NewYork* (Oat City Press). He lives in New Orleans.

Julie Smith is the author of numerous books and short stories, mostly in the mystery and suspense field. *New Orleans Mourning*, the first book in the Skip Langdon series (about a New Orleans police detective) won the Edgar Allen Poe Award for best novel. Her latest book is *Louisiana Bigshot*, featuring PI and poet Talba Wallis.

For the past decade **John Verlenden** has divided his time between the Middle East and New Orleans. "New Orleans, not surprisingly, counts many Arabs among its polyglot population. Not all of them drive taxis either. Since New Orleans is a port city, it lends itself to (im)migrants who then dwell in 19th century flats, architecturally, while residing between (or among) cultures in all internal aspects. I am one of that silent minority of permanent transients who ply our way along Canal Boulevard or Decatur Street, looking for all the world like we belong here, when we never quite feel rooted." Verlenden publishes stories, poems, translations, and essays in a variety of journals, with a book of translation from U. of Arkansas Press. His current work-in-progress is a Middle Eastern memoir.

Mick Vovers was born in an Australian town so small it was replaced by a telephone exchange the size of a cigarette box and a new road into a bigger town. His need to find real people in a "real world" eventually took him to New Orleans where his stories and life have found inexplicably surreal surroundings in which to fester and blossom. The fruit has been published in numerous zines and underworld publications not intended for wide public dispersal. Although he thinks he's a writer his photographs have been displayed in many cities and all sorts of silly places around the world. In amongst other mental breakdowns he's close to finishing a short novel about life's driving force, commensurate greed, and another compilation of desperate snippets of real life disasters.

M.O. Walsh was born and raised in Baton Rouge, LA. After receiving a B.A. from LSU and an M.A. from the University of Tennessee, he is now writing and teaching at the University of Tennessee. His work has appeared in publications such as *The Phoenix* and has warranted invitations to readings in Tennessee, Kentucky and Alabama. His story "A Billion Years or So" won the John C. Hodges Award for Excellence in Graduate Fiction in 2001. He has a dog, a family, and some friends.

Tennessee Williams was a playwright, poet, fiction and screenwriter. His plays include *The Glass Menagerie, Cat on a Hot Tin Roof*, and *A Streetcar Named Desire*. William S. Gray, a friend of Mr. Williams, recalled, "He was very sensitive to the light in New Orleans. We would have long periods of silence while he just watched the light change."

Jason Wiese works in the Vieux Carré as a librarian and archivist specializing in New Orleans history and culture. He has published short fiction and essays in a variety of publications, including *River Oak Review* and *Louisiana Cultural Vistas*, and also served as contributing editor for *Charting Louisiana: Five Hundred Years of Maps*, an historical atlas to be published by the Historic New Orleans Collection in 2003.

Andy Young is the poetry editor of the *New Laurel Review*. Her poems have been featured in journals such as *Concrete Wolf, Exquisite Corpse,* and Dublin's *The Stinging Fly* as well as in jewelry designs, electronic music, and in her chapbook, *mine*. Her latest book is *All Fire's the Fire* published by Erato Press. She has been awarded an Artist Fellowship from the Louisiana Division of the Arts and the Marble Faun Award. She works as an artist-teacher at the New Orleans Center for the Creative Arts.

Acknowledgements

Light of New Orleans Publishing gratefully acknowledges all the writers, and their representatives, for granting permission to use the works in this volume.

"Annie" by Remy Benoit. Copyright © 2001 by Maureen G. Rodriguez.

"Appealing for the Truth (A Sad Joke)" by Mick Vovers. Copyright © 2001 by Mick Vovers. First appeared in *Moments of Madness* by Mick Vovers.

"Bible Thumpers" by Andy Young. Copyright © 2001 by Andy Young.

"Blue Elephant" by Lorin Oberweger. Copyright © 2001 by Lorin Oberweger.

"Brownsville" by Tom Piazza. Copyright © 1996 by Tom Piazza. First appeared in *The Quarterly* (Vintage Books) and in *Blues and Trouble (St.* Martin's Griffin, 1997) by Tom Piazza.

"Burgundy" by Christine P. Horn. Copyright © 2002 by Christine P. Horn.

"A Bus Named Cemeteries" by Jeri Cain Rossi. Copyright © 1989, 1996 by Jeri Cain Rossi. First appeared in *Angel with a Criminal Kiss* by Jeri Cain Rossi (Creation books, 1996).

"Conjure Me" by Jarret Keene. Copyright © 2001 by Jarret Keene. First appeared in *Louisiana Literature* 18/1 (Spring/Summer 2001).

"The Dive" by Jason Wiese. Copyright © 2001 by Jason Wiese.

"Fairy Tale" by Robert Olen Butler. From *A Good Scent from a Strange Mountain* by Robert Olen Butler, copyright © 1992 by Robert Olen Butler. Reprinted by permission of Henry Holt and Company, LLC.

excerpt from upcoming novel "Fleeing the Restoration: A Novel with Architecture" by Andrei Codrescu. Copyright © 2001 by Andrei Codrescu.

Acknowledgements

Foreword: "Quarter Rats" by James Nolan. Copyright © 2002 by James Nolan.

"Go to Hell" by Andy Young. Copyright © 2001 by Andy Young.

"Gregory's Fate" appeared in *The Torturer's Apprentice* by John Biguenet. Copyright © 2000 by John Biguenet. Reprinted by permission of HarperCollins Publishers Inc.

"The House of Mischief" by Julie Smith. Copyright © 2000 by Julie Smith. Originally appeared in *Mary Higgins Clark Mystery Magazine* (Summer 2000).

Introduction by Joshua Clark. Copyright © 2002 by Joshua Clark.

"La Vie En Rose Construction Co." by James Nolan. First appeared in *Hawai'i Review* issue 49, vol. 21.1 Fall/Winter 1997. Used by permission of the author.

"The Land of the Poppies" by Clarence John Laughlin. Copyright © 1982 by Clarence John Laughlin.

"The Last Bijou" by Bruce Henricksen. Copyright © 1997 by Bruce Henricksen. First appeared in *New Orleans Review* (Spring 1997).

"Lost Text: Hotel St. Pierre" by John Verlenden. Copyright © 2001 by John Verlenden. First appeared in *New Orleans Review* (Vol. 25, No.'s 1 & 2).

"Making Groceries" by Marda Burton. Copyright © 2002 by Marda Burton

Excerpt from *Malaise* by Nancy Lemann. Copyright © 2002 by Nancy Lemann. Printed with permission from International Creative Management. From *Malaise* (Scribner).

"Mussolini and the Axeman's Jazz" by Poppy Z. Brite. Copyright © 2002 by Poppy Z. Brite. First appeared in the anthology *Dark Destiny: Proprietors of Fate* (White Wolf), and in *Are You Loathesome Tonight?* (Gauntlet Press) by Poppy Z. Brite.

"The New Orleans of Possibilities" by David Madden. Copyright © 1982 by David Madden. Appeared in *The New Orleans of Possibilities* by David Madden (Louisiana State University Press, 1982).

"The Night Was Full of Hours," Copyright © 2002 The University of the South
Printed by permission of The University of the South, Sewanee, Tennessee.
All rights whatsoever in this work are strictly reserved and application for any use must be made in advance of such use to Casarotto Ramsay & Associates Ltd., National House, 60-66 Wardour Street, London W1V 4ND

About the editor:

Joshua Clark is an economist and writer who founded *Light of New Orleans Publishing* with the sole original intention of collecting an anthology of the best new stories to come out of this neighborhood he loves so much.

Above all, I wish to thank each and
every author for their patience and support
in seeing this project to fruition.

I would also like to acknowledge
the following individuals who willingly devoted
time and energy to *French Quarter Fiction*:

Joseph Ayers, Shelly Calkins, Erin Cotter,
GK Darby, Lee Grue, Kenneth Holditch,
Christine P. Horn, Vidho Lorville, Nick Moschovakis,
Nancy Moss, Diana Shortes, John Travis, Jason Wiese

And lastly, let us not forget the
buildings, streets and characters of a neighborhood
that inspired this whole thing in the first place.

.

…in the summertime. They walked into my bar and I asked,

"How are you guys?"

"Alright."

"Alright," said the other.

They took their seats on one side of the square bar. They already had drinks in plastic cups—one tall and clear, one short and red, the ice melted in both. They could have been sisters—the one on the left clearly older. They did not look at me. They were silent and they looked at each other. Then there were tears and the younger said to the older, "Here is my shoulder. Do you want a shoulder to cry on?" She did. She laid her hair and then her face on the other's shoulder. And there was nothing in the entire bar but the pieces of two people. Two heads and a shoulder. One head hidden in the darkness of a shoulder. One head half lit, the face straight forward facing me, but the eyes looking out of the darkness inside into the brightening graying mourning light framed in the open doorway, filtered gently in the space between the doorway and themselves, their darkness, their pieces, the darkness of the inside that lay on them who were framed by the gray-brown brick of the pub's side wall. And the pieces were quiet. They held together, unflinching, moving only with the whispering fluidity of a body's breath, of two bodies' breath. Three pieces breathing the small sad light of a New Orleans summer day's mourning.